P9-CCK-311

# Chase the Dawn

*Also by Jane Feather
in Large Print:*

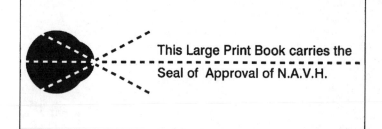

This Large Print Book carries the
Seal of Approval of N.A.V.H.

# Chase the Dawn

## Jane Feather

**Thorndike Press • Waterville, Maine**

LARGE TYPE
F
FEATHER, J

3 1257 01644 8085

Published in 2005 by arrangement with the Bantam Dell Publishing Group, a division of Random House, Inc.

Thorndike Press® Large Print Core.

The tree indicium is a trademark of Thorndike Press.

The text of this Large Print edition is unabridged.
Other aspects of the book may vary from the original edition.

Set in 16 pt. Plantin by Ramona Watson.

Printed in the United States on permanent paper.

---

**Library of Congress Cataloging-in-Publication Data**

Feather, Jane.
    Chase the dawn / by Jane Feather.
      p. cm. — (Thorndike Press large print core)
    ISBN 0-7862-7281-3 (lg. print : hc : alk. paper)
    1. Aristocracy (Social class) — Fiction.  2. Amnesia — Fiction.  3. Large type books.  I. Title.  II. Thorndike Press large print core series.
    PS3556.E22C47 2005
    813'.54—dc22                      2004026824

---

*For my parents:*
*remembering chauvinism*
*and the ninth and tenth redoubts*

As the Founder/CEO of NAVH, the only national health agency solely devoted to those who, although not totally blind, have an eye disease which could lead to serious visual impairment, I am pleased to recognize Thorndike Press★ as one of the leading publishers in the large print field.

Founded in 1954 in San Francisco to prepare large print textbooks for partially seeing children, NAVH became the pioneer and standard setting agency in the preparation of large type.

Today, those publishers who meet our standards carry the prestigious "Seal of Approval" indicating high quality large print. We are delighted that Thorndike Press is one of the publishers whose titles meet these standards. We are also pleased to recognize the significant contribution Thorndike Press is making in this important and growing field.

Lorraine H. Marchi, L.H.D.
Founder/CEO
NAVH

★ Thorndike Press encompasses the following imprints: Thorndike, Wheeler, Walker and Large Print Press.

# Chapter 1

Bryony was going to sneeze. The agonizing tickle built inexorably with the disturbance of dust and straw in the hayloft. She pinched her nose with fierce fingers, squeezing her eyes tight shut as she prayed for deliverance. Through the drumming of her heartbeat, she could hear the low voices in the barn below, the scuffling of booted feet on the flagged floor. They were dragging something, hay bales presumably. But why? And who were they to come out of the night like shades, to come with such clear mischievous intent? They had clubbed old Jebediah to the cold stone of the stableyard without a second thought. What would they do if they found her?

She sneezed, burying her face in her hands as images of rape and murder ran rampant in her head. Such things were common occurrences in this year of revolution, 1779. Or at least they were if the hushed whispers of the women in her mother's drawing room and the pontificating rhetoric of the men around the mahogany dining table were to be believed.

"What was that?" a voice from below demanded, and a dreadful silence fell, a silence during which the creeping paralysis of terror gripped the girl in the loft, convinced her that the sound of her heart could be heard throughout the wooden building.

"Only rats," someone said after the silence had continued into eternity, and the scuffling and dragging began again. "That'll do," the same voice said. Although low, it carried an authoritative ring that was not disguised by an inherent softness that sounded to the wild imaginings of the listener above like spring raindrops. There was a renewed silence, but this time it was clear from the quality that it came from the absence of life.

Had they gone? Bryony came onto her knees, wincing at the protestations of her cramped muscles, held for so long in rigidity. She listened again. Nothing. Then she smelled it. Smoke. She heard it. The insidious crackle of fire taking hold. They had put a torch to the hay bales below, stacking them up to create a funeral pyre for the unseen, unheard watcher in the loft above. She was going to die — burned alive like

Joan of Arc. Did it hurt? Of course it did. She had read enough in the books of the saints extolling the excruciating torments of martyrdom, the blistering skin, the stench of roasting flesh, the sounds of popping and bursting as . . . dear God.

She stumbled to the ladder. Smoke curled, thick and black and impenetrable; flames crackled, then surged in sudden brightness. The smoke filled her nostrils, was dragged into her protesting lungs, and she was drowning in the hot dryness. Hindered by the rigid whalebone of her hooped petticoat, she half fell, half jumped down the ladder into the inferno, her only thought that there was one door, one possibility of salvation.

Flames from the pyre flicked out at her like the venomous tongues of a nest of vipers. She dodged, covering her nose and mouth with the lace-ruffled sleeve of her rose damask evening gown. The thin soles of her matching satin pumps seemed to absorb the heat of the fire, scorching the bottom of her feet, and the warning smell of singeing hair brought tears of desperation to her already streaming eyes. The heat was so intense that it seemed she would not need to be touched by flame to be reduced to ashes. The door, her goal, was lost in the smoke, her sense of direction vanquished by terror, and she stumbled blindly in circles, straining for air that was not forthcoming, every inch of her skin stinging with the pain of the heat. Then, by some miracle, the door loomed in the smoke-wreathed darkness. She cried out in hopelessness as she touched the heavy latch and found the metal heated to an unbearable temperature — unbearable to any but the desperate.

Fighting down the agony as the skin of her palms blistered, she jerked on the solid fastening. As it eased upward, she pushed with her last vestiges of strength against the massive double door. It swung open, letting in a rush of air that caught the conflagration behind her, sending it upward and outward with a great roar of triumph. The flames seized the back of her gown. She screamed in pain and terror, outlined in flame in the doorway. Then she was lost to the world as a smothering black cloud drowned her, rolled her over, knocked her to the ground with head-splitting violence, and light and life dissolved in a starburst of dazzling color.

Benedict Clare left the close confines of the log cabin and went out into the summer evening. The heat of the day was retained by the tall trees surrounding the small clearing, and he wiped his brow with his neckcloth. This evening, that broad brow was buckled with a deep frown. He was a man who considered himself cured of sentiment, immune to the softer emotions. There was no room for them in the life struggle he had been fighting ever since puberty. He couldn't blame the men for their startled disapproval. He had been condemning his own weakness from the moment he had tossed that ruined bundle of scraps and tatters into the wagon, atop the stolen cache of muskets and ammunition, and ridden away from the Trueman plantation, the blazing barn at his back.

But once the raid had been completed successfully, Loyalist weapons appropriated to the Patriot cause, firing the barn had been unnecessary — a self-indulgent act of personal revenge. It was a revenge to which he was entitled, God knew, but the trapped girl bore no guilt, and if he had not indulged himself, she would not have suffered. Some stubborn sense of justice had obliged him to pick up the pieces. He hadn't known whether she was dead or alive when he had borne her off, but he had known that he could not leave her.

She was alive, but for the last twenty-four hours she had drifted in and out of consciousness, caused more by the blow to her head when it had struck the cobbles, he suspected, than by the burns on her back. The latter were not as severe as he had feared and were healing with the sureness of young, healthy skin, although, judging by the soft moans as she moved on the cot and when he dressed them, they were sufficiently painful to cross the boundaries of unconsciousness.

He strolled through the trees to the banks of the narrow creek that ran into the broad reaches of the James River some two miles along. The creek was clogged with bullrushes and swamp grass, navigable only by canoe, and Benedict's only companions were the curlews, pipers, and their like rising to circle above the marsh. Raising his musket, he sighted, squeezed the trigger, and the dark shape fell from the sky. It was a plump plover that would make good eating, and he was in need of a substantial dinner. He had been living off dry stores since the raid on Trueman's, unwilling to leave the girl alone for the time it would take to hunt his supper until he was sure she had rounded the corner. Slinging his musket across his shoulder, the bird dangling from his hand, he made his way back to the cabin.

Bryony became aware of the soreness first, as always. It seemed to be a part of her, exacerbated to stinging rawness by an unwary move, so that, even in sleep, she seemed to move with care or not at all, lying still until her motionless limbs cried out for relief. The muzziness was still in her head, and when she opened her eyes, she looked through a blur as if viewing her surroundings from underwater. It was too much of an effort, so she closed her eyes again, flexing her toes in the hope that her cramped legs would be satisfied with the activity of their extremities. It was a vain hope, and with a groan of sheer misery she inched herself onto her other side.

"Are you awake?"

It was a voice she knew, one that had punctuated her sleep-waking; it went with the hands that soothed her hurts, held the cup of water to her parched lips, lifted her on and off the tin pot with a gentleness that did its utmost to avoid unwary contact with her sores. She did not know to whom it belonged — that did not seem to be of the least importance. Through the watery blur of her vision, she had once in a while

13

registered a bearded face, brightly sharp eyes, but then she had slipped away again into the warm darkness.

"I think so." Her voice sounded strange, an unfamiliar croak, and she realized that she had not spoken for as long as she could remember. Panic flared. "Where am I? Who . . . ?"

"Hush, lass. You haven't the strength yet to get yourself into a fret." The soft voice gentled as his hands moved her onto her belly. She felt a sudden coolness as the blanket was drawn back, then the wonderful, now familiar sensation of the healing oil smoothing into the hurt skin of her back and legs. Her heart swelled with gratitude. The flash of panic receded, and she slept again.

When Bryony next awoke, it was to a world of sharply clear objects, of lucidity of thought, of complete awareness of her body, of its lines and contours, of its place and shape in the world. She lay still, taking inventory, trying to separate confused memories. Her back still hurt, and when she turned her head restlessly on the thin pillow, a bruising soreness stilled her instantly. But she was awake, and she could see without mist, and she could hear without the buzzing in her ears. What she

14

could not do was remember where she was, or why she was here, or how she had hurt herself, or — dear God, she could not remember anything beyond the bewildering turmoil of the last however many days she had lain here, drifting, cared for by some strange man. A memory took shape, sharpened. Slowly, almost fearfully, she placed her hands on her belly, moved them up and down. She was as naked as the day she had been born. She raised the blanket, and her eyes confirmed her touch.

Bryony hastily dropped the blanket and lay staring up at the rough-hewn, smoke-blackened clapboard roof. Her mind stretched to remember, something . . . any-thing! But there was nothing — just an abyss. She knew only that she was in a log cabin, that she was naked, that there was a man somewhere for whom that nakedness had become familiar. What had happened to her? What had he done while she was lying here, defenseless? But she knew what he had done. It was the only thing she did know. He had not harmed her, he had cared for her like a nurse with a baby, at-tending to her intimate needs. And Bryony wished she had died rather than wake to this shaming reality, peopled with only these recent and so mortifying memories.

A creak and a square of bright light heralded the opening of the cabin door. She blinked as the dazzle struck her unaccustomed eyes, then the light was blocked for a minute by the bulk of a figure — an utterly recognizable figure. She retreated behind closed eyes.

Leaving the door open, Benedict crossed to the bedstead and stood looking down at its occupant. The girl had her eyes tight shut, but there was something about her posture beneath the blanket, about the sudden mobility of her face, that told him not only was she awake, she was finally fully conscious. He knelt down beside the bed. "Open your eyes, Bryony."

Bryony! Her eyes shot open, meeting the intent scrutiny of a pair as black and resonant as ebony. "Is that my name?" She forgot the agonies of shame for the moment in this all-important question.

The breath whistled through his teeth as he absorbed the implications of the question. "Can you not remember?"

She shook her head, wincing as the soreness rubbed against the pillow again.

Those hands, with remembered gentleness, turned her head to one side, parting the blood-stiffened locks of raven-dark hair, feeling the lump. "You took a blow to

16

the head to fell an ox," he said, sighing. "I suppose it is not surprising. But it is a damnable complication."

"How do you know I am called Bryony?" Her voice shook a little, as much with disuse as anxiety.

"It was embroidered on your handkerchief and on all your undergarments, what remained of them." He stood up, turning away from the cot, so he did not see the scarlet wave flooding her cheeks. Taking a small ceramic pot from a shelf carved into one of the horizontal logs that formed the wall, he unscrewed the lid and came back to the bed. "Lie on your belly, lass, and I'll dress the burns on your back."

Bryony stared at him in mute refusal for a second, then shook her head gingerly. "It is all right, thank you. I do not feel them anymore." There was a note of pathetic dignity in her voice, pathetic because of the undisguised appeal that lay beneath.

"You are being foolish," he said quietly. "If those burns become infected, they will mortify."

"Then I will do it myself," she countered in a choked whisper.

Benedict frowned. She could not possibly manage such a thing, and it was a task that had to be done. However, per-

17

haps it would be best if she discovered that for herself. He could see little to be gained by coercion, easy though that would be. Shrugging, he placed the pot on the blanket beside her. "As you please. I will bring you something to eat in a few minutes."

The door swung shut behind his departing figure, and Bryony struggled to sit up in the welcome dimness, shafted by bars of sunlight sliding through the gaps in the logs where the moss and clay filling had come loose. She dipped her finger in the oily, aromatic cream and reached a hand behind her. Her blind fingers brushed roughly against the weals, and tears sprang into her eyes. She tried reaching over her shoulder, then upward from her waist, but it was impossible to do more than skim patchily over the burns.

The creak of the door again drove her back beneath the blanket, and the ceramic jar fell to the earthen floor. Benedict placed a steaming bowl on a three-legged stool by the hearth and wordlessly picked up the ointment, replacing the lid. Looking down at her, he quirked a well-drawn eyebrow but said only, "I have some broth for you. Are you hungry?"

The rich, savory aroma from the bowl

filled the cabin, and Bryony realized that she was famished, even as she realized that her body was making another, imperative demand, one that would interfere with her pleasure in food if it was not satisfied. "I have to go outside first," she said, blushing furiously at renewed memory.

Benedict sighed, recognizing the shape of the battle. "I do not think you are strong enough, lass. I will bring the pot."

"No!" With near-superhuman effort, she sat up, tucking the blanket around her breasts, swinging her legs over the edge of the bed frame.

He stood and watched her, impassive, yet with no unkindness. Indeed, he felt more than a hint of admiration for this dogged determination. If she could be this resolute in the face of such odds, what would she be like when well and strong? It was an intriguing thought, but for the moment he would simply wait in resigned patience for the odds to tell and bring her to her senses.

Gritting her teeth, Bryony put her feet to the earthen floor and carefully stood up. But her legs would not bear her weight, and the room spun like a top, bringing a dizzy nausea to tug at her belly as her head pounded viciously. She grabbed the side of the bed with a convulsive movement that loosened the blanket so that it fell with a rustle to the floor.

The tears of weakness, of frustration at her helplessness, rolled down her cheeks, but she made no further protest when he lifted her gently onto the pot. When he helped her up again she put her arms around his neck, clinging in defeat, like a small, wounded animal, to the masthead of his strength.

Benedict simply held her, imparting comfort and reassurance with his body even as he wondered at himself. It was a woman's body he held, and beautiful in its clean-limbed youth, for all its wounds and weakness. The skin under his hands was soft as silk; the raven's-wing hair tickling his chin was richly luxuriant, for all that it was in sore need of a wash. Until now, he had been aware of her only as a responsibility, the consequence of a self-indulgent whim — a consequence to be mitigated at the earliest possible moment. Once healed, she was to have been transported blindfolded to a point close to home and left to make her own way and tell her own story. She would have laid eyes only upon him, and would never see him again. But now that plan lay in ruins — ruined by this amnesia caused presumably when he had flung her to the cobblestones of the stableyard, smothering the flames with his cloak. And its ruin left a gap, a gap that these unwelcome recognitions of her femininity, and of the essence of the awakening personality, rushed to fill.

With grim determination, he pushed these disquieting reflections aside and placed her on the bed, on her stomach. She made no protest this time as, in silence, he anointed her back, his fingers brushing delicately down the long, narrow length, across her buttocks, and over her thighs. For some reason, he seemed to have become acutely aware of the slender indentation of her waist, the flare of her hips tapering to the long, creamy slimness of her thighs. Try as he might for a return to the untroubled objectivity of the past, it remained elusive. Then there was a moment when she stirred beneath his touch. He would have staked his life that it was an involuntary movement, and it was not a flinching from the pain of her burns, either.

Bryony did not question the ease with which she now submitted to the intimacy of his touch. Her earlier protestations seemed simply ridiculous. He was only doing what he had been doing for days, and only a fool would protest the ministrations that brought such wondrous relief. How many days? she asked herself, leaning against his broad chest as he sat behind her, supporting her so that the bowl of broth could rest on her knees. It was delicious, but after a few spoonsful her shrunken belly was sated, and she lay back with a sigh of repletion, too contented to worry about an answer to the question. Time enough after she had had another sleep.

Benedict took the bowl and laid her down on the bed again. "By tomorrow, you will be able to do things for yourself, Bryony. Then we must try to jog your memory."

Bryony responded with an inarticulate mutter and turned on her side — a maneuver accomplished with only a twinge of discomfort. Sleep, warm and welcome, enfolded her.

It was full night when next she opened her eyes. Gradually, the seemingly impenetrable darkness gave way before her accustomed vision, and she was able to make out the shapes of the simple furniture — the plank table and three-legged stools; shelves simply cut out of the log walls; the unglazed aperture that served as a window. Tonight it let in the soft, moist air of a Virginian summer night and the milky illumination of starlight, but the cabin would be bitter in winter, even with the wooden shutters fastened.

She turned her head with the care of experience to look in the direction of the quiet, regular breathing. The man — for that was all she knew of him — lay peacefully asleep on a straw pallet beside the empty hearth. A rudimentary spit and cooking pots were in the hearth below the log-and-clay chimney.

Something told her that this was no backwoodsman. She did not know what it was that convinced her of the fact, maybe an elusive knowledge based on a runaway memory. His voice, perhaps. That soft lilt was tauntingly familiar, though she had heard it so often in the twilight world of semiconsciousness that that memory could be explained. There was something about his hands that didn't match this primitive lifestyle. They were callused, the fingernails squared, short, and practical, but the fingers were long, sensitive, elegant. How did she know that they were not the hands of a man accustomed to tearing his livelihood from the elements?

Bryony frowned and wriggled into a more comfortable position. She did not know who she was; she did not know how she had arrived in this place; she did not know the day or the year or the month. But there were all sorts of things she did know. She knew about backwoodsmen, it seemed. She could add and subtract, multiply and divide in her head. She could remember lines of poetry and Latin verbs. She seemed to be able to reason perfectly well. She could give orders to her body, and they were obeyed — or, at least, she amended ruefully, they would be once she was physically stronger. In short, apart from some significant and clearly selective gaps, her memory seemed to be functioning perfectly well.

She was wide-awake. Was it yesterday that she had had the soup, or just a few hours ago? Impossible to tell; time just ran along without dividing lines when all one did was sleep. The urge to see something other than this log-enclosed space grew inexorably until it would have taken an indomitable will to resist. Since Bryony could see no real reason why she should resist the urge, the battle did not last very long. Casting a wary eye at the sleeping figure on the pallet, she sat up. The room remained on an even keel and continued to do so even when she swung her legs to the floor and stood up with exaggerated care. Her legs rather felt like jelly, but they did not collapse. Clutching the blanket securely around her with one hand, she shuffled to the door, using her free hand to gain support from whatever solidly rooted objects appeared on the way. At the door, she looked again at the recumbent body. He must need his sleep, she thought with a considerate little nod. It would be most unfair to wake him up. And besides, maybe he would raise objections to this expedition. On that convincing thought, she lifted the wooden latch, biting her lip nervously in case the opening door should make some alerting noise in the night stillness.

Nothing occurred to disturb the quiet, and Bryony found herself outside, the door closed softly behind her. She stood still for a minute, breathing deeply of the freshness laden with the scents of pine needles, honeysuckle, damp moss, and river mud. They were all familiar smells, she realized as she identified each one. The ground beneath her bare feet was soft and springy, and she curled her toes luxuriously into the mossy turf, relishing the overpowering sense of being alive — a sense that seemed to carry a curious overlay, as if it were a possession only just now truly valued. Had she nearly died, then, when whatever had brought her to this place had happened? Her mind stretched again, but again there was only an abyss where there should have been memory. At least that was one memory that the man could fill in for her.

The sky was lightening as the first pale streaks of dawn, rose-tipped, showed in the east above the trees. Bryony made her way slowly to the edge of the clearing, sensing her returning strength with each step. Among the trees, her feet sank into the carpet of pine needles, which pricked the soles of her feet, and she jumped back with a little cry. The sensation had brought more than the simple ordinary sting. It felt like something else, something that now hovered as a dark, amorphous shape in the wings of her mind.

Resolutely, she stepped forward into the trees, standing quite still on the prickly needles. All that happened was that her feet became used to the sensation. An owl hooted its farewell to night. A squirrel skittered across the ground in front of her and leaped at a tree trunk. A thrush twittered, and then the forest came alive as the dawn chorus ushered in the new day. The blanket-wrapped figure made her way through the trees in the direction of the water that she seemed to know instinctively was to be found within a few yards.

Benedict awoke as always at the first note of the dawn chorus. He came awake with no intervening drowsiness, and his first action was to look toward the bedstead attached to the far wall. What he saw brought him to his feet in one fluid motion, a soft, explicit curse on his lips. Pulling on his shirt, he went outside. The tracks of her feet were visible indentations in the springy turf leading to the trees. He sighed with relief — at least there was only one set of footprints. At the trees, the tracks stopped. The pine needles were too thick and resilient to bear any mark of her progress. He swore again, tucking his shirt into the waistband of his britches. Wherever she had gone, she had gone alone. But he had no idea what condition she was in, whether her mind was functioning sufficiently to enable her to find her way back, whether she had enough sense to recognize her body's limitations.

"Bryony?" he called, softly at first, then with increasing power, although it went against all his instincts and experience to announce his presence in full voice. One could never be certain that there were no observers, no ears to hear. And Benedict Clare could afford neither. There was no answer, and he stood for a minute, listening intently for any sound that he would identify immediately as not indigenous to the woodland. Nothing. Collecting an iron kettle from the cabin, he made his way down to the creek in search of her, reflecting with customary pragmatism that he might as well kill two birds with one stone.

He saw her at the water's edge as he broke through the trees. The huddled, blanketed figure was sitting on the bank, chin resting on drawn-up knees, her raven's hair falling forward to conceal her profile. She was rapt in contemplation of something, whether of the internal or external world he could not guess. Making no attempt to disturb her immediately, he simply went to the creek's edge and bent to fill the kettle.

"Good morrow, sir." Bryony came out of her daydream as his figure filled her vision.

He straightened, swinging the now heavy kettle easily from one hand, a little frown drawing the fine eyebrows together over glowing black eyes. "Good morrow, Bryony." He trod across the grass toward her, each step seemingly invested with purpose. "You are somewhat restored, I gather?"

"I find myself so," she agreed. There was something a little forbidding suddenly about his expression, and she offered a tentative smile. "You do not object to my taking a walk, I trust?"

He dropped to his heels beside her. "In future, you will do me the courtesy of letting me know before you decide to go awandering."

"But I am not a prisoner," Bryony objected, feeling suddenly uncomfortable. If his statement had been a mere request, she would have felt no need to protest it, but there was a tension in the atmosphere, and the statement had been made in an authoritative tone that admitted no dissension.

"That is perhaps a matter for definition at some later point," he said evenly. "There is much that you do not understand." He stood up and reached down for her hand. "Come, the damp bank of a creek in the dawn chill is not the ideal place for the ill-clad and but newly recovered."

Bryony allowed him to pull her up. "I do not understand what you have said."

"No, there is much that you do not understand," he repeated. "And it is possible that you must remain in ignorance. For the moment, you must do as you are bid, I fear, and control your curiosity."

It was not a declaration to be accepted by anyone with a flicker of spirit, and Bryony possessed rather more than a flicker. "I do not think I can agree to that," she announced. "Apart from anything else, I do not know your name."

"That is easily remedied," he returned, sounding amused rather than annoyed by the stiffness of her voice. "My name is Benedict, and you may call me Ben, if you wish."

Ben . . . Benedict . . . She turned the name over in her head and found it pleasing. It suited him, somehow. Plain, yet elegant; strong, yet sensitive. Sweet heaven, she was becoming fanciful! Or perhaps she always had been? She had no idea what she was like, and no clues, either.

"How did I come to be here?" The question followed the previous thought naturally.

"When you have had some breakfast and I've had another look at your back, I will satisfy your curiosity as far as I am able. And we will see what we can do to jog your errant memory."

The anointing took place under a veneer

of dignity maintained by an apparently indifferent silence that neither of them chose to break. Once Benedict was finished, remarking with quiet satisfaction that she was almost as good as new, she was rewrapped in the blanket, and they returned outside to the sun-drenched clearing. Bryony broached a subject at the forefront of her mind. "Do I have any clothes, Ben?"

He shook his head. "Rags and tatters, lass. Not that they weren't costly scraps," he added. "Rose damask with a hooped petticoat, lawn and lace, and satin pumps." He watched her for some reaction. "You were dressed for dancing." When she looked at him blankly, he said, "What I would like to know is why, dressed like that, you were in the barn — presumably the hayloft, since we didn't see you earlier — at three o'clock in the morning. The dancing at Trueman's had been over long since."

Bryony shook her head helplessly. "I do not know. Are you sure my name is Bryony?"

"Unless you were wearing someone else's drawers, it is." He chuckled. "I suppose it is possible that you dressed up in this Bryony's clothes for the same reason that took you to the barn at that hour."

"What were you doing there?" There was challenge in both her voice and her pansy-blue eyes. "Did you set the fire?"

Benedict chewed on a stalk of grass for a minute, then shrugged. "As it happens. But I was not to know the barn had an occupant other than the rats."

"Why would you do such a thing?"

"My reasons are my own," he told her in that soft, definite tone. "And they are not what concerns us at present. Does the name Trueman mean anything to you?"

Bryony was inclined to reply that if he would not answer her questions, she did not see why she should answer his, but common sense told her that she would be merely cutting off her nose to spite her face. She thought, her expression twisted with the effort, but there was nothing there. "No."

"Bryony is an unusual name," he mused, regarding her through narrowed eyes, hoping that the casual comment would trigger an automatic response. "Always assuming that you did not borrow it for some nefarious purpose."

She smiled a little at that and wondered if it could possibly be true. Somehow she hoped not. At least having a name that she believed was her own gave her some sense of belonging in the world. "It's the name of a flower, is it not?"

"I believe so." He sighed. "We are not getting anywhere, are we? For the most part, your memory is intact; there is just one large chunk missing."

"But it is the most important chunk of all," she maintained, suddenly desolate. "What am I to do?"

It was a question exercising her companion considerably, but more along the lines of what was *he* to do. He appeared to be stuck with this stray waif, and from what he had seen of her so far, she did not strike him as a particularly biddable creature. She had a potentially dangerous curiosity that he dared not satisfy.

A low whistle sounded through the clearing, and he stiffened. He'd told William to come only under cover of darkness. He whistled back, a soft, trilling melody barely distinguishable from a bird call.

Bryony looked at him in astonishment. "You are signaling to someone?"

"Yes, someone that you may not meet." He stood up. "Come into the cabin."

"But why may I not?" She found herself being pulled behind him, as she clutched the blanket convulsively, and there was a quality to his hold that sent a shiver of apprehension down her spine. The gentleness had gone, replaced by a taut determination.

He did not answer her, merely swung her onto the bedstead. As she struggled upright, vociferous protest on her lips, he took a thin strip of rawhide from the shelf. "I am sorry, but this is necessary for your own safety." The mouth, which she had seen only curved with amusement or softened with compassion, was now a thin line within the neat, rich copper beard, and his eyes no longer glowed; they were hard black stones that glittered without warmth. Even as she cried out in fury and sudden fear of this stranger, he took one of her wrists and bound it with the leather band to one of the forked poles that formed the frame of the bed. "I won't be gone long." He ran a finger between the hide and the skin of her wrist. "If you do not pull on it, it will not chafe. Just lie quietly and try to sleep." Then she was left in the dim light of the cabin, a prisoner tied to the bed, with no identity, no name, no sense of self or of her place in the world.

When Benedict came out of the cabin, William was waiting at the edge of the clearing. His heavy peasant face was set in an obstinate glower, which caused Benedict to sigh in anticipation of trouble in the offing. William was spokesman for the band, more because of his natural aggression than for any articulate tact.

Deciding to take the offensive, Benedict strode across the clearing, his face hard. "You were told not to come here in daylight."

"The men want to know what ye be goin' to do with her." William's balding head jerked toward the cabin. "Unless she be dead."

"No, she is not." Benedict moved into the trees, gesturing imperatively to William that he follow. Although he knew the girl could not get to the window, he never dropped the habitual caution that had kept him alive for the last five years. "She is my responsibility. You need have no fear that I will allow her to endanger anyone."

"Who is she?" demanded William, unappeased.

"That I do not know, my friend, and unfortunately, neither does she."

William's button eyes widened in incomprehension. "Don't quite take yer meaning."

"Amnesia, William." The word clearly meant nothing to the other man, so Benedict explained the situation succinctly.

"Then turn her loose," William said with the happy beam of one who has hit upon the perfect solution. "If she's not going to die after the burning, then she can make her own way. She won't know nothing, won't have anything to tell."

"You are a fool," pronounced Benedict with calculated insult, knowing that the other man stood sufficiently in awe of his leader's intelligence and planning ability to be cowed by the accusation. "Do you think I am about to let loose an unknown quantity who was present at the burning of the Trueman barn? When I know who she is, then I shall decide what to do with her."

William struggled with this idea in the long silence that followed. He was not one of the brightest members of the band by any means, but once an idea took root he could be relied upon to stick with it through thick and thin. And he carried a great deal of weight with the others — not least because of those powerful blacksmith's shoulders and brawny forearms, and the huge hands that could wrestle an ox. "Reckon so," he pronounced eventually. "Could be a Trueman, after all."

Benedict shook his head. He had some knowledge of the construction of the Trueman family. "There is no daughter, and the girl wore no wedding ring, so she is not married to one of the sons. Trueman has no kin except his immediate family."

"What's to do, then?" William asked.

"Listen to the gossip and tell the others to do the same. If she's from these parts, the news of a missing girl will take flight soon enough."

"Aye, 'tis true. And ye'll be keeping her close till then?"

You do not know how close, my friend, Benedict thought, remembering the fury and the fear in those deep blue eyes as he had bound her to the bed. But what else could he have done? "Aye, I'll keep her close, but you do not help by seeking me out when it's forbidden." He returned to the attack, sharper now with his own annoyance at what he had been forced to do.

William shuffled his feet on the pine needles and looked suitably discomfited. "I'll be off, then. Ye'll send word?"

"I'll send word." Benedict watched the burly figure melt into the trees as if he were a part of them, then turned back to the cabin in the clearing. The scream reached him before he gained the center — a scream that rose in an eerie crescendo, galvanizing him into a headlong dash for the door.

The figure on the bed twisted and thrashed, the deep blue eyes wide with blank terror. The blanket had fallen to the floor with the wildness of her movements, but Benedict barely noticed as he bent over her, swiftly unfastening her captive wrist. "What is it, lass?" His voice was gentle as he came down on the cot beside her, sliding an arm beneath her to draw her against his length. She came shudderingly into his embrace, tremors racking her slim frame.

"Who am I?" Ceaselessly she repeated the whimpered question. "There is nothing there, nothing but darkness."

"It's there, sweeting, you just have to find it." His hands were all over her, the soft, sweeping caresses insisting that she acknowledge the humanity that in her dream seemed to have been denied her.

"There is nothing, just an abyss. I am at the bottom of a chasm . . . I am nothing, nothing." She sobbed out the black terror of nothingness, struggling for words to describe the devastating knowledge of annihilation.

"You are real, Bryony. Real and alive. Can you feel this?" Urgently, instinctively, he brought his lips to hers, locking on to her mouth in a kiss of honeyed sweetness as a hand moved to one breast, closing over the soft mound, a fingertip circling her nipple.

Bryony inhaled deeply of his scent, the very real scent of sun-warmed skin, of fresh sweat, of the soap-washed linen of his shirt. She tasted salt and sun on his lips, felt the tangible, soft prickle of his beard against her face. And she felt the tightening of her breast's crown beneath the insistent fingertip. It was an exquisitely pleasurable sensation, as exquisite as the feel of his lips on hers, of his other hand stroking over her buttocks as he held her against the long, lean length of him.

One minute there had been only the abyss of a historyless anonymity, an insensate vacuum with no grip on reality, and now there was this. Pure, joyous sensation to fill the chasm, offering the handholds that would wrench her back into the world. Her mouth opened to him, her back arching to thrust her breast against the palm of his hand as she curled her legs around his body, responding in her innocence to the memories of bodily joy.

Benedict's world tilted as he drank greedily of her sweetness, recognized the demand she was making, and wondered for one bewildered second what she was.

Not the innocent he had thought her. The cleft of her body was pressed against the hard throb of his penis, her fingers twining between the buttons of his shirt, twisting in the soft hair of his chest as she brought her lips to his throat, teasing him with her tongue. He groaned, and groaned again as her opened body pressed with increased fervor.

"Love me," she whispered. "Make me feel."

His hands caught her shoulders, flipping her onto her back with the force of desire now beyond control. He was on top of her, his mouth closing again over hers as their tongues warred, then danced, then plunged in a wild spiral of passion that excluded all but their partnered bodies and this utterly imperative passion. He tugged at the waistband of his britches, and she helped him, pushing them off his hips, her hands running in greedy exploration over his chest beneath his unbuttoned shirt, over the narrow hips, enclosing that burning, throbbing shaft that lifted to her touch.

Drawing her beneath him again, he parted her willing thighs and for one instant paused on the threshold of her body. Her eyes were closed, her face lost in joy, but as he gazed down at her, the long black lashes swept up, showing him the appeal and passion in those velvet-blue eyes. "Love me," she whispered.

With a little sigh, he guided his surging entry within the moist tenderness of her core. There was a moment when he sensed the resistance that he had never expected. He checked himself with a soft-breathed curse and the tautening of his muscles, but her hands went to his buttocks, gripping with that urgent demand, and it was too late. She could not breathe for a second as the aching fullness stretched her, then it yielded and her cry of pain was more an exhalation of relief. Benedict brushed his lips over her damp temples, touched the corners of her eyes, trailed to the sensitive corner of her mouth, while he cupped her breast, sliding his thumb over the pliant and responsive peak. As he felt her relaxation, the suppleness of her body, he eased deeper, and her eyes shot open at the prickle of pleasure that ran across her nerve centers.

Watching her, he set the rhythm, which she picked up with the ease of an established lover, but he was too lost in the glory of this fusion to question any further. They rose and fell together, and Bryony was conscious only of the wonder of her need and the amazing wonder of its satisfaction. His hands closed over her buttocks, lifting her to meet him as he reached the very center of her self, and the steadily growing blossom of pleasure inside her burst into full bloom, and she cried out against his mouth. As her body convulsed around him, Benedict thrust once more, holding himself within her as his own fulfillment throbbed.

They lay entwined, sweat-slippery skin molded, hearts slowly settling as the fever abated. Bryony fell into a second oblivion, the sleep of emotional and physical exhaustion, but just before she slipped over the edge, she heard a soft, explosive execration that seemed to make no sense. And then she heard no more.

# Chapter 2

"In the name of the Almighty, man! The girl was in your charge." Sir Edward Paget paced the stone-flagged terrace overlooking the broad sweep of the James River, his agitation more clearly expressed by the fact that his wig was askew than by the heat of his remarks.

"No, Edward, she was in mine," Eliza Paget moaned, dabbing at her beaded upper lip with a lace-edged handkerchief. "You cannot hold Mr. Trueman to account."

"You, madam, have never been able to take charge of your daughter in proper fashion." Sir Edward rounded on his wife, the irascibility that he usually kept in check when talking to her bubbling over under the press of near-ungovernable anxiety. "I should never have permitted the visit, but I cannot forever be accompanying you on your social gadabouts."

Eliza Paget whimpered, and Charles Trueman shuffled his feet uncomfortably.

"She cannot have been taken from the house, Paget," he said, "even if her disappearance had anything to do with those damn bandits. They came nowhere near the house. The arms were stowed above the smokehouse, and the barn they fired was at the far side of the stableyard. Old Jebediah remembers little before they clubbed him, but he swears he saw no woman."

"You have found nothing?" Sir Edward buried his nose in a tankard of nutmeg-laced toddy. "No trace at all?"

"Nothing." Trueman shook his head in bewilderment. "Not a sign of an abduction — or of worse." He looked anxiously at the distraught Eliza, whose sobs became noisy.

"Go inside, woman! Your sniveling doesn't help," her irate husband snapped, and his wife made haste to obey, the streamers pinned to the sides of her lace coif fluttering away from her head as she scurried from the terrace and into the relative cool of the central hall.

"I've had the woods beaten and every inch of the estate combed," Trueman said, his tone businesslike. "The household slaves have been questioned repeatedly. Not one of them saw or heard anything untoward." He chewed his lip for a minute before saying tentatively, "There would be no reason for Bryony to . . . well, to leave of her own accord?"

Sir Edward's generally pale, well-bred countenance darkened. "That is calumny, sir."

"No, I beg you not to take it as such," his guest made haste to conciliate. "It is just that, well, young girls do get strange notions sometimes. I just wondered. . . ."

"Bryony has never had a strange notion in her life," said her father. "She's head-strong, I grant you, but she has more sense in that head than half the women in the county put together."

Trueman was inclined to ascribe this to paternal bias. Who ever heard of a twenty-year-old girl having anything in her head beyond balls and visiting and games? But then, as Mrs. Trueman had remarked only that morning, if Bryony Paget had been wedded and bedded these two years past, as she should have been, none of this would have happened. It was unheard-of indulgence for Sir Edward to agree to a postponement of a wedding that had been arranged since the young couple had been in their cradles. It was actually rumored that Miss Bryony had told her father she was not yet ready for matrimony, and Sir

Edward had agreed without a murmur. No one, it seemed, had given a thought to the prospective groom, so Francis Cullum grew more disconsolate by the day.

Following this reflection, Trueman suggested, "I suppose Francis has no light to throw on the matter? He left to ride home immediately after dinner, complaining of a powerful migraine."

"No, he has nothing at all to offer, beyond the fact that he spoke with her at dinner and she seemed her usual lively self." The English aristocrat took another turn around the terrace, trying to grapple with this near-inconceivable fact: his daughter, in sound mind and body, had disappeared off the face of the earth, transported on clouds, it would seem, from the solid, dependable household of his old friend and under the very eye of her mother. The only other peculiar circumstance of that night had been the Patriot raid on the cache of arms hidden in the smokehouse, and the burning of Trueman's barn.

The bands of Patriots were becoming increasingly bold as the war in the North dragged on and the British seemed incapable of crushing, once and for all, the American forces under General Washington and the Marquis de Lafayette. But abduction of innocent maidens had not so far formed part of their activities. Sir Edward Paget was an Englishman first, a colonist second, but it was surely incidental that the maiden in question was the daughter of one of the most prominent Loyalists in the colony, now that the Crown's governor had fled his palace at Williamsburg as soon as the town had become a hotbed of revolutionary turmoil.

"I will bear you company home, Trueman," Paget said heavily. "Maybe I can elicit more from your household and the man Jebediah than you could. Someone, somewhere, must have seen or heard something, even if they don't realize its significance."

The other man nodded and stood up, settling his sword more snugly against his side, adjusting his crimson brocade waistcoat over a portly belly. "I am more sorry than I can say, Paget."

"Aye," the Englishman said with a curt nod. "But I'll find her if I have to turn over every stone in Virginia." He bellowed a command and the dignified figure of his butler appeared before the echo had died down. "Tell your mistress I am going to Trueman's," Paget instructed. "I'll be gone two or three days. She's to send word there if anything comes to light."

The two men left the terrace, taking the broad walk bordered by large flowering laurels and catalpas, which led down to the river highway and the landing stage where Trueman's boat waited.

Inside the mansion, Eliza Paget flew up the graceful stairway with its carved step ends and newel posts, her hand barely skimming the rich mahogany handrail, to seek refuge in her chamber. She knew her husband blamed her for this dreadful happening. If only she had been able to give him more children, but of the six she had borne, only Bryony had survived to adulthood. The five little graves beneath the oak tree were a constant reproach.

Her husband, that man of stern and rigid principle, a man of short temper who did not suffer fools gladly, was ultimately responsible for anything his daughter might do. He had indulged her from the moment she had said her first words, had encouraged her defiance of her mother, had supervised an education that went far beyond the requirements of a girl whose only role in life was to be a good and obedient wife, a loving mother, and a just plantation mistress.

If only he had insisted that the marriage to Francis Cullum be celebrated on Bryony's eighteenth birthday, as the betrothal contract had stipulated, none of this would have happened. If only his daughter had been taught to recognize the duty she owed her parents, instead of cherishing this shocking assumption that she had the right to dictate the terms of her existence. For that, Edward was to blame. If Bryony carried such an assumption into marriage, she would be storing up a life of misery for herself. Eliza had learned by heart the *Virginia Gazette*'s description of a "good wife," one who was humble and modest from reason and conviction, submissive from choice, and obedient from inclination. A husband had the right to expect such a wife, and it was the parents' duty to ensure that their daughter would fulfill those expectations.

But none of these truths could assuage the mother's grief as she thought of her daughter and remembered only the warm, loving nature, the sunny temper, the quick consideration of others; she forgot the obstinacy, the sharp tongue, the indecorous habit Bryony had of always speaking her mind, no matter to whom, and the exasperating reluctance to devote her time to the embroidery, music, and drawing lessons essential to the education of a well-bred young lady.

Benedict fixed the night crawler on his hook and cast his line into the creek. It was an activity that usually brought him an untrammeled mind and enough clarity of thought to allow for problem solving. But his present problem seemed to defy solution. What in the name of the good God had he done? He had failed to recognize the hysteria of a fevered brain, of a young innocent subjected to a series of physical and mental assaults. He had thought he had an experienced wanton in his arms, and he could hardly have been blamed for thinking so. The way she had moved, had twined herself around him, had aroused him with such devastating instinct; and she had begged with such husky longing for the loving he found himself desperate to give. She had responded in the manner of one well versed in loving. But the devil take it! She wasn't well versed in anything, unless it was female sorcery.

A tug on his line caught his attention, and with a muttered oath, he pulled it in, unhooked the respectable-sized catfish, and tossed it into the bucket before re-baiting the hook and casting again. He had taken the virginity of some scion of Virginian landed gentry, and he'd probably got her with child into the bargain! For a minute he gave himself up to the scourge of self-disgust, permitting the self-flagellation as a necessary penance. Then, with customary decision, he looked again at the problem.

It was twofold, as far as he could see. On the one hand, he had allowed an unknown quantity to penetrate the secrecy that ensured his survival. Until the quantity became known, he must keep her both secure and in ignorance of anything except his first name and her immediate surroundings. She must not be allowed to wander farther afield and thus gain a knowledge of the geography that could be put to good use later. Neither must she be allowed a hint of his greater purpose.

The second thread of the problem lay quite simply in what had happened this morning. It must not be allowed to happen again. He could not possibly complicate further an already impossibly convoluted situation. She was his responsibility because he had made that decision the night of the Trueman raid and would continue to honor it; she was his prisoner by the same token, and her future would remain undecided until he had discovered her identity. Enjoying her body was most definitely not compatible with such a scenario.

Another tug on the line punctuated this satisfactory exposition of problems and half answers. He pulled in a second catfish and decided that two would suffice for their supper. It was also high time he returned to his responsibility, whom he had left dead to the world in the aftermath of passion.

Picking up a flat stone, he put the flapping, gasping fish out of their misery, then took the wickedly sharp clasp knife from his belt and gutted them both with swift economy. After tossing the guts back into the creek, where they would be devoured in the age-old food chain of turn and turn about, he wiped the knife on the grass and made his way back to the clearing.

Bryony had slept throughout most of Benedict's absence, but she had woken feeling bereft and disoriented, until, discovering the traces of that wonderful possession, she remembered why her body was cold and lonely. She lay still, playing with the images of what had happened, hearing her voice, shameless in its wanting, begging to be loved, reliving the sensations of her body as her hands moved slowly, touching herself where she had been touched. She was a spoiled virgin. The loaded phrase popped into her head with the ease of familiarity. Obviously, then, such a thing mattered to whoever she was. To whoever she *was*. It didn't matter in the slightest to who she was *now*.

Bryony stretched with a wondrous sense of well-being, feeling the slight stickiness on her belly and between her thighs. How had she known what to do? What was absolutely the right thing to do? She certainly had not done such a thing before; she seemed to know enough about breaching the maidenhead to be certain that that was what had happened. Perhaps you didn't need to know. Perhaps such knowledge was deeply embedded in the body and didn't need to be learned, needed only the right trigger to release it.

She sat up with a surge of energy and swung herself off the cot just as the door opened and Benedict came in. A wave of shyness paralyzed her, froze her tongue, and she just stood and looked at him as if seeing him for the first time. A slash of sun from the open door behind him burnished the thick copper thatch of his hair, carelessly rumpled as if he had just run his fingers through it. The nose was aquiline, set above that expressive mouth with its long, sensuous upper lip, a lip that her own remembered with tingling vividity. His complexion was bronzed by the sun, his beard as burnished as his hair, and the black eyes held all the sharp perception of a hawk.

His eyebrows lifted as he ran a swift, all-encompassing look down her body. Bryony blushed and pushed her hair back from her face. "I would like to bathe and wash my hair."

"I am not sure that water will be good for your burns just yet," he replied, briskly matter-of-fact, as if she were not standing naked in front of him. Then his eyes flicked to the bed behind her, caught the bright stain of blood on the sheet, and the self-recriminations flooded in again. "I don't suppose it will matter," he said, changing his mind. "They are all but healed. I even have some soap, somewhere." He picked over the shelf and came up with a sliver of the precious stuff. "Only coarse, I am afraid, but better than nothing." A scrap of toweling appeared in his hand. "You can use this to dry yourself."

"Thank you." Bryony took the offerings and continued to stand by the cot, uncertain what to do or say next.

"Come along, then." He moved to the door, a distinctly impatient note in the soft voice.

"Where to?" Bryony asked.

Benedict stopped and looked at her in surprise. "To the creek. You wish to bathe, do you not?"

Baths, Bryony seemed to remember, were generally taken in tubs within four walls. However, if they took place in creeks in this new life, so be it. Shrugging, she wrapped herself in the blanket again and followed him down to the water's edge. Once there, she regarded the rather murky water with some misgiving. "It does not look very clean."

"It is perfectly clean," he said shortly. "It flows constantly."

"But there will be fish in it." She looked at him, the huge eyes wide with appeal.

Benedict's lips twitched. He could not possibly manage to maintain his distance when she looked at him like that. "You will cause them more trouble than they will cause you," he said, taking the blanket from her. "Now, in with you, lass. I have to cook our supper in a minute."

Bryony took a tentative step into the bullrushes, her toes sinking with a squelch into mud. A shoal of tiny fish shot out from the reeds in alarm. Bryony jumped backward onto the bank. "I think I would prefer to fill a tub."

"I do not have a tub," he told her, his shoulders shaking with suppressed laughter.

"Well, perhaps I will wait until tomorrow." She picked up the blanket.

"You are in sore need of a bath, Bryony, and having got this far, I think we should complete the task." He pulled off his boots and unfastened his britches. "I will come in with you and frighten away the fish."

"I am not afraid of a little fish," she denied with total lack of conviction, her eyes locking without volition onto his body as he pushed off his britches.

"Then prove it!" He tossed his shirt onto the bank and strode toward her. "In!" Spinning her round so she could no longer look at him with those hungrily speculative eyes, he pushed her ahead through the rushes. "Get right under the water and wet your hair. I'll wash out the blood by that cut."

His voice was brisk, his hands as impersonal as he could make them, pressing on her shoulders to encourage her submersion. Bryony obeyed because she appeared to have little choice, but as she ducked below the water, her hand brushed against his flat belly. The muscles tautened involuntarily, and Benedict drew in a sharp breath. Deliberately, he made no further move, telling himself that the touch had been accidental. They were standing very close to each other, after all. But then her fingers whispered across his thighs in a knowing, arousing caress that only an insensate fool could pretend had been accidental. With an oath, he yanked her up.

"Just stop that!"

"You seemed to like it," she observed with a mischievously sensual smile, her hand reaching for the powerful evidence of his liking.

Dear God! Where had she acquired this wanton assurance? "Bryony, listen to me." He grabbed her wrist, holding it tightly. "What happened this morning was an aberration, and it is not going to happen again."

She looked at him, bewildered. "Why ever not? Why was it an aberration?"

"I do not make a habit of deflowering maids," he said bluntly. "If you had not convinced me you were no maid, it would never have happened."

"But I wanted it to," she said simply.

"You made me whole again. I still have no history, but I do not feel annihilated anymore. I have a present, and a future, which you helped me create."

"That is well and good, then; I am glad to have been of help," he said briskly, turning her back to him so that her hands were out of the way. "But it is not going to occur again." He lathered soap into her wet hair, carefully circumventing the lump behind her ear as he rubbed at the blood-clotted strands. "Once we discover who you are, you will be able to put it behind you, see it as a dream. So long as there are no repercussions," he added, pushing her under the water again to rinse the soap from her hair.

"What repercussions?" Bryony came up choking, in such a hurry to ask the question that she took in a mouthful of creek water.

Benedict sighed. "Think."

Bryony thought. "A child, you mean?"

"Just so."

"Then we would marry, would we not?" It seemed simple enough to Bryony. "I don't think I am already, and I could learn to live in a log cabin very easily."

Benedict wondered if she were being deliberately simpleminded, but, of course, she knew nothing about him at all. He told her so, succinctly.

"Well, I know that you are not a back-woodsman, really, for all that you are living like one at present," Bryony informed him, serenely soaping herself.

Benedict stiffened. "How do you know that?"

"Your hands, for a start," she replied, turning back to him, raising her arms to wash beneath them, the movement lifting her breasts clear of the water. "They are too fine, too elegant. And the way you speak. There is something about your voice, a lilt that I do not think I have heard before, but I do know that you don't have the speech of a peasant farmer or woodsman."

Benedict averted his gaze from the creamy swell where the tight bud of her nipple had hardened in response to the cool water and the fresh air. "Knowing what a man is not, my dear girl, is a long way from knowing what he is."

"Then tell me what you are." She looked at him in frank curiosity, her square chin tilted in unconscious challenge.

That combination of deep blue eyes, raven-dark hair, and skin like clotted cream was common to the beauties of his homeland, Benedict reflected absently. Perhaps she had Irish ancestry. "Come, you will catch cold if you stay in the water any longer. You are still not as strong as you should be."

"Why will you not answer me?" Her voice was low and insistent as she took his arm with sudden urgency.

"Because I cannot," he said briefly. "Do not ask again." Shaking off her hold, he turned his bare back on her for the first time and waded to the bank.

Bryony stared, appalled. The broad, muscled back was crisscrossed with ridged white scars from his neck to his waist. "What happened to you?" Her voice was barely a whisper; she knew the answer well enough, and a wave of nausea churned in her belly, surged acid bile in her throat.

From the bank, Benedict turned to look at her — standing waist-deep in the creek, her hand pressed to her mouth, her face the color of chalk, her eyes pools of horror. His lip curled; the black eyes seemed to flatten as all emotion left them. "Have you never before seen the scars of a flogging, Miss Bryony?"

She had. Many times. But never on the back of a white man. "Why?" she whispered. Her feet seemed to have taken root in the muddy bottom of the creek, and a shudder of cold and revulsion shook her, bringing goose bumps pricking on her skin.

"You will have to forgive me if I choose to keep my private affairs just that," he drawled, pulling on his shirt, which clung immediately to his wet skin. "You were obviously not taught the difference between pertinent and impertinent questions." He stepped into his britches, tugging them up roughly, pushing his shirt into the waistband.

"I am sorry," Bryony apologized wretchedly. "I did not mean to pry. It was just such a shock."

"You may count yourself fortunate if you receive no worse in your life," he stated, thrusting his feet into his boots. "I am going to start the fire for supper." He strode off through the trees, leaving the girl to uproot herself and stumble onto the bank.

Who was he? What was he? What could he possibly have done to invite that torture? She knew he was tender, caring, humorous. But he had tied her to the bed without compunction, and she also knew he had fired the barn where she, for some unknown reason, had been hiding. Had she been hiding? There were too many questions — all without answers.

Bryony dried herself with care, dabbing at her back, which had begun to sting again. The sensation brought renewed images of horror, and she bit her lip fiercely as she rubbed the water from her hair. Somehow, she had to discover the truth. And she was *not* going to accept his proscription on that wonderful activity to which she had just been introduced. Wrapped in the blanket, she marched determinedly back to the clearing, seeking refuge from her disturbing thoughts with action.

Ben was squatting before a fire laid in a circle of stones. A flat stone rested on the ashes, and on its hot surface lay the catfish. The marvelous smells of wood smoke and broiling fish set her saliva flowing, and she swallowed, sniffing hungrily. He glanced up, and she saw with relief that the dead, expressionless look in his eyes had vanished. In fact, they held a gleam of understanding humor as he read her expression. "Hungry?"

"Famished," she agreed, sitting down beside him.

"You must do a little work, too, you know, if you expect to be fed," he said with gentle irony.

Bryony felt her cheeks warm, and she stood up again. "I am quite willing."

He smiled at the stiff dignity in her voice. "In the cabin you will find a stone jar. It contains a loaf of wheaten bread. There is butter in the crock on the shelf, where you will also find knives and platters. There is a jar of cider in the corner, by the hearth, tankards on the shelf."

"It would be easier to fetch and carry if I did not have to hold the blanket around me," Bryony pointed out. "There must be something I can wear."

He frowned in thought. "I suppose you could wear one of my shirts for the moment. You will find one in the chest."

The chest was battered, bearing the scars of rough handling and much use. Made of leather-bound cedarwood, it was of the kind that Bryony's selective memory identified as a sea chest. She knelt to open it. The sweet fragrance of cedar filled the air and had impregnated the stack of linen. There were shirts of holland, fustian, and kersey, but beneath these working garments was a pile of the finest lawn, sleeves edged with Mechlin and Brussels lace — the shirts of a gentleman, and a wealthy one at that. Not the shirts of a man who bore the indelible marks of the whip upon his back.

"Is there not a nightshirt in there, at the bottom somewhere?" Benedict spoke from behind her, and she started guiltily as if caught prying. "I have no use for them, so you may as well have it." Bending over the chest, he flicked carelessly through the contents as if there were nothing at all extraordinary in the contrasts there revealed. "Yes, this should do." He shook out the folds of a white linen garment as soft as silk, with voluminous sleeves and a high, lace-edged collar. "You will drown in it," he said, chuckling, handing it to her. "You can use a cravat as a sash." This the chest also supplied. Then, whistling cheerfully, he swung up the jar of cider and took it outside.

Bryony dropped the luxurious, cedar-fragrant folds over her head. She was of more than middle height, but the night-shirt did, indeed, drown her. She rolled the sleeves to her elbows, where the folds billowed over her forearms, and caught the skirts up at the waist, confining them with the linen cravat. It was a strange costume, but infinitely preferable to the blanket, and the body beneath felt wonderfully cool and clean. She combed her drying hair with her fingers, shaking her head vigorously so that her hair swirled around her face to settle in a shining blue-black cloud over her shoulders. Then, her makeshift toilet completed, she set about the task of gathering up the required articles for supper.

"Shall I set the table inside?" She popped her head round the door. Benedict looked up, and could not hide his astonishment. Gone was the waif, tattered and bruised in her blanket; in her place stood this radiant young woman. He had known she was beautiful, but dirt and distress had done much to conceal the reality. She was also older than he had thought.

"How old are you?"

"Twenty," she replied instantly, then gasped. "I remembered."

"So you did." He smiled. "Can you remember your birth date?"

Bryony shook her head. "That still escapes me."

"It will come," he said with confidence. "Where do you wish to eat?"

"Outside. I have spent long enough confined."

He nodded easily and turned back to the fish. If only her memory returned soon, he could be rid of her before this damnable mess became even messier. And it would, he thought glumly. Never one to avoid the truth, Benedict was well aware that he would not be able to resist her if she decided to be irresistible.

A contented silence fell between them for the next half hour, until Bryony sighed with repletion. "That was wonderful." She scraped the last morsel of fish from the wooden trencher with the tip of her knife and sucked it off. "I don't think I have ever eaten anything so delicious."

Benedict laughed. "I am sure you have. But food in the open air always tastes better. Now, since I both caught and cooked our supper, you may take responsibility for clearing it away."

Bryony gathered up the trenchers, knives, and pitch-lined leather tankards. She looked uncertainly at the pile of fish bones. "What do I do with these?"

"Throw them back in the creek before you rinse off the platters," he told her.

"But I just bathed in the creek!" Bryony exclaimed. "I don't wish to bathe in water full of old fish bones and grease."

"Nature will look after it, lass." He shook his head. "The water is changing constantly with the river tide. Obviously, your education has been somewhat limited."

"I don't think I have ever washed dishes before, either," she declared, looking with distaste at her burdens.

"New experiences never did anyone any harm." He lay back on the grass with a contented sigh, gazing up at the sky, where the first stars were just beginning to appear.

When Bryony returned from the creek with the now clean dishes, the sleeves of the nightshirt sopping wet where they had fallen over her hands as she had bent to her task, Benedict was on his feet with the air of a man on the move. "I am going to leave you for an hour or two," he said without preamble. "And I want your parole before I do."

"My parole?" She stared, her eyes riveted on the pistols in his belt. "But I am not a prisoner."

"As I said this morning, that is a matter for definition." This was the other Ben, the man who set fire to barns. "Since I will not permit you, under any circumstances, to leave the clearing except to go down to that one part of the creek, you might say that you are a prisoner."

"Why?" Bryony was suddenly angry. She owed him her life, but that did not give him the right to impose imprisonment for reasons that were not vouchsafed. It wasn't as if she had done anything to deserve it; quite the reverse, since it was his fault that she was here at all.

"My reasons are my own," he replied quietly. "But they are sufficient. Will you give me your parole?"

"Not unless you tell me why I should," she said, her mouth taking a stubborn turn.

"Because if you do not, I shall have to confine you as I did earlier, and I do not wish to do that." There was patience in his voice, but it could not disguise the implacability of the statement.

"Tie me to the bed?" She glared in disbelieving anger.

"If you give me no choice." He glanced up at the sky and frowned. "I must leave now. Your parole?"

"No," Bryony heard herself say. "Not without a reason." She yelled as he lifted her as if she weighed no more than a kitten. But her twisting and writhing, the curses and imprecations, availed her not a whit. She was dumped in the middle of the bedstead and her wrist secured with the rawhide to the frame.

"Give me your parole, Bryony." He stood looking down at her, showing no satisfaction at his easy victory.

It was her last chance, and as much as she feared being left alone and helpless in this degrading fashion, the stubborn refusal to submit to what she saw as clear injustice, a reaction that Eliza Paget would have recognized instantly, made her shake her head in mute denial.

Benedict shrugged and lit an oil lamp on the table.

"What if something happens to you and you do not come back?" she demanded through a throat of leather. "There are bears in the woods."

"I will be back within two hours." Then he was gone.

Bryony wrestled the knot with her free hand, but it was an intricate series of twists that evaded all her efforts. There was sufficient play in the strap to allow her to sit up, even to get off the bed, and to lie in whatever position she chose. Still, tears of angry frustration not unmixed with fright poured down her cheeks. At least she was not in darkness. Had he any cruelty in him, he would have left her alone without the comfort of the lamp. Instead, with an air of grim resignation, he had simply done what he decided he had to do. It was just another facet of the man, another piece of the jigsaw.

She fell into a fitful sleep eventually, and woke with pounding heart at the sound of the door opening. But it was Benedict. He came over to the cot and unfastened the strap from the bed, although leaving it attached to her wrist. "Do you wish to go outside?"

Bryony wished that she did not and could answer him by disdainfully turning away, but her body was not prepared to be accommodating. When she returned, he was standing quite naked by the table, trimming the lamp. Even in vexation, laboring under a powerful sense of injustice, she could not help the little thrill that ran through her at the sight of that slim-hipped, broad-shouldered, vigorous figure, where there was only muscle and sinew, the bronzed skin stretched taut over the large frame. In silence, she climbed up onto the straw-filled mattress and tugged crossly at the strap still on her wrist. Benedict brought the lamp over to the cot, setting it on a stool; then, as silent as she, he swung himself onto the bed beside her. Taking the free end of the rawhide, he calmly fastened it around his own wrist, blew out the lamp, and lay down, pulling the blanket over them.

Bryony lay rigid in the dark, feeling his warmth so close to her, the length of him, lean and muscled, against her softness, and her hurt and anger seemed to evaporate.

He was going to win this battle of the parole because she did not want to fight with him; she wanted to make love with him. And that was clearly not a possibility in the present atmosphere. She edged closer, but to her disappointment there was no response. His breathing was deep and even, as if he had slipped instantly into sleep the minute he had lain down. Of course, she was swathed in yards of lawn, so it was hardly surprising that he could ignore her closeness. But there was always tomorrow.

# Chapter 3

The wood exploded with the joy of the dawn chorus, and Benedict slipped the knot on the strap that attached him to the still-sleeping figure and propped himself on one elbow to look down at her. That coloring was very Irish, he thought again, resisting the urge to trace with a fingertip the delicate flush of sleep high on her cheekbones. But whatever her history, he would stake his life that she had no firsthand knowledge of that strife-torn land.

"You are to be drawn on hurdles to the place of execution, where you are to be hanged by the neck, but not until you are dead; for, while you are still living, your bodies are to be taken down, your bowels torn out and burned before your faces, your heads then cut off, and your bodies divided each into four quarters, and your heads and quarters to be then at the King's disposal; and may the Almighty God have mercy on your souls."

The penalty for treason, but not if you were a Clare. When a Clare rebelled against the Crown, he was condemned to hear that ultimate sentence for his compatriots and then to hear for himself the mercy of a court presided over by a judge in the Clare family's pocket: fourteen years of penal servitude as a bondsman in the Colonies. And to spare the family further disgrace, he would no longer bear the name of Clare. That had been his father's sentence, and the bondsman had bowed his head in submission.

Until . . .

Benedict Clare sprang off the bed and strode naked to the door. At the creek, he swam vigorously, as he had swum in the rivers of his boyhood, cold, clear, pure Irish waters that drove the devils from the soul and the bleakest memories from the mind. But the devils and memories of boyhood had not the power of those that bedeviled maturity, and a Virginia creek was no Irish river.

She stood on the bank, watching him, waiting for him, feeling his pain across the distance that separated them, not understanding its whys or wherefores, but pierced by his agony, nonetheless. When he came out, his soul bared in his eyes, as

73

naked as his body, as scarred as his back, she went to him, enfolding him in her arms, the soft white folds of her gown billowing, clinging to his dampness; and as he had used his body to create a whole out of the fragments of her self, she used hers to heal, offering the essence of her womanhood to enclose and nurture.

Afterward, as they lay entwined on the bank, still wrapped in the magic of their union, she caressed his ruined back, learning each scar with her fingertips as her lips pressed into his neck, nipping and nuzzling like a foal against the salt-sweet skin. This time, she asked no questions, knowing with an age-old wisdom that the answers would emerge in their own good time and in the place of their choosing.

"You have unmanned me, sweeting," he whispered at last, breaking the spell. "Destroyed my resolve, decimated my defenses."

"Did you imagine I intended otherwise?" she returned in soft teasing, taking the free end of the strap that was still attached to her wrist and drawing it around his neck, pulling his head down to hers, tasting his lips with the tip of her tongue as a bee sips nectar. "I hold *you* prisoner now, do I not?"

"I fear so." His hands reached up to grasp her wrists. "And it is a pretty tangle in which we are enmeshed, lass." She felt the languor leave the hard body, the muscles tauten in thigh and belly as he prepared himself to move away from her. She pulled the strap tighter.

"Tell me, Ben. Tell me why it is such a tangle."

"Were I to do that, my sweet Bryony, I should not 'scape hanging." His voice was very sober, and the hands imprisoning her wrists gripped tighter, then broke her hold as if he were prying loose the little fingers of a baby, and slipped the strap from her wrist. He rolled off her and stood up. A glint of laughter in the black eyes chased away the somber expression.

"For a wood nymph, you are shockingly disheveled!" Bending, he caught her beneath the arms and pulled her upright, picking moss and twigs from the shining mass of black hair, brushing off dirt and grass that stuck to her sweat-slick skin. He shook his head in mock defeat. "I fear that it will have to be the creek again." She protested, laughing, as he scooped her up and waded into the water. Still holding her, he dipped her beneath the surface, and she relaxed into his hold, lying heavy in his arms as she gave herself to the cool water lapping silkily over her skin.

"What an indolent creature you are," he murmured, smiling down at her peaceful face, eyes closed in lazy pleasure, the raven's hair streaming on the surface of the water. "It seems you cannot even take a bath for yourself."

Her eyes shot open at the mischievous note, but the alert came too late to save herself. Before she could grab on to him, Ben dropped her. Chuckling, mightily pleased with himself, he left her floundering and sputtering in laughing indignation and waded to the bank.

"Bully!" Bryony accused, standing, hands on hips, in the waist-deep water.

"Not at all," he denied, sounding hurt. "I am going to prepare your breakfast. I look after you very well."

Which was undeniably true, Bryony reflected, watching him stride, wonderfully naked, through the trees. There was much softness in the man. Why would he not trust her with the truth?

She made her own way to the bank and picked up the soft lawn nightshirt that had been discarded in such haste during those wondrous moments when their bodies and minds had touched. The garment was

much the worse for wear, she thought ruefully, shaking out the folds. Then her eye
caught something she had not noticed before — two letters embroidered in white at
the back of the collar: *B.C.*

*B* for *Benedict.* That was easy enough.
What did the *C* stand for? And, more to
the point, did she dare ask? It would be a
perfectly understandable question, quite
natural, under the circumstances. She
dropped the shirt over her head, rolled up
the now grubby sleeves, and fastened the
limp cravat at her waist. Her hair dripped
chilly water onto her shoulders, and she
shivered uncomfortably. High summer it
might be, but water was still wet and
tended to be cold when it clung to the
skin.

She ran through the trees back to the
clearing, her bare feet now hardly noticing
the prick of the pine needles. There was no
sign of Ben, but a fire had been lit in the
stone ring, and she sat down beside it,
holding her wet hair to the warmth.

"It seems to me you need something a
little more practical to wear." Ben's voice
came from the cabin door, and she turned
curiously. "Put this on." He dropped
something creamy and soft into her lap.

Bryony made haste to obey. It was a

tunic of doeskin, the kind worn by Indian women, and it was the most comfortable garment Bryony could remember having worn. "It's lovely. Where did it come from?" She smoothed the butter-soft hide over her hips. It came to just below her knees and seemed to accentuate the slimness of her calves and the neat turn of her ankles, she thought with complacent vanity, tossing back her hair and smiling at him.

Benedict laughed. "You vain creature! However, it does suit you quite admirably."

Bryony flushed both at the accurate accusation and the compliment. "But where did it come from?" she asked again.

He shrugged. "A friend of mine. I acquired it last night." He took a kettle from the fire and poured boiling water onto coffee in a pewter jug. "How does fried hominy appeal?"

Bryony frowned. "I don't know. I don't think I have ever had it."

"Not a sufficiently refined dish, presumably," he observed with a dry smile. "Pour the coffee."

"I do not see why you should make mock in that manner," she retorted, stung. "I would imagine that in your past life, you were too refined to eat it, also."

If she had hoped for a reaction, she was disappointed. He merely shrugged and said, "Possibly."

"What do the initials *B.C.* stand for?" There seemed little to be lost by the question, but Benedict sighed wearily.

"If you are going to persist in this inquisition, lass, we are going to have another falling out. I have told you that my private affairs are just that. It is for your safety as much as mine." He spooned a mess of maize porridge onto a wooden trencher and handed it to her, advising, "Use your mouth for something other than questions."

Bryony scowled but accepted the inevitable. The hominy was quite palatable, particularly when one was ravenous. She cleared the plates and utensils afterward without Ben's prompting, but when she returned to the glade, it was to find him slinging a musket over his shoulder, counting bullets in the palm of his hand before dropping them into the deep pocket of his coat.

She felt a sudden flash of apprehensive premonition. "Where are you going?"

"Business," he said shortly, and it was as if the morning by the creek had happened to two other people. "Do we have to go through the lesson of last night again?"

She bit her lip, hating to give in, yet knowing she had little choice. Reluctantly, she shook her head. "I will stay by the cabin."

Benedict's face cleared with relief. "I know it's hard for you to accept, lass, but just trust me."

"Oh, I do," she replied with complete truth. "I trust you implicitly, which is why I don't understand why you will not trust me."

"It is not a question of trust," he said quietly. "I do not know exactly how long I will be. If you become hungry, you will find bread and cheese in the stores."

"But it is dangerous, what you are going to do, isn't it?" She looked at him, the blue eyes clear and determined, showing no fear of the answer.

Slowly, he nodded. "But no more than usual."

With that, Bryony must be satisfied, and she turned back to the cabin, strangely unwilling to see him out of sight. It was while she was putting away the dishes from their breakfast that she remembered something. It was nothing that seemed to have any direct relevance to herself; at least, it turned no keys in the locked area of her mind. But it seemed to have relevance to a great many other things. Bryony remembered the war.

It had been going on for just over four years, ever since British troops had arrived on a military exercise in Lexington, Massachusetts, where they had come across some seventy American minutemen gathered on the common in the mist of early morning. A series of blundered orders and misunderstandings, a volley of musket fire from each side, and eight minutemen lay dead in the dawn. At least, that was how she had heard it had begun, and in the years following, the fighting continued in the North, neither side winning a decisive victory. There had been no fighting south of Delaware. No, that was wrong. Something had been said. . . .

She frowned, struggling to place the echo of a voice, to grasp elusive threads, knowing that they were somehow important. All she had were the bare bones of a story, but she could not find the flesh. She could not even remember why there was fighting. Benedict could tell her about the war. There could be nothing secret about that. Or could there? Was this dangerous business that he pursued tied up with the struggle?

She went to the door, intending to sit in the sun and worry at those facts she had, in the hope of elucidation. But at the door, she froze, her heart thudding against her ribs. An Indian brave stood in the trees at the edge of the clearing. He carried a musket and was clad in a pair of britches made of the same doeskin as her tunic. He was standing quite motionless, almost as if his body were an insect's antenna picking up signals from the warm, summer air. A low whistle sounded as Bryony ducked behind the door, peering through the crack. Two more braves slid out of the trees.

There had been no Indian trouble for years, she told herself in an effort to quiet her pulse. But there were always renegades. She crept to the window at the back of the hut, stood on tiptoe to peer through. She could see no sign of life in the trees from here. But that didn't mean that the Indians weren't there. The forest was their home, an environment in which they blended without trace. Perhaps they were not interested in the cabin. Perhaps they would just disappear as soundlessly as they had come. And perhaps pigs could fly.

Bryony had climbed through the unglazed aperture and dropped to the ground beneath almost before this thought had come and gone. As she cowered against the back wall, she heard the squeak of the door and then the slight shuffle of a moccasined foot on the earthen floor. Her tunic, she noticed, seemed to blend into the earth as she wormed toward the trees on her belly, expecting any second to hear a shout or feel a clutch at her ankle. But she reached the green, shady refuge safely. She did not get to her feet, however, until she had crawled on pine needles several yards farther. Trembling, filthy, and wearied by that unaccustomed mode of progression, she stood up and set off on tiptoe through the trees.

"Tod, you will take your men to the right wing." Benedict's forefinger jabbed at the spot on the map spread out on the long oak table in the farmhouse kitchen. "Joe, to the left. I will take the front. There are sentries posted at each entrance, shifts changing every four hours. We make the raid one hour into the night shift, at one o'clock. That should give us time enough to be well away before the shift change." He glanced up at a dour, heavyset farmer whose corncob pipe filled the already stuffy atmosphere with acrid fumes. "You're responsible for the wagons, Joshua."

"Aye." Joshua nodded phlegmatically. "Three of 'em should do it." Sun poured through the two glazed windows that pierced the walls whose plaster of oyster-shell lime shone dazzling white under this illumination.

"Knives only?" said Tod, upending a rum bottle into his tankard.

Benedict nodded bleakly. "Absolute silence, or we're lost." He sliced into the raised crust of a giblet pie and carried the pewter spoon to his lips. "My compliments to your lady, Joshua. This is a fine pie."

"We'll all be lost if the British take Charleston," muttered a young man with a shock of bright red hair and an educated voice. "Georgia was lost as soon as they took Savannah. South Carolina'll go the same way, you mark my words. And what's the South to do without its major seaport?"

"Don't be such a pessimist, Dick." Benedict spoke briskly, pushing the pie toward the young man. "If Lincoln fails to hold Charleston, General Washington will send reinforcements from the North. And we'll be ready to welcome them with an entire armory and a band of Patriot soldiers well trained in the underbelly of this war." A smile lit his eyes, and he helped himself to the rum bottle. "Every weapon we take, my friends, is one less for the Tories."

"And every dead sentry, one less to fight," someone growled.

"True enough," Ben said without expression. He looked at the grandfather clock and pushed back his chair. He'd been away from the cabin for three hours, and it would take him an hour to return, on foot and by way of the little-known trails. "Rendezvous in the usual place, the first night of the new moon." He waited until they had all gone, except Joshua, whose house it was. Farmers, gentlemen, laborers — a diverse group with a shared aim. They would drive the British occupation from American soil and fulfill the goal of independence asserted with such magnificence three years earlier. Benedict Clare would help them, avenging his own wrongs and those of his friends as he fought the same enemy he had fought in his homeland, fighting for the same cause. He had lost once, but he would not do so again. Next time, he would die first.

With a gesture of farewell to his monosyllabic host, he slipped out into the July afternoon. The farm was isolated, set well back from the river and the main thoroughfares on land. It could be approached from any number of directions and, as such, provided the ideal meeting place for men who did not wish to be seen traveling in one another's company. Benedict made for the trees, seemingly uncharted to the ignorant eye, but for one who knew them they were a positive maze of intersecting trails easy enough for the educated eye to read.

He reached the clearing an hour later. The three Indians sitting around the stone fireplace hailed him cheerfully. Benedict returned the greeting in correct form before asking where the girl was.

"She crawled off into the woods," one of them said easily. "But we came to see you, Ben, not her."

"When did she go off into the woods?" he asked, apprehension prickling his scalp.

"When we arrived." The Indian looked up at the sun. "Some three hours past."

"Death and damnation!" Ben swore. "Why did you not stop her?"

"Came to see you, not her," the other repeated calmly. "Heard you'd got a woman, though." He offered a serene smile of congratulation that was not returned.

"Which direction did she take?"

"Over yonder. Went through the window at back." His informant gestured behind the cabin. Then a rather surprising thought seemed to strike him. "You want to find her? It shouldn't be difficult — not if she doesn't know the woods."

It was not an offer to be refused. These men would see tracks invisible to Benedict, and the woods were vast. What on earth had possessed her to break her word? There was nothing remotely alarming about his three visitors, who would have arrived perfectly peaceably . . . unless you were an aristocratic planter's sheltered daughter whose head had been stuffed with the old stories of savage massacres. It would not need many promptings of a rich imagination to send such a one scuttling in panic. Understanding reduced his anger to exasperation, but it could do nothing to allay his fears for her — an inexperienced baby loose in the woods with only half her memory.

His companions read answer in his expression and loped off into the trees at the rear of the house. Benedict stood irresolute. It was a waste of time and effort to join them; it was not as if he could be of any assistance. And she might find her own way back. In which case it would be better if he was here.

Bryony, in fact, had long ago given up all

hope of ever being able to find her way back. The world consisted of trees — monumental, gnarled oaks that blocked the light of the sun; huge, spreading chestnuts whose leaves filtered the light that dappled the mossy carpet at her feet. There were bright animal eyes, too, and rustlings; the knocking of a woodpecker, much less alarming than the funny snaking slithers that brought clammy sweat to the palms of her hands. Every now and again, she would remember that some snakes lived in trees, waiting curled against a gray branch for a movement beneath; and when she remembered that, Bryony thought that death was probably preferable to the terror of anticipation. It seemed that, except when she was with Ben, there was only terror.

She stubbed her toe on an upthrust root and dropped to the ground with a moan of misery, rubbing the injured foot. A sudden shiver ran down her spine. Abruptly she looked up — into a grinning bronzed face. Bryony screamed, leaping to her feet. She continued to scream, drowning out the words of the Indian, who was joined almost immediately by his two companions. Then a flat palm slapped against her right cheek, and she fell silent with a sobbing breath.

"Your pardon," the Indian who had struck her apologized carelessly. "But you weren't listening. Ben wants you back." He gestured with a flick of his hand to the right, and Bryony belatedly came to her senses. She had run needlessly from Ben's friends. The doeskin tunic she was wearing — hadn't he said it came from a friend? Tears of mortification at her foolishness stabbed, and she blinked hastily. A finger prodded her in the small of the back, and she realized that she was still standing in the same spot. "Not good for a man's woman to run off," the owner of the finger declared.

Bryony's tears dried miraculously. "I am *not* Ben's woman!"

A disbelieving "humph" came from behind her, and the finger jabbed again. She set off in the required direction, thinking with an absurd and slightly hysterical bubble of laughter that her three captors obviously did not realize they were responsible for her flight. And how would Benedict see it? The thought sobered her instantly. She had violated her parole. But surely he would understand.

She found herself in the clearing in a ludicrously short time — an embarrassingly short time! No more than a quarter of an hour, yet she had been wandering, lost, for an eternity.

"Sweet Jesus!" Ben strode toward the little group. "You gave me your word!" His hands closed over her shoulders, his eyes charcoal embers as he shook her. Bryony pushed vigorously against his chest with clenched fists.

"I was frightened!" she protested, instinctively adopting the policy of attack as the best form of defense. "I do not know who your friends are! I know *nothing* about you. You left me here alone —"

Ben silenced her with his mouth, hard in its enforcement, yet making his own statement of relief. Their audience, appearing to find nothing untoward about the spectacle, returned to squat at the open-air hearth as they had done throughout the afternoon. The trouble with the woman had simply delayed their talk with Ben, but patience was a quality they had in abundance.

"Where have you been?" Benedict demanded, releasing her lips at last.

"I do not know," she said miserably. "To hell and back, I think. There is so much to be frightened of, Ben, when you have neither comprehension nor memory to make sense of things."

Slowly, he nodded as he made space in the circuitous turmoil of anger and relief for empathetic understanding. He smoothed the tumbled hair from her brow, his thumbs massaging her temples as a rueful smile played over his lips. "Poor lass. You are having a rough time of it, these days. A little brandy, I think, is called for. Come and be introduced properly to my friends."

"I thought I was not supposed to meet your friends." In spite of a distressing afternoon followed by inordinate relief, Bryony was still capable of challenge.

"That depends on the friends," he said in a level tone, refusing to pick up the glove. "You can do no more harm to these than they can do to you."

Bryony frowned. "The Indians are not connected with your 'business,' then?"

"A logical enough conclusion," he said with an easy nod. "They'll not, however, expect you to participate in our conversation, so you will not embarrass me by remaining after you have been introduced, I trust."

"I am not an Indian woman," Bryony pointed out.

"That is not in dispute, but it won't alter their view of the matter. And as they are my guests, I will not offend their principles." It

91

was said very gently, accompanied by a smile, but Bryony was in little doubt as to the nature of the request — it was not one that brooked refusal.

"I have remembered about the war," she said, preferring to allow his statement to go by default. "At least, I have remembered some. I would like you to tell me the bits I have forgotten."

"We will discuss it later." Without further ado, he led her over to the fire stones, where with immaculate formality he introduced her to the three men. Then he asked quietly, "Would you bring us the bottle of brandy, lass? Take some for yourself, first."

So, in addition to absenting herself from the conversation, the woman was required to wait upon the menfolk. Something niggled at the back of her mind as she went into the cabin — a sense of déjà vu. Somewhere, sometime, she had felt this same irritation, yet knowing, as she did now, that the irritation was not considered acceptable or justified. Rules were rules, and one should not attempt to change them. Or, at least, that was the received wisdom.

Bryony poured brandy into a cup, which she left on the table, then took the bottle outside, presenting it with a mock curtsy to Benedict.

The black eyes sparked with laughter. "So, you haven't forgotten your manners, then," he murmured, taking the brandy. "Try to rest a little now. You are still not fully recovered, and I don't wish to have an invalid on my hands again."

She smiled appreciatively, recognizing the delicate way he had ensured her compliance with his guests' rules while giving her the perfect self-motivating excuse for her absence. And truth be told, she was very weary.

An hour later, Benedict's guests took their leave. A glance in the cabin told him that Bryony was fast asleep, and he took his gun and went out in search of their dinner. It was the devil's own nuisance that she had recalled the war. Once he had satisfied her hunger for the details, she would draw the obvious conclusion — that he himself was hip deep in the civil strife.

His eye caught a flash of gray in the undergrowth. His musket bellowed, and the flash became still. It was a plump hare, more flavorsome than squirrel, which was an acquired taste and one that it was reasonable to assume had not so far been acquired by Miss Bryony.

"Are you fighting for the Patriots or the Loyalists?" Bryony asked him as he came back toward the cabin. "I have been trying to light the fire, but I do not seem very good at it." Her cheeks smudged with soot and her hands caked with ash were ample evidence of this fact — that and a very dead fire.

So, she had already reached the correct conclusion without help from him. Her sleep had obviously renewed more than her physical strength. There was little to be gained by further concealment. He dropped the bloody carcass on the grass and squatted down beside her. "Let me show you. It's just a knack."

Bryony sat back on her heels and watched him with undisguised admiration. "You are so competent, Ben." Her eyes flicked to the dead hare. "I suppose you are going to skin that now."

"Unless you wish to eat it with the skin on," he suggested with a gravity belied by the curve of his mouth. "Or do you care to attempt the task yourself?"

"No," she said with repugnance. "If I were not so hungry, I do not think I should care to eat it, either."

"Well, there are some carrots, turnips, potatoes, and onions that you can peel and chop," he said cheerfully, indicating a small sack leaning up against the cabin. "A gift from our friends this afternoon. In the pot with the hare, they will make an excellent stew."

"I suppose so." Bryony sounded a little doubtful. She was quite sure that she had never peeled a vegetable. "You did not answer my question."

Ben pulled his clasp knife from his belt. "No, I did not." Dragging the hare toward him, he turned it over and slit its belly.

Bryony averted her eyes. "You don't really need to, because I think I can guess. You are a Patriot. I remembered what the war is about, you see, when I woke up, and I do not think that Loyalists live in woods."

"And what are you?" he asked, pausing in his task.

Bryony sighed. "I don't know," she said. "I've made my head ache with thinking, but there is still nothing there. I know that I must be one or the other, because everyone is, are they not?"

"All but the dying and the lunatic," he agreed.

"Well, what do *you* think I am?"

"Impossible to say." He shrugged, wiping his bloody hands on the grass. "Trueman's Tory, though, and you were at his house."

"He would not entertain a Patriot?"

95

"He might." Ben quartered the hare and threw it into a pot. "There's been no real fighting in these parts, yet. Rhetoric, certainly, gathering of arms and training of militia; but families and friends are living with split loyalties. When it comes time to bear arms, then the divisions will make themselves felt."

"And that time will come soon?" The deep blue eyes held him with their intensity, their passionate need to people the wasteland of her mind with sense and facts.

He could not refuse her that understanding; could not condemn her to wander in the confusion of a suddenly imposed, arbitrary ignorance. "Georgia and some areas of South Carolina have fallen to the British expeditionary force and the Loyalists. Charleston has been under attack since May. If it falls to Clinton and Cornwallis, then the rest of the Carolinas will follow. Virginia, logically and geographically, comes next."

*That* was what she had been trying to remember this morning. But the voice that accompanied the revived memory still remained an elusive echo. "So you are preparing for this? Preparing to meet the Tories and the British if . . . when . . . they come?" It was presented as a question, but it was fundamentally rhetorical.

Ben opened the sack of vegetables and upturned it on the ground before her. Wiping his knife clean, he presented it to her, handle politely forward. "Your job, Miss Bryony."

She grimaced but attacked the task with grim determination. "You were working for the Patriot cause when you fired the barn that night?"

"Yes." He sat back and watched her, a smile tugging his lips at her struggles with a potato.

"Doing what?" She held up the potato for inspection. "It doesn't look very clean."

"Stealing arms." He stood up. "I'll fetch water from the creek. When they're washed, I expect they will do."

"And you did not want me to know of these things because when . . . if . . . I remember who I am, it might be difficult for us?"

"Basically," he agreed, picking up the kettle. "If I find I've a passionate Tory under my roof, one who knows a great deal more than she should about me, we would both be in danger. As would those with whom I work."

"But now I do know."

"Yes, you do." A sheen of mockery filmed his eyes — a mockery that encompassed them both. "The road to hell is paved with good intentions, lass. I held out for as long as I could against the odds presented by a somewhat determined waif with a wonderfully passionate hunger for the glories of loving."

Bryony smiled with pleasure. "It was quite unexpected," she announced, almost smugly. "I do not think I had felt it before."

Benedict roared with laughter. "There is a world of difference between feeling such a hunger and satisfying it, sweeting. I suspect that you have been tormented with the feeling for quite some time, but its satisfaction is customarily confined to the conjugal bed. And you appear to have no husband, for all your advanced years."

"Well, what happens now that I know about you?" Bryony found both his laughter and his statement a little galling and reverted to the original topic.

His laughter died. "We will have to wait and see what your memory turns up. There's no point crossing bridges until we reach them."

He went down to the creek, leaving Bryony to wrestle with recalcitrant vegetables, and to reflect that, in truth, she still knew very little of the man. His history was as closed to her as her own, and was likely to remain so if Benedict had anything to say about it. It was a history that had scarred him, and she was somehow convinced that the worst scars were those she could neither see nor touch.

# *Chapter 4*

A stray wisp of raven's-wing hair was tickling Ben's nose. Smiling, he moved it aside and rolled over to examine the hair's sleeping owner. Miss Bryony was, he decided complacently, a little too good to be true. Long summer days in the sun had kissed her complexion with a delicate gold and produced a most surprising scattering of freckles over the bridge of her small, slightly upturned nose. A certain deep contentment, engendered by the soul's peace and the body's fulfillment, lent a suppleness to her features, a translucency to her skin, a languid grace to her movements. The slight hesitancy of the unsure had yielded to the full, rounded beauty of the mature woman — one who took as much pleasure in the giving as she did in the receiving.

His smile broadened as he slowly drew the blanket down her body, carefully because he didn't want to wake her just yet; he wished to savor the moments when her body lay in all its sensual beauty, for the moment uninhabited by the vigorous spirit, the bubbling energy, the eagerly inquiring mind that led her to plunge into new experiences, from baiting fish hooks to making love in company with the fish in the creek. The lady's soft and so very white hands were now brown, the nails broken and not always perfectly clean.

It was near impossible to look and not touch, Ben decided, teasing himself with his restraint as he allowed his hands to imagine that they were globing the small, soft hillocks of her breasts, now flattened over her rib cage as she lay on her back, arms flung above her head, hands curled like those of a sleeping child. Just the lightest flick of his fingertip, and the sleeptight buds of her nipples would lift and harden and her hips would writhe in sympathetic arousal.

He allowed his gaze to roam with lazy anticipation over the delineation of her ribs, the slender curve of waist and belly, the soft flare of her hips, the raven-black fleece at the apex of her thighs. With a little sigh of resignation, he yielded to the inevitability of needy passion and placed his hand at that apex, fingering the mound beneath the silky fleece, one questing finger pursuing its own course until she stirred, her hips lifting, a contented little moan escaping her lips, parted in the relaxation of sleep.

Bryony luxuriated in the twilight world of half sleep, where nothing existed but this dreamy arousal as lips nuzzled, a tongue stroked hot and demanding, teeth nibbled with playful intensity, and hands possessed every inch of her sleep-warmed skin until the prickles of pleasure ran like wild fire, connecting every nerve ending, until she was forced to abandon all pretense of sleep and enter the world of powerful sensations that refused to be denied.

He rolled her onto her side, her back to him, molding himself against her curved shape so that he could continue to play, to probe, and to stroke over the exquisitely sensitive center of her arousal as he slid within her moist, welcoming chamber. His breath rustled against her neck on an exhalation of supreme joy when his turgid flesh, in throbbing intensity, found its home. Bryony whispered her own pleasure, moving backward against him, her bottom warm against the taut flatness of his belly as she held him within the enclosure of her body.

"I've a powerful need, sweeting," he murmured into her hair. "Bear with me."

She smiled, a woman's secret smile at the knowledge of her power to arouse and of her unique ability to satisfy that arousal. Her body softened, welcoming his release, and she drew her own pleasure from this moment of giving, knowing in her new-found wisdom that the pleasures of loving came in many and varied forms and it was not necessary for two always to share the same form at the same moment. Her own moment came, as she had known it would, when the inexorable spiral of sensation coiled her body beneath his fingers, clamped the muscles in belly and thighs, and her blood sang in the joy of expectancy; then the spiral burst asunder, the coil unraveled, and utter languor flowed like butterscotch through her veins.

Later that morning, Bryony, according to instruction, was husking ears of Indian corn. Benedict, a preoccupied frown corrugating his brow, paused in the process of untangling a fishing line that she had earlier contrived to snarl in the branches of an overhanging tree by the creek. "There is going to be a slight disturbance in the even tenor of our existence, lass."

Bryony looked at him curiously. The announcement had been made in that soft, determined tone that she knew meant business and certainly would not permit objections. Did it mean that he was expecting her to object to whatever he was about to say? "A pleasant disturbance?" she asked.

He shook his head. "Not really. But tonight I have something planned — something that means I must put you in a safe place, in the care of one who will be able to look after you until you regain your memory in case I should find that I cannot."

"If you're killed or taken?" Bryony demanded directly. A small nod was her answer. "What are you going to do?"

"The less you know, the better, lass." He frowned over a particularly recalcitrant knot in the line. "I must teach you to be a little less enthusiastic when you cast."

"Oh, bother the fishing line!" she said with a gesture of impatience. "Why won't you tell me what you're planning? I know so much already, what difference can it make?"

"You know a great deal more than I am happy with," he informed her in the same soft tones. "I am not about to add to the sum."

"Then I'll husk no more corn." Bryony tossed the ear to the ground and glared at him.

"Then you'll have no dinner," he responded, serenely unperturbed. "After the dinner that you won't be having if you refuse to do your share, I shall be taking you to the farm of a friend of mine. His wife will care for you until I return."

"He, of course, will be going with you." Bryony resumed work on the corn. She was always far too hungry these days to contemplate going supperless over a pointless defiance that would not achieve her object anyway.

"That is so." He smiled at her. "Don't scowl, lass. If the wind changes, your face will be stuck like that, and it is not at all pretty."

That made her laugh, as he had known it would. "My nurse used to say that to me."

"What was her name?" He asked the question casually, hoping, as always, that this unexpected memory, produced so naturally, would start a chain reaction.

But Bryony shook her head ruefully. "I do not recall. But she did say it."

"How can you be so sure it was a nurse and not your mother, perhaps?"

"I don't know." A look of desolation crossed the mobile countenance. "How long is this going to continue, Ben? It is so frustrating to have these little, tantalizing glimpses into the abyss and then . . . nothing!"

"Just give it time." Ben smiled reassuringly as he stood up with the now untangled fishing line. "Come along. Let's see if you can catch our dinner without catching a tree first."

Bryony did what she could to put aside thoughts of the coming night. It was clear that Benedict intended to be no more forthcoming than he had been, which left her in possession of remarkably few facts and a wealth of anxious uncertainty. She did not want to be disposed of like a child in need of a caretaker, but neither did she want to spend the night alone in the cabin wondering if he would ever return. If only he would tell her what he was going to do, then the dread would at least have a shape, and she could perhaps calculate his chances of returning safely.

"You're not concentrating," Ben chided, standing behind her, holding her hands tight around the fishing rod. "What did I just tell you to do?"

Bryony nibbled her bottom lip. Even if she had not been preoccupied with her fears of the coming night, she would have found it difficult to concentrate in this proximity. The skin of her back was alive and rippling at the feel of his chest, bared and warm, pressed against her. Her eyes seemed riveted on his fingers, long and strong, linked around her hands. "Why don't you catch the fish and I'll sit on the bank and watch you?"

"Because you will never learn like that and you cannot spend your days in idleness. Just flick your wrist, like this." Her wrist flicked under the tutoring of his fingers, and the line snapped across the surface of the creek in perfect order. "See how easy it is." He released his grip. "Do it on your own this time."

The attempt was a miserable failure, and she looked mournfully upward as the line took on a life of its own and doubled back into the branches of the weeping willow overhead, twisting itself with malevolent momentum round and round a branch.

Benedict sighed. "You are not trying, Bryony. At this rate, we are going to go very hungry."

"Oh, why won't you do it?" she implored. "I do not think I want to be a fisherman."

"Well, this time you are going to have to untangle that line yourself," he said briskly, picking up a second rod from the bank. "I will catch our dinner while you do so."

Untangling fishing line was a most unpleasant task, Bryony discovered, her fingers slipping and sliding over the slick twine, which had a nasty habit of slicing deeply into her hands when she was least expecting it. The cuts were tiny but bled copiously and hurt like the devil; only her innate stubbornness and a refusal to admit further failure to her effortlessly competent companion prevented her from throwing in the towel.

"Finished?" Ben glanced over his shoulder in inquiry. Two shining silver mullet flapped on the bank at his feet.

"Almost," she said, wiping her bloody palms on the grass, swallowing a yelp of pain.

"What in the name of the good God have you done to yourself?" Ben exclaimed, dropping his rod and coming over to her. "Show me your hands."

"There's nothing the matter with them," she said in emphatic denial, holding them curled against her sides. "See, I have almost finished."

Benedict would not be distracted. He went down on one knee beside her. "Show them to me."

Reluctantly, she uncurled her palms and turned up her hands for his frowning inspection. "Why on earth didn't you stop?" He looked at her in exasperation, and Bryony's mouth set firmly.

"I like to finish what I have started. I cannot help being incompetent, but I'm not going to admit defeat in a battle with a piece of twine."

The exasperation in his features faded, and he chuckled. "Such an indomitable will is an unusual possession for a young woman of your kind. You are supposed to be submissive and accepting of your fate." His voice was teasing, but Bryony had the feeling that he was at least half serious.

"I wonder why I am different, then?" she said.

"We shall find out soon enough. Go back to the cabin and put some of that salve on those cuts." He returned to his fishing, lips pursed thoughtfully. In his far-from-limited experience, young ladies of good parentage and substantial estate received only the most rudimentary learning, the main focus of their education being on acquiring the skills to equip them for marriage and motherhood — in short, to ensure that they were able to provide the necessary degree of comfort in a man's life, whose life would form the pivot of their own. Miss Bryony, he had discovered, possessed a knowledge of the classics to match his own, and her skill at mathematics far exceeded the simple demands of housekeeping. She had an analytic turn of mind that had clearly been fostered by someone. She accepted nothing without question and gave in only when the odds were insuperable. He somehow doubted that she would willingly subdue her own needs and desires to those of another, be he her lord and master according to the laws and vows of matrimony or not.

The sickle of the new moon hung low in the sky, offering only slight illumination, when Benedict extinguished the oil lamp in the cabin and followed Bryony outside. He stamped out the last glowing embers of the fire in the stone hearth and took one final look around the clearing. The black eyes, sharp as a hawk's, saw nothing untoward, and he gave a short nod of satisfaction. "Let us go. It's an hour's walk through the woods."

Bryony, who had never walked in the woods at night, found herself prey to her vivid imagination. Every rustle, every whispering murmur made her jump. Her companion, on the other hand, strode unerringly along almost invisible trails, no wider than the span of a man's hand, where the undergrowth was barely trodden down. Bryony pressed on behind him, grateful for the hand he held at his back, into which her own occasionally disappeared, her fingers clutching convulsively around his. Benedict didn't seem disposed for conversation, and since Bryony could think of nothing but the questions she wished to ask, questions that he would not answer, silence reigned supreme.

After an hour of this, they broke through the trees into a field. Across the field, the lights of a building winked in welcome.

The group of men waiting in the kitchen, dark clad, their faces smeared with soot or burned cork, stared at the figure blinking bemusedly beside their leader.

"What's she doing here?" William demanded.

Benedict ignored the question. "Joshua, is your wife around?"

"Aye, shutting up the chickens, I reckon," the farmer said, puffing on his pipe.

"I want her to look after the girl." He gave Bryony a little push in the direction of the oak settle by the hearth. "Sit over there, lass."

"You be leaving her here, then?" William

spluttered. "So she can tell about this place, about us, about —"

"She knows nothing," Benedict interrupted. "How's she going to recognize you, blacked up as you are? And we came through the woods. She'd never be able to find her own way."

"Aye." Joshua nodded sagely. "Makes sense, and he couldn't leave her alone in the cabin. Bertha'll be happy to have her company." He got to his feet. "There's three wagons out back. The lads and I will bring them along once ye're well on the way."

"Right." Benedict glanced round the circle. "Everyone knows what to do. Let's get to it." He gave Bryony a smile as he stood at the door, and her heart lurched. What would become of her if he did not return? Would he not kiss her in farewell? But she knew that he wouldn't, in order to save her embarrassment. His men might think what they pleased about what went on in the cabin in the woods, but Benedict would give them nothing on which to base their conclusions. The fact that Bryony did not care in the slightest what they thought would probably not weigh with him, so she kept her seat on the settle and watched them go, all but Joshua and two lads in their mid-teens.

"How long do you wait?" she asked tentatively. "Before you follow them?"

The farmer shrugged. "A quarter hour. They'll be off through the fields. Us with the wagons must take the high road. Take us half the time."

"I see." Bryony nodded and thought fast. She was not going to stay here in this isolated farmhouse with the unknown Bertha, waiting in trepidation for the return or not of the only solid factor in her present trackless existence. She would hitch her fate to the Patriot's, embrace his destiny this night, because at the moment her life without him was unthinkable.

Bertha, a comfortable woman in holland apron, linen cap, and heavy boots, plodded into the kitchen. She listened to Joshua's laconic explanation for the stranger on the settle, accorded Bryony a friendly nod, and began to bustle around the room, trimming lamps, straightening the rush-bottomed chairs left askew by the departing men. Bryony sat quietly, waiting until it became clear that Joshua and the two boys were preparing to leave.

"I've a need of the necessary house, ma'am," she murmured in polite explanation, slipping out into the dark yard. The three wagons, already hitched, stood in the shadow of the barn. It was the work of an instant to hop into the back of the lead cart and to burrow beneath a pile of coarse sacks whose generally dusty condition suggested that they had been used to transport flour. She would look like a wraith, Bryony thought, her hair floured, her face deathly white. But such considerations were of little importance. She cowered against the side of the wagon, praying that the men would come to start their journey before the length of her visit to the necessary house became marked. Once she was away from here, there was nothing Bertha could do about her truancy.

After what seemed an eternity, a square of light showed from the farmhouse door, and low voices drifted across the yard. She dived back beneath the sacks, praying that she would not sneeze from the irritating burlap and the dust. The wagon creaked in protest, the frame shaking as someone clambered onto the bench. Joshua, she thought. The other two were too slightly built to have that effect. A soft clicking noise encouraged the horse forward, and the wagon moved out of the yard with its unseen passenger.

It was a long journey on a warm night, and Bryony struggled for breath beneath the sacks, not daring to raise her head from the hard planking of the wagon's floor. It was a bumpy ride since she had nothing with which to brace herself, and just when she was beginning to regret the impulse that had condemned her to this suffocating, jolting, bruising misery, the motion mercifully ceased. Holding her breath, she waited. Discovery at some point could not be avoided, but it mustn't be too soon. If Joshua found her before his rendezvous with Ben, he might decide to take her back to the farm, and that would defeat her object, as well as jeopardize whatever goal this mission carried. That last consequence was one she was not prepared to face.

The wagon creaked and sighed as Joshua descended. Bryony lay motionless, concentrating on every sound in the blackness of her hiding place. A whisper on the wind, and then there was silence, utter silence. Gingerly, she emerged from the sacks, shaking her hair free, wiping her sweating brow with the back of her hand. Smearing dirt and flour dust, no doubt — she dismissed this half thought as totally irrelevant. The crescent moon was visible but shadowed in mist, the stars blanketed in high cloud, the air filled with the near-hysterical chorus of cicadas — an inevitable part of the backcloth of these summer nights.

Bryony dropped to the ground; grass underfoot, bushes encircling the wagons. The three horses chewed their bits and stood, placid and resigned to the waiting. There was no sense of human activity anywhere, yet Joshua and the boys had been gone no more than five minutes. Ben and the others must be somewhere near.

Ben's last visit to his Indian friends had produced a pair of moccasins, as silent as they were comfortable, and Bryony now trod with the utmost stealth across the grass, pushing through the screen of bushes. Then she stared at the sight before her. A low building of wood sheathed with chestnut planking stood within a pallisade. The double doors of the building stood open, and dark-clad men moved silently in and out, adding muskets and sacks to a growing pile. She recognized Benedict immediately, as much by his bearing as by his face, the only one not blackened with burned cork. He was clearly directing the operation even as he seemed to do his share of the fetching and carrying.

A cough and a shuffle of feet screeched in the quiet, and she ducked back behind the bushes, her heart pounding. Someone was standing within five feet of her — a lookout, perhaps? They would have to have them posted all around. Bryony stood and thought. She did not want to announce her presence just yet. It would distract Ben, and she didn't wish to give him further cause for the wrath that would inevitably fall upon her head when she was discovered. Somehow, the idea of waiting meekly by the wagons for that moment did not appeal, either.

Moving away from the activity and the lookout, Bryony slipped through the bushes at the far side of the clearing and found herself on a cart track. It was presumably the track the wagons had taken to bring them to this spot, and it continued past the concealing bushes. Bryony wondered whether they had come from the south or the north; she had had no way of telling from beneath the sacks. She started down the track in the direction of the north star, curious to see if there were any indications of human habitation. The building that housed the armory that Ben and his men were so efficiently plundering presumably had not sprung out of nowhere.

The sound of voices raised in raucous laughter above the cicadas, the smell of wood smoke and tobacco brought her up short. She shrank into the shadows. Did Ben know that there were others abroad tonight? Others this close? Bryony crept forward to the bend that hid the owners of the voices from view. Around the corner she saw a sight to chill the blood. In a field bordering the track, about a dozen redcoat soldiers were sprawled around a fire. Judging by their opened coats, the weapons scattered carelessly on the grass, the flagons that were being passed from mouth to mouth, they were not on active duty, were not expecting anything to disturb their roistering. Someone played a few haunting notes on a pipe, and voices joined in singing accompaniment.

Bryony crept back around the bend, and once there took to her heels, flying down the dry mud-ridged track as if all the devils in hell were pursuing her. Her hair streamed, as black as the night, as the warm, moist air rushed past her with the speed of her progress, and the sweat ran on her body so that the doeskin tunic stuck to her skin. She arrived, panting, at the wagons and was about to rush through the bushes and down to the armory when something grabbed her from behind. She opened her mouth to yell, but a hand, hot and hard, clamped over her mouth. She could taste the salty sweat of the palm pressing against her lips, could smell the sourness of unwashed skin and hair as she writhed in terror. Her feet left the ground as an iron band at her waist lifted her into the air. She was carried, kicking and struggling, through the bushes. It was only then that she was sure she had fallen into the hands of one of Ben's men and not one of the soldiers, and her struggles ceased. When she was still, she was set on her feet again, although the gagging hand remained in place and one of her arms was pulled behind her back, held there with painful pressure as she was propelled forward.

She was marched across the enclosure, toward the open doors of the building. Just as they reached the entrance, she heard Ben's voice, authoritative yet with that inherent softness that reminded her of spring raindrops. When had she had that fanciful thought before? The instant before she was thrust into the building, Bryony remembered. She was in the hayloft, listening to the voices of the intruders who had clubbed Jebediah just as she had been about to leave the stableyard and return to the house, her problem unsolved, but at least the solitude had brought her some peace. Her problem . . . Francis . . . oh,

God, it was better not to have remembered! Her father, Sir Edward Paget . . . a king's man to his backbone, to his last drop of blood . . .

*"What the hell are you doing here?"* The soft voice, infused with incredulity, exploded her rapt trance. Bryony shook her head free of the memories that, now unleashed, threatened to overrun her senses. The hand at her mouth was lifted.

"Redcoats," she said. "About half a mile to the north, along the track."

"Coming here?" The question snapped in the sudden stillness.

"No." She shook her head. "Camped and well away with drink, I think."

"Sentries?"

"I did not see any, and I nearly fell over the camp, but no one saw me. There are perhaps a dozen of them, but I didn't stay to look around carefully. It seemed more urgent to warn you."

He looked at her closely, the black eyes narrowed. "If you're due any gratitude, you will receive it with what else is owed you for this night's work." There was no misunderstanding him, and Bryony swallowed nervously. This was the Benedict who set fire to barns, stole weapons, tied innocent people to beds in order to prevent their getting in his way. This was the man who bore the scars of the whip upon his back, inflicted for some unknown crime.

He swung away from her and began to rap out orders in a sharp staccato. Bryony backed out into the enclosure, where men were moving swiftly and silently, the pile of weapons diminishing as they were transported to the waiting carts. She stepped sideways to avoid a man with a heavy sack and tripped over something soft and yielding. A rapidly quelled scream emerged from her lips as a strangled whimper of horror. The man at her feet was dead, his eyes staring wide and blank into the night sky, a red stain spreading untidily across his tunic.

"Get over to the wagons." It was Benedict's voice, harsh, bearing no resemblance now to spring raindrops.

"He's dead," she said, looking up at Ben.

"And he'll not be the only one before this night is over, unless we have uncommon luck," he replied shortly. "Have you any idea what you've walked into?" He shook his head impatiently. "I don't have time to deal with you now. Get over to the wagons and stay there until you are told what to do next."

"Would it not be more helpful if I kept watch on the track?" The shock of her discovery of the dead man shaded her eyes, but her voice was strong and she met his anger with lifted chin, her mouth set in a determined line. "It seems you can ill spare one of the others to stand guard."

Benedict struggled with himself for barely a second. She was quite right, and he could not, for the moment, afford the luxury of chivalrous concerns for her safety. They were pointless, anyway, since she had obviated his earlier attempts to protect her. "Go, then. But stay within sight on the track. You are not to approach the camp again, do you understand?"

Bryony nodded and ran back to the cart track. What was Benedict intending to do with three wagons loaded with purloined arms? They couldn't use the cart track again, surely. Not with British soldiers half a mile up the road. The men would be able to disperse across the fields, through the woods, the way they had come, presumably, but carts and horses needed more clearly defined paths.

Dear Lord! What was the daughter of an Englishman of Sir Edward Paget's standing and conviction doing hiding in the grass, wearing an Indian tunic, on the lookout for a troop of British soldiers in order to betray them to a man who treated dead bodies as nonchalantly as if they were all in a night's work? Which, of course, they were. Death and war were bedfellows, she remembered with bleak chill. Somehow, in the loving idyll of a log cabin in a clearing, the world's reality held at bay across the abyss of unremembering, the connection had escaped her. And what would Benedict say when she revealed her identity?

"How many did you say there were?"

Bryony jumped. He had come up behind her like the proverbial thief in the night . . . like the soldier that he was, well versed in stealth and trickery. "About twelve," she whispered. "Merry and somewhat befuddled."

"Should be easy to take, then," he said with a twist of his lips that sent a shiver down her back. "Locked in swinish merriment, betrayed by that damned English arrogance, as usual, they'll never know what hit them. The pleasure will be all mine."

"But why must you take them?" she asked with all the naivete of a noncombatant.

"In order that the wagons can get away. We cannot risk them hearing us, now, can we?" That same smile disfigured his face.

There was nothing about this Benedict

that remotely resembled the one she knew. He was glorying in the prospect of ambushing the unwary troop, with a pleasure that seemed to have little to do with the need to secure the safety of the laden carts. Black-faced men were slipping out of the shadows, forming a circle around their leader. They had knives in their hands, the blades dull gleams in the dimness, and pistols in their belts. Was Benedict going to order and supervise the deaths of those men who were laughing and singing in the unwariness of drink? Bryony knew that it was not a question she could bring herself to ask, yet her eyes asked it.

His own became flat, expressionless, opaque as they read the question and denied the answer she wanted so desperately to hear. "Little girls should not wade in waters too hot and too deep for them," he said, his voice tinged with mockery. "You will go now to the wagons. Joshua is responsible for you. It's a responsibility that he would as lief not have, so I suggest you avoid making your presence felt."

"I would prefer to remain with you."

Anger, dark and fearsome, engulfed his expression, and she took an involuntary step backward. "Your preferences are of *no* importance," he said with soft finality.

"Your safety is all that concerns me at present. It is a safety that you have wantonly jeopardized, but I will not do so. Neither will I risk that of my men for some foolhardy whim of yours." Without waiting to see if she obeyed, he turned from her. His hand moved in a brief signal to those around him, and they seemed to melt into the shadows as they stole toward the unwitting redcoats.

Bryony went back to the wagons. Joshua and the two boys were in position, ready to drive the carts out. Tarpaulins covered their mounded contents. She hesitated at the lead wagon, waiting for some sign of acknowledgment from Joshua. She received nothing, so she clambered aboard to sit beside him.

"Ye've no business here," he growled.

"If I hadn't been here, you'd have had a nest of redcoats on your backs," Bryony retorted.

Joshua's eyes flicked sideways, a glimmer of surprise in their depths. Then he snorted, a curious sound, half laugh, half exclamation. The silence in the clearing became almost palpable, and Bryony could not get out of her head the image of the dead body lying by the plundered armory. How soon before it would be discovered?

Were there more? And what in the name of all that was good was happening down the road? She waited in dread for the sound of shots, the clash of steel, shouts, but there were only the cicadas, shrill and monotonous.

Hours seemed to pass, but she knew it was only a matter of twenty or thirty minutes before Joshua raised his hand to those behind, clicked softly at the horse, and the wagons moved onto the track. The journey seemed infinitely longer this time, even though she could breathe and see and was not in fear of imminent discovery. But she could feel the tension in the burly figure beside her, the straining into the darkness for the sounds of pursuit, and her own thoughts were a roiling turmoil of fear for Benedict, of the avalanche of awakened memories, and of how the disclosure of those memories was going to affect the idyll in the woods.

# Chapter 5

Dawn was streaking the sky when the wagons turned into the yard of Joshua's farm. They were driven into the barn, and the solidly comfortable figure of Bertha appeared immediately, tucking her hair into her cap.

"I've been worried sick wondering where you'd got to!" she scolded Bryony, wagging a ferocious finger. "If you were one of mine, I'd take a switch to you . . . going off like that without a word."

"Leave her be, Bertha. She'll have trouble aplenty with Ben," said Joshua, unhitching the horse from the traces. "Besides, she did us a good turn." He handed the reins to Bryony. "You can do us another one, and get this old lady out of harness and bedded down in the far stall."

Bryony, glad to have something useful to do and not at all unwilling to be out of the way of Bertha's rough tongue, took the horse off cheerfully. It was not a task she was accustomed to performing, Sir Edward's stables being amply staffed, but she set to it with a will, reflecting that recently she had learned to do a great many things that Miss Bryony Paget in normal circumstances would never have expected to tackle.

Bertha was caring for the other horses while Joshua and the two lads were pitchforking hay over the wagons. Bryony, having fed and watered her charge, grabbed a fork and joined in. It was backbreaking, scratchy work, with dust and straw flying around, sticking to the sweat on her brow, and getting in her nose and mouth. Her hands, still sore from their combat with the fishing line, blistered rapidly, but she persevered, refusing to give up before anyone else. Bertha joined them and seemed every bit as strong as the men, swinging the pitchfork with an enviable rhythm. She glanced at Bryony and pursed her lips.

"Not used to this sort of thing, are you?"

"Is it that obvious?" Bryony paused for breath, leaning on her fork.

"Clear as day," the other woman said bluntly but without rancor. "You're all wore out, I shouldn't be surprised. Go on up to the kitchen. There's a pot of coffee in the hearth."

It was a tempting offer. "No, I'll do my share." Bryony resumed the forking, feeling that in some way she had to redeem herself in the woman's eyes.

"How long do you think the others will be, Joshua?" The question didn't manage to sound as casual as she had hoped, as calmly confident that they *would* be turning up at any moment.

The farmer grunted, paused in his efforts for the time it took to wipe his brow with a bright spotted handkerchief. "Only Ben's coming here. The others'll be off their separate ways. We got to lie low for a while after this night's work. Don't want to draw attention to this place . . . not with this lot under the hay." He gestured to the three haystacks that had replaced the wagons.

"So, how long do you think he'll be?" she persisted, tossing another forkful onto the haystack.

The answer was unhelpful. "No telling. Depends how much of a fight the redcoats put up." He propped his fork against the barn wall. "Reckon that'll do. Let's go up to the house. My belly's cleaving to my backbone."

Bryony, however, found the keenness of her own appetite blunted by apprehension. She was quite incapable of doing justice to the steaming pile of griddle cakes that Bertha set before her, or to the ham and beef that the farmer's wife carved in lavish thickness. Bryony's eyes kept sliding to the door, her ears pricked for the sound of footsteps, and several times she slid off the long bench to go to the window.

The sun was now high, shedding its merciless illumination on anyone who was abroad and wished to be inconspicuous. There was bound to have been a hue and cry when the theft and the body at the armory had been discovered. And what about the redcoats? Twelve men lying with their throats cut! Oh, God, if it had taken that to bring Benedict back safe and sound, she would live with it.

"Ben's got himself out of worse trouble than this, m'dear," Bertha said, her eyes softening as she came to put an arm around the younger woman's shoulders. "He'll not come here until he's certain there's no pursuit. He'd not risk us, so he might not come till dark."

"I don't think I could endure waiting that long!" exclaimed Bryony. She was filthy, almost febrile with exhaustion, yet quite incapable of doing anything about either condition. "I could make my way back to the clearing."

"If you even think of running off again, my girl, you'll be a lot more miserable than you are now!" Bertha threatened. "Ben left you here in my charge, and here you'll stay. You understand?"

Benedict certainly picked convincing guardians, Bryony reflected with a rueful grimace, returning to the bench. She had just reached for the coffeepot when the door opened. Benedict strode into the kitchen. His face was drawn and tired, the black eyes heavy with weariness. He was as dirty and disheveled as Bryony, but much of the fatigue seemed to leave him when he saw her, relief lightening his eyes.

"Ben!" She skittered across the floor and into his arms. "You're safe!" He smelled wonderful, of dirt and sweat overlaid with earth and sun and the acrid tinge of gunpowder. His hands moved briefly over her head resting against his chest.

"All well, Joshua?"

"Aye. And with you?"

"All but Tod."

Bryony looked up into his face and saw the gray cast of sorrow, the dark agony of remorse in his eyes. He was not indifferent to death, then, at least not to the death of his own.

"We thought we had them all," he continued, his voice expressionless. "Then one came out of the bushes with a knife. He stabbed Tod a second before I shot him."

There was a long brooding moment of silence while the loss was absorbed, the colleague mourned, then Bryony heard herself ask in a voice that sounded stiff, as if after long disuse, "Did you kill them all?" She stood back from him, meeting his gaze.

Ben said nothing for a minute, and his expression was unreadable. Then he spoke, slow and soft. "They were drunk and unarmed, all but the one who knifed Tod. Only he died. I cannot bring myself, even in bitter hatred, to perpetrate murder in cold blood, but . . ." A low intensity entered his voice and his eyes burned. "I would have given much to have had them sober and armed. There would have been no quarter then."

Bryony shivered at the power of the hatred, the force of a feeling that could so transform the gently humorous, tender lover. Surely it went deeper than the quarrel between American and British, Patriot and Loyalist? But he had not killed in cold blood, and the relief was naked on her face.

"*You* have some explaining to do now,"

Benedict said suddenly, taking her wrist.

A pot clattered in the hearth under Bertha's busy fingers; a chair scraped on the wooden floor as Joshua rose ponderously to his feet and made for the outside door.

Bryony met the black hawk's gaze steadily. "I caused you no harm — quite the opposite, as I recall."

Ben took her chin between thumb and forefinger. "You could have been killed." It was a stark, uncompromising truth.

"So could you," Bryony returned with equal absence of adornment.

"I am prepared for defense, and I do not take risks without understanding their nature or their gravity."

"And you assumed that I did?" Bryony shook her head vigorously in spite of the fingers that remained on her chin. "I decided that I preferred the risks of embracing your fate last night to those of finding myself alone, without memory, with no present or future either, if you were not there to inform them." Now was the moment to tell him that she no longer wandered in the trackless wastes; so, why didn't she?

"Mmm." A slight smile appeared in his ebony eyes. "A lawyer's defense, Miss Bryony. You appear to have turned aside my entirely legitimate wrath." The copper head bent and he kissed her, his lips warm and reassuring. With a shuddering little sigh, she dropped her defenses and her fears and cuddled into his hold.

"You'll eat some breakfast, Ben," Bertha pronounced with another expressive clatter from the hearth.

"Gladly." He straightened but kept his arm around Bryony. "I reckon I've walked halfway round the county this night, in an attempt to ensure I wasn't followed."

"Is that why you were so long?" Bryony poured coffee for him and perched on the corner of the table as he took a seat on the bench.

"Mmm." Ben nodded through a mouthful of pancakes. "We split up, and it's to be hoped everyone made it home. We were well away by the shift change, at least."

"Change of guards at the armory?" The image of that dead body intruded, sullying her newfound tranquillity.

Ben looked up at her, read her expression, and spoke briskly. "Yes. Now, no more questions. The answers are not those I wish to give or that you will wish to hear."

Bryony played with her fingers for a minute as she accepted the inevitable. She had strayed of her own free will into that dark corner of Ben's life, and if she did not care for what she found there, then she had only herself to blame. She still knew almost nothing about him and seemed to understand even less. And she could not tell him about herself yet, not until she had had time to become thoroughly reacquainted with that self.

Ben laid a calming hand on her fiddling fingers. "You are repulsively dirty," he said with a teasing smile. "Just what have you been doing?"

She returned the smile. "Hiding under flour sacks first, then running like the wind, forking hay . . ." She shrugged. "I cannot think of what else."

"It's quite enough. I think we're both due for a dip under the pump." He put down his beaker and wiped his mouth. "Bertha, that was the best breakfast ever to pass my lips."

Bertha protested this flattery, but a betraying flush tinged her cheeks. "If ye're to use the pump, I'll find ye some toweling." She bustled over to a chest of drawers made of black walnut.

Bryony stared at Benedict. The pump? She mouthed the two-word question incredulously, and he burst out laughing.

"Yes, lass, the pump in the yard. It'll make a welcome change from the creek. No fish in it."

"But . . . but . . ."

"Dear me, has the cat got your tongue?" he inquired with feigned solicitude as she struggled to express the problem that he had already guessed.

"You are detestable!" she declared. "You know quite well what I mean."

"You haven't said anything yet, so how can I know what you mean?" His eyes widened innocently.

Bertha came to her rescue. "If it's an audience you're worried about, m'dear, ye need not. Joshua and the boys are out in the top field, and there's no one else but me, and I doubt ye've anything under that tunic to surprise me."

"No, I do not suppose I have," Bryony said wryly, accepting the towel with a smile. "But there's those amongst us who might refrain from taking advantage of a momentary embarrassment." She glared at Benedict, who was rocking with laughter.

"Come now, you did not expect to escape completely unscathed after last night, did you, Bryony lass?"

Her jaw dropped. "If you think, after that warning, I am going anywhere near the pump in your company, Benedict, you must think again."

"Truce." He held up his hands in a gesture of peace. "I swear I will take no unfair advantage."

"We should perhaps agree on a definition of *unfair*," she said, eyeing him warily.

Her wariness was entirely justified. For answer, Ben lowered one shoulder and swept her over it before she had fully realized what was happening. "That definition is mine, and not subject to interpretation," he declared, striding with her out into the sunny yard, where he set her down and dusted off his hands with an air of great determination. "Take off your clothes."

"I will not!" Bryony stamped one foot to express her indignation, but her dancing eyes expressed much more.

"Oh, is that so?" He advanced on her, and with a squeal Bryony turned and fled into the barn. The three cart horses moved restlessly at this disturbance of their peace as Ben pounded after her, diving for her knees as she reached the ladder to the loft. They collapsed together into the thick, fragrant nest of straw, where laughter yielded to the surge of passion, renewed when the spring of the night's tension finally broke. He held her with the weight of one leg across her thighs, arms braced on either side of her as he gazed down into her eyes.

"I very much fear, Miss Bryony, that for your sins you are about to be tumbled in the hay like any farmer's lusty wench." The light words, the teasing note could not disguise the throb of desire, and he could read the matching hunger in the slight narrowing of her eyes, the way the tip of her tongue peeped from between her lips.

"Then I must sin more often," she murmured, raising her hand to touch his face in almost wondering exploration.

Shifting his weight onto one elbow, Benedict brought his free hand to palm the knee revealed by her tunic, which had climbed to mid-thigh during their wrestling. He ran the hand down over the firm, slender length of her calf, feeling the skin beneath his fingers quiver with anticipation. Her body stirred in the rustling hay. Slowly, his hand retraced its path over her knee to trail up her thigh, pushing up the hem of the tunic inch by inch.

Bryony felt the wondrous tension build as the tunic slipped up over her belly and the warm air stroked her bared skin, adding to the sense of vulnerability, of her openness to the invasion of the stroking hand and the piercing intensity of the black-eyed gaze that seemed to encompass every inch of her. Her thighs parted beneath the insistent pressure of the leg that held her, and his lips whispered across her stomach as his fingers danced over the satin softness of her inner thighs before sliding beneath her, lifting her bottom to free the tunic, which he then drew up her body and over her head.

"That is better," Benedict murmured contentedly, cupping one breast in the palm of his hand, lifting the nipple with a grazing finger. "I find the dearth of underclothes in your present wardrobe to be a matter for great satisfaction. It gives me much pleasure to know that these treasure centers are so readily accessible."

Bryony shivered at the words so expressive of possession, a possession that with hands and lips and tongue he was now making complete. The callused hands of the soldier-woodsman spanned her waist as his tongue brought moist fire to her breasts, stroked deeply in the hollow of her throat and upward, tracing the length of her slender neck to tickle beneath her chin. He laughed softly when she squirmed, and stilled her with the weight of his imprisoning leg, moving his hand to hold the now moist and throbbing center of her body as his tongue plundered her ear with the wicked knowledge of its keen sensitivity. She thrashed wildly beneath this exquisite torment and each movement thrust her core against the warm hand that held her. She was mounting now toward some turbulent, ravishing plane of bodily bliss where the mind holds no sway, and he was taking her there with unerring knowledge of the paths that would lead her, allowing no pause in the wild spiral of delights succeeding each other in ever-ascending intensity, until she reached that space and time where only the trembling paroxysm of pure sensation existed.

Ben kissed her gently as the violent pulsating of her body's core slowly subsided against his warm palm, and her heart juddered into its normal rhythm. She smiled weakly at him, touching his face, running her fingers over his lips in benediction and gratitude for the gift of love.

"Have I taxed you beyond further endurance, sweeting?" he asked with a quizzical lift of an eyebrow. For answer, she unbuttoned his shirt, pushing it off his shoulders, raising herself to kiss his nipples, to run her tongue through the light dusting of silky copper curls on his chest. He unfastened his britches and kicked them from him before lowering himself over her.

"This straw is very scratchy," Bryony teased, curling her legs around his hips.

"That is easily remedied." Spreading his hands beneath her back, holding her locked against him, he rolled over, reversing their positions. Bryony gazed down at him, a startled look in her eyes, and he chuckled softly, running his hands down her back, molding every curve and hollow of her body to his length. "This way can bring you much pleasure, lass, as I trust you are about to find out." She nodded with a considering gravity that brought laughter sparking in his dark eyes, then she lowered her mouth to his, savoring the pleasures of initiation as her body, already alive with sensation, registered the feel of him, the silky tickle of the hairs on his chest against her breasts, the steady jarring of his heart, the ridged muscles of his abdomen against the soft roundness of her own, the taut hardness of his thighs, and the throbbing heat of his manhood pulsing against her lower belly.

With a soft groan, Benedict seized her hips in an urgent clasp, raising her and guiding her onto the impaling shaft. Bryony gasped as she took him within herself, finding the sensation quite new. He smiled. "You are in control of your own pleasure now, sweeting."

"And yours, also?" She palmed his nipples, her lips curving in a smile as knowing as his.

"And mine," Ben agreed, drawing one breast into his mouth, suckling with a hungry fervor that seemed to tug at her belly and fill her with a host of sensations hitherto unexperienced. She wanted to make him a part of herself, blood of her blood, bone of her bone, sinew of her sinew. She moved around and over the part of him she possessed, drawing him ever deeper within, consuming him with her own fires, discovering the nerve centers of her own pleasure as she moved, and imparting that pleasure to the one whom she possessed at this moment as surely as she had been possessed. He was moving with her now, reaching up into her depths, seeking the refuge and the joy she offered. And the joy burgeoned, surging between them under the savage, thrusting tempo of their fusion, to burst finally in an explosion that ripped through them, ravaging in its completion.

Bryony lay beached upon him in the straw, as wanton and as thoroughly tumbled as any farmer's lusty wench, and the image of Sir Edward Paget, the leanly ascetic, fastidious aristocrat, rose unbidden and unvanquishable. She laughed with what little strength remained to her, her face buried in Benedict's shoulder, inhaling the musky, earthy fragrance of his skin that mingled with the glorious pungency of their loving.

"What has amused you, sweeting?" He patted her bottom in a soft caress, a note of sympathetic laughter in his voice. But Bryony could not begin to explain, and, unfortunately, neither could she stop laughing. "Hey!" The pats became a little more forceful. "If you cannot share the jest, my love, it is only common courtesy to desist." He sounded a little puzzled, a little uncertain, and Bryony realized that after such a shared loving, her laughter could well appear a strange reaction.

"I beg your pardon," she gasped. "I think that you have quite overset my reason. Coming after so many other shocks, you understand?"

"I am not sure that I do, but I do have the cure." With a monumental heave, he lifted her, heavy in the languor of fulfillment, onto the straw beside him. He stood up and reached down for her hands. "Bath time."

"I do not think I could stand the shock," she implored, resisting the pull of his hands. "I am so warm and languid . . . and *sleepy!*" The last word was a cry from the heart.

"You will sleep better when you do not reek of sweat and the stable; as will I." With a degree of callousness that Bryony found impossible to resist, he pulled her to her feet and shepherded her, protesting feebly, into the yard.

"I am unaccustomed to taking baths in public," announced Bryony in dignified accents, the effect somewhat diminished by a wide-mouthed yawn.

"The only audience I can see is a somewhat ancient dog, six chickens, and a pig," Ben responded cheerfully, seizing hold of the pump handle. "You can perform the service for me, afterward. It will warm you up and give you full opportunity for revenge."

Bryony howled and danced under the stream of cold water, but she made no attempt to run from it, and Benedict correctly interpreted her gyrations as the entertainment they were designed to be. She moved with the lithe grace of a dancer. Presumably, it was an activity that had occupied much of her time, coming as she

144

must from that pleasure-centered faction of Southern society whom he had cause to know so well, and to remember with so much bitter loathing. His lips tightened at the thought and the memories — the women, fluttering their fans, passing their days in idleness and gossip, issuing orders in that careless manner that implied that those who fulfilled them belonged to some lower form of life; and the men, as idly dissolute as their womenfolk, and as blindly, dangerously contemptuous of those who were responsible for ensuring their comfort. And Bryony? Where did she fit into the pattern? Even as he asked himself the question, watching the mischievously sensual invitation of her dance, he realized that he did not want to know the answer. This Bryony, with only a present, belonged in some way to him. The Bryony of the past and future had other allegiances, ones that perhaps ran counter to his own, ones that would assuredly bring an end to their shared idyll.

"Your turn, sir!" Gasping and laughing, she ran out of the stream and laid her hands over his on the pump handle. "I am so clean, I squeak." The deep velvety blue eyes held the residual glow of loving, and the sun-brushed complexion had a translucent radiance that, as she looked up at him, seemed to dim for a minute. "Why so somber, Ben? You look quite forbidding."

"Heaven forfend!" Taking the wet mass of her hair, he wrung it out between his hands, and his smile chased the shadows from his expression. He kissed her lightly before yielding his place at the pump handle.

Bryony put all her remaining strength into the task as the sensuous embrace of the sun dried her skin and the effort of pumping sent the blood coursing through her veins. Benedict's bath was very thorough and as much designed for her entertainment as hers had been for his. "You are outrageous!" she exclaimed as he paid considerably more attention than strict hygiene demanded to certain portions of his anatomy. "Whatever will Bertha think?"

"If she's watching," he replied, chuckling, "then she must accept what she sees."

Half an hour later, they bade farewell to the farmer's wife and set off across the field to the woods.

It was a steamy afternoon, and the woods were infested with clouds of midges and mosquitoes. Bryony's weariness was bone deep, and she could barely put one foot in front of the other, stumbling along the single-track paths behind Benedict's broad back, her eyes on the ground because her head was too heavy to lift, feebly swatting at the darting insects that seemed to find her blood maddeningly sweet.

At last they reached the clearing and the log cabin that to Bryony's eyes this afternoon appeared more welcoming and luxurious than the Pagets' elegant country mansion above the James River, or their handsome town house in Williamsburg. She fell onto the straw mattress with the sigh of pleasure she would have accorded her own bed of hand-carved cherrywood with its sumptuous hangings of richly embroidered brocade, and the deep feather mattress and pillows.

Benedict removed her moccasins then raised her against him to pull off her tunic. "It is too hot to sleep in," he said when she protested this postponement of promised bliss.

"Are you coming to bed, too?" she managed to mutter as her eyes closed under the leaden weight of their lids.

"I'll doze in the sun a little," he replied, tossing the sheet over her, but Bryony didn't hear the answer.

When she awoke, enveloped in the most wonderful dreamy lethargy and aware of a powerful hunger, it was to find the cabin in darkness, no hint of daylight coming through the ill-filled cracks between the logs or through the square window. Benedict was sleeping beside her, sprawled on his stomach, one arm curled heavily around her waist. She could feel the dampness of her skin beneath the weight. Far from being uncomfortable, it was a reassuring sensation of the immediacy of their bodily intimacy, of its earthy existence, which seemed both to spring from the vibrant world of reality and also to shape it. The rounded edge of her shoulder prickled as his head moved on the pillow and his beard brushed against her skin. Francis Cullum's beard was coarse against her cheek when he offered the chaste salute permitted between betrothed couples, but the texture of Ben's was as silky smooth as the glossy thatch on his head.

Bryony stared up at the clapboard roof. Francis — her dear friend Francis. She allowed her mind to drift back to that evening, the evening that had brought her to this cabin in the woods and the arms of a loving stranger whose past held some savage secret and whose present was informed by the violence of war and the embrace of its bloodshed.

Two more different men would be impossible to find; yet, until the events of that evening, she would have married Francis cheerfully enough, once her father's patience exhausted itself and he decided that she had had her freedom and could no longer hold off the yoke of family duty. Francis was her friend, and there were many worse fates than to be wedded to one's friend. But Francis did not care for women — at least, not as wives and lovers. . . .

She could still feel the amazed disbelief that had held her rooted to the spot in the doorway of the little pantry, staring at the sight of Francis and the Truemans' young serving man locked in a passionate embrace amid the silver and the china. She had been so stupefied that she had been unable to whip herself out of the room before they became aware of her. She would never forget Francis's face as his eyes opened and he saw her over the shoulder of his lover. Incongruous words of apology had formed on her tongue and found their way into the room, then she had turned and left, closing the door softly behind her.

Once the shock had abated a little, her first thought had been, peculiarly, one of anxiety for the servant. If his part in such a scandalous business was ever discovered, he would be lucky to escape with his life. For these deviations from acceptable practice, Francis could surely have chosen his partners from the ranks of those capable of looking after themselves. But then, justice and common sense had told her that in essence it was no different from the customary use of serving wenches to satisfy masculine hungers; at least there was no danger of Francis's young man being left to bear alone the living consequences of such carnal indiscretion.

The absurdity of that thought had served to bring an element of humor and perspective to the situation. She had never heard such a practice discussed; indeed, it would be extraordinary if any of her mother's social circle could imagine such a thing, let alone believe in it as reality. But Bryony had had the advantage of a rigorous education under the supervision of her scholar father, and such an education could not help but embrace the classics. Sir Edward had not been unduly squeamish, either, about providing the answers and explanations to texts that puzzled his daughter, although he had permitted no discussion or expansion of the subject. As a result, Bryony found herself shocked, not so much by what had been revealed about her fiancé as about his deception of her. He had never given the slightest indication of reluctance to agree to the marriage arranged by their parents, and in recent months had been pressing Bryony to agree to an early wedding. In fact, he had given the exemplary performance of a lovelorn suitor.

Not that she had believed for one minute that he was truly lovelorn. They had known each other from the cradle, were fond of each other in the way of old friends, and could neither of them see any just cause for disobeying parental ruling in the matter of their marriage — not when such disobedience tended in general to have uncomfortable consequences. Disinherited, neither of them would be in a position to find another suitor, and there was little reason to imagine that either father would treat the defiance of his child with greater lenience than was customary. It was a marriage arranged with the children's best interests at heart. They had grown up together, liked each other perfectly well, and the merging of the two fortunes would create vast wealth for the new dynasty that such a young and healthy couple would be sure to create.

But what was to happen now? Bryony

had gone into dinner with the question no closer to solution and had found herself, as usual, seated beside Francis. His condition was pitiable — his face gray, his hands shaking so violently that he was barely able to hold his knife, and his wineglass clattered against the heavy silver platter on the infrequent occasions that he set it down. Bryony had maintained a light, matter-of-fact conversation throughout the interminable hours of the formal meal that was to precede the ball, her cheerful chatter filling the silences of her companion so that nothing untoward would be noticed by the others around the table.

He had been one of the first to join the ladies in the drawing room after dinner. His expression as resolute as his complexion was pale, he had come over to Bryony with the quiet request that she walk with him in the garden. Eliza Paget had nodded her permission for the unchaperoned excursion. It was not a consent she was likely to withhold since her main object these days was to bring Bryony rapidly to the altar. Had she been a party to the conversation that took place between the so-called lovers in the garden, she would most probably have fallen into strong convulsions.

Remembering the excruciating embarrassment of that conversation, Bryony fidgeted on the straw mattress. Francis had all but wept, promising that such an aberration would never occur again, that he had no idea what had come over him. He had implored her to set a date for their wedding, maintaining that the two years of waiting to which he had been subjected by Bryony's whim — a whim that no one could understand except as the selfishness of a spoiled child — had taken great toll on his peace of mind.

Angry at this cowardly evasion of responsibility, Bryony, never one to mince her words, had snapped back with brutal frankness, which she had regretted the minute Francis had left, making excuses of ill health to his hosts before riding home to the Cullum plantation. Bryony had danced the night away, and if anyone noticed a brittle quality to her laughter, a certain inconsistency in her conversation, they were too polite to comment. And when the household was abed, she had crept, still in her ballgown, out of the bedroom that she was sharing with half a dozen other visiting young ladies from neighboring plantations, and out of the house, seeking the solitude of the quiet night. Only to find herself caught up in a conflagration . . .

Her stomach growled in loud and vociferous protest at its empty condition.

"That is a most unladylike sound," a sleepy voice murmured in the darkness. Ben's warm palm flattened over her complaining belly.

"Mayhap, but a farmer's lusty wench does not tend to be ladylike," she said with a laugh that sounded awkward to her suddenly oversensitive ears. "And even ladies can be hungry." It was a conversation too close to home, one that could have taken place without artifice when she had not known exactly who she was. Why did she not simply tell him the truth, now that she had it? Because to do so would mean making decisions, decisions that she did not wish to contemplate, let alone to make. And because she would have to tell the Patriot, in his Patriot hideout, that she came of Loyalist stock, just as he had feared. She would never betray him, and he would know that, but after what she had witnessed last night . . .

"I did try to wake you for supper," Ben murmured, still sleepy and apparently not noticing the awkwardness that she had heard in her voice. "You were beyond all stimuli."

"I find that hard to believe." Bryony rolled into his arms, nuzzling his shoulder. "There are some stimuli I am never beyond."

"I tried them all, lass, but to no avail, I swear it." There was a comically mournful note in his voice now, and the drowsiness seemed fast disappearing.

Bryony put memories and insoluble problems aside. She needed solitude if she was ever to come to terms with either, and, at some point, she must. But for now, there was this warmth, this languid arousal, the joining of bodies that kept all specters at bay and brought the peace of a union that had place only in the universe that was their own, untouched by other worlds.

# Chapter 6

"Why so sad, lass? You look as if you lost a guinea and found a groat." Benedict crossed the clearing early one morning several days later, a rabbit dangling by its hind legs from his hand, his musket slung across his shoulder.

Bryony, who was sitting hunched over on the grass by the stone fireplace, was well aware of her wan appearance. "I have the bellyache," she muttered.

"I told you to be a little more circumspect with those plums last night," he said, passing a stroking hand over her hair as he dropped his burdens to the grass. "You must have consumed at least two pounds."

"It has nothing to do with the plums." Bryony sounded more than a little snappish, and Ben frowned, dropping onto his heels beside her.

"Someone got out of bed on the wrong side this morning." A long finger beneath her chin tilted her face to meet his scrutiny. "What has occurred to make you as cross as two sticks?"

156

"Nothing!" Perversely, she twisted her head away, scowling into the distant trees.

Ben shook his head in frustration. "Am I supposed to persevere in my efforts to find out what is the matter, or am I supposed to leave you alone? The message is not clear."

"I told you, I have the bellyache and it is making me feel miserable," Bryony offered, still staring into the trees.

"Well, if it is not caused by a surfeit of plums, what is it?" he asked.

"It's private," Bryony muttered rather feebly. She could not imagine why she should be so embarrassed after the intimacies that they had shared, but some deep-rooted reserve seemed to be holding her back from complete candor.

Benedict's frown deepened, then he said, "Ahhh," and stood up and went into the cabin. He emerged within a few seconds with a beaker. "A little brandy will help, lass."

Bryony took the beaker. "How do you know what will help?"

He smiled. "I have not spent my life in a monastery, sweeting. Drink it up, now. It will relax you a little."

She took a sip of the fiery liquid and felt its warmth slide down into her belly, loosening the cramped muscles. "The ache doesn't usually last long," she said, feeling immeasurably easier with him. "And I suppose we should be thankful." She looked at him over the lip of the beaker, searching his face for reaction.

"And are you not?" he asked quietly, sitting down beside her again.

"Yes . . . yes, of course I am." She was, but at the same time could not help the niggling thought that if she were with child, then they would be forced to make some decisions about a shared future, to face a reality outside the fairy ring of this glade in the woods. She could tell him of her identity, of Francis, of her father, and the knowledge of her background would not seem important or divisive if something over and above those facts joined them in love. And her father would accept the reality, would make the best of it, after the initial explosion. She would not have to betray Francis to Sir Edward, either, in order to break the marriage contract, since her own disgrace would be more than sufficient reason. And she could go to her father soon, put him out of the torment that she knew he must be enduring at her disappearance. Loving him as deeply as he loved her, Bryony had been stretched upon the rack of guilt these last few days at keeping him in ignorance of her safety.

"My love, it would not work," Benedict said gently, smoothing back her hair. "There can be no future for us. I am not the kind of man of whom husbands are made."

How had he read her mind with such accuracy? Bryony felt her cheeks warm. "What kind of man are you, then?"

"No more and no less than you know," he replied in that soft tone that signified an end to the subject. "Finish your brandy. I'll excuse you your chores this morning, so you may pass the time in idleness in the sun, like any other grand lady." He gave her a smile that seemed to combine gently resigned understanding with the firmness of his resolution.

Bryony watched the competent economy of his movements as he fetched wood from the pile by the cabin and laid and lit the fire in the stone ring, then made coffee and ground maize with pestle and mortar to make the porridge for their breakfast. She had never met a man who could do those things and all the other tasks that he performed with such unthinking ability. The brandy and the warmth of the morning sun were making her drowsy, and she closed her eyes, resting her head on her drawn-up knees. The sun created a red glow behind her eyelids, and she could feel its rays, concentrated and hot, on the back of her head. What kind of man was he? A warrior with an all-consuming cause; a supremely skilled woodsman and hunter; a man of considerable learning, with many of the attributes of an aristocrat; a wondrously tender and experienced lover; a humorous man; a ruthless man of invincible purpose — and heaven help the person who stepped between the man and that purpose.

Benedict paused in his tasks to observe the hunched figure, arms wrapped around her knees, lost in her reverie. In spite of his overwhelming relief that she was not with child, he was conscious of a certain sadness. Their exchange had told him clearly what he had known but had tried to ignore. Bryony was not going to be able simply to accept what they had for as long as they had it. Hopes of permanency had entered her soul, and they were hopes that he had had to dash without explanation. It was time to bring an end to the idyll in the woods before she got in any deeper.

Before *she* got in any deeper? A mirthless smile quirked his lips. Before *he* found himself in waters too hot and too deep. If he were truly honest with himself, Miss Bryony was well and truly under his skin, and he could not afford such an encumbrance — for either of their sakes.

He poured himself a beaker of coffee and sat back on his heels, still watching her covertly since it was clear she was not asleep. He knew very little about amnesia, but surely her memory was taking an unconscionably long time to return? It was not as if the loss was complete, and for a while she had been remembering little things on a daily basis, but that seemed to have stopped in the last few days. Benedict sighed. He would have to go in search of her identity himself. It would mean going into town, where news of a missing girl in the neighborhood would surely have been circulated by now. Maybe some of the men who worked in town had picked up some gossip. It was something he should have done days ago, but he had been curiously reluctant, telling himself that someone would bring the information to him when they had it. In truth, of course, he had been afraid to find out, knowing that it would signal the end of the idyll, one way or another.

Her head turned on her knees, and she opened her eyes, looking directly at him, without saying anything. Her expression was grave, with a resignation that he knew was mirrored in his own.

"Come and have some breakfast," he said quietly, pouring a second beaker of coffee.

She came over to the fire, taking the offering with a tiny smile of thanks.

"I'm going to leave you for a little while this morning," Ben told her casually. "I should be back by mid-afternoon."

"May I come with you?"

"No."

Bryony shrugged. In another mood, she would have demanded a reason for his refusal, but she could not summon up the energy, somehow.

Benedict considered softening his denial with the explanation for his absence. But then she might be frightened at the very idea of his going in search of her identity. It would be a terrifying notion, he thought — if one had lived in the trackless wastes for such a time, creating a self out of the present, suddenly to contemplate the imposition of a past over which one had no control. No, better to leave her in ignorance for the moment.

"I hope you do not expect me to skin that rabbit whilst you are gone." Bryony attempted to lighten an atmosphere that seemed heavier than the maize porridge on her trencher.

"I do not expect you to do anything but lie in the sun until your ache is better," he replied in similar accents.

"Then I shall take the brandy bottle to the creek and lose myself in a sodden, swinish, sun-soaked stupor."

Ben regarded her through narrowed eyes. "If that was an attempt at provocation, lass, permit me to tell you that it was successful. It is only your present delicate condition that restrains me."

"From doing what?" she bantered with a mischievous gleam.

"Don't ask, you might not like the answer," he returned smartly.

When he left thirty minutes later, the despondent gravity had dissipated completely, more by conscious effort on both their parts than by chance. Bryony pottered around the cabin, performing her customary tasks, although Ben had told her to leave them for today. She actually found the business of tidying, sweeping the earthen floor, and straightening the coarse holland sheets on the bedstead relaxing. It freed her mind while her body moved along accustomed paths, and there was considerable satisfaction in the efficient performance of even these small tasks for one who hitherto had been unaccustomed to tying her own shoelaces.

Benedict's destination was a forge in Williamsburg. But he went first to Joshua's farm, where he borrowed a sturdy cob that would carry him the seven miles rather faster than his legs. For all that the town was strongly supportive of the Patriot cause, habitual caution led him to avoid the place as a rule, on the principle that the fewer people who saw his face, the better. He was not remarkable in clothing or bearing so long as he remembered to walk like a backwoodsman and not with the challenging stride of a Clare. But he had learned to disguise the aristocratic bearing — to lower his head and gaze, to round his shoulders and scuff his feet a little as he walked — during the years of his servitude, when the natural arrogance of his birth and breeding had so exacerbated his master. Now no one would look twice at the bearded man in jerkin and britches, wearing his own hair unpowdered, like any workman, hands callused from hard work, long legs astride an unremarkable if stolid mount.

William barely acknowledged him when

he appeared in the doorway of the forge and watched the young lad who assisted the blacksmith vigorously pump the bellows. Sparks flew with the clang of steel upon steel as William hammered a sickle out of the glowing, pliant iron upon the anvil. The heat from the roaring fire was oppressive, and both the smith and the lad, in their heavy leather aprons, were pouring sweat. Ben wiped his brow with his checkered neckcloth and sauntered out into the street again.

Now that William knew Ben was in town, he would round up the others and they would congregate in the loft above the baker's, ready for whatever emergency had provoked his coming. It had been agreed that they would have no contact for two weeks after the raid on the armory, except in the case of emergency. The weapons were still hidden beneath the straw in Joshua's barn, waiting for the hue and cry over the raid to die down before they would be transported to the Patriot armory up-river, on the plantation of Paul Tyler — the man who provided the overt rallying point for Virginia Patriots. For those whose work for the cause was as yet covert, Benedict Clare provided leadership.

Benedict strolled around the town, an inconspicuous figure whose ever-open ears and eyes would not be remarked upon. He had no need of the commodities offered in the shops, and little coin with which to purchase them even had he the need. Escaped bondsmen tended to be impecunious. What he could not hunt, catch, or fashion for himself, he acquired by barter with the Indians and with those farmers and tradesmen who could use the skills of an educated man. Beneath the earthen floor of the log cabin lay a pouch of gold sovereigns and those possessions of Benedict Clare that could be turned into hard currency when the right moment came; it was an inheritance that his mother had pressed upon him in those minutes of farewell, as agonizing as they were brief, before he had been dragged back to the stinking jail to be held, shackled among the rats, until the vessel that would bear him into slavery set sail for Charleston, South Carolina.

A rich yeasty fragrance rose on the air outside the baker's shop, steaming in enticing, aromatic invitation through the door that stood open to the street.

"I give you good day, Bart," Benedict greeted the broad back bent over the enormous brick oven set in the wall beside the stone chimney.

The baker turned, his usually ruddy face scarlet, hands coated with flour. "Good day to ye, Ben." He wiped his hands on his apron. "I'll join ye abovestairs just as soon as I've taken this batch out."

Ben nodded easily and went up the rickety stairs set in the corner of the shop. The small loft contained six men, all of them showing signs of varying degrees of agitation.

Ben greeted them casually and perched on a corner of an upturned barrel. "Let us wait for Bart," he suggested, seeing William about to launch into speech. "There is nothing amiss."

"Oh, but there is!" exclaimed William. "Summat dreadfully amiss. I was coming to ye tonight if ye hadn't come to town."

"True enough, Ben," one of the younger members of the group put in. "Jack here only found out yesterday eventide and we've not known which way to turn, waiting for dark to bring ye the news."

"Well, now I am here, so you need wait no longer." Ben smiled, the smile that generally soothed and reassured as it reminded them that he was in control, that he had never yet met a situation he could not handle, never yet let them down in a moment of crisis.

"It's that girl," William pronounced. "I told ye no good would come of it." The rather bovine features settled in an expression of morbid satisfaction as he looked around the room. "Should have left her to take her chance at Trueman's. I always said so."

"Yes, William, so you did." Ben sighed with ill-concealed irritation. "However, I chose to do otherwise."

"And we'll all have cause to regret it —"

"That is enough, William!" The crisp, incisive tones reduced the blustering blacksmith to silence. They were tones Ben rarely used with this group, accepting that his position as leader was by democratic decision and depended entirely on his continued success at preserving their safety and accomplishing their goals. He had no authority but that which they gave him. However, there *were* times when he was forced to exert the natural authority of his breeding and education.

"Jack?" He turned to the man with the information. "Enlighten me, pray."

The vintner scratched his head with both hands, clearly in vigorous search of an active louse. "I was making a delivery up at

Carter's plantation last even. A butt of fine canary," he added, as if the matter were of some relevance. "Anyways, there was talk in the kitchen about a Miss Paget gone missing from Trueman's. Seems her father — Sir Edward, he be — has come to town in a great taking. They couldn't turn up nothing at Trueman's plantation, so there's to be a proclamation by the criers in the town square — a reward for any information." Tale told, Jack subsided against the wall and returned to his head-scratching.

Bryony Paget. Benedict felt the cold bitterness seep into his veins. Almost any other identity would have been easier for him to accept — even if she had been the Crown governor's daughter. No wonder she had that Irish coloring, although he'd lay considerable odds that she had almost no knowledge of his homeland. The Pagets were one of the wealthiest absentee landlords in that beleaguered country, denying their own heritage, even as they milked the land and their tenants of their life blood in order to maintain themselves in luxury in England — and here in the Colonies, too, presumably. He felt sickened as he always did when he thought of the abuses visited upon the peasant farmers whose cause he had fought for, turning against his own

169

kind and ultimately against his king — a traitor who had not paid the traitor's penalty but had still paid dearly at the hands of Sir Edward Paget and his like. Bryony Paget — the daughter of a man who embodied everything Benedict Clare had sworn to fight, everything against which he had sworn vengeance; the daughter who had presumably imbibed contempt for the Irish peasantry together with the Loyalist cant of a true blue Englishman from her first waking moments!

"She's got to be got rid of." William spoke again, with even greater truculence than before. "If ye're too squeamish to do it, then I've no such qualms."

"Do not be ridiculous!" Ben snapped. "I'll not have gratuitous killing. I've told you before."

"William's right, Ben." Bart appeared at the head of the stairs. "She was at the armory, saw us all. . . ."

"And saved our bacon, as I recall," Ben said sardonically.

"But she didn't know who she was then," Jack pointed out. "What happens when she remembers? She'll run to her pa with a fine story. There's Joshua's farm and the cabin, Trueman's barn, the armory, and every one of us."

Benedict shook his head. "You'll have to trust me. She'll not betray us, I promise you that."

"The only way to be sure of that is if we still her tongue for good," William muttered. "Ye can't keep her with ye for always, stands to reason. And she can't go back home to her folks, knowing what she does."

"She'll not betray us," Ben repeated with absolute conviction. Sickened though he was at the knowledge that she came from a family who embraced everything he most detested, he knew instinctively that she would be loyal to him and to the memory of their time together, regardless of any opposing loyalties and principles she might hold.

"It'll be more than *your* head that'll roll if she does," Bart said. "We can't risk it, Ben."

"What are you suggesting? That I cut her throat while she's asleep and throw her body in the river?" He raised his eyebrows as if the idea were laughable.

"Easy enough," said William with a shrug. "We know she's been keeping yer bed warm, so I'll do it for ye, if she's made ye softhearted."

"I said no." He spoke very softly now, his

eyes narrowed with anger and purpose. His hand drifted casually to the pistol in his belt, and a slight ripple ran through the men in the loft. "I take responsibility for Miss Bryony Paget, now and at all times. And she is not to be harmed." The hawk's eyes roamed slowly around the circle, stabbing each face until the owner dropped his gaze under the glittering black challenge.

"What's to be done, then?" Bart asked with a resigned shrug. He, for one, was not prepared to pick up Ben's gauntlet. The younger man was all too handy with knife and pistol, and he'd never given them the least cause to mistrust either his loyalty or his ability to fulfill his promises.

Ben stood up. "It is time Miss Paget was returned to her own," he said with a briskness that hid his pain. "It was in the hopes of discovering her identity that I came here today." He went toward the stairs, then paused. "I say again, none of you have anything to fear. I have never yet given you cause to mistrust my word, have I?"

Again, he scanned the circle of faces, and slowly the heads nodded in agreement, William's head last, but none the less definite.

"Then, I bid you farewell. I'll send word when we're to move the arms from

Joshua's to Tyler's." His hand lifted in a parting gesture, and he sprang lightly down the unstable staircase, through the bakeshop, and out into the street. The afternoon air was heavy and humid, adding to his feeling of oppression as he made his way to the forge, where Joshua's cob waited. Dust rose, dry and thick from the streets, under the wheels and hooves of carriages and horses traversing the town that a short time ago had been the seat of government of King George's colony of Virginia; but the business of government was for the moment in abeyance as the king's men battled throughout the thirteen colonies for the continued right to govern the king's colonies.

The same oppression hung over the clearing, rendering Bryony languid and depressed throughout the hours of waiting for Benedict's return. The morning's conversation had crystallized one important fact for her: she did not want to leave Ben, wanted no other life but this secluded woodland intimacy. Yet, the realistic Bryony Paget knew that such a want was not achievable, even had Ben been less resolute in his statement that it could not be. He did not belong in the woodland for longer than he needed the seclusion for his present purposes. He would soon leave to fight the battle in the open, and there was no place on the battlefield for the loving play of fantasyland. So, what was to be done?

She had found no answer to the tormenting question by the time Benedict finally returned, appearing without warning at the edge of the trees. The minute she looked at him, Bryony knew that something was seriously amiss. He held himself taut, without the rangy ease to which she was accustomed. The black eyes were somber, and the light that usually sprang to life in them when he saw her remained dimmed.

"What is it?" Hesitantly, she approached him, her bare feet curling in the grass, one hand pushing her tumbled hair away from her face in a curiously nervous gesture.

"What is what?" he responded with the wraith of a smile. "How is your bellyache?"

"Better." She looked at him closely. "Something has occurred to trouble you."

"I have been into Williamsburg." He strode toward the cabin. "I had better skin that rabbit if we are to have any dinner."

Bryony found herself trotting after him — like a spaniel pup hoping for a pat or some such sign of affection, she thought with self-denigrating unease. Ben disappeared into the cabin, presumably to fetch their as-yet-hirsute supper, and she followed him inside, standing by the door uncertainly as he filled a beaker with cider from the stone jar, drinking deeply before wiping his mouth with the back of his hand and setting the beaker down on the plank table with a gesture indicative of finality. He spun on his heel and regarded her gravely.

"You have discovered who I am." Her voice was low.

"Aye." He nodded, picked up the rabbit from the table, and moved toward the door. Bryony stepped aside hastily and followed him outside.

"I did not think it would upset you quite so much," she said. "I know my father is a fervent Loyalist and that —"

"You *know?*" Ben dropped the rabbit and swung around to face her, his eyes seeming to impale her so that she stood motionless, pinned in the doorway.

"I remembered everything the night of the raid on the armory," she said in the same low voice, aware that she was suddenly afraid, but she did not know of what. "You are not angry with me, are you?"

Benedict sighed. "You could have saved

me a journey and a somewhat tiresomely acrimonious meeting. Why did you not tell me before?"

"I suppose because I needed to become reacquainted with myself first," she said slowly. "And . . . well, I had hoped that I would turn out to be a stalwart Patriot." She gave a nervous little laugh and shrugged. "A vain hope, as it happens." Ben did not respond and turned his attention to the rabbit. Bryony looked down at the bent copper head touched by a finger of late-afternoon sun, the strong column of his neck rising from the open collar of his shirt, the long-fingered hands performing their bloody task with such efficiency. A lump of tears clogged her throat, and she swallowed hard. "I do not, myself, seem to hold any strong opinions on the matter, but even if I did, you know I would not betray you, Benedict."

"Yes, I know that." He wiped his knife on the grass. "I am going to wash my hands and fetch water for the pot."

"I picked a basket of mushrooms this afternoon," she offered. "I think they are the right ones this time." Her last attempt at mushroom picking had been a lamentable failure since she had had no idea that mushrooms could come in a poisonous variety as well as an edible one.

"I had still better look them over before they go in the pot." He walked off in the direction of the creek, swinging the iron kettle, and Bryony realized forlornly that he had not looked at her properly since she had made her disclosure. It would have been better if she had told him herself, she realized now. Keeping her returned memory a secret, obliging him to hear of her identity by accident, had been an unfair deception.

She wandered in his wake down to the creek, feeling somehow as if she had been cast adrift from her moorings. "I should have told you before, Ben. Will you forgive me?"

He was squatting on his heels at the edge of the creek, washing the blood and debris from his hands with almost exaggerated care. "I am not sure that there is anything to forgive. I would have preferred you to tell me, certainly, but your reasons for not doing so were your own and strike me as sufficient."

"Then why are you so angry?" She touched his back between the shoulder blades, and he seemed to recoil as if from a burning brand. Tears sprang into her eyes. "You cannot be this angry just because I am the daughter of an Englishman and a Loyalist."

And the daughter of one of the abusers of his homeland, of the same breed that had convicted him of treason and sentenced him to bondage because he chose to champion those whom they exploited. But he could not tell her that. It was a past he could share with no one in this new life. "I am not angry with you, lass." He stood up, trying to make his voice light as he cupped her face with his wet hands, brushing his lips over hers. Her eyes were wide with distress and incomprehension, and a wash of remorse swept through him. "Come, let us talk no more of this for now. I am much in need of my dinner. On a full belly, we will be able to look at the situation with more clarity." Taking her hand in a firm clasp, he hefted the now full kettle in his other hand and led her back to the cabin.

"What did you mean about an acrimonious meeting?" asked Bryony, washing the mushrooms that had been declared edible.

"Your identity, Miss Paget, has caused some alarm amongst the men," he told her dryly. "They were all for cutting your throat and throwing your body in the creek."

Bryony gasped. "They think I will betray them?"

He shrugged. "In all fairness, why should they think otherwise? Had you not included yourself in the raid on the armory, they would have been less alarmed. But you do know some rather incriminating facts about this operation."

"But I could only tell someone about you by incriminating myself," she pointed out. "And I warned you about the soldiers."

"True enough. But that was a Bryony with no allegiances except those she had formed in the very recent past. Amnesia and captivity would be considered sufficient excuse for any aberrational behavior on your part."

"You are not going to do it, are you?" She regarded him warily, and for the first time since he had returned, Benedict laughed.

"No! I don't think you deserve such a fate."

"And I will not betray you," she reiterated with sudden fierceness.

The laughter died from his face. "No, I know you will not. But the fact remains that we must contrive some explanation for your disappearance that will satisfy your family and any other inquisitive souls, who, I rather imagine, will be legion."

"I do not want to go back, Benedict." She plucked at the hem of her tunic with agitated fingers. "If it were not for my father, who must be out of his mind with worry, I would stay disappeared."

"You are being a little childish, if you don't mind my saying so." His tone was calmly neutral — a schoolmaster correcting an erring pupil — and Bryony flushed, recognizing the truth in the reprimand.

"If I return, I will either have to marry Francis Cullum or expose him . . . his . . ." She stumbled wretchedly, unsure how to describe delicately what she now knew about her betrothed. "I will have to expose him to my father, because Papa will not accept any excuse for my withdrawing from the contract except the truth. Not after all these years," she added. "Perhaps two years ago, if I had said the marriage was distasteful to me, instead of simply asking for a grace period, he would have agreed to break off the betrothal. But after everyone has been so accommodating to my" — her tone unconsciously imitated Eliza Paget — "to what Mama refers to as my self-indulgent whim, it would be unthinkable of me to cry off at this point."

Benedict frowned, absorbing as much of this somewhat jumbled speech as made sense. "I am all at sea, lass," he said after a long, frowning silence. "To what self-indulgent whim was your mother referring?"

"It's all a little complicated." Bryony plucked a long stem of grass and began to suck it thoughtfully. "Francis and I have been betrothed from our cradles. He is also an only child, and there is a large inheritance. Sir Francis and my father decided it would be a good idea to merge the two inheritances." Shrugging, she chewed the succulent stem. "It's not exactly an unusual arrangement."

"No," he agreed with a tight little smile that fortunately Bryony did not see. "Quite customary. You made no objections?"

"I did not really have any, until . . . well, I did not have any. We have known each other for years and have always liked each other. One does not marry for love, after all." She shot him a challenging look. "If one did, matters would be a little different, would they not?"

Ben simply inclined his head. "So, why are you not married to this worthy gentleman?"

Bryony bit back the angry retort at his thinly veiled sarcasm. "I wished for a little time . . . time to be free and to be myself — a self-indulgent whim, you understand?" She glared at him. "But Papa agreed that the marriage should be postponed until my twenty-first birthday. Francis and his father could not really argue, so . . ." Another shrug.

"I see." Sir Edward Paget must be an indulgent father, he reflected. Indulgent, understanding, and loving. But the way a man conducted himself in his private affairs was not always reflected in his public conduct. He could be as gentle as a lamb with his daughter, and yet be as roughly brutal as he pleased to those unfortunates who depended on his generosity for survival, without anyone remarking on any dissonance.

Bryony felt a graveyard shiver run down her back at the stark, bleak bitterness on his face. Nothing she had said could have caused that look. Hesitantly, she put her hand out to touch his. "What is troubling you so, Ben?"

He shook his head briskly, as if to dispel whatever cloud hung over him. "Continue with your story, Miss Paget. I am fascinated. What has this Francis done to cause you to wish to break off such a mutually advantageous arrangement?"

Bryony flinched at the cold, ironical tone. "You're not really interested," she said, exchanging the chewed stem of grass for a fresh one. "I think I will go to bed."

"You have not yet had your dinner," Ben pointed out, laying an arresting hand on her shoulder. "And the sun has only just gone down."

"I am not hungry, but I am sleepy." She made to rise, but the hand on her shoulder held her down.

"I crave pardon, Bryony lass. I have had an uncomfortable day," he apologized softly. "I am truly interested in the story. There are times when my dark side makes itself felt, and I cannot always prevent it."

"It is my fault. I know it is, but I don't truly understand why." She gazed, wide-eyed with the appeal for enlightenment.

Benedict sighed, running a hand up the back of her neck. "Sweeting, you must accept it when I say it is not your fault. More than that I am not prepared to say, and you should be aware by now that there are things about me you may not know. I have told you this often enough."

It was so much easier to relax against the hand massaging her neck, to let her head rest against his shoulder, to accept that this dark side would soon give way to the sun's light and everything between them would be as it was before this morning. So much easier to believe that than to fight to understand what had happened, to shiver in the chill of hurt and incomprehension. Hesitantly, feeling for words, she told him about discovering Francis in the pantry, about his passionate, despairing appeal that she continue with the wedding, about the confusion that had led her to the stableyard in the early hours of the morning that had brought her and Benedict together.

Ben listened in silence, amazed at the matter-of-fact acceptance of Francis Cullum's predilections exhibited by this tender, well-bred young lady. Some devil in him found aspects of the situation hilarious, but he controlled the reaction severely. It was not in the least amusing for Bryony Paget, for all that an outcast from that society might take wicked delight in such an overturning of well-laid plans.

"So, you see, I really do not know what to do," she finished. "If Francis wishes to take his pleasure in that manner, then it's nothing to do with me, but I cannot marry him, knowing that he prefers men to women. I don't think I could even if he said he liked women, as well," she added thoughtfully, and Benedict, his control finally defeated, whooped with laughter.

"Now, what's amusing?" Bryony looked at him in puzzled indignation. "It doesn't strike me as in the least funny."

"Forgive me. It is you who are amusing, sweeting. Young ladies of your background and expectations are not supposed to know of such peculiarities, and you are certainly not supposed to condone them."

"Oh," she said. "Well, I have had an unusual education. I am very well-read in the classics, you understand, and in ancient times such fancies were perfectly acceptable."

"Yes," he agreed solemnly. "I seem to remember that from my own schooling."

"You are making fun of me again," she accused.

"Heaven forfend!" His hands lifted in horror, and she fell on him, fists flailing in feigned indignation. They rolled together on the grass, burying the real emotional disharmony in a mock physical battle. Each knew that this was the case, and each, in cowardice, eagerly grasped the opportunity to retreat from the pain by denying, for the moment, the rift that had so suddenly sprung between them.

# Chapter 7

Try as she might during the next few days, Bryony could no longer deny that rift. Ben was preoccupied and took to going off into the woods for hours at a time. True, he always came back with game of some kind, but Bryony could not deceive herself that hunting for the dinner table was his sole motive for these expeditions. If it were, he would have allowed her to accompany him, as she frequently had done in the past. But the first time since his return from Williamsburg that she tentatively suggested bearing him company, he produced a list of tasks around the cabin that were apparently imperative and would keep her busy for the better part of the day; the second time, he responded with a blunt, unadorned refusal. She hid her hurt as best she could, and greeted him cheerfully and without recrimination on his return, but she did not again risk the pain of rejection. Instead she waited in forlorn patience for the invitation that was not issued.

On the fifth day, Bryony decided that something had to be done. She had racked her brain for some way in which she was responsible for his withdrawal, but she came up with nothing that could have caused this degree of resentment. Her Loyalist background was problematic, but surely no more than that. She would not betray Ben and his men, and she was no fervent proponent of the king, so there should be no cause for quarreling between them on that score. Perhaps, therefore, it was nothing to do with her. Perhaps something had occurred that Ben would not — or could not — share with her. Perhaps she should offer him comfort and reassurance, attempt to take his mind off whatever was distressing him in the only way she knew, offering the healing love of her body with a generous spirit that would make no demands of its own.

Benedict, although he slept beside her every night, had made no attempt to touch her beyond a brief good-night kiss. She had assumed he was exhibiting a natural delicacy about her monthly indisposition, but such consideration was no longer relevant and maybe he was waiting for her to signal that fact.

With a plan of action came relief. She

had spent too long agonizing in indecision and incomprehension. It was time to take matters into her own hands. Humming cheerfully, Bryony found soap and towel and set off for the creek. No longer bothered by sharing her bathwater with fish and water beetles, she washed her hair and every inch of skin, then lay on the bank, allowing the sun to dry her before she returned to the cabin.

Instead of the doeskin tunic, which by now had most definitely seen better days, she donned Benedict's nightshirt, freshly washed and sun-dried, taking as much care as if she were dressing for a dance as she rolled the sleeves artistically. She gathered the material at her slender waist, wrapping a cravat around as her sash, tying it in a neat bow at her back. Ben had a comb — missing several teeth, certainly, but a comb, nevertheless — and she put it to good use, drawing it through the shining blue-black silken waterfall until not a tangle remained. There was no mirror, but somehow she knew that her eyes were bright, her skin clear; Ben, in the time before this estrangement, had told her so often how he loved the way the sun had colored her complexion that she could picture her features without difficulty.

Then, as eager and as carefully prepared as any bride anxious to please her groom, Bryony went outside to sit in the evening sun and await the returning hunter.

Benedict, in the company of three Indians, a deer slung on a pole between two of them, emerged laughing into the clearing and then stopped, the smile fading from his face as Bryony stood up, turning to greet him. The fine weave of the lawn nightshirt did little to conceal the shape of her breasts, the dark shadow of her nipples, the soft lines of her body. Her eyes, in the instant before she registered his companions, shone with the luminous glow of anticipation — the glow they always bore when she contemplated lovemaking — and her arms lifted toward him. Then they fell to her sides so rapidly that he could almost have imagined the invitation.

He felt a sick sinking in his belly, remorse mingling with compassion, as he understood what she had been intending as she waited, so fresh and eager, for his return. He knew he had behaved abominably to her in the last few days. Somehow, whenever he saw her, heard her voice, watched her move with the unconscious certainty of privilege, all the memories so firmly controlled, the bitterness carefully reined so that it provided only constructive force rather than destructive inefficiency, were triggered into life again, obscuring clarity and rational purpose. Bryony Paget bore no personal responsibility for the horrors that he and others had endured, but she belonged to the perpetrators, had learned their values and ideals, had absorbed a self-image that placed her without personal effort on the pedestal of the master race, both in Ireland and here in the Colonies — the English. And that image, as well as her unquestioning acceptance of the privileges that accompanied it, was manifest in every move she made, every word she spoke, so that constantly and quite unconsciously she exacerbated the deep-rooted sores on his soul and he reacted with blind unkindness.

Ben pulled himself together as one of his companions cleared his throat. Bryony should not be standing there in that semitransparent shift, her loving purpose nakedly revealed as much to his friends as to himself. He strode rapidly across to her, leaving the Indians, who, standing utterly motionless, seemed to fade into the background of trees as if understanding that their presence was for the moment awkward.

"Sweet heaven, lass! We are in the middle of the forest, not in the boudoir of a bawdy house!" The low-voiced exclamation sounded harsh when he had wanted it to sound gently teasing. He kissed her quickly, before the deepening hurt and embarrassment in her blue eyes could overwhelm him. "You are a sight to enflame even the most jaded spirit," he whispered, his lips brushing the sensitive corner of her mouth. "But it is not a sight I am prepared to share. Where is your tunic?"

Bryony shrugged with a fair assumption of carelessness, fighting back the wave of mortification. "I felt like wearing something clean after my bath, that's all." Her eyes went over his shoulder to the three men and the dead buck, and the joyful glow, the energy of decision, ran away from her like drops of oil on stretched hide.

"Go and put it on," he insisted. "It is hardly fair to torment those who may not accept the invitation."

"I did not know . . ." she began, then turned with a helpless little shrug to the cabin. "I will stay inside until they've gone."

"They will stay to sup with us," Benedict told her. "We must divide the buck, since we caught it together, but we intend to roast a haunch and share it tonight."

"My company will be unwelcome, in that case," she said in a dull monotone. "Your friends will not choose to break bread with a woman."

Benedict caught her arm as she moved toward the cabin. "You will eat with us, and you will help me prepare the meal," he stated. "I have told them so already, and they expect it."

"And if I do not wish to?"

"Why would you not wish to?"

"Perhaps for the same reason that you do not wish for *my* company." Her voice was dull, flat, and she stood passively, still turned toward the cabin, waiting for him to release her arm.

Benedict's hold tightened. "I am not going to embark on an unseemly squabble in front of my guests. We can discuss this later, but for now you will please change your dress and come back out here. If you refuse to join us, you will insult them and humiliate me."

"When last they were here, my *presence* would have done both, as I recall," she snapped. "What has changed so radically?"

Benedict sighed, hanging on to his temper by a thread as he recognized that she did have a point. "I invited them to share our meal," he said quietly, "making it clear that if they accepted the invitation, they must also accept the rules of my fireside. They are most courteous men, Bryony, and having accepted graciously both the invitation and the condition, any alteration in either would cause them grievous insult. Do you understand that?"

She did, of course, although definitions of courtesy were obviously open to interpretation. "Yes. I'll go and change."

"Thank you." Releasing her arm, he offered her a small bow that in different circumstances would have entertained her. But now, with her healing plan in ruins, her grievances relegated to the status of an unseemly squabble, there seemed little reason for amusement.

When she came outside again, once more respectably clad in her tunic and moccasins, her hair tied back with the cravat that had served as a sash for the nightshirt, she found the fire already blazing and the four men occupied in butchering the deer. Bryony picked up the kettle and headed for the creek, averting her eyes from the butchery. Mint and cress grew in lavish profusion around the creek, and she gathered a bunch for a salad, reflecting that since meeting Ben she saw her surroundings with new eyes — recognizing in perfectly ordinary plants, grasses, and bushes the makings of a quite tasty dish or accompaniment to the abundance of fish, fowl, or game. He had taught her with painstaking care on those occasions when they had roamed the woodland together — on those occasions when he had seemed to welcome her companionship.

Absently, she sat back on her heels, gazing across the creek to the reed-thatched marsh beyond. She had to return home. There was nothing to keep her here anymore — no hope for a permanent future — and she could not evade the responsibilities of her identity for much longer. But she did not want to part from Benedict like this, unable to understand and therefore unable to change his abrupt, bewildering indifference to her that had come out of the blue and at times seemed close to dislike.

"Bryony? What the devil are you doing? This is no time for daydreaming!" Ben's voice, raised in exasperation, brought her to her feet automatically. "I need this water, and I need your help," he declared testily, taking the kettle from her. "In case you have forgotten, you are not lounging around on a terrace, sipping orange-flower

194

water and waiting for your dinner to appear as if by magic, prepared and presented by unseen hands! If you wish to eat, you do your share."

Tears pricked behind her eyelids at this blatant injustice. "I do do my share!" She yelped as he pushed her in front of him with a light but definitely scolding smack on her bottom. "Don't do that! I am not a donkey!"

As rapidly as it had arisen, his irritation seemed to vanish under the indignant glare she threw at him over her shoulder. "I beg your pardon," Ben said in perfunctory apology. "I cannot imagine how I could have made such an error." His lips twitched and he put the kettle down, grabbing Bryony around the waist, bringing her hard against his body. "Cry truce, sweeting."

"But it is you who are quarreling, not I," she said. "I don't understand what has happened. I cannot seem to do anything right." The temptation to sink against him, to drop her defenses and melt into his strength sang a siren song, but she resisted it, afraid of another rebuff, which painful experience had taught her could follow this moment of warmth, without a word of warning.

His expression softened and a long finger traced the straight line of her mouth. "I am an unmitigated bastard," he said remorsefully. "I must wrestle with my own demons, sweet Bryony. I cannot help it if I must do so alone."

"I should leave you, then," she said. "Return home, become again Miss Bryony Paget with an insoluble problem." There was no note of question in her voice, no request for reprieve from the inevitable.

"You must decide that for yourself," he replied, wondering why he was not endorsing a resolve that he had made for himself and was the only avenue open to either of them. "Come now, we cannot talk of this further with venison to cook and guests to entertain."

It was a strange evening that Bryony passed. Their visitors barely acknowledged her presence, but neither did they show her the least discourtesy on the occasions when they were obliged to notice her. The stone cider jar emptied over the course of the evening, and Bryony, interpreting correctly a glance from Ben, fetched the brandy bottle from the cabin. Benedict, she noticed, showed little sign of being the worse for drink; his three visitors, on the other hand, began to have difficulty putting their words together coherently and coordinating their movements.

A heavy yellow moon hung in the purple sky, and the air was redolent of wood smoke and roasting venison. Mosquitoes whined in the close, humid night, and Bryony gave up slapping at them since they only renewed the attack when her hands were elsewhere.

"Go to bed," Ben said into her ear. "They will bother you less inside if you hang the blanket over the window."

She had been intending to wait up with him until the visitors left, had been hoping that the moment of warmth beside the creek could be kindled anew, and, as they took pleasure in and of each other, that they could touch truth, reach some point of understanding. But she rose, bade them all a soft good night, and retired into the cabin. The blanket over the window kept out the mosquitoes, but it made the atmosphere in the cabin insufferably hot. She lay naked, sprawled on the bedstead, the sheet cast aside, feeling the sweat dew her skin simply with the effort of breathing. The rise and fall of voices murmured beyond the door, broken by an occasional crack of laughter and the sound of liquid slurping into a beaker.

What were Ben's demons? In what hellish depths of his soul did they dwell? She knew every inch of his body, every millimeter of skin; the feel and the scent of him were almost as familiar to her as her own. And yet she knew nothing of the man beyond those aspects of his character and personality that he permitted her to see. He bore the scars of the whip upon his back, the dark secrets of his past upon his soul. And without a single clue, she could not begin to speculate about either. But until she discovered that history, she would never understand what had wrought this bewildering change in him, of that she was quite convinced.

She fell asleep eventually, despite the suffocating heat. When, toward dawn, Ben gently rearranged her outflung limbs to allow room for himself on the bedstead, she barely stirred, rolling against him as his weight pulled the mattress down. He slipped an arm beneath her, stroked the thick mass of her hair away from her damp brow as he lay down beside her in the darkness. The three Indians lay beside the now dead fire, their snores resounding in the clearing.

Later this morning, Ben thought, he would make plans to return her home.

Bryony would presumably be able to suggest a secluded spot at which he could safely leave her to make her own way to the house. What story she decided to tell, he would leave to her considerable ingenuity, and then they could both pick up the reins of the lives that had been postponed during this interlude. And he could concentrate with an untrammeled mind on the pursuit of his vengeance, which he would achieve by the annihilation of Sir Edward Paget and his ilk and all that they stood for. It was not a goal compatible with the lusty enjoyment of Paget's daughter, as he and she had discovered to their shared misery.

When Benedict woke, it was full day and his bedfellow had disappeared. He lay for a moment taking stock. His head was a trifle heavy, but nothing that dousing with cold water would not cure, and his mouth tasted foul, but that was as easily remedied. What was not as easily remedied was the heaviness of spirit that the night's reflections had engendered. He went outside, to find the clearing deserted, his three visitors departed, and not a sign of Bryony. He stood for a minute, yawning and idly scratching his bare chest in the sun's warmth, which was already showing signs of becoming uncomfortable. From the sun's position, he judged the time to be around nine o'clock. So, where, in the name of all that was good, was Miss Paget?

No attempt had been made to light the fire, judging by the stone-cold ashes, and the kettle stood empty and forlorn on a trivet beside the hearth. Fetching water was a task that fell to Bryony's hand, as was the setting up and clearing away at mealtimes. There was no sign of platters, utensils, or ingredients for breakfast. Her attempts at fire-lighting tended still to be hit or miss, so he was not unduly surprised that she had neglected that chore this morning, but he would have welcomed the wherewithal to make coffee, even had she been unable to prepare it herself.

The dereliction did nothing for his temper. Bryony Paget was, when all was said and done, a rich little girl from the ineffably cushioned, leisurely background of the Southern aristocracy! He swung up the kettle and strode off to the creek. He had good cause to know the breed — the simpering, idle, petulant, pampered misses who could not bear the slightest thwarting of desire; whose mouths opened in wide wails of complaint when all was not as they wished it; whose eyes shone with vindictive pleasure when the offender paid the penalty. . . .

God dammit! Bryony was not like that, as he knew perfectly well. She had applied herself with eager willingness to whatever task he had assigned her, her mouth set in a determined line as she struggled to master the unfamiliar. Ben smiled in spite of himself as he remembered the way she had fought with the fishing line at the expense of her hands. He filled the kettle at the creek and stood looking around for some sign that she had been there before him. The night dew had dried from the grass several hours earlier, so there were no footprints on the bank — none, either, in the mud to indicate that she might have waded into the water for a bath. The reeds were not broken or bent to indicate human passage, and the bird and animal life along the creek showed no signs of disturbance as it rustled, flew, called, and scampered about its business.

He waded into the creek, plunging beneath the tepid water, which offered little refreshment but was better than nothing. Shaking himself dry, he returned to the clearing. There was still no sign of Bryony, and the first flicker of anxiety made itself felt. She just went for a walk, he told himself, firmly repressing the flicker. He laid and lit the fire, setting the kettle on the trivet above it. Coffee was his most imperative need at this point, and maybe the aroma would bring Miss Paget running. She would receive short shrift, however, he decided, pulling on his britches over his now dry limbs. She knew the rules: there were no handouts in the backwoods.

Coffee was made and drunk with gratitude, but the fragrant steam curling in the moist air failed to produce a breakfast companion. The flicker became a flare. Benedict stood up, sipping his coffee and listening. Bryony was not in the habit of disappearing alone into the woods — not after her last experience. He could hear nothing untoward above the shrill monotone of cicadas, the *rat-tatt* of a woodpecker, the scuttle of a squirrel. But as he stood still, allowing himself to merge into his surroundings, to become an integral part of the forest as his Indian friends had taught him, he felt the hairs on his skin lift. He was being watched, and not with the casual eye of a fellow woodland creature, or the fearful eye of a potential victim for the pot, or the hostile eye of a predator. Slowly, he put his beaker on the ground and walked into the middle of the clearing.

There he stopped and listened again.

"Bryony?" he called, softly questioning. There was no response, but he was certain that he was not alone in the glade. His eyes ran around the uneven circle, across the brown-patched grass, dried by the summer's drought, up into the trees with their broad, gnarled trunks and the wide, dusty green umbrella of their foliage.

He called her name again, imperatively this time as annoyance swelled with his conviction that for some juvenile reason she was hiding from him, as if there was some amusement to be gained from such a prank, as if there weren't tasks to be accomplished, a host of problems to be solved, as if the seriousness of the world could be dissipated by a tiresome joke. Miss Bryony Paget, like other young ladies of her world, had been so sheltered from the problems and seriousness of the reality lived by the majority of the population that she presumably saw nothing inappropriate in this piece of teasing mischief. Well, Benedict Clare had ceased to be amused by the game of hide-and-seek many years ago — at the point when the game had taken on for him the deadly purpose of life preservation.

There was still no reply. Hands resting

on his hips, legs apart as he rocked easily on the balls of his feet, Ben declared in a soft yet carrying voice, "Bryony, if you have not ceased this childish game by the time I count to three, you are going to find yourself in some very childish hot water!" He had reached three when she dropped from the broad branches of a spreading beech tree at the edge of the clearing. Picking pieces of twig and leaves from her hair, Bryony walked slowly toward him.

"I fail to see why you should have to sound so schoolmasterly. Why should I not climb trees, if I choose?"

"I have neither the time nor the energy for foolish games," he snapped. "You neglected to fetch water in your enthusiasm for pranks, so you will go hungry until noon."

Bryony discovered to her dismay that being treated like a recalcitrant babe had the effect of reducing one's temper and reactions similarly. "Since you are oblivious of my presence, it seems extraordinary you should find my absence remarkable, sir."

"Now, just what is that supposed to mean?" He made no attempt to moderate the acerbity of his tone, the weary sigh that said all too clearly he was preparing for a familiar whinging complaint.

It was the last straw. For six days now, she had borne the indifference, the occasional disconcerting flashes of loving warmth, the prolonged absences, the irascibility, the blanket refusal to discuss anything beyond the practicalities of the immediate present. She *had* been playing a game, certainly, had enjoyed watching him go about his business when he did not know he was observed, had waited with considerable interest to see whether her absence would concern him. But there had been nothing malicious or even particularly juvenile about her behavior, and the Benedict of a week ago would have laughed and exacted a playful penalty when she had dropped from the tree.

"It means that I am sick to death of receiving less attention than a mosquito!" A bare foot stamped in the grass as she tossed her head in a swirl of raven-black hair.

Benedict inhaled sharply, his vision blurring as the image of Margaret Martin transposed itself on the face of Bryony Paget, and he heard the former's petulant whine demanding the intimate attentions of her father's bondsman on a bright, sunny August afternoon in Georgia three years ago. He could feel the smooth wood of the ax handle in his palm as he stood sweating beside the woodpile, striving to control his anger at this insolent importuning of a Clare by an overindulged, ill-educated, ill-mannered, conceited miss who had neither birth nor breeding to her advantage, only the superimposed pride of the rich and the master.

"So, you lack attention, do you, miss?" he drawled, as he should have done that August afternoon — taken his revenge by giving Margaret Martin what she was insisting upon, instead of yielding to the temptation to send her about her business with all the contempt a Clare would show an importunate bawd. "Attention of this kind, I assume." A hand caught Bryony at the nape of her neck, and he brought his mouth to hers. But what followed no more deserved the name of kiss than a blow is a caress. Bryony's shout of outrage and alarm died, suffocated by the ferocity of the assault. Her neck, bent back under the pressure of his lips, felt as if it would snap, but then the hand at the nape moved up to palm her scalp, supporting her head even as it held her fast, making her unable to escape the ravaging tongue driving deeply within her mouth. Bryony reacted with unthinking terror. Her teeth sank into his bottom lip.

Benedict tasted blood, felt the piercing pain in his lip. . . . He had bitten through his lower lip that long-ago afternoon, had tasted the salt taste of his own blood as he'd fought to keep back the screams clogging his throat under the torture of the lash. But they had broken out eventually, the inhuman screams of a man entering the dark world beyond endurance. And Miss Margaret, who, denied her stud, had transmuted the private complaint of neglect to public complaint of assault by her father's bondsman, had watched and heard the agonies of his degradation, soothing the savage soul of the scorned.

He thrust a hand upward between the thighs of the woman he held, probing with rough intimacy, as the lines between past and present blurred and he relived the horror, intending at last to exact the brutal and appropriate revenge on the one who had delivered him to the whip.

For a moment Bryony was paralyzed, disbelief and incomprehension warring with the physical reality of those delving fingers whose skillful play was a hideous mockery of the glories of their lovemaking. Somehow the knowledge came to her that Ben was living in one of the dark corners of his past to which hitherto she had been denied entry. Now she had strayed inadvertently across the boundaries and was playing a part in the living memory. The paralysis passed and she writhed violently, trying to twist away from the dreadful skill of that hand, which knew her yet denied her. Her bare foot kicked against his calf, her hands punched and pulled at whatever part of his body they could reach. With a muttered expletive, he freed her head, seizing her flailing fists at the wrists.

"Ben!" Wrenching her head away from his mouth, Bryony yelled his name with all the force of which she was capable.

Ben stared down at the face, white beneath the light suntan; the deep blue eyes, enormous with distress; the soft mouth, bruised and swollen as if it had been repeatedly struck. A deep shudder went through him as the fearful blackness retreated, returning the nightmare memories to that corner of his mind to which he had relegated them two years ago, when sanity had finally come back to him. "God in heaven!" he groaned. "What have I done?" Taking her face between his hands, he visited her lips, her eyes, her deathly pale cheeks with the tender healing caress of his mouth as his hands spread across her back, holding her against the warm support of his body. "As I have wounded you, sweeting," he whispered, "let me salve your hurts."

Bryony could only shiver in his hold as he drew her down to the grass, her head cradled in the hollow of his shoulder. The power of speech seemed to have deserted her under the shock of a rapine assault delivered by a stranger in familiar guise, then this sudden volte-face, the intensity of his remorse, the exquisite gentleness with which his hands returned to the sites that they had ravished, bringing first a healing peace to the sore, throbbing flesh — a peace that finally yielded to the sweetness of arousal.

With lips and tongue and fingers, he brought her to the soft, verdant fields of release; in penance, he denied himself the union that would heal his own hurts, concentrating only on the giving that would make her whole again. Bryony was wandering so deeply in the realm of pure sensation, gulping the ether that anesthetized the pain of the past, that she simply received and failed to notice that the giver did not also take his due.

Much later, as she still lay cradled in his arms, she whispered, "Why? Why did that dreadful thing happen, Ben?"

"I cannot tell you, love." Laying her gently on the grass, he got to his knees, leaning over her to brush the tumbled hair from her brow, to pull down the tunic over her bare thighs, which were gleaming pale against the green-brown ground. "You must put it behind you and try to find it in your heart to forgive me."

"I have done so long since." She sat up, reaching to touch his face. "But it is so hard to be denied understanding."

The black eyes became opaque in the way that she knew and dreaded. "Do not persist in this, lass. It will serve no useful purpose." He rose to his feet in one easy movement. "Are you hungry?"

Bryony shook her head, trying to hide the disconsolate bleakness that had replaced the ephemeral serenity of physical release. "No, I do not find that I am." She watched him go into the cabin and return with his musket. "You're going hunting?"

"No. I must go to Joshua's to meet with the others." He looked down at her and offered a smile where apology mingled with regret. "I cannot take you with me, lass. They would take ill to your presence at a planning discussion."

"Yes, I understand that." Bryony extended a hand for him to pull her to her feet. "How long will you be?"

"Three, maybe four hours," he said. "We have to plan for the removal of the weapons from the armory. They have lain beneath the straw in Joshua's barn quite long enough."

"When you come back, we should plan how best I may return home without causing difficulties," she stated matter-of-factly, although her eyes slid past him lest he read the different message there.

"Yes, it is time," he agreed quietly, and then the silence hung heavy in the clearing, expanding to enfold them in the deadening truth of inevitability. Ben tilted her chin and lightly kissed the tip of her nose, the corner of her mouth, the cleft of her chin. "Farewell, sweetheart."

"Have a care," she bade softly.

For an hour, Bryony wandered aimlessly around the cabin and clearing, but she could settle to nothing when her thoughts seethed in such turmoil and her soul was leaden with unhappiness. Eventually, deciding that she had learned enough in the last weeks for the woods to hold no perils, she set off along one of the paths that she had taken with Ben, reasoning that if she did not deviate from it, she could simply retrace her steps later. She recognized the little crossroads where four narrow trails met. She and Ben had branched off to the right, as she recalled, but, sticking to her original plan, Bryony continued straight ahead.

She walked for about two hours, until fatigue had driven off turmoil and despondency. She had made no plans, but the calm of resignation lay upon her. She was about to turn back when she noticed a difference in her surroundings. The trees seemed spaced farther apart, the light was brighter, pouring down through foliage much thinner than in the center of the forest. The sounds of woodland life were somehow muted, as if the creatures of the wood did not inhabit this part, or, if they did, wished to keep their presence unmarked. Then, quite suddenly, Bryony broke through the trees and found herself on a road.

She stood and stared. It was a broad thoroughfare, and well traveled, judging by the wheel tracks and hoofprints in the dust. Where did it go? Williamsburg, of course. Hadn't Ben said the town was some seven miles away? The highway would have to pass alongside the woods. Even as she stood, blinking at the first sight of the wider world — if one did not count the armory or Joshua's farm — that she had glimpsed since waking in the log cabin all those weeks ago, a horse and rider rounded a bend on her right. Instead of obeying her first instinct to duck back into the trees, Bryony could not resist indulging her curiosity to see this fellow traveler.

The horseman drew closer. He was dressed in buckskin britches, a brown cloth coat and matching waistcoat, and a tricorn hat on his unpowdered hair, which was drawn into a queue at the nape of his neck. He had a small, neat brown beard. Bryony was rooted to the spot, no longer having the option to run.

As the horse drew level, the rider cast the Indian woman a cursory glance, then pulled back on the reins with an almost vicious tug, bringing his mount to a rearing halt.

"Bryony Paget! Dear God, is it really you?"

Bryony looked blankly at Francis Cullum and shook her head, rubbing her temples in a gesture of total confusion. "I do not know," she said. "Who are you?"

# Chapter 8

This time, Ben knew that the clearing contained no mischievous watcher in the trees. He could feel the emptiness, the absolute solitude as he stood listening under the dying rays of the evening sun. So certain was he that he did not even bother to call her name, turning instead to the cabin in search of some sign of her whereabouts. Everything was as he had left it that morning, except that the covers had been straightened on the bedstead and some attempt had been made to tidy up. But it seemed to have been a half-hearted attempt. He shook out the damp, scrunched ball of towel lying on the plank table and took it outside to dry. Where the devil was she?

A minute search of the immediate wood and creek produced no clues, and by nightfall Benedict's iron control had yielded to the terrors of uncertainty. There were perils aplenty in the forest for the unwary, particularly after dark, and he greeted the appearance of his Indian friends with undisguised relief.

"Run off again, has she?" one of them said with a shrug that seemed to imply, What else could you expect of such an unpredictable creature? "She needs a leash, if you ask me."

Ben refrained with difficulty from replying that he was not asking for such advice, instead requesting quietly, "I'd be grateful for your help in tracking her. If she's lost in the woods, there's no knowing what could have befallen."

Somber nods of agreement ran around the small group. With one accord, they loped off into the trees, Ben this time accompanying them. They picked up Bryony's trail easily enough, following it to the outskirts of the forest.

"Reckon she took the road."

"Aye," Ben concurred tersely, turning back into the trees. "There's nothing more to be done. My thanks." The set of his shoulders and the angle of his head indicated to his friends that he did not wish for further company, and they melted into the woods, leaving him to make his solitary way back to the cabin.

Had she left him deliberately or by accident? Not that it mattered either way, he thought with a light shrug. She had gone and that was the only significant fact. It would have happened within a day or so, anyway, but at least if it had been planned there would have been some ceremony, some dignified rounding off of the loving idyll, instead of this jagged ending where the rawness of this morning's horror still pulsed, only half healed.

News of her safe return would run like wildfire through the district, and once he had heard it for himself, then he would be able to put Bryony Paget behind him and devote his undivided attention to the vital business that had never before left the forefront of his waking mind.

Benedict Clare went into the log cabin and slammed the door on the deserted clearing and the star-filled sky. The night-shirt that Bryony had made her own lay on the sea chest. He folded it carefully and put it back in the fragrant cedar interior, beneath the pile of shirts.

A few hours earlier, Francis Cullum, on the Williamsburg road, had struggled to find his wits. "What do you mean, you do not know?" He sprang down from his horse. "Are you hurt, Bri? Where have you been? Why on earth are you wearing that tunic?" The questions tumbled over them-

216

selves. He took her shoulders and pushed back her hair as if to assure himself that she really was the missing Miss Paget.

Bryony continued to shake her head in apparent bemusement, although her brain was racing. Of all the damnable ill luck! At no point had she given thought to the story she would tell if and when she returned to the bosom of her family — to have concocted an explanation would have emphasized the finite nature of the idyll, and she had not been ready to face that. But now it was upon her, and Francis was staring, his green eyes puzzled, anxious. Amnesia was a familiar enough state for her to be able to feign it convincingly, which would at least buy her time.

"Am I called Bryony?" she asked blankly. "I do not appear to remember." The deep blue eyes widened as if with the effort of thought. "I don't remember you, either, sir, for all that you seem to know me."

Francis swore softly. He had known Bryony Paget since the dawn of memory, and it seemed utterly inconceivable that she should be looking at him in that blank, featureless fashion — particularly after their last meeting. He could feel a dull flush stain his cheekbones at the thought and wrenched his mind away to deal with the problem at hand. It was clearly incumbent upon him to restore this sun-browned gypsy in her Indian tunic to her father with no more ado. Let Sir Edward deal with the situation from then on. It would surely not be beyond his powers. Indeed, Francis doubted whether anything would be beyond Sir Edward's powers.

"Your name is Bryony Paget," he said gently. "I am Francis Cullum and I am going to take you home."

A frown fluttered over the smooth wide brow. "Home?"

For answer, Francis took her by the waist and lifted her onto his horse. He swung up behind her, circling her waist as he reached for the reins.

"How do I know that you are not kidnapping me?" his passenger inquired in stricken tones. "Why should I believe —" She began to struggle and he tightened his grip.

"For heaven's sake, Bryony, be still! You'll have us both off!" he expostulated. "Dirk is no pony!"

Bryony became prudently still, deciding that she had put up sufficient protest to be convincing. Francis was no fool and knew her too well to be deceived by her present ploy if she overstepped the mark. She

218

would have to be careful with her father, too — the slightest exaggeration and he would instantly smell a rat. "Where are you taking me?" she asked in a small, hesitant voice.

"Home," he replied, "as I told you. Your parents have been frantic since you disappeared."

"When was that?" Bryony swiveled on the saddle to look at him with what she hoped was convincing curiosity.

"Six weeks ago," her companion told her. "You vanished from Trueman's on the night of the ball." He frowned at her upturned face, his voice suddenly intense. "Are you sure you have no memory of that, Bri?"

Bryony dropped her eyes hastily, turning to face forward again as she murmured a soft negative. The agonizing memory of that evening was obviously as vivid to Francis as it was to herself. "I have been with the Indians," she offered as the story sprang ready-made to her lips. "I woke up one day in a hut in a village. They said they found me wandering in the woods. I had a bump on my head . . . but I don't know how I got it or why . . . I remember nothing before waking up. They were very kind to me. . . ." She allowed her voice to fade a little, then to pick up as if with sudden resolution. "I went for a walk this morning and arrived on the road by accident." That, at least, was God's truth, Bryony thought. The nearer she could keep to the truth, the better would be her chances of pulling off the deception until she could safely appear to regain her memory.

"Dear Lord," Francis muttered. "What a tangle!" Sir Edward was going to have a fine time worrying at it, and he wouldn't let go until it was unraveled. The English aristocrat was as tenacious as a bulldog once he got his teeth into a puzzle, particularly when matters concerned his precious daughter.

They rode in silence for a while — a silence that Bryony welcomed, as it gave her the opportunity to take stock and plan her next moves. The thought of Ben was a dull ache, one that she knew waited only for solitude before it blossomed into pain, but she could not allow it to intrude now; she needed to keep all her wits about her. It took her but a few minutes of serious reflection to acknowledge that she would not be able to deceive her father with the pretense of amnesia. Her own desire to see him was too strong for her to pretend convincingly not to know him at the moment of reunion, so she had best recover her memory under the shock of that reunion. There was no reason, however, why the events that led to her disappearance should not remain lost to memory as a result of the bump on her head, just as there was no reason why she should be able to retrace her steps to the Indian village where she had supposedly been cared for in the intervening time. The woods were vast and Indian settlements plentiful. So long as she could swear that she had come to no harm, her story would produce no demand for action.

Bryony was not prepared, however, for her reaction as Francis turned his horse onto the long driveway leading up to the Paget mansion. The great house stood a mile from the road, but in sight of it, high on a hill. It was served both by the road at the front and the river at the rear, and Bryony had never been able to decide which view of the house she preferred. Both front and back of the large, square, two-storied brick building were distinguished by their imposing entrances, pillared and stepped, neither one obviously the superior.

She had always loved the house, and

now, as they rode up the drive between the sweeping lawns and terraced gardens hedged with boxwood and lilac, her heart filled with nostalgia. She wondered why she had not missed her home while she had been living in the log cabin, but it was a question all too easily answered. Her surroundings were of no importance beside the loving companionship of a certain Patriot, and if a wave of her hand would cause this elegant, solid grandeur to disappear, a log cabin and Benedict put in its place, she would gladly have waved.

She shivered suddenly. Francis's arm tightened around her waist. "What is it, Bri?"

"I am afeard," she said slowly, realizing that she spoke only the truth. The prospect of the imminent meeting with her mother and father was terrifying in the depths of emotion that she knew would accompany it. How could she keep her head clear? Benedict's life, as well as the lives of the others, depended on her ability to maneuver her way through the maze. One false step and her father would wrench the truth from her. He was the only person capable of doing so, but he *was* capable.

"There is no need to be," Francis said gently, and Bryony felt a sudden stab of regret at the twists and turns of fate. He had always been a good friend to her, and if things had been different they probably would have dealt with perfect amity in marriage. But *now* such a prospect was inconceivable — the original impediment compounded by her knowledge of what passion, love, lust, and friendship combined really meant. Such a knowledge precluded the acceptance of its counterfeit. So, what was she to do?

Sir Edward Paget walked to the long window of his study at the front of the house, gazing almost absently out onto the broad gravel sweep before the landward entrance. He recognized Cullum's horse immediately and wondered with a snap of irritation what could have brought the young man here to this grieving house. Then an icy stillness enveloped him as he stared fixedly. There was no mistaking that blue-black hair cascading over her shoulders, no mistaking the set of those shoulders, the proud angle of her head. A strange sound, half sob, half expletive, broke from his lips, and he flung himself out of the study into the central hall, which ran through the house to connect its two fronts. He was through the door and on the steps above the sweep as the horse and its two riders reached the entrance.

"Papa!" Bryony tumbled from the horse and into Paget's arms. Father and daughter clung together in the afternoon sun, heedless of the now bemused Francis, who remained mounted, uncertain quite what he should do next. Bryony appeared to have recovered her memory somewhat abruptly.

"Where have you been, child?" At last Sir Edward drew back to look at the returned wanderer, disbelief, wonder, and amazement all mingling on the lean, aristocratic face.

"I found her on the Williamsburg road, sir," Francis offered diffidently. "She had lost her memory, but . . ."

"I remember now," Bryony said hastily. "It must have been the shock of seeing Papa that made all the pieces fall into place again."

"Yes, I expect so," Francis agreed, wondering why he was not convinced. "I will leave you now, sir. You do not need intruders on your joy." He took off his hat with a courtly gesture. "Perhaps I may call upon Bryony in a day or so, when she has quite recovered from —"

"Call upon me tomorrow, Francis." Bryony went swiftly toward him, extending her hand. "There is really nothing from

224

which I must recover, you know. I am perfectly well, just a little confused. But tomorrow I will be able to thank you properly for your kindness."

Francis leaned down and took the proffered hand, examining her face intently. Something was lurking behind that innocent smile, he decided. She'd best have a care if she wished to keep whatever it was from Sir Edward. "Until tomorrow, then," he said blandly. "Pray accept my congratulations, Sir Edward."

"Yes . . . yes," said the Englishman with a degree of impatience at these elaborate courtesies. "I owe you much. By all means, call upon us tomorrow, when I have discovered the truth of this tangle. Lady Paget, I know, will be glad to welcome you. Bryony, come inside. Your mother has been out of her mind these last weeks, and I am much in need of an explanation."

Bryony cast a backward glance at Francis as her father hustled her indoors. She could not resist a mischievous wink, which she knew Francis would interpret correctly. Sir Edward Paget was never at a disadvantage for many minutes; not even the miraculous return of the daughter he had presumed dead could disturb his self-control for long.

An excited crowd of slaves stood chattering in the doorway, witnessing this extraordinary reunion, and Bryony was instantly engulfed as they exclaimed over her and touched her as if to convince themselves that she was indeed flesh and blood. Sir Edward sent them about their business tersely, propelling his daughter into the relative cool of the hall, where the loftier members of his household, the paid staff who ensured its smooth running, were gathered in wide-eyed astonishment.

Eliza stood on the stairs, one hand pressed to her bosom, shock and disbelief on her face. She had not believed the housekeeper who had rushed in upon her where she knelt at the prie-dieu as she had been doing continuously once hope had finally left her, praying for forgiveness, for salvation, for knowledge, at least, to bring an end to the agonizing uncertainty. Mary had gasped that Miss Bryony and Mr. Cullum had just ridden up to the door, that Sir Edward had run out, and that it was a heaven-sent miracle that the poor child was restored to them. The old woman's eyes had rolled incredulously, her hands clasped tightly at her heart, and Eliza had been obliged to move the rapt figure bodily from the doorway before she could venture forth herself to discover the truth of this marvel. Now she looked upon the miracle and, with a mother's instinctive knowledge, knew that her daughter was unharmed though she had lived through some life-defining experience.

"Mama." Bryony moved away from her father, toward her mother, reading the agony of the past weeks in her face and feeling a wash of remorse that she had not put an end to that agony sooner. In fact, if it were not for the accident of finding the road and Francis, she would still be in the clearing with Benedict, still clinging desperately to the last shreds of a fairy tale. Benedict . . . oh, Ben, she thought with her own agonizing wrench as the ache threatened to blossom. Why could it not have been different? Then she had her arms around her mother, who was crying. Her own tears began to fall, and she could no longer distinguish who or what it was for which they fell.

That night, she lay in her own big poster bed, the light summer hangings drawn back to allow what little air there was some freedom of movement. There had been more tears, a little laughter, endless questions, so that her head spun with the effort to keep her story straight, the continuity accurate. But there had been no serious questioning of the truth of her tale. Eliza had wanted to summon the physician from Williamsburg, but Bryony had protested so vociferously, had demonstrated so clearly that she was as healthy as she had ever been, that her mother had yielded. However, when she had tucked Bryony into bed as if she were again a little girl, she had sat beside her, taking her hand, and had gently probed into the details of her life among the Indians.

Bryony flung herself on her back, kicking off the sheet. The feather mattress was somehow smothering after the hard, resistant surface of the straw mattress on Ben's bedstead, and even the slight river breeze drifting in through her opened casement was no compensation for the unutterable loneliness of an empty bed.

Was she doomed to spend the rest of her life in this emptiness? To condemn a body that had known the glory of fulfillment to eternal deprivation? Having known Ben, she could not imagine sharing the glory he had taught her with anyone else. And what had her mother suspected? Not the truth, surely? That her daughter was a spoiled virgin, no fit bride for Francis Cullum or for any other young man.

The thoughts circled, viciously relentless, and the great well of grief at the suddenness of her loss, the denial of the time to draw matters between them to a civilized close, swallowed her in abject wretchedness. She wrapped her arms tightly around herself as if they could replicate the hold that had carried her through sleep for the last six weeks, and finally she fell into an exhausted oblivion as the dawn crept into the sky.

The rich, familiar fragrance of hot chocolate brought Bryony out of sleep. She blinked bemusedly in the brilliant sunlight, her first thought that it must be sinfully late and Ben would greet her appearance with an eyebrow raised in admonition and some wry comment about slug-a-beds who neglected their allotted tasks. And then Mary's face, beaming and hovering over her, filled her vision, and she remembered.

"Dead to the world you were, Miss Bryony," Mary said, plumping up the pillows behind her young charge, who was struggling to sit up. "Your mother said to let you sleep, but it's all of three o'clock in the afternoon!"

"It cannot be!" Bryony stared in horror, pushing back her tumbled hair as Mary placed a silver tray on her lap. "I cannot have slept so long."

"Well, you did," Mary affirmed stolidly. "I'll have your bath prepared in no time. Sir Francis and young Mr. Cullum are bidden to dinner at four o'clock."

Bryony poured the dark, richly scented stream of chocolate from the silver jug into the shallow, fluted cup and sipped appreciatively, watching as Mary bustled around the large sun-filled chamber, pouring steaming water into the porcelain hip bath before the empty hearth. Every piece of furniture in the room, as elsewhere in the house, had come from England, carefully chosen for the elegant simplicity of master cabinetmakers, bearing the hallmarks of Thomas Chippendale and George Hepplewhite. A Wilton carpet of deep rose covered the floor, matching the hangings at the bed and windows, and on the walnut chest of drawers reposed the heavy silver-backed hairbrushes and combs that had been her betrothal gift from the Cullums.

Anything further from the primitive simplicity of Ben's log cabin in the woods would be impossible to imagine, she reflected, flexing her toes beneath the fine linen sheet. It was no wonder he had teased her so often about her luxurious tastes and overly refined habits.

Bryony bit her lip. Such thoughts were

not going to facilitate her return to the life to which she had been born, and she could not allow herself to be distracted by melancholy in company. Her mother already seemed to suspect something untoward and must not be given further food for suspicion.

"Why, whatever's the matter, Miss Bryony?" Mary, her face twisted with concern, came over to the bed. "You look as if you've seen a ghost."

*That* was what she must guard against! "No ghosts, Mary," she responded cheerfully. "I am still trying to become used to being home again, that's all." She offered a teasing smile. "I have not had anyone to wait upon me in the last weeks, and it is proving a novel experience."

The explanation appeared to satisfy Mary, who turned her attention to the contents of the armoire while Bryony took a bath in a tub within four walls for the first time in an eternity. Half an hour later Bryony stood in front of the pier glass, examining her reflection with critical curiosity. She should look different, surely? But, apart from the freckles on her nose and the delicate suntan, she appeared to be quite unchanged. Her stays felt uncommonly constricting, and she toyed with the idea of telling Mary to loosen them, or to remove them altogether, but the elderly housekeeper would probably swoon away at such a sacrilegious request.

Mary shook out the folds of an elegant French sacque of turquoise silk and dropped it over Bryony's head. The flowing gown fell unconfined from her neck to her ankles at the back while molding her figure at the front and the sides. The elbow-length sleeves were edged with lace ruffles threaded with dark blue velvet sleeve-knots. A similar ribbon held the luxuriant mass of black hair away from her forehead to tumble artlessly to her shoulders. Would Ben approve of the effect of this finery? This amazing transformation from grubby gypsy in a doeskin tunic to lady of the first style of elegance, the epitome of the English aristocrat . . . No, he would not like it. He had loved the Bryony who had no history, no family, only a present that he shared . . . but shared no longer.

"There, now." Mary finished fussing over the set of the gown. "You'll want to wear the pearls, I daresay." She opened a japanned jewel case on the dresser, drawing out the rich creamy string of pearls, then clasping them around

Bryony's neck with a little sigh of satisfaction. "Beautiful," she pronounced. "To look at you now, no one would ever know what you have been through."

Exactly so, thought Bryony desolately. It might never have happened. She went downstairs, praying that her armor would hold, would be strong enough to withstand sharp eyes or keen questions or, more dangerous, the sudden, unbidden surge of memory and wanting that would show on her face. Was Ben worried about her? Had he searched for her? The news of her safe return would be around the town already. Someone would have told him. . . .

"Bryony, dearest. Are you quite rested?" Eliza stood up from the brocade upholstered sofa in the drawing room in a stiff rustle of lavender satin. She wore a crimped cap with lace lappets hanging down the sides of her face, a style that Bryony privately thought made her mother look older and dowdier than she had any need to. But Eliza was most insistent on dressing according to her perceived advanced matronly state, for all that she was barely six and thirty. "See, Sir Francis has come to offer his congratulations on your safe return, and Francis is here, of course." Eliza gave a satisfied little nod. "He was far too anxious to know that you are in good health to stay away another minute. Is that not so, Francis?"

Francis bowed and murmured that, indeed, it was so. Bryony received a chaste salute from both Cullums then was subjected to her father's minute scrutiny before he, too, kissed her in greeting.

"It's a relief to see you looking like my daughter again," Sir Edward declared. "There was a moment yesterday when I wondered if you would ever appear respectable again."

"Oh, dear," Eliza fluttered, fanning herself vigorously. "The least said the better, sir, do you not think?"

"I am not about to be ashamed of my dress, madam, when it was furnished by those who offered me only kindness," Bryony said, thus indicating to all in the room that her conduct and personality had undergone no changes during her disappearance. However, she smiled and took her mother's hand, kissing the faded cheek. "Indeed, Mama, I do not know what would have become of me without them."

"No, no . . . and we are forever in their debt," Eliza said hastily. "I wish I could tell them so myself. I only meant that . . . well . . ."

"That my scandalous disappearance and equally remarkable reappearance will provide food for the gossips as it is," Bryony finished for her, taking a glass of sherry from the silver tray held by the butler.

"For which reason we shall not broadcast any details, miss." It was the nearest to a reproof that Sir Edward was likely to come, and his daughter simply inclined her head in acknowledgment.

"Quite so . . . quite so," concurred Sir Francis heartily, patting his wig with one hand as he held his glass to be refilled with the other. "Best to withdraw from society for a while, my dear, on account of your ordeal, you understand. It'll be a nine days' wonder, you mark my words."

Nothing had changed, absolutely nothing at all, Bryony thought, except for herself. *She* was radically changed and could allow no one to see the change. How was she to confine her expanded soul in this rigid mold again?

Dinner was interminable, and Bryony found that her belly had grown unaccustomed to the richness and variety of a meal where woodcocks on toast vied with roasted turkey and buttered apple pies, where the aroma of roast beef surrounded by horseradish and pickles at one end of the table fought with the scent of gravy soup and chicken and bacon at the other. Catfish broiled over an open fire on a flat stone, hare in a pot with turnips and carrots, fried hominy . . . She placed her fork carefully on her delicate delftware plate. Ben, like most backwoodsmen, had only knives and spoons and wooden trenchers and leather tankards.

"Are you not hungry, dearest?" Eliza inquired anxiously across the expanse of snowy damask, where silver glinted and the late-afternoon sunlight was trapped in the intricate cuts of the glassware.

"Perhaps if I wait for a little while, I will be able to eat a bit more." Bryony smiled reassuringly at her mother and picked up her glass, holding the rich ruby claret up to the window to catch the light. The wine was making her feel light-headed. She had drunk only cider, ale, and some brandy in the last six weeks.

"I would dearly love to hear something of your life among the Indians, Bryony." It was Francis, uncannily tuning into her thoughts. She looked at him sharply and saw speculation in the green eyes.

"Why, I would tell you gladly, Francis, but details are not to be broadcast, as I recall." She smiled with a trace of her old mischief, hoping thus to set his mind at rest, to still the speculation.

"Your fiancé is entitled to hear as much of the story as he wishes, child," Sir Edward pronounced. "Indeed, I think you are obliged to satisfy his curiosity to the most minute detail."

Blue eyes met green across the table. "But of course. After dinner, perhaps we could walk a little, Francis? If Mama permits?"

"By all means, dear, but you must not overtire yourself," said Eliza. "You are by no means recovered from your ordeal and must have a care how you exert yourself."

Nods of agreement ran around the table, and Bryony, with a rueful little smile, accepted the role she must play for public consumption. Despite the fact that she was in the best of health after six weeks of Benedict's woodland regime, she would lie upon a sofa in a darkened room when considered well enough to receive the courtesy visits from neighbors. She would remain in seclusion until all talk died down, this tale superseded by another. It was a role that suited her own purposes perfectly. It would allow her time enough for the raw throb of memory to fade and some practical path through the turmoil to reveal itself.

She played with a lemon syllabub, sipped her wine, and when the covers were removed, drank the toast to King George without the blink of an eye. Then she rose with her mother to withdraw and leave the gentlemen to their wine, talk, and further toasts.

Francis appeared in the drawing room within a very short time, and they received leave to stroll about the garden from a smiling Eliza, who was looking forward to a nap before her husband and Sir Francis decided to join her.

"Do not go out without a hat, Bryony," she adjured. "The sun has not gone down yet."

"No, Mama," her daughter murmured meekly. "I will send someone for it." She went into the hall, followed by Francis, and made straight for the door opening onto the rear terrace overlooking the James River.

"Your hat, Bri?" Francis reminded. He only used the childhood shortening of her name when they were alone, and somehow its use always established the mood of friendly sparring and teasing with which they were most comfortable.

"Bother the hat!" she replied with a dismissive wave of her hand. "I have not worn one for six weeks and have been out in the hottest sun and come to no harm." She stepped through the door that had opened as if by magic, perfectly in accordance with the smooth running of Sir Edward Paget's household. "Let us go down to the river."

"Yours to command." Francis executed a magnificent leg and they both chuckled. Then the merriment died as they each remembered that they had little to be merry about. Bryony walked across the terrace and onto the broad walk flanked by lawns studded with curving borders in full bloom.

"Shall I tell you of the Indians, Francis, or shall we talk of what concerns us both most nearly?"

"You remember, then?" His voice was so soft as to be almost inaudible, but, unlike that dreadful night at Trueman's, he was perfectly collected.

Bryony nodded. "I went for a walk in the early hours of the morning, trying to clear my head, to decide . . ." Her shoulders lifted in a gesture expressive of helpless resignation. "Something happened to me while I was walking. . . . I hurt my head, and the rest you know."

"Did you decide anything?" The question was asked almost casually, but Bryony was not deceived.

She laid a hand lightly on his silk-clad arm. "Only that I know I cannot marry you, my friend. It is not that I am any the less fond of you . . . but —"

"But what?" he broke in, softly but urgently. "I have promised that it will never happen again, and if you still regard me with friendship —"

"How can you promise that it will never happen again?" Bryony turned across the right-hand lawn in the direction of a thicket of young oaks. "From what I understand, Francis, such desires do not strike once, like lightning." She looked sadly at him over her shoulder. "Let us be truthful, at least. I have no desire to hurt you, but you hurt me by deception."

"It is no deception when I swear that you would not suffer in the least degree from marriage to me. I would make no demands, would not curtail your freedom in any way."

"And children?" she asked bluntly as they moved into the seclusion of the thicket.

"It would be expected," Francis responded as bluntly. He swallowed and cleared his throat. "I see nothing to preclude such a happening."

"By which you mean you would perform a distasteful duty in order to keep matters straight in the eyes of the world. You must pardon such unmaidenly candor, but you know that I am not one to pretend to false ignorance and a delicacy that I do not possess." Bryony stopped and turned, leaning back against a tree trunk. "That was not meant to be unkind, Francis, but the unvarnished truth is often hard to hear."

He was very pale and his hands shook slightly as he brushed an imaginary speck of dust from the sleeve of his emerald silk coat. "A marriage of convenience," he said. "Is it so unusual?"

"No." She shook her head. "But I wish for more or for nothing at all." Now more than ever. But that was a thought Bryony kept to herself.

"I do not understand why it need be any different now from the way it would have been." His voice held the desperate ring of a man who knows he is fighting the last-ditch battle, who recognizes the shape of his inevitable submission. "You would never have known from the way I would behave with you, from the way we would conduct our marriage, and there is no reason why that should alter. There will be no indication ever."

"No!" She pushed herself away from the tree trunk and began to walk briskly away from him, out of the thicket. Francis caught up to her as she emerged onto the lawn in sight of the house. She slowed instantly, and they resumed their walk down to the river as if they were discussing nothing of more moment than the pleasant evening and local gossip. "I am sorry, Francis, but I could not live that lie. We would make each other wretched, and I would rather die an old maid."

"You cannot understand to what you condemn me?" he said with a painful throb. "To be reviled, cast out, brought to trial, even —"

"No," she interrupted swiftly. "I will not betray you. You cannot imagine I would do such a thing."

"Then what reason will you give for wishing to break off the betrothal?"

Bryony gave a deep sigh. They had reached a large fish pond graced by an ornamental Roman temple standing on a small mount in the middle. "That is what I have not yet decided." She sat on the grass beside the pond and drew her fingers absently through the water, pushing aside the huge flat lily pads. "Have you ever seen the monstrous carp that lives at the bottom of this pond?"

"No." Francis stood above her. "I don't actually believe it's there. You've promised to show it to me so many times, and it has never appeared to order."

Bryony smiled. "Matt, the gardener, says it must be at least a hundred years old. When you reach such a great age, you learn a few tricks." A huge goldfish swam serenely in the gloom beneath the bright surface, and Bryony flicked at it with the tips of her fingers. "Can you think of a reason for crying off, Francis?"

"For me?" He looked startled. "There is only one reason, as you well know, why a man might be permitted to withdraw from an engagement."

"Mmmm." Bryony said nothing for a minute, trailing her hand in the water, feeling its silkiness coat her fingers, remembering what it was like to immerse oneself naked in the cool, clear waters of a creek. She could give Francis his reason. Could tell some of the truth of her experiences, release him, and shoulder the blame. But the disgrace could destroy her father, drive her mother over the brink of sanity. It was not a right she had — not when there was no alternative bridegroom to make all right.

Shaking the water off her hand, she held

it up to him imperatively. Bending, Francis took the hand and pulled her to her feet. "We can buy a little time," Bryony declared, smoothing down her skirt. "I am supposed to be recovering from a horrendous ordeal. No one will expect wedding plans to be made for a while. Maybe something will occur to us during the respite."

"Was it a horrendous ordeal?" Again that speculative scrutiny from the green eyes.

Bryony shrugged, averted her gaze. "It was not always pleasant." That, at least, was true.

"It must have been very strange," Francis responded with careful neutrality. "A very different way of life."

"Oh, it was quite different! Incalculably so," she agreed. "It will take a long time for such an experience to fade into memory."

Her arms crossed over her breasts in an involuntary, unconscious hug, which did not escape her companion. But he made no remark, merely suggested that perhaps they should return to the house since she was not to overexert herself. The conspiratorial smile she gave him in response was designed to return their relationship to its customarily easy footing, but it was a very thoughtful Francis Cullum who eventually left the Paget mansion. There was a lot more to Bryony's story than she was pre-pared to reveal, of that he was convinced; but in what manner, if any, such a revela-tion would bear upon the problem he and she shared had yet to be seen.

# Chapter 9

Ben saw the man fall even while the cold hard press of the trigger remained imprinted on his finger.

"My thanks, Ben." Dick Jordan, bleeding copiously from an ugly gash in his shoulder, his face blackened with smoke, struggled to his feet from where he had fallen, an exposed target for the rifleman on the bank below them. "That was too close."

"The entire operation was," Ben responded shortly. "Someone must have alerted the guards. Get going now. I'll cover you." He raised the musket again.

Dick vanished into the trees at Ben's back, leaving the man with the musket firing steadily down into the crowd of men milling around in the river shallows where the flat rafts floated aimless and upturned, the barrels that had contained their shipments of gunpowder bobbing, now empty, on the surface.

Ben swore softly and fluently to himself.

They had lost two men on this raid, and three, counting Dick, had been injured, and the mission was only half-successful. They had intended overpowering the Loyalist guards and floating the rafts with their precious cargo downriver to the waterfront of Tyler's plantation, where men waited to unload and secrete the purloined explosives. Instead, they had succeeded only in destroying them, emptying the barrels into the river so that neither side would gain the benefit. He had been told to expect two guards to a raft, and there had been four, clearly alerted to the possibility of a raid.

Was there a traitor in their midst, or was it simply that the Loyalists were getting wise to the fact that the local Patriots were a force to be reckoned with? It was high time they did, of course. In the last seven months, Ben and his band had carried off enough arms and ammunition to supply a small army, their ability to do so facilitated by the arrogant indolence of their Loyalist opponents, who neglected to take sufficient precaution against an enemy they had consistently underestimated.

A musket ball whined, almost clipping his ear, and Benedict judged it time to make his own escape. He stepped backward into the line of trees and seemed to vanish as a separate figure distinct from the dark shapes of the nighttime forest. It would be dawn before he reached the cabin in the clearing, but he found that he preferred to sleep during the day. For some reason, the simple bedstead had become hard and unyielding, emphasizing the loneliness of the nights. Miss Paget, of course, would be luxuriating in featherbed comfort, sleeping until the sun was high in the sky, waking to a day where her every need would be attended to by those whose sole purpose in life was to ensure her comfort and minister to her pleasure. Had she forgotten what fried hominy tasted like? How to peel a potato? Wash dishes? Of course she had. Of course she had put such aberrational knowledge behind her in the last seven months, together with whatever memories she might have carried of that strange intermission in the even tenor of her privileged existence.

He had seen her just once, in Williamsburg, during the winter season when, despite the war and differing loyalties, all the prominent families had followed established routine and moved into town from their country estates. She had been entering one of the imposing mansions, a Persian quilted cloak over a ballgown, her hair dressed fashionably high and lightly powdered. He had heard her voice with those well-remembered clear tones expressive of the effortless superiority of the elite. They were tones he knew he shared, but somehow that knowledge had not prevented a surge of irritation as the outcast had drawn back into the shadows. He had wanted to strip the finery from her, to take down that magnificent raven's-wing hair, to see it disheveled under his twisting, twining fingers, to drown those crystal accents under the throaty murmurs, the little cries and whimpers of pleasure as she lay beneath him, above him, beside him. . . .

Dear God! He was haunted by her. Even in the midst of battle when his mind should be on killing, he thought of loving.

"Those damn Patriots!" Sir Edward paced the long drawing room, twiddling his eyeglass, which was suspended from his neck on a thin silver chain. "How the devil do they dare call themselves by such a name! I'll see them all hang, the murdering bastards!"

"Sir Edward!" Eliza protested this virulent language with a faint bleat, which her husband ignored.

Bryony stilled the quiver of her fingers and asked, "What has happened now, Papa?"

"Destroyed hundreds of pounds' worth of gunpowder," spat her father. "At least they didn't manage to make off with it themselves this time. Those damn British commanders have at last decided that they are not playing in a sandpit with a group of babies and are making some attempt to fight back. Got two of them last night." This last was uttered in tones of savage satisfaction, and Bryony felt the sick dread tug at her belly again. Every time she heard of yet another Patriot raid on Loyalist property, another skirmish, heard the tally of dead and wounded, she waited to hear that the bearded leader was one of either group. With the same terror, she waited to hear that one of the captured wounded had revealed under questioning the identity and whereabouts of the mysterious man who planned and orchestrated the increasingly daring succession of raids.

"Two dead?" she asked now, casually, as if the question was of only minor interest.

"Yes, and not from these parts, so we can't identify them." Her father sighed. "If those dithering idiots would finally take Charleston, maybe we could get somewhere."

Sir Henry Clinton and Lord Cornwallis were in the process of mounting a third attack on the seaport, two previous attempts having failed, and there was much grumbling among the Virginia Loyalists these days, who saw their own side frittering away the advantages of manpower and training while the dogged revolutionaries continued to wreak undercover havoc, proliferating like mushrooms, bouncing back seemingly undeterred by reversals.

"If Washington and Lafayette come south of Delaware to back up Benjamin Lincoln at Charleston, the entire South could go over," the Englishman continued, still pacing restlessly. "Those damn Patriots don't wage war like gentlemen. They are forever stinging us with these damned hit-and-run raids."

"They do appear to be remarkably adept at purloining your weapons," murmured Bryony.

"Not *my* weapons, daughter!" Sir Edward snapped. "*Our* weapons. Or do you not consider yourself to be a part of this struggle?"

"Of course, Papa." Bryony made haste to

recover her slip. "But work with weapons is the province of men."

It was a deft answer and one that seemed to satisfy her father, who merely humphed and demanded to know if she intended to ride with him that morning. Bryony, deciding that the conversation had strayed dangerously close to her own forbidden boundaries, agreed with alacrity. Exercise in the soft March air would do much to restore her equilibrium. However, her father's conversation took an even more unwelcome turn once they had attained one of the bridle paths running through the woods bordering the plantation.

"You attain your majority at the end of May," he began without preamble.

Her heart sank as she recognized what was to come. She and Francis were no nearer a solution and, indeed, she had allowed the issue of their marriage to lapse from memory and thought when it seemed that her father was also prepared to let it fall into abeyance. Now she murmured an assent and waited.

"It would please me if you were to celebrate your marriage on the same day," Sir Edward said. "Do you see any difficulty with such a plan?"

"I must talk with Francis," Bryony offered hesitantly. "Perhaps he has some idea of his own."

Her father stared at her incredulously. "My dear child, I trust you will show your husband obedience and respect in all things, but the day of your wedding is yours alone to decide. Your bridegroom will accept whatever date you choose, so long as he is physically empowered to do so."

"I would still like to discuss it with him," she replied. "I myself would prefer to wait until Christmas."

Sir Edward sighed. "I have been uncommonly patient with you, Bryony. Indeed, foolishly indulgent many would say, including your mother, but you cannot procrastinate further. You have had seven months to recover from the extraordinary business of last summer, and now you *must* resume the pattern of your life. Unless . . ." He looked at her sharply. "Unless you have some unassailable reason for not wishing this marriage."

It was worth a try, Bryony thought. "I do not wish for any marriage, Papa. Francis is aware of this and would release me willingly —"

"That is enough!" her companion thundered, and the raking bay he rode skittered in alarm. "I have never heard such foolish-ness and have always thought better of you. You sound like a half-witted female with no more sense than a loon. Next, you'll be telling me you wish to become a bride of Christ."

"No, I won't," she said. "I am not that simpleminded." She laughed deliberately and shrugged, as if the subject were easily dismissed. "Will you not allow me until Christmas?"

There was a short silence while Sir Edward wrestled with the familiar conflict between ensuring his daughter's happiness and insisting that she do something she did not care to. "I will put it to Sir Francis," he said eventually. "But if he does not like it, then I will not argue with him further. You will marry on your twenty-first birthday."

Bryony made no further demur. It would be up to Francis to persuade his father to agree to another postponement. Not that procrastination was any long-term solution, but she knew Francis believed that the longer the final confrontation was delayed, the better were his chances that she would agree to the convenient marriage. And perhaps, in the end, she would, Bryony thought with a dull stab of painful recognition. As memory faded, and her knowledge of the glories that could exist between man and woman were blunted by time, maybe she would settle for a deadening mediocrity. At least marriage to Francis would hold no surprises — pleasant or otherwise.

"What the devil's going on!" Sir Edward's exclamation broke the silence that had continued between them for the rest of their ride. They had just turned into the gravel drive leading to the house, only to find it much resembling a major highway. A barouche was bowling up the drive ahead of them, two horsemen could clearly be seen approaching the house, and a riding chair stood at the steps leading to the front door.

"Mama is not receiving, is she?" Bryony asked, frowning. "She would have expected me to be at home." The sound of hooves behind made her turn her head. Francis Cullum cantered up to them.

"Have you heard the news, sir?" He was clearly in a state of great excitement.

"It would appear not," Sir Edward said dryly. "Although the world and his wife seem to have descended upon me in the two hours of my absence."

"Oh, what is it, Francis?" demanded Bryony as images of Benedict hanging from the gibbet in the town square blocked her vision.

"Major Patrick Ferguson of the British army," Francis told them. "He has come to take command of the Tory forces. He is a career soldier and will know just how to deal with this Patriot rabble."

"About time," rumbled Sir Edward, nudging his bay into a canter. "Now, perhaps, we can organize ourselves and cease this hole-in-the-corner skirmishing."

It was come at last, Bryony thought, following at a more sedate pace. The time Ben had talked about, when men must bear arms and fight for their loyalties, was upon them. That would mean that Ben, too, would come out of hiding, would wage war in the open, probably far from here, wherever the battle took him, and she would never know what became of him.

The house was in an uproar, servants and slaves running hither and thither with trays of refreshment, little knots of women fanning themselves and whispering their fear and excitement as they looked at their menfolk engaged in serious, ponderous conversations.

Now that the governor had left, the Paget house was always the focal point for any local excitement, since Sir Edward was the man everyone turned to when community decisions needed to be made. It was inevitable, therefore, that when news of the imminent arrival of Major Ferguson had reached the community, the world had flocked to the Pagets'.

Bryony ran upstairs to change out of her riding habit, then, correctly attired in a morning dress of blue-patterned chintz over a quilted silk petticoat, she descended to the drawing room to play the role of daughter of the house, assisting her mother in the reception of this unexpected influx of guests, which, it could now be anticipated, would continue throughout the day. Dinner must be provided for however many chose to join the family; later there would be tea and then supper; and even beds would be provided for those who decided to avoid the perils of returning home in the dark in various stages of sobriety. Such was Southern hospitality, and it would not occur to anyone, be they guest or host, to question the obligation of the mistress of the household to provide, or the rights of the guest to receive without stint.

Bryony, as usual, was more interested in the men's talk than in the wailing and flutterings of the women toying in titillated fear with images of the horrors of war, of how they would manage when their men went off to do battle.

"We need men, arms, and money," Sir Edward was declaring in all-encompassing fashion. "Ferguson cannot be expected to do the job without the right tools. We must set up a committee to organize a series of rallies. There are those amongst us who still sit on the fence; they must be brought down upon the right side."

Bryony could find it in her heart to feel a little sorry for those unfortunates who were about to be brought down by her father upon the "right" side. And the Lord have mercy upon those who chose to jump the other way, or were even slightly dilatory in offering up themselves, their worldly goods, and whatever else might be demanded of them by the zealots. Smiling, curtsying politely, she apologized for interrupting such serious talk and invited the gentlemen to repair to the dining room if they so desired.

"Have my study prepared after dinner for a meeting, Bryony," her father said. "You will ensure that we are to be disturbed by no one except yourself, who will answer the bell should I require anything."

"Yes, Papa," Bryony said with another

demure curtsy. Whatever was to be discussed was clearly not for the ears of servants. If she played her cards correctly, Bryony thought, she could contrive to remain in the room throughout the deliberations and planning. Her father would not object, so long as she was not obtrusive, and no one would be impolite enough to question their host's decision in such a matter. She needed to know what was planned for one reason, and one reason only: so she could imagine what Ben would be doing, where he would be directing his activities; as long as she could do that, she still felt as if they were in some way connected. Just as at night she would re-create the feel of the straw mattress beneath her, see the dim light of the cabin, the shadowy shapes of the primitive furniture, and she would feel that the distance between them was not infinite, even though she knew that it was.

"Ferguson? What do we know of him?" Benedict Clare twirled the delicate stem of his wineglass between his fingers as he posed the question to Paul Tyler.

The planter frowned, helping himself to a dish of pickled crab on the low table between them. "A British career soldier of some repute. He was with Howe in Philadelphia and, if rumor has it right, was not backward in his criticisms of that general's tactics."

Ben's mouth quirked in a sardonic smile. "One could hardly have praised Howe, could one?"

Tyler laughed. "No, indeed not. An extended rest period in the city of Philadelphia and dalliance with the wife of a fellow officer were hardly aggressive tactics. But I think we must avoid underestimating Patrick Ferguson. He commands the respect of the most zealous Tories, and is not averse to the use of plunder, burning, and murder if they will serve his purpose better than a gentlemanly pitched battle."

Ben nodded, pursing his lips. Then he rose and went to the window, where the curtains were drawn tight against the night and any prying eyes. He drew the drapes aside, gazing out into the midnight blackness. The plan took shape, the lines solidifying, and the tremor of excitement flared, sending a surge of energy to the very tips of his fingers. It was outrageous, reckless, but to carry the battle into the enemy camp, to perpetrate a monumental deception on that arrogant breed . . . oh, it was irresistible! And he would see her again.

She would not betray him any more than he would betray her. No harm would come to Bryony Paget through his plotting, except in as far as his attack was aimed at her castle.

Did Benedict Clare have the right to satisfy his own passionate need to see her again at the expense of whatever peace and resignation she had gained in the seven months of her return? It was not a question he wished to ponder. He had a job to do and that came first. Whether he wished to see Bryony Paget again or not, the battle whose victory would bring him sweet revenge was paramount. The fact that it might also satisfy a secondary, personal need was basically extraneous. Quibbling conscience thus dismissed, Benedict turned back to his host, who had been watching him in interested silence.

"What are you brewing, Benedict?"

"Oh, a most powerful potion, my friend; one of wormwood and gall, fire and brimstone." Ben chuckled and rubbed his hands. "I shall require a little help, however."

Tyler refilled their glasses. "I am at your service. Whatever I am able to do, I will."

"I need to turn some articles into hard currency," Ben said directly. "For obvious reasons, I do not wish to be identified with the transactions, so I need a broker. Will you act for me in this?"

Tyler nodded. "Am I to be a party to your plans?"

"But of course." Ben sat down on a velvet-covered chair and picked up his glass. "Listen well, Paul. . . ."

Half an hour later, Paul Tyler, momentarily rendered speechless, stared at his companion. "You are run mad, Ben! It will put your head in a noose."

"Only if I am discovered prematurely," Ben replied calmly. "There is no reason why that should happen." Tyler knew nothing of Bryony Paget's sojourn with the Patriots, and Ben deemed it unnecessary to tell him of it at this late stage. It would only add to his concerns. "You must admit it is a sound plan. Dangerous, I grant you, but one does not achieve much by risking little."

"And it is time you came out of the woods," Tyler mused, almost to himself. "I had not imagined quite such a dramatic re-entry, but perhaps, knowing you as I do, my friend, I should not be surprised."

"And you will help?"

"Without question."

The two shook hands and Ben slipped

out of the house by the side door, making his way, just another shadow in the gloom, down to the river, where his canoe was tied. Paul Tyler was the only person living who knew that Benedict Clare, scion of one of Ireland's oldest families, was also a runaway bondsman from Georgia. And it was to Paul Tyler that Benedict owed his life and his continued freedom. The filthy, emaciated, fever-ridden man, his back a mess of infected sores, whom Paul Tyler had stumbled upon on the riverbank nearly three years earlier, bore but superficial resemblance to the man now paddling his canoe through the network of creeks that would take him back to his own run without venturing onto the main river highway.

He owed Paul Tyler his sanity, too, Ben reflected. The planter had taken him in, healed his body, asked no questions until the day Benedict, his strength regained but the soul's agony still as raw and infected with bitter hatred as ever, had attempted to take leave of his benefactor. Ben had shouldered the chest that contained all his worldly goods and his history, to which he had clung throughout his flight with all the desperation of a limpet. He had had no plans beyond the conflicting needs to keep running and to exact vengeance. Tyler, with quiet resolution, had called in his debt, demanding to know Benedict's full history.

Benedict stopped paddling for a moment, allowing the canoe to drift over the dark water. When he had placed his trust in Paul Tyler, he had taken the first step on the road back to spiritual health. It was Tyler who had suggested he pull together the disparate threads of his life by serving the Patriot cause, doing what he had done in Ireland, fighting the same enemy for the same cause, though in different form. He would turn his hatred to good use, channel the destructive energies to serve the political ideals he had held for so long, and in the destruction of the colonial world, he would achieve his own revenge for the wrongs visited upon him.

Ben dipped his paddle in the water again, a soft, slicing motion that sent the small craft skimming ahead. From the moment he had taken up residence in the clearing in the wood, had begun the task of recruiting the undercover soldiers for the Patriot cause, had carried off the first successful raid, he had found himself again whole and strong in mind and body — the only lapse that dreadful moment with

Bryony when past and present had merged, triggered by the black mood brought on by the knowledge of her albeit innocent ties with the two strands of his hatred.

God, how he missed her! How he ached for her with an unremitting need. He was longing for the impossible, but how could he pass up the opportunity to see how she was, how she was managing, discover whether she had solved her problem with her betrothed? He would allow nothing to endanger her position, but one final meeting was surely not too much to ask for — the chance to tidy up the threads so rudely torn apart, to close the episode with grace. It was surely something she needed, also, even after all these months.

"How many guests do you expect this weekend, Mama?" Bryony walked into the small parlor at the rear of the house, where Eliza conducted her household business. "Mary is getting in a great fuss about sheets. She says that she will have to use darned ones for some reason."

"Oh, that is absolute nonsense." Eliza rose hastily, smoothing down her lawn apron. "There are a dozen pairs of fine cotton sheets but newly made in the linen press. She knows that perfectly well. Sometimes I think she does it deliberately to add to my burdens!" She bustled out in search of the housekeeper, leaving Bryony chuckling to herself at this familiar domestic pattern.

"Where is your mother, child?" Sir Edward spoke from the open doorway. "I wish to ensure that she understands the music must be interrupted at the ball tomorrow night in order for Major Ferguson to make his speech."

"I am sure she understands, Papa," Bryony said reassuringly. "At the moment she has sheets much on her mind."

"Sheets!" Sir Edward looked nonplussed. "What have they to do with anything?"

"It is customary to put them upon the beds before people sleep in them," she explained with an innocent smile.

"Impertinent miss!" But his eyes twinkled. "I trust your mother is intending to accommodate Major Ferguson and his party in the guest house?"

"I believe so," Bryony said. "Also those in Lord Dawson's party. The lesser folk must fight for bed space within the house."

"There is no shortage," rumbled Paget. "The youngsters may bundle in usual fashion."

"I hope you do not expect me to do so," Bryony stated. "My own bed to myself seems little enough to ask for in the face of all the other disturbances."

"I expect you to make sacrifices for your country as everyone else is doing," came the sharp response.

"By all means." Bryony smiled, but her eyes held a glint of determination, which her father recognized well. "I will cheerfully sacrifice my bed and sleep in the hayloft, so long as I may do so without company."

"Bryony! You must not talk to your father in that fashion!" expostulated a shocked Eliza, pausing in the doorway as her daughter's clear tones reached her on her way through the hall.

"She always has done so," said Paget. "I do not think you will stop her now, my dear wife."

"I think it is for you to stop her," said Eliza, greatly daring.

Her husband simply laughed. "Since I do not appear to have felt the need to do so before, madam, I cannot see why I should now. However" — he shook a warning finger at the smiling Bryony — "there'll be no sleeping in haylofts, miss."

"La, husband, she would not dream of doing such a thing!"

Paget regarded his wife with a degree of resigned compassion. "You do not know your daughter as well as you should, wife. If you did, we might perhaps have avoided the incident of last summer." With that, he stalked from the room.

"Oh, Mama, I am sorry." Bryony hugged her mother as the tears stood out in Eliza's eyes. "He does not really mean to be unkind. It was not your fault. Papa knows that."

"It *was* my fault," Eliza said bitterly. "I should never have permitted you to leave the house at that hour."

"But you did not permit me," Bryony told her logically. "How could you have? You didn't know of it."

"No, but if I had been a proper mother to you, you would never have dreamed of going out on your own in the middle of the night. I know of no other well-bred young lady who would have done such a thing."

"No, they would have been in fear and dread of a whipping." Bryony smiled. "And Papa would never permit such a thing, and I do not think you would have been capable of it, either. So don't pretend that it's all your fault that I am such an undisciplined creature and such a disappointment to you."

"Oh, dearest, you are not a disappointment." Eliza smiled mistily. Bryony could always manage to return matters to correct perspective. "I wish only . . ."

"That I would get on with becoming a respectable matron and provide you with a quiverful of grandchildren," Bryony finished for her soberly.

"Why will you not?" Her mother made no attempt to deny the statement. She looked closely at her daughter, who stood very still, a certain dark shadow in the deep blue eyes. "It has something to do with what happened to you when you disappeared, does it not?"

Bryony tucked a stray wisp of hair into the ribbon that banded her forehead and wished that she could confide in her mother, could drop the burden for just one minute, could describe the glories of that loving idyll, the ache of loss, and the whole glutinous mess with Francis. But, of course, she could divulge none of it. Eliza would not survive such shocks, and it would be unforgivably selfish of Bryony to unburden herself at the expense of her mother's peace.

"I think that perhaps such a strange experience took its toll," she said now, carefully. "I find it hard to contemplate a major upheaval again. It feels so safe here at home." So safe, so wrong, and so boring! Bryony despised herself for the twisted truth even as she saw with relief that it had served its purpose.

Her mother's face cleared and she patted Bryony's shoulder. "I understand, dearest. But Francis is no stranger, and he will look after you, I am sure of it."

"Yes." Bryony nodded, suddenly brisk. "Of course he will. I would like to wait until Christmas, that is all. Sir Francis has agreed, I understand. Should we not put talk of weddings behind us for the moment and concentrate on this gala entertainment that the Pagets are about to host? The first guests will be arriving in an hour or so."

"Great heavens, is that the time!" Eliza threw up her hands in horror. "Will you wear the cherry-striped taffeta with the embroidered petticoat? It is so becoming."

"But if I wear that tonight, how shall I follow it for tomorrow night and Sunday?" Bryony teased. "Should one not save the best for last? Was that not the point of the parable of the wine at Canaan?"

"Oh, be off with you! I do not have time to bandy words, child. You are worse than your father."

"Not worse, surely! Simply an apt

pupil!" Bryony kissed her mother and left, satisfied that matters between them were returned to their usual footing.

Mary was too busy to offer her usual assistance with Bryony's toilet, although she popped in and out of the bedroom to give crisp orders to the young maid who was deputizing for her. Bryony, who would have preferred to be left to dress alone, swallowed her irritation, knowing that the girl would assume she had been at fault if her mistress sent her away.

It promised to be a tedious weekend, one with a dual purpose — to offer three days of lavish hospitality to the prominent county families, and to give the leading Tories the opportunity to wring support for the king's cause from any hangers-back. There was to be a rousing speech from Major Ferguson at the ball tomorrow night, the ball that would be the high point of the occasion. There would be conferences and informal discussions as play alternated with the serious business of the war effort, and Bryony would be expected to play as hard as any of the other young unmarried girls — except that she was nearly two years older than the oldest of them. Her peers for the most part sported swollen bellies and a clutch of nurslings. At least she was respectably betrothed, so she escaped the pitying glances accorded the old maids who remained on the marriage mart beyond their nineteenth year.

The first carriages arrived as the little maid was fastening the delicate silver filigree fillet that held the rich black mass of hair away from Bryony's face while allowing it to fall unconfined in soft ringlets to her shoulders, which rose, bare and creamy, from the scalloped neckline of the cherry-and-white-striped taffeta gown. Her hooped petticoat was embroidered with a fantastic design of wildflowers, twisting and twining their delicate shapes and colors in glorious profusion. A chased silver pendant to match the fillet in her hair nestled in the cleft of her bosom. Similar bracelets encircled her wrists.

"Lordy, Miss Bryony, but you look so beautiful!" the young maid gasped, surveying her handiwork. "It's a wonder Mr. Cullum hasn't carried you off long ago. . . . Oh, I beg pardon!" Her hand shot to her mouth and she gazed in wide-eyed distress.

Bryony laughed easily. "That is all right, Bridget. I am complimented, and you should be, too. It's all your good work, after all." She moved to the door of her bedchamber, bracing herself for a long afternoon and evening.

At the head of the gracious, curving staircase leading down to the central hall, she paused, listening to her parents' voices raised in welcome. She heard Lord Dawson's unmistakable drawl as she moved lightly down the stairs, one hand running over the polished banister, the other holding up her skirt. She reached the bend in the staircase and peered down at the group in the hall. A voice as soft as spring raindrops was responding to her mother's greeting. Her feet in their pink-and-white-striped satin pumps froze in mid-step. Her breath froze in her lungs.

Benedict Clare turned from her mother, turned slowly to look up at the stairs. Black eyes, sharp as a hawk's, locked with hers in glittering warning.

# Chapter 10

Sir Edward's eyes followed Benedict's. "Ah, there you are, child." He held out a hand toward her, smiling in invitation and very obvious pride. "Gentlemen, most of you are already acquainted with my daughter, I believe."

The blood that seemed to have stopped in her veins began to flow again. Her lips curved in an answering smile. Benedict released her from the captivity of his gaze, and she came down the stairs with becoming grace. "Lord Dawson." She curtsied with impeccable depth, swimming upward as his lordship raised her hand to his lips.

"Miss Paget. You grow more beautiful, it seems, with each passing hour." The elderly roué seemed to swallow her with a distinctly lascivious smile. "Young Cullum is a lucky dog, I swear it."

"You are too kind, my lord," Bryony murmured. The blood was pounding in her ears as she wondered how she would respond to her imminent introduction to the clean-shaven, copper-haired, black-eyed gentleman dressed in sapphire velvet and Mechlin lace, an enormous diamond pin nestling in the ruffles at his throat. He wore his own hair, unpowdered, but that was the only infringement of sartorial rules and it was a minor one.

Then she was curtsying to a Mr. Benedict Clare — B.C., she thought with wild, poignant memory — and her hand was in his. She dared not raise her eyes, instead gazed fixedly at his fingers, brown but long and elegant, the nails squared and neatly manicured, a heavy gold signet ring, intricately worked, encircling the little finger of his right hand. The pressure of those fingers increased, imperceptible to the eye but most definitely felt, a message of warning, not of conspiratorial passion. Somehow she managed to respond to the introduction with a murmured word of welcome, a flickering smile, before her hand was returned to her and she switched her attention to the rest of the party.

The conversation seemed to drift over her head as she stood, smiling inanely, nodding like a marionette on a slack string. Mr. Clare was but newly arrived in the Colonies from Ireland, Lord Dawson was explaining. Sir Edward knew of the Clares, of course. Did not the Paget estates march with the Clares in their Irish homeland?

That explained that lilt, the softness of spring raindrops in his voice, Bryony thought. She was not sufficiently acquainted with the Irish accent to have recognized it without prompting, and Ben's was far from pronounced. But now it seemed obvious.

Why would an Irish aristocrat bear the marks of the whip upon his back? What in God's name was an active Patriot doing in this Loyalist stronghold? How long could she stand here, close enough to touch him, to be touched by him, yet keep from melting into the embrace whose memory had haunted her lonely nights and tormented a body aching with loss?

More carriages rolled up to the front of the house. Major Ferguson and his retinue mounted the steps. The Dawson party moved aside politely to allow their hosts to greet the new arrivals. Bryony, still feeling as if she had entered a strange dream, part nightmare, part heavenly trance, retreated into the safety of the role she could play by heart — that of daughter of the house, affianced to Francis Cullum — every step quite clear, every word and gesture simply part of the ritual, and there was infinite safety in ritual.

Benedict Clare watched her. Even when he could not see her, when social demands obliged him to have his back to her, he felt as if eyes in his back were upon her. He heard her voice, clear and true, speaking the expected words, never missing a beat, and he acknowledged with quiet satisfaction that she was as strong as he had always believed her to be. There had been but one moment when he had feared she would give way beneath the shock, but her recovery had been faultless.

God, was she beautiful! Somehow all his resentment at the ease with which she took her place in this elite, privileged world had vanished as he took his own place in it. He had found, to his rueful chagrin, that he had had no difficulties in resuming a status and position that had been his until five years ago. He had thought that his detestation of all those who lived in this ivory tower would have prevented his easy reabsorption into their world — but old habits died hard, it would seem.

"Bryony, child, your father wishes you to partner Mr. Clare at dinner." Eliza spoke softly at her daughter's elbow, and Bryony spun round, swallowing the little startled gasp at this interruption of her self-induced hypnosis. "Francis will understand that you have other duties this weekend," her mother continued, blithely unaware of the effect her words were having on the still, pale figure. "Mr. Clare is a most honored guest and must be shown extra courtesies."

Extra courtesies, Bryony mused as a sudden imp of mischief came surprisingly to her rescue. She could imagine furnishing some extra courtesies to this honored guest that Eliza would not dream of, even in her wildest nightmares. "I shall be delighted, Mama," she responded promptly. "I shall be more than happy to make Mr. Clare my particular charge."

Eliza smiled happily at this evidence of daughterly docility. "Then I will leave you to ensure that he lacks for nothing."

Bryony inclined her head in acceptance, but that same mischievous smile played over her lips. She moved across the drawing room to where Benedict Clare stood with Lord Dawson.

"Mr. Clare, I have been charged by my father with ensuring your comfort this weekend." A small curtsy accompanied the smile and the soft words. "I do trust that you will be quite candid in expressing your slightest wish. It is a prospect that affords me much pleasure."

Minx! Benedict thought with a sudden surge of relieved merriment. Not only had she recovered from the shock, but she was prepared to play games — games at which two could play. He bowed. "It cannot afford you as much pleasure as it will afford me, Miss Paget. I am deeply honored."

"Lucky dog!" rumbled Lord Dawson in customary fashion. "The undivided attention of the most beautiful girl in Virginia, indeed!"

"Do not put me to the blush, your lordship," Bryony demurred. "Mr. Clare, do you care to take a turn upon the terrace? The view of the river is quite magnificent."

"By all means." He proffered a sapphire velvet arm. Bryony placed her hand upon the sleeve, smiled graciously to the assembled company, and moved toward the doors opening onto the terrace.

Benedict's head lowered for an instant. "Say and do nothing out of the ordinary until I deem it safe. You understand?" he whispered against her ear, straightening up again almost in the same movement.

She nodded just perceptibly. "How long have you been in the Colonies, Mr. Clare?"

"Some three months, Miss Paget. But I have been in the North until recently."

"Do you come to take part in the king's struggle with the revolutionaries?" Her gaze met his in direct challenge.

The black eyes became opaque in the way that she knew of old. Without answering, he walked away from her to the edge of the terrace, and Bryony followed, knowing that she had erred, not so much with the question as with the obvious challenge that went with it. His warning had encompassed looks and movements out of the ordinary as well as words. "Spring is a beautiful season in Virginia, sir," she said. "You've timed your visit well. It's somewhat colder in the North, I understand."

"A little," he agreed gravely. "I should be loath to feel another chill in the air in these parts."

In other words, don't do it again, Bryony understood wryly. "That is most unlikely, Mr. Clare. We are unused to cold snaps after the middle of March."

He smiled. "I'm relieved to hear it."

"Bryony, I have been looking all over for you to pay my respects." Francis Cullum spoke with gentle raillery, and she turned, smiling, to greet him.

"Francis, have you met Mr. Benedict Clare? He is a guest of Lord Dawson's, newly arrived in Virginia from the North."

She turned back to Benedict. "May I introduce Mr. Francis Cullum, sir."

The two men bowed and murmured pleasantries. Then Benedict said, "I understand from my host that you have the great good fortune to be betrothed to Miss Paget, Mr. Cullum. May I congratulate you?" A smile flickered over the well-shaped mouth. "And, of course, Miss Paget."

"You are too kind, sir." She could not look at him as she wondered if possibly he had forgotten the agonizing problem that had led to her presence in the hayloft that memorable night, or whether he was merely responding as politeness demanded.

Francis felt the tension immediately and was puzzled by it. Bryony was as taut as a plucked string, and there was an air of containment about the Irishman that bespoke a type of strength, both physical and spiritual — the kind of strength that developed through long years of adversity, through confronting oneself and coming to an acceptance of what one found. It was a process that Francis Cullum understood, being deep in the midst of his own personal struggle.

"Let's stroll down to the fishpond,"

Bryony suggested, anxious to break the awkward silence and her own train of thought. "Do you accompany us, Francis?"

"If you will have me," he returned with a slight smile, which conveyed both puzzlement and speculation, and Bryony felt herself shy like a nervous colt. She covered the involuntary movement by stepping hastily off the terrace onto the broad path running between the lawns. The high wooden heel of one satin pump caught in the gravel, and she tripped, seeing the path come up to meet her even as Benedict caught her, his arm an iron band around her waist, the contours of his body pressed against her own. The quiver that ran through her sparked against his skin. One hand was beneath her breast, his thumb splayed against the rising curve. Bryony's breath seemed suspended in the agony of expectancy and memory as she felt his own breath, coming suddenly fast, whispering across her forehead.

Then he was putting her from him as she blushingly apologized for her clumsiness in a voice that did not sound like her own. Her legs were shaking so violently that for a moment she doubted whether they would support her.

She smoothed down her skirt with rapid

little fluttering movements and pushed back her hair in the way Benedict remembered so clearly as denoting uncertainty or embarrassment. It wrenched at his heartstrings, and the urge to take her again in his arms, to rediscover the satin softness of her, the richnesses of her body, threatened to overwhelm him. For a second it showed in his eyes, then the control that had kept him alive in the last five years reasserted itself. "Steady, now," he said quietly as if she was indeed a nervous colt. Then he turned to Francis, who was standing very still to one side of the path. "It amazes me how ladies manage not to break their ankles regularly with those heels, don't you agree, Cullum?"

"Uh, yes . . . yes," Francis muttered. "Bri, are you feeling all right?"

"Yes, of course. It was just clumsiness," she insisted reassuringly, pulling herself together. "I am very grateful to Mr. Clare for his swift reaction. I was about to take a most undignified tumble." She managed a tiny laugh. "Shall we continue on our way, gentlemen?"

"I have just remembered that I must pay my respects to Mrs. Hall," Francis said suddenly. "I'm charged with a message for her from my mother. Would you excuse me if I left you to continue your stroll without me?"

"Of course." Bryony bit her lip, her brows drawn together in a deep frown as he turned and disappeared among the throng on the terrace. Francis was intuitive enough to know that something peculiar was afoot.

"Stop frowning in that manner," Ben instructed in a sudden urgent whisper. "You will have everyone looking at us in a minute." He took her hand and tucked it firmly under his arm. "Smile and talk nonsense if you cannot think of anything sensible to say."

Bryony smiled obediently and said through her lips, "I must talk to you." Except that I don't really mean "talk," she amended silently. Touch you, kiss you, become one with you again . . .

"All in good time, lass," Ben replied, his voice neutral, his smile calm. "*I* will decide when that is, and you must wait patiently until then." He pointed in the direction of a large, square bowling green sunk a little below the level of the garden. "Is that a game you play, Miss Paget?"

"Not really," she replied. "My father is very fond of it. Why must I wait for you to decide?"

"I share Sir Edward's fondness," he said. "Because I am more aware of the dangers than you are and a great deal more experienced. Say no more!"

It was almost as if they were back in the clearing and he was asserting the mastery of one who knew his own business a great deal better than she did. It was quite true, of course, but Bryony could not help the tight bud of anger forming as she thought of the monumental disadvantage at which he had so callously placed her. *He* had been prepared to see *her*, but had not thought twice of the dreadful shock she would experience at the sudden, stupefying sight of him in her father's house. It was a miracle that she had not betrayed him, betrayed them both, in that first paralyzing moment, and now he was giving her instructions as calmly as if she were a willing but inept accomplice in whatever dangerous game this was that he played.

The gardens were littered with strolling couples and small groups enjoying the warm spring air, butterfly bright in their gay dress whose richness of color and material drew no distinction between the sexes. Benedict Clare was regarded with the frank curiosity of a community that was required to rely upon itself for all forms of entertainment. A newcomer, particularly one so personable and well connected, was a considerable addition to their usual amusements. The presence of their host's daughter at his side was considered quite right and proper, and Miss Paget, although only Ben could guess at what cost, played her part, word perfect. At one point, Benedict turned to look up at the gracious two-storied mansion, its many windows winking in the sunlight. There was a space in the eddying crowd around them, and he said softly, "Which is your chamber?"

"On the second floor, the third casement from the right," she replied with equal softness.

"Do you have a bedfellow?"

"Not at the moment." Her heart beat fast against her taffeta bodice as the possibilities of the exchange blossomed in her mind. But surely Ben would not take such a blatant risk? Not when he had forbidden her to behave in any way that could be construed as even slightly out of the ordinary. But then Bryony was coming to the conclusion that there was one rule for Benedict Clare and one for others on the knife edge that he trod with such insouciance.

The afternoon and evening dragged interminably, and Bryony's head ached with the need to stifle the questions that surged and tumbled. Why was he here? Who was he really? What danger was he in? The backwoodsman seemed to have disappeared entirely, a figment of her imagination. In his place was this suave, elegant aristocrat. The clean lines of his jaw and the set of his mouth were clearly revealed now that the curly, burnished beard was gone. She did not know which she preferred. Her eyes were continually riveted upon his hands as she remembered the feel of them on her body, the wonderful deftness as they tackled whatever task came up, the strength of them. The same hands that now held the heavy silver cutlery and twirled the delicate cut-glass stem of his wineglass, had gutted fish and skinned rabbits, had killed at least one man to her knowledge, and in her heart of hearts she knew that there had been others.

His voice, soft and carrying, was constantly heard during the long hours of dinner. Whenever he spoke, Bryony noticed, he commanded instant attention without once raising his voice. His political allegiances were assumed quite naturally to be those of his hosts — an assumption that, breathless at his mendacious audacity, she heard him confirm with every authoritative statement, blandly smiling, although the hawk's eyes were flat and opaque.

Bryony shivered, realizing that she was seeing at work the Benedict whom she had known only infrequently — the man who had tied her to the bed an eon ago; the man who treated dead bodies and contemplated the dealing of death with a matter-of-fact, case-hardened indifference; the man who bore the marks of the whip upon his back and kept his own counsel; the man who carried a world of horror in the recesses of his mind, a world that could produce a terrifying transfiguration of the laughing, loving, gentle Benedict.

The moment came when trays of nuts and raisins, bowls of olives, and baskets of fruit appeared on the table, together with the decanters of port and madeira, bottles of sherry and sauternes. Bryony felt a great stillness enter her soul as she waited, her eyes on Benedict's hands, her body sensitive to every ripple of the powerful one beside her. Decanters were passed and glasses filled. Sir Edward Paget rose from his great carved chair at the head of the long mahogany table, where candlelight gleamed. A sea of smiling faces, roseate with his bounty, turned expectantly toward him.

"My lords, ladies, and gentlemen, I give you the king." He raised his glass.

"The king," came the fervent response as chairs were pushed back and the company rose to drink the Loyalist toast. Benedict Clare rose with them, his glass went to his lips, and only Bryony saw the white knuckles on his free hand, clenched against his side. *What was he doing here?*

Laughing, mightily pleased with themselves, the company resumed their seats. The drinking of toasts was a matter both serious and amusing. The truly serious one having been attended to, they were now ready for amusement. Sir Edward glanced down the table and with a smile called upon Bryony.

"Daughter, a toast, if you please."

Bryony nibbled her bottom lip for a minute, well aware that she was required to be both apposite and gracious if she was not to disappoint either her father or the company. She raised her glass. "When passions rise, may reason be the judge." Her father's eyebrows lifted with his glass, and she could read his mind without difficulty. While he could not fault her toast, he had expected something in a rather lighter vein. Bryony was not in general given to the pronouncement of precepts.

"A sentiment we must all carry in our hearts, Miss Paget," declared Major Ferguson. "In such stirring times, passions may well run high to the detriment of good sense."

"How very true," murmured Benedict Clare, his eyes shaded with sardonic humor as they met those of his neighbor. "Passion makes a poor master, Miss Paget."

"Indeed, sir, I believe it does," replied Bryony with barely a flicker. "A most untrustworthy one, at least." Then further exchanges became impossible as the round of toasts continued, and at its end the ladies left the table.

Bryony did not talk to Benedict again that evening. When the gentlemen were called to the drawing room for coffee and tea, he paid court to Eliza and offered gentle attentions to the matrons, rapidly earning himself the title of the most delightful addition to the county. Eschewing the pleasures of the billiard table and the card room, he remained in the drawing room, attentively listening to the various musical performances. On one occasion, to Bryony's speechless amazement, he accompanied on the flute Miss Violet Drysdale's indifferent playing of the pianoforte.

"What an accomplished gentleman is Mr. Clare." Francis, soft-footed as usual, had come up beside her as she stood at the back of the room, listening and observing. "You look a little startled, Bri, at his accomplishments. It's not very polite, you know, to appear quite so dumbfounded when someone comports themselves so well."

Bryony flushed with an annoyance directed as much at herself as at Francis. "You must confess, Francis, that Mr. Clare does not strike one as a gentleman so at home in the drawing room," she countered, opting for the near truth as being the safest with her uncomfortably perspicacious betrothed.

Francis smiled. "More of a warrior, I agree. There is a quality about him . . . a certain power, or do I mean 'menace'?" He glanced at Bryony out of the corner of his eye. "He disturbs you in some way, doesn't he, Bri?"

She tried for a light, dismissive laugh, but it sounded as hollow and unconvincing to her as it clearly did to her companion. "I find him interesting. But then, so does everyone else." She shrugged carelessly. "You know how the county thrives on new blood, Francis."

"I wonder if he intends to join Ferguson's army," Francis said thoughtfully. "I cannot imagine why else he would be a guest of Dawson's, can you?"

"No," Bryony prevaricated. "I cannot imagine why he should be a guest of Dawson's." That last was the absolute truth at least.

It was midnight before the evening ended. Lord Dawson and his party, together with Major Ferguson and his group, were escorted to the guest quarters in the separate house set some two hundred yards distant from the main house and furnished with the utmost luxury and elegance. Bryony finally reached the peace and solitude of her own chamber, having endured an hour on tenterhooks lest her mother suddenly decide that her daughter must sacrifice her privacy to the comfort of some young lady. However, either Sir Edward had stepped in or Eliza had decided that Bryony had done as much as should be expected of her for one day. At any event, all the guests were dispersed throughout the mansion, and none made an appearance in Bryony's bedchamber.

Mary fussed over her for an unconscionably long time, it seemed to Bryony, whose muttered complaints at having her hair brushed the requisite one hundred times were completely ignored. At last she was tucked up in the poster bed among lavender-scented sheets and embroidered pillow-cases. Mary blew out the lamp as she left the room, and Bryony lay for a minute in the darkness. Then she hopped out of bed and turned the key in the door before relighting the lamp and opening the casement, letting in the cool night air with its river tang. Propping her elbows on the windowsill, she gazed out over the dark garden, where massive trees stood sentinel and not a shadow stirred.

She sat there for a long time, waiting as her eyes grew heavy in spite of mingled anxiety and excitement. The air grew chill, and she shivered beneath the thin covering of her lawn shift. It was not as if he had said he would come. All he had done was ask which was her chamber, and for some reason she had assumed that he would take the appalling risk of coming to her in the night, a reckless Lothario who would spring nimbly up the creeper that clung tenaciously to the brickwork, to drop into her waiting arms, as desperate as she to assuage the ache, to fill the void. . . . She was being ridiculous. Passion had obscured reason and common sense.

Bryony laughed in self-mockery, remembering her toast at dinner — one that had been intended as reproof to Benedict Clare lest he allow political passion to rule his head. Curiously, she had not then been thinking of this other passion that was threatening to deprive her of a night's sleep. There was no reason, after all, to assume that Mr. Clare was a slave to it, even if she seemed to be.

Resolutely, Bryony went back to bed, for a second hesitating as she bent to blow out the lamp. Then, with a little shrug, she left it burning, flickering in the breeze from the open window, and snuggled down beneath the covers. Her eyes closed. . . .

The dark-clad figure flung a leg over the broad sill and dropped soundlessly to the carpeted floor. He crossed to the bed and stood looking down at its sleeping occupant, a tiny smile playing over his fine mouth. He reached a hand to brush a tumbled lock from the wide, alabaster brow, and the thick dark lashes swept up, revealing a sleepy, startled pair of blue eyes.

"O, ye of little faith," Benedict chided with gentle mockery, placing a knee on the high mattress beside her. "My pride has suffered a sore blow, Miss Paget. I had expected to find you barely managing to curb your impatience, not lost in the land of dreams."

She smiled, wondering why she had ever doubted that he would come. "I left the lamp burning and the window open."

"So you did." He leaned over her, bracing his arms on either side of her body, and looked at her, the hunger of the long deprived glowing in his eyes as they explored her countenance. She reached up a hand to touch the burnished copper hair where the lamplight set a series of flickering fires, then her fingers stroked down the smooth planes of his face to trace his jaw. "Will you miss your hirsute lover?" he asked, turning his head so that his lips pressed into her palm.

"The backwoodsman of no name," she murmured, reveling in this moment when they were barely touching, except with their eyes. The postponement brought a deep, wondrous tension coiling in the pit of her stomach, prickles of pleasure darting across her skin, her nipples straining against the softness of her shift. "Who are *you*, Benedict Clare?"

"For tonight, simply a man who once knew you in the ways of love and lust and wishes to renew the acquaintance." He drew back, bringing his other knee onto the bed astride her, then slowly pulled down the covers. Bryony quivered, the shape of herself in familiar space dissolving under the radiant heat of fast-spreading passion. The crowns of her breasts stood out, dark and urgent beneath the near-transparent lawn, begging for the touch that was a long time acoming. Slowly, so very slowly, he moved a fingertip to hover over the rounded silhouette, sketching in the air the contour and its keen peak. Her breath sped with longing; her blood ran hot in her veins under the swift rise of ardor; her body shifted slightly in an urgent movement beneath him.

Ben smiled, running a finger over her lips. "I am like a parched man at an oasis, sweeting. I must take my pleasure with care after such long denial, lest I founder and fail us both."

"You will not founder." She sucked his finger into her mouth, her tongue stroking, hot and sensuous. "No more than I shall." Her eyes locked with his as she continued the wicked caress of his finger, a caress that danced with symbolic promise, until he could bear the suspense no longer and placed his hand along the fragile line of her jaw, lifting her chin as he took her mouth with his own, gently at first. But when she strained against him, her hands linking behind his neck, his tongue thrust within the warm, moist cavern, seeking her own to join in a dance of spiraling desire.

Her mouth burned, bruised beneath the demanding pressure, but she felt no discomfort, only the towering need to lose herself in his body. Utterly absorbed in the magic of this desperate compulsion to be one with the other, they lost all sense of the room around them, of the bed beneath them, seeking only the limitless rapture of the present.

Benedict, without loosing her mouth, slid down beside her, smoothing his hands over her back, spanning her hips as he pressed her to his lower body so that the hard throb of his need pulsed against her thigh. Bryony whispered her pleasure at the feel of him as she unclasped her hands from his neck and brought them down to the waistband of his britches, sliding her flat palm within. She felt him draw up her shift, uncovering her knees, her thighs, then upward to raid the curves and hollows of her body, the deep secret places, with an inexorable trespass that sent shivers of fire and ice rippling across her bared skin. In her urgency, her fingers fumbled with the buttons at his waist, and he drew back from her long enough to rid himself of his shirt and britches before taking the hem of her shift and peeling it off over her head.

Bryony gave a deep sigh of joyous satisfaction as her nakedness at last met his and their tender explorations could continue unobstructed. They were revisiting each other's body, rediscovering the pleasure centers, and finding that the long months of denial had sharpened rather than blunted the keen edge of joy. Her fingernails trailed over the hardness of his flanks as his tongue swept the curve of her breast before circling the hard, tight bud at its crown. She groaned, bringing her hand round to the front of his body, twisting in the crisp triangle of hair that snaked down from his belly to the point where sprang the silken shaft of his manhood. She took him between her hands even as her body arched upward to the caress of his roving tongue, and she heard his soft exhalation of pleasure, felt it as a zephyr undulating across her belly.

He swung astride her then, reversing his position so that they could both play freely, and for an eternity it seemed they cavorted in sensate bliss, running the gamut from savage delight to the most sensitive inventiveness. If Ben had been truly afraid of failing her, it had been a baseless fear. Buried in her sweetness, he took her from peak to peak, nibbling and probing at her essence until tears of joy stood out in her eyes and she felt as if she had no more to give, and could receive no more. But she was wrong.

When at last his own need could no longer be delayed, Ben turned and moved over her, slipping his hands beneath her buttocks, lifting her to meet him as he surged within the moist, welcoming entrance to her body. His face melted with pleasure as her velvety softness tightened around him, and she curled her legs around his hips, pulling him deeper.

"Oh, lass," he whispered softly. "I have missed you beyond words." He brushed her eyelids with his lips, took her mouth again so that she could taste herself upon his lips and tongue, then, intent and powerful, he swept her with him beyond the barriers of sensation. With each ever-deepening thrust, the golden world of ecstasy swelled. Bryony could feel his body thrumming with the vibrations of his pleasure as he plumbed the very depths of her soul, and she yielded herself unsparingly, meeting his need with her own, in the rise and fall of fusion. And at the last, when the bright bubble of rapture burst around them and they soared in elemental joy for the moments that seemed infinite, he stifled her cry with his mouth, holding her tightly as the convulsions shuddered her slender frame, racking her from head to toe.

"What are we going to do?" Bryony whispered as a totally unexpected, utterly inappropriate wave of sadness washed through her. She clung to him, her deep blue eyes tear-bright.

Ben wiped the salty smudges from her cheeks with his thumb and kissed her again. "It's all right, lass," he said gently. "Don't fight the sadness. It happens sometimes when one has touched the peak of bliss. Coming down is not easy." He disengaged slowly, delicately, rolling onto the bed, drawing her into the circle of his arms.

"But what *are* we going to do?" she repeated. "I don't understand anything anymore. Why did you come?"

He brushed back her hair, asking prosaically, "Do you have a handkerchief somewhere, sweeting? You are making me very soggy."

She thrust her hand under the embroidered pillow, pulled out a scrap of lace-edged chiffon, and blew her nose vigorously before offering him a watery smile. "I beg your pardon. I can't imagine what came over me."

"I can." Tugging the pillows behind him, Benedict propped himself up and drew Bryony with him. "Ask your questions, lass, and those I can answer, I will."

"There are so many." A final, decisive sniff and Bryony pushed back her hair in that characteristic gesture. "I don't know where to begin."

He chuckled. "Then I will tell the story and you may interrupt me as you wish."

Bryony listened without interruption as he told her that he intended to become a party to Major Ferguson's plans for his Loyalist army; that when he had learned enough, he would take his information to the American forces, at which point he would himself join with them in open battle; that this was his last undercover operation.

"You are here, in my father's house, as spy, then?" she queried slowly when he had finished.

Benedict looked at her sharply. "Have you discovered that you are, after all, a committed Loyalist, my little patrician?" he asked, unable to prevent the shaft of derision in his voice, which had nothing really to do with her.

"No," Bryony replied, ignoring his tone, recognizing its irrelevance, even though she did not yet understand it completely. "I do not appear to care much one way or the other. But I *am* loyal to my father."

"And you will betray me?"

"You know I will not. But it is uncomfortable to be torn between two such allegiances." It was a quiet, dignified statement, which told him more clearly than a passionate outburst would have done how deeply she could be hurt by his mission. He had seen her with her father, and the closeness that existed between them would have been obvious to a blind man. Much as he abhorred everything that the Pagets stood for, he could not deny the power of a familial love that had nothing to do with the world's struggles.

"I, also, am torn," he said softly. "What I feel for Bryony Paget cannot come in the way of my work. Miss Paget is her father's daughter, is she not?"

"Then why did you come to me tonight?"

"Because it would take a stronger man than I to resist the promise of such bliss. My reasons for entering your father's house were twofold. I wished also to see for myself how you were faring, perhaps to tie up the loose ends that lay between us."

"And now that you have done so?"

A rueful smile touched his lips. "We have tied no loose ends, lass, merely unraveled another strand."

"And I ask again, what are we to do?"

"Enjoy what we have for as long as we have it," he replied, knowing it was no satisfactory answer for either of them, but it was all he had to offer. "You remain betrothed to Mr. Cullum, I understand." It was but a slight shift of subject.

"Only until one of us comes up with a means of breaking the engagement without telling the truth," she replied. "I have managed to achieve an extension of the betrothal until Christmas, but it's merely postponing the inevitable." Her fingers plucked restlessly at the sheet, and he laid his own over them, stilling the nervous gesture with strong warmth.

"The gentleman is most fond of you, Bryony. It's very clear in his manner."

"As I am of him. But it does not alter the facts." She sighed. "Francis is also very perceptive, and he has always been quick to see things that concern me, sometimes even before I realize them myself."

Benedict nodded. "And what do you think he has seen now, lass?"

She shrugged. "Nothing specific — except for that moment when I tripped on the path and you caught me."

"It was innocent enough."

At that she smiled. "It was not, and you know it. I am not an accomplished conspirator, Mr. Clare, unlike yourself."

Benedict let this pass for the moment. "Will Mr. Cullum keep his own counsel?"

"He'll not betray me, if that's what you mean," she responded swiftly. "But he may press for explanations, and I am a poor liar."

"A poor liar and an inexperienced conspirator!" Benedict laughed in a deliberate attempt to lighten the mood. "My sweet, there are devious pleasures to be gained from being successful at both. I will teach you."

"Well, I hope you have more success than you had trying to turn me into a fisherman." Bryony picked up the cue deftly, turning to snuggle into his hold, flicking his nipples with the tip of her tongue, tasting the salty sweetness of his skin. If she could see it as a game — a game with high stakes, certainly — then she would not have to think about loyalties and betrayal, and they could deal in the present without the intrusion of a divided future.

There was peace and happiness, exquisite joy to be garnered as fruits of the present, so why should she not eat, drink, and be merry? For who knew what tomorrow would bring.

# Chapter 11

"Bryony, I would like you to attend us in the library after breakfast." Sir Edward addressed his daughter the following morning as she came into the hall, drawing off her riding gloves. "Mr. Clare, I am certain you will wish to join our deliberations." He looked questioningly at his daughter's companion.

Benedict handed his whip and gloves to the servant waiting to take them. "By all means, Sir Edward." He brushed a smudge of dust from his sleeve. "Miss Paget has been showing me around your estate. I must congratulate you on your excellent husbandry."

Sir Edward smiled with pleasure. "It is a poor landowner who neglects his land, Clare."

"True enough," replied Benedict. "But that is a lesson not taken to heart by most Irish landlords. I might venture to ask when you last paid a visit to your estates there?" The light smile took all possibility of offense from the question, offered rather an understanding complicity. Only Bryony, seeing the sudden flatness of the black eyes, was able to detect the hint of contemptuous anger, which puzzled her mightily. What had the Pagets' Irish estates to do with Benedict Clare?

Paget laughed, laying a friendly hand over his guest's shoulders, easing him toward the dining room. "I leave such matters to my steward, Clare, as you so rightly guessed. Nothing else to do with them. The tenants are an idle lot, more interested in the shebeen than in farming, and they breed like rabbits." He stood aside to allow his guest and daughter to precede him to the breakfast table.

A shiver ran through Benedict's powerful frame, communicating itself like ground lightning to the slender figure beside him. Gazing up at him, Bryony gave a little gasp as she met his opaque stare, which seemed to bore straight through her. He was looking at her as he had done during that last miserable week in the woods after he had discovered her identity. It was a look of intense dislike and, as then, she could not imagine what she had done to warrant it. And she could not ask him, not here in the crowded dining room, where the weekend guests were consuming in leisurely fashion the substantial breakfast that must fortify them until late afternoon.

With a muttered word of excuse, she left his side and made for the door. "Bryony, where are you going? You have not breakfasted," Eliza called from the sideboard, where she was supervising the refilling of the silver chafing dishes.

"I must change my dress, Mama," Bryony responded with an effort. "I have been riding." She fled before her mother could make further comment. Riding dress was quite acceptable at the breakfast table, although most definitely not at dinner, and there was no reason at all why she should feel the need to change.

"It's most unlike Bryony to worry about coming to table in her dirt," Francis Cullum observed casually, pulling out a chair beside his own for Benedict. "She's much more likely to be sent off by Lady Paget to wash her hands and comb her hair — even these days." He laughed, and Benedict, putting away the dull anger that had filled him at Sir Edward's words, returned the laugh, finding himself accepting the little intimate confidence as if he had a right to it. And then he remembered what Bryony had said about Francis Cullum's perspicacity.

"You have known Miss Paget for some time, I gather?" He helped himself to a slice of cold venison.

"Since we were children," Francis replied.

"Then you must know her very well." Ben sipped his coffee, his tone pleasant and neutral.

"I usually understand her, Mr. Clare," responded his neighbor. "You had a pleasant ride, I trust?"

"Most pleasant, I thank you."

"Mmm." Francis sounded distinctly skeptical. "I wonder what could have happened to upset her, then."

Benedict's lips tightened. "Not having the advantage of childhood intimacy, Mr. Cullum, I regret to say that I had not realized that anything had upset Miss Paget."

Francis merely smiled and pushed back his chair. "You will excuse me, Mr. Clare." He sketched a bow and sauntered out of the dining room, leaving a very thoughtful Benedict to complete his breakfast. That conversation should not have taken place between two strangers about a woman who was betrothed to one and supposedly only slightly acquainted with the other. But what on earth could the man suspect? Not the truth, not in a millennium!

Bryony, having changed and composed herself, returned to the dining room. Benedict was still there, protracting his meal in the hope that she would reappear. She wore a gown of sprigged muslin with a flowered gauze apron that emphasized her tiny waist. The rich dark hair was piled on top of her head, held with a knot of ribbon, and her face was pale and set, hurt bewilderment lurking in her eyes.

Benedict cursed himself uphill and down dale as she responded to his greeting with the merest flicker of a smile that barely touched her lips. It had only been a moment, that flash of intense fury, but she had got in the way of it again, and now he must try to make amends while withholding the true explanation.

"Might I beg a favor, Miss Paget?" he asked with a conciliatory smile.

"I am yours to command, sir," she responded dully. "It is my duty to ensure your comfort, and I am ever dutiful."

Ben whistled soundlessly. He caught Sir Edward glaring at Bryony, who flushed beneath the reproving scowl. It was her tone rather than the words that offered discourtesy, and Ben decided to ignore it, hoping thus to deflect her father's ire. "You have been the soul of kindness and attention,

Miss Paget," he said swiftly. "As I mentioned on our ride, I am most interested in examining the workings of an estate of this size and was wondering if you would accompany me on a tour of the various service buildings. It's a matter of some fascination to me to compare the way business is conducted here with the way it is at home."

"With pleasure, sir," she replied promptly, and to Ben's relief, her father seemed to relax and return his attention to the sirloin. Bryony rose from the table. "Do you care to go now?"

"Pray finish your breakfast first," Benedict protested politely.

"I am finished, Mr. Clare, and am at your disposal."

"You will join us in the library on your return," Sir Edward said. "We would welcome your suggestions, Mr. Clare."

Benedict bowed his assent, Bryony curtsied politely to her parents, and they moved through the open doors onto the rear terrace.

"My thanks," Bryony said a little stiffly, once they had rounded the corner of the house and were walking across the paved courtyard toward the kitchen, in the sight only of domestic workers. "You rescued me from certain reproach."

Ben smiled ruefully. "It seemed hardly just that you should suffer censure for something that I caused."

"I do not understand what I did to provoke you. I have never understood it. But sometimes you look at me as if you hate me. How can you, after . . . after last night?" she whispered passionately.

"I do not hate *you*, lass."

"But you have a powerful hatred for something . . . someone." It was a statement, not a question, and Benedict offered no response.

They reached the low building that housed the kitchen and storerooms. "Do you truly wish to go in?" asked Bryony. "We shall only be in the way. There is much to be done with thirty guests in the house."

"No, I don't wish to go in." Ben turned aside. "I thought that the pretext would afford us a degree of privacy. We'll just walk around, and you'll pretend to point out the various buildings and explain their functions."

"Are you really Benedict Clare?" Bryony asked as they reached the smokehouse.

"Yes, I am a Clare."

"But why is such a one hiding in a Virginian wood, living like a backwoodsman, plundering and raiding those who fight for their king?" Bryony realized that for some reason, maybe in penitence, Benedict was more accessible to her questioning than he had ever been, and she fought to keep her head clear, to ask only the truly important questions so that she would not fritter away the opportunity.

"There are plenty who do the same across the land, Bryony," he responded. "Notwithstanding social position. There are those who wish for independence from a rule that takes but endows nothing. Is that so very wrong?"

"There are those who would call it treason."

"And what do you call it, Miss Paget?" This time there was no mockery in his voice.

"Does it matter what I think?" she asked softly. "Am I not tarred with the enemy brush, regardless?"

"On occasion," he answered frankly. "But I will learn to curb an irrational and unjust response if you will be patient with me."

They followed their noses toward the bakehouse. "There is more to this hatred than simply that of Patriot for Loyalist,"

Bryony said, taking the bull by the horns. "Feelings run high, I understand that, but such a powerful detestation that I have felt and that you sometimes can't separate from everyday matters, that has deeper roots, roots in the soul." She waited and it seemed that she would wait forever. Scurrying figures cast them curious glances as they strolled across the cobbles, exchanging the rich aromas of the bakehouse for the soapy steam of the washhouse.

"I'll not argue with you, lass," Ben said eventually. "Leave it at that."

"It has to do with your back, does it not?" Unwisely, she persisted, willing to risk rebuff rather than lose through cowardice an opportunity to pry loose one more crumb of confidence.

"Did you hear what I said?" The tone was curt, the words clipped, and Bryony bowed to the inevitable. At least his refusal to deny her statement told her that she was correct. She must once again accept his right to privacy.

"I heard you," she said. "We should perhaps return to the house, since your presence is expected at the planning session, and I am sure you would not wish to miss the opportunity to do what you came here for."

"Is the sarcasm entirely necessary?" Ben inquired. "I freely admit that spying is not the occupation of a gentleman, but I ceased to lay claims to such a status quite some years ago. Except when it suits me," he added with a grin, hoping thus to divert the gloom that threatened to descend upon the sunny morning. The attempt, however, was not entirely successful.

"I wish it were not you, or, at least, I wish that you were not spying on my father," Bryony declared. "I must sit in the library and listen to the deliberations, knowing that there is a spy in the room and that I am colluding in the deception."

Ben sighed. "I understand that it's very uncomfortable for you, sweeting. But it can't be helped, I am afraid. Why are you involved in the meeting?"

Bryony shrugged. "My father would have it so. It pleases him to include me in matters that might traditionally be the sole province of men. He has done so since I was a little girl and proved that I would not prattle and could listen to good purpose." She smiled softly. "I am, after all, the nearest to a son and heir that he has."

"You love him very much."

"Yes," she affirmed simply.

They had reached the terrace, and all

conversation that was not suitable for general consumption had to be dropped. A select group of men were gathered in the library, Lord Dawson and Major Ferguson among the most prominent. They greeted the arrival of Benedict Clare without surprise, and Bryony realized that he must have been laying the ground for this apparent active participation in the Tory cause with great care. Knowing her own role, she took a seat in the corner of the room and settled down to listen, to form her own opinions — opinions that would later be sought by her father — and to keep an attentive eye on the needs of the men in the room. The ostensible reason for her presence was to ensure that their glasses were kept filled, the platters of salted fish, nuts, and olives passed around, to summon a servant if necessary without causing any disruption to the vital business being conducted by her elders and betters.

At least she was allowed to remain in the room, Bryony reflected with an inner chuckle, unlike with the Indians, who expected their womenfolk to wait upon them from a distance. She thought with a little stab of nostalgia of that first time in the clearing when Ben had banished her to the cabin because her presence would offend his guests. She had had that curious sense of déjà vu then, as her irritation had blossomed at the assumptions of male superiority that lay behind the Indian rules. It was an irritation that she had often felt at similar assumptions at home, an irritation that her mother bewailed as being so unwomanly and indecorous. Her father simply laughed and encouraged his daughter to consider herself any man's equal — so long as she kept such considerations to herself, of course. Bryony's lips curved in a sardonic smile as she settled back to listen to the flowery rhetoric that seemed to be preceding any serious deliberations of the formation and deployment of Major Ferguson's Tory forces.

Ben kept his own expression well schooled, his eyes showing none of the contempt he felt at the elaborate compliments, the extravagant statements of commitment, the passionate trumpetings of loyalty and condemnation. Sir Edward, he noticed, was much more restrained than the others, and once or twice glanced at his daughter with an almost complicit, slightly weary smile, which Bryony instantly returned. Somehow, Benedict had given no thought to Bryony's position when he infiltrated her family. The idea that she would have such an unusually close emotional bond with her father had never occurred to him. It was not an experience with which he was familiar. His own father had been with all his children a distant parent at best, a hostile one more often than not.

Several times in the past, Ben had wondered who had taught Miss Bryony to be so independent and resilient, who had fostered that analytic turn of mind, who had ordered such a broad education. The answer was now clear, and he recognized with a pang of remorse that by forcing her to choose sides, he had put her upon the rack of divided loyalties. Unfortunately, there wasn't a damn thing he could do about it, and he was obliged to admit, looking at her creamy beauty, the memory of her body imprinted on his own, that even had he realized, he would not have done otherwise. The temptation to see her again once the opportunity arose had been insurmountable. Now, wrapped in the selfish coils of passion and love, he didn't know what to do, except let matters take their course.

"May I refill your glass, Mr. Clare?" Bryony spoke softly against his ear, leaning over him, too close for either comfort or necessity, to reach his wineglass.

"My thanks," he murmured, inhaling the fresh rose-water fragrance of her hair and skin, resisting with the greatest difficulty the urge to run his hand over the provocative curve of her hips. Lying behind this risky teasing was that imp of mischief he had noticed before. It was the same imp that had led her to hide in the tree that last morning in the clearing, that had produced the wickedly suggestive remarks she had made in front of Dawson the previous day. This playfulness seemed to spring free when matters were at their most tense — an unconscious means of deflecting the tension, perhaps, or of rendering it manageable for herself.

Whatever the reasons for it, Benedict decided that he would enter into the spirit. It had to be a better reaction than castigating her for childish pranks. He dropped his hand below the edge of the table and pinched her thigh through the muslin gown, all the while smiling with apparent interest at Lord Dawson across the table. Bryony squeaked and her hand shook, spilling claret on the rich cherrywood table.

Pink-cheeked and muttering apologies, she mopped up the spill before hastily removing herself from the danger zone. Benedict continued to smile placidly as if he had noticed nothing, but both Francis and Sir Edward were eyeing Bryony with a degree of puzzlement as she resumed her seat in the corner of the room.

Ben gave her ample opportunity throughout the rest of the day to recognize that when it came to mischief he was every bit as adept as she was. He never lost the opportunity for a surreptitious pat, stroke, or pinch, and Bryony was on tenterhooks lest another involuntary gasp or yelp should escape her. "Tormentor!" she hissed when for a moment no one was within earshot. "I am probably black and blue!"

"Nonsense," he scoffed. "You are not made of porcelain."

"Next time I shall scream," she threatened, and Ben chuckled.

"I promise I'll kiss it all better as soon as I get the chance."

Sharp desire arrowed through her at the thought, and she felt color flooding her cheeks and her legs turning to jelly. "Excuse me, but I think my mother wants me." With as much dignity as she could muster, Bryony gathered up her skirts and fled his side, utterly outsmarted and knowing it.

Ben grinned and picked up a copy of *The Lady's Magazine* from a small table. "Not the most absorbing literature, Mr. Clare," came Francis Cullum's quiet voice. "Although one assumes that the ladies find it so."

"I daresay." Ben flicked idly through the pages. "I suppose recipes and needlework patterns and maxims on conduct have their appeal."

"It's generally considered that more difficult subjects might not only intoxicate weak brains but turn them," Francis remarked solemnly. Ben glanced sharply at him, and they both laughed at their shared thought.

"She has not been educated to believe in her mental inferiority," Francis continued with the unquestioning assumption that his companion would know to whom he was referring. "But I expect you've already realized that."

"It would be a little hard not to," Ben agreed neutrally. "It takes but little conversation to recognize an informed mind. And Miss Paget does not appear to subscribe to the precept that a woman's learning should be kept a profound secret."

"Indeed not." Francis chuckled. "Such want of delicacy, I take it, does not disgust you, Mr. Clare?"

"Not in the least." Benedict wondered how long this fencing would continue before Mr. Cullum decided to come out into the open with whatever was exercising him. "You are to be congratulated on the prospect of acquiring a wife who will partner you in the fullest sense."

Cullum seemed to shiver into absolute stillness, and his eyes narrowed into thin green icicles. Then he smiled and bowed in graceful acknowledgment. "I am aware of my good fortune, sir, every waking moment."

"Gentlemen, dinner will be served at half past four." Eliza bustled over to them. "The ladies are retiring to change their dress."

"Then, perhaps we should do the same," replied Ben with a small bow and a warm smile, which caused Lady Paget a little flutter in the general region of her heart. He was the most charming man!

Bryony remained unconvinced of Benedict Clare's charm as she dressed for dinner and the ball that was to follow. There was nothing charming about a man who deliberately put one in jeopardy because he felt like taking a game to its outer limits. And there was nothing charming about a man who could bring one to weak-

kneed, liquid arousal by a wickedly un-
scrupulous suggestion in the midst of a
crowded room. She had had absolutely no
defenses all afternoon, and there were no
guarantees that she would be spared this
evening unless she could keep out of his
way. Perversely, such a prospect seemed to
afford little pleasure, and she sought out
Eliza as soon as she had reached the
drawing room.

"Am I to escort Mr. Clare at dinner
again, Mama?"

Eliza regarded her daughter appraisingly
and then straightened the lace fichu at the
neck of Bryony's turquoise satin gown. "I
think that perhaps tonight you should,
dear, although I am sure it is most irksome
for you, and Francis is being very patient.
But tonight is the most important event of
the occasion, and I would not like to appear lacking in courtesy and respect to our
honored guests. It would look a little
strange if you were to abandon Mr. Clare
now, when you have been attentive so far."

"Quite so, Mama." Bryony curtsied duti-
fully. "But perhaps Mr. Clare has some
preference . . . Sally Fordyce, maybe."
Bryony was not at all sure what devil was
prompting this line of conversation, unless
it was the idea that she should appear a

little reluctant to perform her duties as regards Benedict Clare. It would never do to give the impression that she took an inordinate amount of pleasure in his company.

Eliza gave the suggestion frowning consideration. "Well, of course, Sally is most personable, and unattached into the bargain. But I do not think Mr. Clare is hanging out for a wife at the moment."

"He doesn't have to be to enjoy being seated beside an attractive and unattached young lady," Bryony pointed out, quite unable to resist teasing her mother. "Why don't you ask him, Mama?"

"That would be most indelicate, Bryony. One does not expect a gentleman to make such a choice."

"But they do it all the time," her obstinate daughter persisted. "The choices *are* made, and since women do not make them, one can only assume that such decisions, like so many others, are the province of men."

"This sounds a most fascinating topic, Miss Paget. Might I inquire as to the nature of these decisions that fall to the lot of my sex?" Ben's soft, amused lilt came from behind her, and for the barest instant she felt his hand flatten against her hip. It was so swift she could almost have imagined it, except that her skin beneath the turquoise satin seemed to retain the warm handprint.

"My daughter is inclined to have some fanciful notions, sir," Eliza said, distinctly flustered. "I beg you will take no notice of her. It is merely playful."

"I was only speculating, sir, on whether you had a preference for a dinner companion," Bryony said sweetly, blind to her mother's distress under the lamentably selfish urge to indulge her quick wit in a little wicked fencing with Benedict. "There are many young ladies I am certain would be overwhelmed by the honor of being your choice."

Eliza whimpered a little but was quite unable to halt her outrageous daughter without creating an even more embarrassing scene. Ben smiled reassuringly at her, his gaze warm and containing not a trace of sarcasm. "Your daughter flatters me, ma'am, but I must confess to feeling chagrin at the thought that I am to be denied my customary partner." He directed a mock bow at Bryony.

"Oh, no, Mr. Clare, there is no question of any such thing," Eliza hastened to correct this unfortunate impression.

"I meant no discourtesy, sir," Bryony interjected. "Quite the opposite. It was your pleasure that was my concern and it seemed possible that you might prefer a little variety in your companionship."

"Oh, yes, indeed, just so, just so . . ." stammered Eliza, patting at her towering coiffure with nervous hands. "I beg you will excuse me. Bryony, you will look after Mr. Clare."

"Of course, Mama." Bryony curtsied at her mother's departing back and cast a look brimming with mischief at Benedict. Only to suffer something of a shock. Mr. Clare did not appear to be in the least amused.

"I fail to see what pleasure you can achieve from embarrassing the poor woman in that manner," he said.

Bryony's jaw dropped. "Are you taking me to task?"

"There was no call to make game of your mother in front of me," he said shortly.

Bryony began to feel distinctly uncomfortable, but she retorted, "How very pompous you have become, Mr. Clare. You hold my family and all it stands for in such disdain that I cannot imagine why a little filial teasing should produce this display of righteous indignation."

Ben's eyes narrowed. "Do not confuse

opposition with disdain. I hold neither of your parents in contempt for all that I am bitterly opposed to your father's politics. If you must tease your mother, I suggest you do so in private." With that final piece of advice, he strolled away from a thoroughly discomfited Bryony, who, even through her annoyance, was obliged to admit the justice of the rebuke. She had not been able to resist the byplay with Ben and had thus thoughtlessly embarrassed her mother.

"Why so mournful, Bri?" Francis sipped a glass of punch and regarded her pensively over the rim.

"I am a prey to self-reproach," she returned with a little laugh. "My wretched tongue got the better of me, again, and poor Mama suffered, I fear."

"Not an unusual occurrence," her companion observed. "Was Mr. Clare a witness to this unseemly display?"

Bryony flushed slightly. "Why should you think so?"

The color of his eyes deepened. "Don't play me for a fool, Bri. I don't know what is between you and that gentleman, but if it concerns us, then I should like to be told. I have the right, do I not?"

"What possible reason can you have for imagining that there is anything between

Mr. Clare and myself?" Bryony tried to infuse the question with lighthearted indignation, but she knew she had failed.

Francis, however, merely shrugged. "It's as plain as day for those with eyes to see. I suppose you'll tell me in your own good time."

The gong sounded for dinner, bringing a reprieve, although for how long, Bryony could not guess. She was obliged to return her attention to the still grave Benedict, who offered his arm without a word as they joined the procession into the dining room.

"May I help you to some salmon, Mr. Clare?" she asked with soft hesitancy once they were seated and she found the fish at her elbow.

"Thank you." He passed his plate, and for a while she was fully occupied in serving the salmon to all those near her who desired it.

"If I might have a little of the curlew, sir," she ventured when her own serving duties were in abeyance. Benedict took her plate and expertly dissected one of the little birds on the silver platter before him.

"There may still be some bones," he said solicitously. "Take care as you eat. I should not wish to be responsible for one becoming lodged in your throat."

"You are already responsible, sir, for the taste of contrition," she murmured, "which does not enhance enjoyment." She watched his expression out of the corner of her eye as she toyed with the meat on her plate.

Ben smiled, his eyes warming, and moved one hand beneath the table, where it became lost in the stiff folds of the damask cloth until it found Bryony's knee and her own hand, which had followed a similar path. A firm squeeze signaled that the matter was at an end, and Bryony, for one, felt an immense sense of relief. It was not at all pleasant to be at odds with Benedict, as she had discovered long ago, and most particularly not when she had been in the wrong.

The dining room's long windows stood open to the driveway, and Bryony heard the pounding hooves before the horseman came into view and swung his mount around the gravel sweep to pull up sharply before the steps leading to the front door. Several others whose seats also faced the windows looked curiously across the mahogany table with its handsome burden of silver and china, and the steady flow of conversation faltered. Neither Sir Edward nor Lady Paget made a move as sounds of commotion from the hall filtered unmistakably into the room. After a minute, the butler made stately, measured progress into the dining room, treading ponderously to where Sir Edward sat at the head of the table.

There was a low-voiced consultation, then Paget, with a smile of excuse to the ladies on either side, rose, paused to say something in Major Ferguson's ear and again in Lord Dawson's. The three men went into the hall.

"Something unprecedented has occurred," Bryony stated matter-of-factly. "I don't remember a time when my father has left his own dinner table with such lack of ceremony."

"Wars tend to cause people to behave in unfamiliar fashion," said Benedict, equally prosaic, but Bryony could feel the tension in the muscle-hard thigh against her own. The buzz of voices around the table increased in volume as excited speculation rose, transcending the rules of civilized social congress. Interest in food waned as interest in the contents of the wineglasses waxed; eager anticipation of some momentous news hovered over the group.

The three men came back to the dining

room, the solemnity graven on their features belied by the springing step, the sparkling eyes, the joyous air of messengers with portentous news.

Bryony felt Ben relax, leaning back in his chair, his fingers now loose on the stem of his glass, twirling it idly, his breathing slow and even. How did she know that the pose was requiring a supreme effort, that he was somehow preparing himself for the worst, ensuring that he would evince no visible effects of whatever this news was?

"My friends." It was her father speaking, his eyes alight. "You will excuse this interruption of our dinner, but I feel sure you would not wish me to waste an instant in imparting to you the news that has just reached us." He paused, smiling down the long table in the expectant hush. "My friends, Sir Henry Clinton and Lord Cornwallis have taken Charleston, and General Lincoln's entire defending force is captured. Finally, victory over those damn traitorous rebels is in our hands!"

The room exploded in laughter and cheering, and Benedict Clare sat smiling quietly in the midst of the joyful throng. He glanced sideways at his host's daughter and, with a mocking lift of one eyebrow, raised his glass in silent toast.

# Chapter 12

"You don't seem in the least concerned." Bryony sat on her bed, hugging her drawn-up knees beneath the demure white nightgown, her hair tumbling over her shoulders and around her face as she looked in intent puzzlement at the insouciant visitor to her bedchamber.

Benedict chuckled. "I have other things on my mind at present, lass. Much pleasanter matters." Leaning over, he twisted a lock of hair around his finger as he brought his mouth to hers. Bryony resisted, pummeling his chest, trying to turn her head away from the capturing mouth. Ben laughed, his warm breath mingling with hers. Taking her face between both his hands, he held her still, her fists imprisoned between their bodies, until he had finished what he had started.

"But I want to know what you are going to do!" Bryony gasped breathlessly, fighting the insidious surge of desire creeping up from somewhere in the region of her toes.

"I will tell you what I shall do if you don't decide to be a little more accommodating," he said, beginning to unbutton his shirt. "I did not climb that creeper at great risk to life, limb, and honor simply to discuss a turn of events over which, at present, I have no control."

"But why are you not upset?"

"Persistent creature!" He swooped down on her, catching her beneath the knees and toppling her backward on the bed. "When will you learn to accept the inevitable?"

Bryony's indignant squawk was reduced to a snuffle as her legs were doubled over her head, and she struggled vainly to pull down her nightgown to achieve some degree of modesty, a condition that Ben seemed determined to deny her. It was at this interesting point that there came a soft but determined knock upon the door. Ben released his hold, and Bryony's legs swung down to the bed. She looked up at him, pink-cheeked and disheveled, her eyes bright with the promise that had been on the verge of fulfillment.

The latch on the door rattled. "Bryony? Are you asleep, child? Why have you locked the door?" It was Eliza — and a most insistent-sounding Eliza, at that.

"It may smack of farce, but sometimes

the old ways are the best ways." Ben dived for the floor, rolling beneath the bed to keep company with the dust balls and the chamber pot.

A bubble of almost hysterical laughter welled in Bryony's chest. She mumbled something that would hopefully reach her mother through the door and stumbled off the bed, kicking Ben's shoes beneath it as she ran to the door.

"I beg your pardon, Mama. I must have been asleep." Bryony rubbed her eyes vigorously with the heels of her hands in an effort to appear red-eyed and drowsy. "What is it?"

"You must have fallen asleep with the lamp burning." Eliza in nightgown and cap bustled into the room. "Your father noticed the light beneath your door when he came up to bed and wished to be sure that you were not unwell."

Bryony sat down gingerly on the edge of the bed, afraid to put her full weight on the mattress lest the bed ropes sag onto the flattened figure beneath. "I'm quite well, Mama. Just very tired. It's been a fatiguing evening, after all." She offered a tentative smile, but Eliza did not respond. She was frowning deeply.

"Why was your door locked, child? You

can have no secrets, surely?"

She had committed a cardinal sin, Bryony knew. Privacy was a rare condition, the desire for it most unusual, and the right to it unheard of. Only mischief could be taking place behind a locked door. Her eyes dropped to her lap, and she played restlessly with her fingers. "Forgive me, Mama. I know it's silly, but . . . but I have had such a fear since . . . since that night last summer." She did not dare look up to see how her confession was affecting Eliza and continued in the same hesitant little voice. "Supposing I had walked in my sleep? It could happen again."

"Oh, my poor child." The bed ropes creaked in protest as Eliza sat stoutly on the bed beside her, wrapping her in her arms. "Why didn't you say something earlier? I will have someone sleep in here with you."

Sweet heaven! thought Bryony as that dreadful bubble of laughter threatened to explode with devastating consequences. If you only knew! "No, please, Mama, that is not necessary. I can't sleep with a bed-fellow, you know that."

Eliza patted her daughter's back and said diffidently, "You will have to become accustomed to it, dearest. There must be no parting of beds in marriage."

Bryony wondered desperately if this was really happening. Beneath the bed lay Benedict Clare, spy in her father's house and seducer of her father's daughter. While upon the bed, her mother seemed settling in for a maternal exposition of the facts of connubial life.

"It will be different then, Mama," she managed in a choked whisper. "I do understand that." A prodigious yawn engulfed the words and she allowed her head to fall heavily upon Eliza's shoulder.

"Well, we will talk a little more about it another time," Eliza stated, rising. "It's time you were in bed, Bryony. We have another full day tomorrow with the picnic, and the men will have so much to prepare for now that the war, thank God, is so nearly finished. One final effort, your papa says, and it will all be over." This last was said in tones of complete confidence.

Bryony, making no response beyond a weary smile, allowed herself to be tucked beneath the covers, but when her mother bent to kiss her, she put her arms around Eliza's neck and hugged her tightly, wishing that the absurd charade did not have to be played, that they could behave in a fashion that more accurately expressed their relationship than this socially dictated mother/daughter inequality that they both knew was not really applicable to their situation. Eliza returned the hug, blew out the lamp, and left the chamber, adjuring Bryony to be sure to sleep soundly.

Total stillness and silence reigned in the moonlit room for long minutes, neither of its occupants daring to make a premature move. Then Bryony hopped out of bed, relit the lamp, and ran to the door, once again turning the key. She stood still, curious as to why Benedict did not reappear, and for one dreadful moment wondered if he had suffocated under the weight of the bedropes and the clouds of dust. "Ben?" She tiptoed back to the bed and then yelped in shock as her ankle was suddenly grabbed.

Ben dragged himself out of hiding, hauling on her ankle as he did so, and lay on his back, laughing up at her. "It seems I have occasion to scold you yet again for a lamentable lack of respect to your mother," he said. "What a disgraceful pack of lies! Sleepwalking, indeed!"

"What would you have had me say?" she demanded, laughing with him, although she felt a little quavery quite suddenly as the fearful tension dissipated.

"Not the truth, I grant you. Come down here." A swift jerk unbalanced her, and she toppled onto him, lying along his length, relaxing against him as his arms encircled her, holding her tightly as if he understood that the last minutes had been no real laughing matter.

He ran his hands through the fragrant mass of her hair, drawing it forward to enclose them both in a dark silken tent as his lips sought hers in a kiss of searing sweetness that for the moment contained no passion, and she drew hungrily at the well of comfort and reassurance, feeling his heart beat steadily against her breast, seeming to calm by example her own tumultuous pulse. When he felt the peace enter her, Ben spread his hands over her back and rolled sideways, turning her to feel the rich carpet beneath her shoulder blades. Propping himself on one elbow, he leaned over her, brushing a stray lock of hair away from her brow, tracing the delicate planes of her face with one long finger.

Bryony lay still, waiting for him to articulate the thought that she could sense forming behind his pensive midnight-dark eyes. When he remained silent, she extended her own hand and ran a fingertip over his lips. "What are you thinking?"

He smiled, nipping her finger. "A thought that I had best keep to myself, lass."

"You have so many secrets," Bryony said in a fierce whisper, surprising herself with the force of an anger that had arisen unbidden and without warning. "I don't understand why I am not to be trusted. What have I done to deserve your mistrust? I cannot help who I am, but I have never —"

"Hush!" He spoke sharply. "It's not a question of trust, as I said to you once before. If I did not trust you implicitly, would I be here at all? Running the risk of a noose around my neck, or worse?"

"You are here because you have a task to perform and this is the best place to perform it," she said dully. "My presence, I assume, is simply a bonus. And you must take some considerable satisfaction out of hoodwinking so dramatically and completely a man you hold in such enmity."

Silence wreathed them; stillness held them. Bryony, unable to meet his steady gaze, turned her head on the rug and wished she had not said those words. What good did it do to wish for more than one could have? It just created this sourness that curdled the sweetness and left a bitter void. She waited for him to get up and leave her, back through the window and into the darkness.

Then Ben spoke very softly. "I was thinking that I loved you."

She turned her head again to look up at him, wonder shining with the tears in her eyes. "I love you, too. Why would you not tell me?"

He sighed. "It is not a fact that can profit either of us, lass, and is best left unacknowledged."

The words of denial rose to her lips, but by some stroke of witchcraft they were stillborn. The answer to Bryony was so simple, so obvious that she could not imagine why Ben did not see it, but some saving grace warned her that now was neither the time nor the place. "Love me," she commanded, drawing his head down to her bosom. "Love me now, Ben."

"So importunate," he murmured, unfastening the tiny pearl buttons of her bodice, parting the sides to bare her breasts. "Will you be had on the floor, sweeting, or shall we repair to the softness of feathers?" His breath whispered across her skin as he pushed the nightgown off her shoulders, his palms cupping their soft roundness. The urgent arching of her body was sufficient answer, and he slipped the garment down to her waist, kneeling astride her as he played with the creamy, lamp-lit swell of her breasts, smiling as the deep languid glow of desire built in her eyes. The raven's-wing hair, spread out in startling contrast to the gold and ivory tones of the rug, shimmered against her skin. A skin like mother-of-pearl in the lamplight, he thought, needing suddenly to see the rest of her, to have her laid out before him in all her glorious wanton nakedness.

Slipping a hand beneath her, he raised her hips, drawing the wadded material of her gown from under her, holding for a minute the warm roundness of her buttocks on the shelf of his palm. He could feel the wire-sprung tautness as her muscles tensed in anticipation of what she knew was to come; the banked fires in her eyes flared as, still holding her up, he bent his head to stroke her stomach with his moist tongue. Her hips arched in involuntary invitation, her thighs falling open to the dewy caress.

"I want you," Ben stated, softly, definitely. "I want all of you, my Bryony." His tongue darted, flicked, probed with deep eroticism until she could no longer hold back the soft moans of submission to the joy he was bringing as she yielded her self.

The lamp burned low during the long hours of play, and Bryony, aware that Ben wanted her passivity tonight, her total acceptance of his loving, gave herself unreservedly to that loving. He turned her, positioned her as the fancy took him, possessed himself of every millimeter of skin, every pulse, every vibrant nerve center until Bryony ceased to belong to herself, to exist in any universe but this one, where the heady scent of her own arousal filled the soft night air, where the hands on her body were not her own, yet were inextricable from herself, where her skin and the rich texture of the carpet were enmeshed.

Ben gazed down at her, ivory and pearl, the blue-black triangle at the apex of her thighs matched by the fanned mass spread, as abandoned as her body, across the carpet. He wondered how he would manage to leave her, to face the life that stretched ahead without her. His clothes had been shed long since, and now, with fierce urgency, he knelt between her widespread thighs, drew her legs onto his shoulders and drove deep into her center.

Bryony gasped as her body stretched to receive his length, felt the throbbing press of him filling her more completely than ever before. He held her hips high as with each thrust she took him into herself, bound him in the silken toils of her body, and watched his face melt in joy, glorying in her turn in the power of the pleasure giver, possessing him in joy as he had possessed her. And then, even while she thought she was in control of her thoughts, draining the last dregs of conscious delight from the observation of her lover's pleasure, the wave of her own satisfaction engulfed her. So intent had she been on Ben that the slow, seeping sweetness had crept insidiously upon her, now to burst in full flower.

As before, Ben stopped her climactic cry with his mouth, gathering her tightly to him even as he withdrew from her body the instant before they fell from the heights, the world settling again on its axis.

"No, don't leave me." As he moved infinitesimally, preparing to roll onto the carpet beside her, she ran her hands over his back, every ridge now familiar to her fingertips, the scars intrinsic to the beloved body.

Weary with the night's exertions, he kissed the corner of her mouth and lay heavily atop her as her slow caresses continued, and the couple drifted in peaceful, fulfilled languor until the flickering lamp finally guttered. They lingered on the moon-washed carpet, readying themselves for the now unavoidable moment of separation.

"Sweeting, I must leave you," Ben groaned, "if I am to touch ground before the break of dawn." Kneeling, he took her hands and hauled her into a sitting position. "Come, into bed with you." He stood up, drawing her upright, toppling her onto the bed.

"Stay with me." The plea encompassed much more than the immediacy of the moment, but if Benedict realized, he gave no sign.

"Do not be foolish," he chided with a teasing smile, tucking the covers around her. "I cannot spend the entire day in hiding beneath the bed! And I shall not succeed in escaping unseen down the creepers once the household is up and about."

For the moment, she would accept his inevitable loss. Bryony met and matched the lingering touch of his lips in farewell, then watched as he dressed, then swung himself with an agile twist through the casement. The right moment would come to bring him to an understanding of the realities and the possibilities, and she would begin preparing the groundwork in the morning.

Bryony wasted no time. Her plan required Francis's cooperation, and as soon as breakfast was over, she followed him out of the dining room, catching him in the hall. "Francis, I would speak with you for a minute."

He turned, looking at her with surprise at the whispered urgency of her tone. "Speak away."

"Not here," Bryony said, glancing around the thronged hall. "In private."

"Now?"

"It may as well be now as later." She turned toward the door leading to the rear terrace.

"I give you good day, Miss Paget." Benedict strolled across the terrace from the garden. "It is a beautiful morning, is it not?"

"Delightful, sir," she agreed, somewhat distracted as memories of the night flooded back to mingle awkwardly with the need to avoid his company for the next few minutes as naturally as possible. "Mr. Cullum and I are going to walk down to the landing stage before Reverend Elstree conducts Sunday prayers." The absence of invitation to join them was glaringly obvious, and with Francis standing beside her, smiling blandly, Benedict could hardly invite himself.

He bowed. "Then I'll delay you no longer." Frowning, he watched them move off. Miss Paget had not seemed at all pleased to see him. What was she up to? Had she taken some notion into her head to allay her betrothed's suspicions? If so, Ben strongly suspected that she would tie more knots than she would unravel. Francis Cullum did not strike him as easily deceived, and a less than truthful explanation would only give rise to further questions. A horrible thought struck him. She could not be intending to make a clean breast to Francis Cullum, could she? The thought was father to action, and he set off toward the thicket of oaks that had just swallowed the two figures.

In the center of the thicket, Bryony stopped and Francis solemnly halted beside her. "This is very cloak and dagger, Bri."

She shrugged. "You will understand why soon enough."

"I am all ears." He lounged against a broad trunk and regarded her with a smile

346

in his green eyes. "You look as if you are about to unburden yourself of a weighty pronouncement."

"Do not mock, Francis. Normally, I don't mind, but this is very serious." She flicked at the lace-edged apron ornamenting the rose cambric of her gown, and the impatient gesture set her hoop swinging. "You said yesterday that I would tell you in my own good time about what lies between Benedict Clare and myself. You also said, rightly, that if it affected our situation, you were entitled to know."

"And I am about to?" The smile had left his eyes, his languid air now masking the tautness of his body as he waited for something that he knew he would not enjoy hearing.

"Yes. You should know that Benedict Clare and I are lovers —"

"What?" Francis interjected before he could stop himself. "Are you run mad, Bri?"

She was very pale but continued resolutely. "I am not run mad. I tell you this so that you will have an unimpeachable reason for breaking off our engagement. It is, as you once said, the only acceptable reason you could have, and I wish you to use it."

"And what of you?" He stared. "You will marry Clare?"

A smile trembled on her lips. "It is what I wish, yes. But there are difficulties. However, I think I can persuade my father that —"

"Your powers of persuasion are not in doubt."

Bryony whirled around in a swirl of rose. Francis pushed himself away from the tree. Benedict stepped into the enclosure, where the sun barely showed through the umbrella of April foliage and the air was as soft as the greenish light.

"Ben . . . I . . . I haven't said anything about —"

"Then do not start now," he interrupted in those quiet, decisive tones that she knew well. "Go back to the house, please. Mr. Cullum and I have some things to discuss."

Bryony stood her ground. She had every right to take Francis into her confidence without betraying Ben, but Benedict at this moment bore the mien of the man who fired barns and killed sentries and tied people to beds. She took a deep breath. "I don't imagine you can have anything to discuss that does not concern me."

The hawk's eyes impaled her, held her motionless, the only sounds the insistent call of a blue jay, the rustle of some small scuttling animal. Even Francis seemed immobilized, standing on the sidelines watching a play whose outcome would bear upon his own life, yet whose action had nothing to do with him.

Ben said in the same soft tones, "You will not, I trust, oblige me to compel you, lass."

Bryony drew breath sharply, memories of the clearing, of his demand for a parole that she could see no justification for giving taking on the lines and contours of reality again. She could not imagine how he would compel her to leave, but she knew that he would do whatever he deemed necessary, and she was not prepared to face a humiliating defeat in front of Francis. Without a word, she turned and walked away, a gauzy shimmer of rose, her hoop swaying gracefully as she slipped through the gray trees, the dark crown of her hair gleaming in the dim green light.

"My God!" murmured Francis in awed tones. "I think she believed you would."

Ben looked at him, uncomprehending. "I beg your pardon." Then his frown cleared and he shrugged, saying dismissively, "She knew I would." Francis smiled slightly and leaned back against the tree, folding his arms. "What did she tell you, Mr. Cullum?"

"Very little, as it happens," replied Francis. "You appeared on the scene somewhat prematurely."

"That I doubt," Ben said dryly. "I should, however, be glad to know what little she did tell you."

"I rather think that Bri intends marrying you, Clare." Francis found that once the first shock had dissipated, not only did he have no difficulty with the idea, it seemed to take on an appropriateness, an inevitability, as if he had known all along. And he could not imagine why, once he himself was removed from the scene to Paget's satisfaction, such an alliance should not receive society's blessing. The Clare lineage was unimpeachable, after all. Ben inclined his head in invitation, and Francis went on. "She explained only that you and she were lovers. I find it hard to believe that such an extraordinary occurrence should have had its genesis in the last two days." His eyebrows lifted. "Does it perhaps go back to last summer? I am well aware that something more occurred then than Bri has admitted."

"Let us leave it at that for the moment, Cullum." Ben drove his hands into his britches pockets. "Do you happen to know why Bryony decided to make this inopportune revelation?"

"As I said: she intends marrying you. Only there is one small impediment." Francis could not help chuckling at the utter absurdity of the situation. "She is already betrothed to me. By informing me of her shockingly immoral conduct, she hoped to provide *me* with the only permissible excuse for breaking off our engagement."

"And do you intend to use that excuse?" The question was asked quite calmly, but Francis was under no illusions as to the importance of his answer. As far as he knew, Benedict Clare assumed that he was in the presence of a betrayed fiancé, one who might well seize the opportunity for revenge.

"Not without a great deal more persuasion that it is in Bri's best interests," he said with due consideration. "Sir Edward adores her, but I can't see him becoming easily reconciled to the idea that his daughter is a fornicator. I suspect Bri's plan is rather more elaborate and will involve the presentation of an alternative future that will satisfy her father — a future in which I assume you are to figure largely." Again his eyebrows lifted interrogatively.

Ben sighed. "Do not misunderstand me,

Cullum. If it were possible, I would have it so. But it is not."

Francis's eyes narrowed. "Why should it not be possible, Clare? You cannot mean to abandon her."

A change came over Benedict Clare. His expression hardened, his eyes becoming flat and cold as ebony. "What lies between Bryony and myself, Cullum, now or in the future, is no concern of yours. You will do well to remember that, despite Bryony's foolish attempt to involve you."

"You forget that I am betrothed to her," Francis snapped. "It seems to me that what lies between you two is very much my business."

Ben shook his head, his lips tightening. "As I understand it, Cullum, your betrothal is in name only. Bryony could break it at any moment she chooses, if she were prepared to expose you to considerable unpleasantness."

Francis paled. "She told you? I cannot believe she would do such a thing."

The tight anger left Benedict, and both face and voice softened. "She told me a long time ago, Cullum, at a time when the possibility that you and I should meet was so remote as to escape consideration. It was a problem much exercising her at the time. I don't think you should consider it a betrayal. She had no such intention."

Francis chewed on a knuckle for a minute, then he shrugged. "So be it. You may despise me as you please, Clare. It could hardly matter less."

"I do not despise you," Ben said gently. "Apart from the fact that I could never despise anyone whom Bryony holds so dear, I am not in a position to judge you in anything and would not presume to do so." He paused, then continued in the same quiet fashion. "I would ask the same courtesy of you. Bryony will come to no harm at my hands."

"And suppose you should get her with child? Not even Bryony's ingenuity would be able to find a way around that."

Ben scratched his head thoughtfully. "I suppose you have a right to ask the question, although it is somewhat personal. You may rest assured that I have become most scrupulous in ensuring that such a thing will not happen." He did not add that, having had one stroke of good fortune in avoiding such a consequence, he had not been prepared to tempt providence a second time.

A dull pink tinged Francis's cheekbones at this undeniably intimate revelation, but no suitable response seemed to come to mind, so he merely nodded.

"Then can we agree to let this matter rest?" inquired Benedict.

"As far as I am concerned," replied his companion, "but I do not think Bri will be so easily put off."

"I think you can leave that to me." Ben held out his hand. "She will not suffer, I swear it."

Francis took the proffered hand but said gravely, "She may not suffer physically, but the wounds of the spirit are sometimes the worst."

"Do you think I don't know that, man?" Ben exploded with shocking suddenness. "In that we will both suffer. But there are times when one must accept the blows fate deals." Turning, he strode off with the long, loping stride that gave physical expression to his surge of agitation.

Francis followed slowly. He could do nothing to resolve Clare's problems, whatever they might be, which were keeping Bryony and her lover from the conventional consummation, but he could take into his own hands those problems that concerned him. If he were out of the way, Bryony would have one less impediment, and for the first time, Francis saw a solution.

# Chapter 13

Ben broke from the thicket and marched across the lawn, back to the house. A welter of emotions roiled in his head: anger with Bryony, and with himself because he should have known from experience that she would not meekly accept a proscription without just cause; anticipatory pain for both of them at the certainty of the grief they were going to feel when the time for parting came; sorrow at the nearness of that parting; and irritation at the knowledge that Francis Cullum now knew that there was more to Benedict Clare than met the eye. Inadvertently, Cullum might pass on this impression to others. Once the seeds of suspicion were sown, there was no knowing what monstrous crop they would produce.

He reached the terrace, his intention to seek out Miss Paget without further ado and express his opinion of her foolhardy action in no uncertain terms. But the voice, the voice from the nightmare past, shivered him into immobility. The bright day dimmed, and cold fingers groped his spine, lifting the scarred skin of his back to the memory of horror.

Roger Martin, his nasal twang rising above Sir Edward's even tenor, stepped out onto the terrace. He was sweating profusely in heavy broadcloth, an elaborately curled and powdered wig contrasting with the raddled cheeks, the pale blue eyes bloodshot as he raised his tankard of brandy and drank deep. "Those damn rebels have sent General Gates to take command of their forces in the South," he boomed. "But he'll do no better than Lincoln, you mark my words."

"It's to be hoped not," Paget said. "I much appreciate your bringing us this news, Martin." He saw Benedict, still standing at the edge of the terrace. "Ah, Mr. Clare, we have another visitor. Mr. Martin has traveled from Georgia to bring word to Major Ferguson from Cornwallis." Smiling, Sir Edward introduced Benedict Clare to the man Ben had sworn to see dead.

Somehow, the icy death lock holding his muscles rigid began to relax, and Benedict stepped forward. His mouth moved and conventional words came forth. His eyes showed nothing. Martin frowned and shook his head as if puzzled by something. "Met before, haven't we?"

"Not to my knowledge," Ben replied without a flicker, the soft lilt in his voice rather more pronounced than usual. "I have not been in the South very long. In fact, I only arrived in the Colonies three months since."

Martin shook his head again. "Must be mistaken." He drained his tankard. "Somethin' demmed familiar about you, though." He turned away rudely as if Benedict Clare could hold no further interest for him and, espying Major Ferguson, bellowed a greeting and stalked off.

"Brandy this early in the day tends to confuse," Ben murmured gently, and Sir Edward tendered a rueful smile.

"Martin works untiringly for the king's cause," he offered as if apologizing for the presence of such a one under his roof. Ben had little difficulty imagining Paget's discomfort. The Englishman was courteous in the extreme, and transgressions of the rules of correct social congress would be bound to offend, even while, as host, he could not allow such a reaction to show. Roger Martin might be a vicious, boorish drunkard, but he was as much entitled to impeccable, unstinting hospitality as the most mild-mannered abstainer.

"D'ye mind missing Sunday prayers, Clare?" Paget asked now. "The ladies will attend, of course, but Martin's news needs discussion, and Lady Paget will be most upset if the picnic has to be postponed for business. She has her heart set on it."

Benedict made the correct response, and Paget went off to round up those others whose religious commitments could be as easily displaced. Ben, knowing that he must have a few minutes of absolute privacy in which to deal with this shattering turn of events — the arrival of his former master, the man who still legally owned his labor — went off in the direction of the guesthouse. Once he was able to absorb the shock, to bring the overpowering, destructive hatred under control again, he would be able to decide what steps were now necessary.

Bryony, making polite if abstracted conversation with a group of young ladies poring over the engraved illustrations of the latest fashions in an edition of *The Lady's Magazine*, felt rather than saw Ben passing by the long drawing room window. She had been waiting for his reappearance with mingled anxiety and eagerness. A confrontation was inevitable and she found herself unsure whether her anxiety to avert his anger was greater than either her own annoyance at his high-handedness or her eagerness to discover what had transpired between the two men. With a muttered excuse, she left the circle and went into the hall, sauntering with apparent aimlessness onto the terrace. There was no sign of Ben, but he had been going in the direction of the guesthouse, and she turned her steps unhurriedly along the same route.

Once round the corner, out of sight of all but a couple of gardeners trimming the box hedges, she saw him striding rapidly along the path ahead, the tails of his coat of blue superfine flying under the speed of his progress. Although hampered by her hooped petticoat, she hastened her step, almost running along the gravel. "Ben!" His pace did not slow, and she was afraid to call louder; her running in this fashion looked strange enough. He reached the low brick building with its gabled roof and went in through the open front door. Bryony pounded in after him. "Ben!" she called, breathless, her throat aching.

He turned in the small square hallway, his hand on the latch of the door that gave onto his own chamber. "Not now."

He seemed to look right through her,

Bryony thought with that now familiar tingle of dread. She put her hand on his arm. "Ben, I must talk to you."

*"Not now!"* The harshness grated, raw, flaying, and he shrugged off her hand, swinging away to enter his chamber, slamming the door.

Bryony stared at the closed door and swallowed the threatening tears. He had withdrawn from her again, refusing to discuss what lay between them. It was a tactic that had had consistently bad results in the past. Stiffening her shoulder blades, she put her hand on the latch.

"Ben, we have to talk." She spoke as she pushed the door open and then stopped, transfixed in the doorway. Ben stood in the middle of the room, his face a mask, wiped clean of all personality, all expression, the black eyes looking at something not in this quiet room — something that could have no possible existence in this quiet, well-ordered luxury. A miasma seemed to take shape around him, defiling all that her father's peace and comfort stood for, and Bryony stepped back into the hall, closing the door softly behind her. . . .

Ben was standing again on the dockside at Charleston, filthy, bearded, crawling with vermin from long months spent at sea, shackled hand and foot. He was indistinguishable from his fellow convicts except for the set of his head, which not the vilest degradation could lower, and the directness of his eyes, which met — with an arrogant defiance of his position — the appraising stares of those who had come to buy.

Roger Martin had examined him as if he were cattle and had laughed in his face when he had encountered the proud glare. He had demanded that he lower his eyes, and when Ben had refused, had cut open his cheek with the pony lash. The buyers knew only the number of years of servitude they were purchasing, had no interest in the crimes or the identities of the bondsmen. Thieves, murderers, political extremists — it mattered not a whit, so long as they could be drained of every last drop of strength in labor for those who bought them. They could be used as their owners pleased. If they died in service, who was to ask why? Unlike slaves, who were a lifetime's investment and needed the care one accorded such possessions, bondsmen were purchased for a limited period, and there seemed little point in wasting money on food, clothes, and a roof. It was cheaper to work them until they dropped; there were always more to take their places.

Ben had known these facts as he had stood on the wharf, had recognized in Martin the savage inhumanity that he had fought against in Ireland and that had brought him to this fate; he had known absolutely that his own arrogance and his refusal to yield were a challenge that the man would take on with a pleasure that would be an added bonus to the acquisition of slave labor. Yet he could not bring himself to offer the submission that might cause Martin to move off down the line deciding to look for more worthy grist to his mill. And, in spite of the privations of the voyage, Benedict Clare, now known simply as Nick, the distinguishing Irish lilt disguised, was in good condition beneath the filth, the shoulders strong and broad, his limbs straight and powerful. He would provide many years of labor before deprivation and unremitting toil took their inevitable toll.

And for nearly two years, Nick the bondsman had slaved and sweated through all the hours God made, had been taught to lower his head and walk like a man owned, because defiance brought humiliation far worse than submission, until the

362

day Miss Margaret had demanded that he serve her, too. For months, he had accepted his role as tame lapdog for the young lady of the house, who had so manifestly inherited her father's viciousness. He fetched and carried to order, drove her pony cart into town, groomed her horse, held his palm for her booted foot when she mounted, stood rigid, seemingly without ears or feelings, while she taunted him in front of her friends, boasted of how amenable he was, how he would attend to her every need. And the sniggers and the prods and the covert glances had apparently left him unmoved. Until that August afternoon when he had refused her, and they'd strung him up to the oak tree . . .

Ben slowly came back to himself in the quiet, sun-filled chamber in the orderly guesthouse of Sir Edward Paget. He had sworn that one day he would ensure the death of the man who had broken him. The paralyzing rage had left him, now that he had revisited the memories with the detachment that Paul Tyler had taught him, and his mind was clear. The first rational thought concerned the degree of danger. Martin had sensed something familiar about the clean-shaven Irishman, but he had been easily put off. He would never, not in his wildest dreams, see his runaway bondsman in the person of an Irish aristocrat, and if he was not looking for it, then surely he would not find it. But what if he did?

The consequences of that happening were not to be borne — to be dragged back in shackles, to face torture again, an inevitable, pitiless death. Was the risk unacceptable? Should he make his excuses and leave immediately to join Gates's forces? Leave Bryony this time, in haste and without explanation, once and for all? There would be no coming back to tie up loose ends — not this time.

If he stayed, then the opportunity to revenge himself upon Roger Martin might well present itself. He would have time to talk with Bryony — to love with her just once more so that they could part with grace.

The decision made itself. He left the guesthouse and returned to the great house, where the men were congregated in the library. Major Ferguson, with his band of Tories and loyal American militia, was planning a campaign that would reinforce the British expeditionary force in South Carolina — a force that, it was now presumed, would proceed to roll up the

Southern colonies one by one.

Francis Cullum sat quietly, listening as the discussion tensed under competitive offers of financial support, and those who were either less willing or less able to pledge grew heated. Benedict Clare sat opposite him, tapping a fingernail on the cherrywood tabletop, a frown between the well-drawn brows denoting both interest and question.

"You have said nothing, Mr. Clare." Sir Edward spoke in his position as unofficial moderator. "We would welcome your opinion." He turned with a frown at the sound of the door opening behind him. Then the frown cleared. His daughter smiled, offered a small curtsy to the room at large, and quietly began to refill the table decanters from the bottles on the sideboard.

"I think Major Ferguson's plan is a sound one," responded Ben. "It seems wise to concert both British and Tory forces in the South, although one assumes that General Gates could be no match for either."

A rumble of satisfied agreement rolled around the table. "Can I count on more than your approval, Clare?" Ferguson demanded suddenly. "I could use a man of your caliber on my staff. There'll be little fighting in that position, I fear — can't afford to waste good planners. But if you don't object to being denied the opportunity for heroics, I'd welcome the opportunity to pick your brain."

Bryony's hand held in midair, the bottle of port angled toward the neck of the decanter. Ben bowed his head. "You do me too much honor, Major. I will serve you in whatever capacity you require." His smile was bland, and only Bryony noticed that it failed to touch his eyes.

Francis breathed deeply. For a minute he had been afraid that his own plan was about to be rendered in part worthless. There was little point in removing himself as impediment to Bryony's eventual conjugal felicity if the prospective bridegroom embraced the same dangerous course. But as a staff officer, Benedict Clare would not see much of the battlefield. Francis spoke firmly. "Major Ferguson, I beg to offer my own humble services as a member of your force." He smiled. "But I would prefer not to be denied the opportunity for heroics."

Applause and laughter greeted this statement.

Two members of the group, however, did not receive Francis's pledge with overt signs of gratification. Sir Francis Cullum and Sir Edward Paget looked at each other, their shared thought needing no words between them. Neither of them could venture the opinion that a young man on the brink of matrimony, the only heir to the family name and fortune, had no right to endanger himself. With one accord, their heads turned toward Bryony, who was placing the refilled decanters on the table. She appeared quite unmoved, and Sir Edward felt that familiar tug of paternal pride. He had bred a worthy Paget, for all that she was a woman.

Major Ferguson, however, was less reticent. "I trust Miss Paget is willing to accept your sacrifice, Cullum. It is always hardest on the ladies who are left behind to worry and wait whilst we are engrossed in action."

"There are wives and mothers, sisters and daughters aplenty, Major," Francis said soberly. "They all wait and fear." A pair of black eyes were regarding him steadily across the table, and they contained both knowledge and acceptance. Francis Cullum, on the horns of an impossible dilemma, had chosen his own way.

"In such a matter of duty and honor, Major Ferguson, I would count my own wishes as naught," Bryony stated formally, trotting out the expected sentiment even as her spirit revolted against this means Francis had chosen to resolve their problem. Francis was a Tory by default rather than invincible conviction. It was too slight a commitment to die for. But he had chosen his own way, and she had neither the right nor the power of veto.

"Not something women should have an opinion on," growled Roger Martin, removing his mouth briefly from his tankard in order to make the pronouncement. "Man does what he has to, nothing to do with his women." He glared at Bryony. "Seems to me, miss, you should be at your prayers with the rest of the ladies."

There was a moment of silence while those around the table attempted to recover from this extraordinary rudeness. Sir Edward spoke with icy disdain. "You object to my daughter's presence, Martin? I can assure you that she is here at *my* invitation." He looked slowly around the table. "Please feel free to express an opinion, gentlemen, if anyone else finds Bryony's presence inappropriate."

"On the contrary," Benedict said smoothly. "Such a charming and attentive addition to the company could only be welcomed." He smiled at Bryony, who felt

a ridiculous urge to giggle as she murmured some vaguely grateful words and
appeared suitably confused.

Roger Martin directed his bloodshot
glare at Benedict. "Seems we have a
courtier in our midst. Pretty words, sir, but
pretty words don't get a man far." He
snorted, oblivious of the contemptuous
stares he was receiving from the rest of the
group. "Demmed sure I've seen you somewhere before." He buried his nose in his
tankard again.

"Shall we return to business, gentlemen?" Sir Edward pointedly turned his
head from the boorish Martin, excluding
him from the question, and the discussion
resumed.

Bryony slipped from the room, deciding
that she had heard more than enough to
occupy her thoughts for the time being.
What puzzled her mightily was the change
in Benedict. It was as if that cold stranger
of barely an hour past had existed in another body. He looked his usual debonair,
calm, controlled self, and his eyes, when
they had rested upon her, had contained
only warmth. What on earth had happened
to bring about such a dramatic change?
She would probably never find out, Bryony
reflected gloomily, making her way up-

stairs. It would be just another of the mysteries that surrounded the man she loved.

And what of Francis? Had he decided to make such a sacrifice simply because of her revelation that morning? Her nimble fingers paused in their work of braiding the dark mass of hair tumbling over one shoulder. He could never back down now, not after such a public avowal. Bryony knew, in her heart of hearts, that Francis would ensure that he did not return. It was a cold, hard truth. But why would he not take the way out she had offered? It was too late now, anyway. The milk was spilled, and Francis was going to war.

She twisted the braid into a coronet around her head and put on a bonnet of Angoulême lace, which framed her face in a thoroughly satisfactory manner. Ben was going to war, too. Cold fingers touched her spine. He had offered his services to Ferguson, so obviously he was intending to leave here before being required to make good his promise. There was so much to be achieved in such a short time. But she would not be dispirited. Putting on a pair of lace-edged mittens and straightening her apron, Bryony prepared to go downstairs and join the throng gathering at the water's edge for the boats that would transport them to the picnic spot upriver. It ought to be possible, in the crowd and during the riotous games that would be played, to snatch a little privacy with Ben. No one would notice if they slipped away from the festivities for a few minutes.

There was much laughter punctuated by girlish squeals as the house party boarded the flotilla of rowboats, each craft manned by two oarsmen. Hoops swayed, a mass of brilliant colors, as their occupants each tried to control the unruly garment that took as much space on the narrow thwarts as three individuals. However, good humor prevailed despite the cramped and occasionally precarious conditions. Canoes loaded with hampers, crates of wine, and servants accompanied the procession. The sun shone, bright and warm but without the savage battering power of its summer self, and there was a merciful absence of irritating insect life — an absence that would last for just a few more weeks. It seemed as if nothing could occur to spoil their entertainment.

"May I assist you, Miss Paget?" Ben jumped lightly into a boat and stood, one foot on the stern, the other on the dock, holding out his hand.

"Thank you, sir." She placed her

mittened fingers into the strong, callused palm whose most intimate touches she knew so well. His hold tightened and, as she stepped onto the stern, his other hand went to her waist, firmly steadying her as the boat rocked beneath them. The entire surface of her skin seemed to contract, and the crowns of her breasts went small and hard, burning against the bodice of her gown. Oh, the power of passion, Bryony thought almost desperately as her eyes sought for the same reaction in his. It was there, and then his eyelids dropped. He pushed her lightly in front of him; she stepped down into the boat and he took his hands from her.

"Pray sit beside me, sir," she invited, squishing her hoop with more hope than success. "Francis, will you take my other side? I've a mind to earn the envy of all with two such cavaliers." Her tone was lightly bantering, acceptably flirtatious for such an excursion, and Francis smilingly obliged. Her hand found its way into his for a second in the wordless communication that was all that was available to them at present. The boat rocked violently, shipping water over the sides, and Bryony exclaimed indignantly, lifting her sandaled feet and the hem of her gown. Roger

Martin, who had jumped with completely unconcerned clumsiness into the center of the boat, now pushed his way forward without a word of apology, depositing his large bulk on the bench opposite Bryony and her two consorts.

Bryony shot him a look of pure dislike and made even greater play of trying fastidiously to avoid the water slurping around her feet. Martin wiped his sweating brow with a none too clean handkerchief. "Demmed hot!"

"And wet, too, it would appear," Bryony said with sweet venom. "But perhaps you do not object to wet feet, sir." The gentleman merely looked at her in drunken incomprehension, but Bryony lost all interest in Roger Martin as her entire body became vibrantly aware of what was happening to Ben beside her. He had not moved a muscle, yet she could feel him coiled like a jungle cat waiting to spring. Worse was that miasma that seemed to surround him again, so that she fancied them both wrapped in cold, slimy tendrils of some defiling emotion more dreadful than anything she had ever experienced or could have imagined. Unable to hide her shock, she looked at him, but his expression was completely impassive, the eyes opaque. She nudged him, but he did not respond, and she realized that he was locked again in whatever nightmare world he inhabited on these terrifying occasions. If only she knew what triggered them. Deliberately, she put her foot on his and ground it down with all her might.

Benedict came back to himself with a jolt, removing his foot abruptly. He glanced at her in surprise and met the troubled question in her eyes. Only then did he fully realize how far he had slipped away in the last moments. "Do you know our destination, Miss Paget?"

He smiled, his gaze warm and reassuring, yet somehow Bryony was not reassured. She knew his body in all its moods, was attuned to his emotional self almost as if it were her own, and Ben was somehow fragmented, the calm, certain core obscured.

"It is a favorite spot of mine." She managed to respond quite normally. "One of my old childhood haunts. Papa used to take me in a canoe when I was very small. Francis knows it well, also." She turned to include her other neighbor, and the three of them carried on a polite conversation, quite unremarkable to any audience, offering not the slightest hint that the holders of the conversation were bound together in a conspiracy of knowledge and silence.

The boat rounded a bend of the James River, and the trees that crowded the banks right down to the waterline gave way on the right to a broad, lush stretch of green grass. Smoke curled from a fire pit that had been dug on a small beach cutting into the bank. An ox was roasting on a spit over the pit, as it had been doing for the last twelve hours, tended by a succession of slaves who formed part of the army busily seeing to the arrangement of the long trestle tables set up upon the bank and the positioning of chairs in the shade of bush and tree for the elderly members of the party. As one body, the workers ran down to help beach the rowboats, assist their passengers to dry land, and unload the canoes. Laughing, chattering like so many bright-plumaged birds, the guests clambered up the bank, took glasses of punch and negus from napkin-covered trays presented by beaming servitors, and exclaimed delightedly at the pleasures of alfresco dining.

"I must talk to you," Bryony said in a low voice as she mounted the bank with Ben's assisting hand at her elbow.

"I will come to you tonight," he replied, barely moving his lips.

"No," she hissed fiercely. "I cannot wait until then. No one will notice if we wander away a little. The usual rules are suspended on occasions of this kind." She moved away from him, saying over her shoulder in tones as clear as a bell, "I will show you the plant I mean, Mr. Clare. It grows just within the woods. I am certain it resembles the Solomon's seal that you talk of."

Benedict followed the rose butterfly because to refuse would assuredly give rise to comment after such a public statement of intent. Not even Eliza looked disturbed by her daughter's going away with their guest. Once within the shadow of the trees, Bryony stopped. "I don't understand what has happened, Ben."

"What has happened, lass, as far as I can see, is that you chose to involve Cullum, both dangerously and unnecessarily, in matters that do not concern him," Ben replied sharply. "What you hoped to achieve, I tell you now, once and for all, is not possible. Do you understand *that?*"

"Just listen for a minute," Bryony pleaded, feeling the ground slide from beneath her feet under the unexpected attack. She had been concentrating so much on the strangeness Ben was exhibiting that she had put aside the business of the early morning. "Papa will accept you as son-in-law, once he is forced to face the truth about us and Francis steps aside willingly. He need not know that you are a Patriot until it's too late. . . . I hate to deceive him in that way," she rushed on before he could get a word in edgeway, "but it seems the lesser of two evils —"

"Enough, Bryony!" He took her by the shoulders, his eyes holding hers with the power of his own invincible truth. "It cannot be. You *must* accept that for both our sakes."

"Why?" Her voice sounded weak beside the strength of such conviction. "In love —"

"It is not sufficient, lass." He sighed, relaxing his grip. "I have told you before, sweeting, that there is much about me that you do not and may not know. I must leave here in the morning, take to General Gates the news that Ferguson is marching to South Carolina. . . ."

"No, please, you cannot go in that manner." Her fingers scrabbled on his sleeve, desperation etched her voice. "You cannot sever love for principle. I will embrace your principle."

"It is a severance that cuts far deeper than mere principle, my love." He spoke gently.

"Then tell me what it is!"

Tell her that he was a traitor, an escaped bondsman whose life was worth not a day's purchase. Tell her who and what and why he fought. Tell her that he was a man with no roots, no family, no future but the ephemeral one that he would carve for himself out of war — a future based on the wormwood of hatred. No, he could not tell her those things.

She saw his face close, the eyes dull, as he withdrew into himself, and slowly she stepped back from him, drawing on pride now to salvage what she could. "Then we must take from one night a lifetime's sweetness. You will come to me?"

"Aye, love, I will come to you." He touched her lips with a finger. The blue eyes were shaded by the brim of her bonnet, but he could feel the haunting power of them, cutting him to the quick. The rich creamy luster of her complexion glowed against the dark of her hair and the crisp white of her hat, and a lifetime of loss waited in the wings. "If it could be otherwise, I would have it so, my sweet Bryony. I beg you to believe that."

Her mouth curved in a sad smile against his finger. "I do believe it, Ben. Just as I also believe that it can be otherwise. But if

I cannot convince you, then . . ." She shrugged. "We should return to the picnic. Even a search for wildflowers must come to an end or draw remark." She walked away from him, back to the sounds of laughter and the chink of glasses, back to those intent on merriment, for whom the bright day contained no shadows.

# *Chapter 14*

Roger Martin sat glowering in the shade of a tall poplar. His sweaty scalp itched beneath his wig, and he pushed it up irritably to scratch at the shaven skin. It was too damned hot for this cavorting about on riverbanks. His belly was stretched, drum tight, pushing against the waistband of his satin britches, but he continued to fork the rich ox meat into a mouth already shining with grease. He took a deep draft of claret, chewing stolidly as he did so, and belched profoundly.

The scene in front of him should have gladdened the most jaundiced eye, sweetened the sourest temper. A boisterous game of blindman's buffet was engaging every picnicker below the age of twenty, the noise vying with the scraping of a fiddle and the pipe of a flute as the next generation performed an informal galliard on the bank. What the dance lacked in ballroom elegance, it made up for in enthusiasm, and the elders of the party, those who were awake, sat smiling and nodding, tapping their toes on the grass as they reminisced about the pleasures of their own youth.

Roger Martin's temper, however, was not to be sweetened. Through the fumes of alcohol befuddling his brain, something nagged at him as it had done since he had arrived at the Paget house that morning . . . or rather, since he had been introduced to that damned supercilious Irishman. Martin was a tenacious man as well as an impatient one, and this thing — whatever it was — that hung on the periphery of sense was driving him to distraction. He stared at the Irishman, who had moved out of the dance, some pretty little filly on his arm. And as Roger Martin stared, it was as if an invisible string tightened between them. Benedict Clare raised his head and gazed directly back. The power of the hatred in his eyes would have pierced the thickest hide, and Martin felt a strange cold prickle touch his scalp. He had been on the receiving end of that same stare from those same black eyes before. But God's blood! Where and when?

Benedict cursed himself silently as he turned without apparent haste to look away from his enemy. He should avoid eye contact at all cost. He knew that perfectly well, just as he knew that he must control the surging temptation to close his hands around the man's neck, to squeeze the life, slowly, chokingly, from him, to see those pale bloodshot eyes start from their sockets. . . .

"Mr. Clare, are you quite well?" A hesitant voice spoke at his elbow, and he realized that he had drifted away again.

"Why, Miss Millicent, what man could be otherwise in your company," he said with a smile that set the maiden's heart aflutter. "But I think I should return you to your mama. She was most anxious that you should not spend overlong in the sun, and one can only commend her concern for such a delicate complexion." The pretty words came so easily, he thought with a sardonic quirk.

The young lady was returned, and Ben left the circle of embroidering matrons and went in search of wine and a little peace and quiet for thought. By this time to-morrow, he must be on his way south. The party would break up in the morning, and it would be assumed that he would then join forces with Ferguson on the march to South Carolina. Was there an excuse he could find to delay his recruitment so that his true allegiance would remain unknown for a few more vital days? The longer the Tories remained in ignorance of the spy they had harbored in their camp, the greater time advantage Gates would have when Ben brought him the news of Ferguson's movements.

"How long d'ye say ye've been in the Colonies, Clare?" God dammit! That truculent voice rasped in the remembered belligerence that habitually preceded some needling taunts that would hopefully prick the bondsman to a punishable insolence. Ben could feel himself slipping back, could feel his shoulders drooping slightly, his eyes lowering as he concentrated on breathing, deep and even, as he sought for the innocent, placatory response. And then he remembered that he was no longer Nick, that he was Benedict Clare, guest of Sir Edward Paget, that to behave like Nick in such a situation would be as dangerously revealing as a bold declaration of the truth.

"Three months," he replied briefly, continuing to saunter across to the still-laden tables.

"Where'd ye land?" Again that belligerence.

"Boston." The Irish lilt became yet more pronounced. It was not something Martin would associate with Nick. Ben reached for a glass, took the chased silver ladle from the matching punch bowl, and filled the glass with the potent brew. "Do you care for punch, Martin?" Still holding the ladle, he reached for another glass.

An expletive derived from the barnyard greeted the polite inquiry. "That muck is fit only for milksops! Give me the brandy." This last was bellowed at a hovering slave. When the boy hesitated, looking for the required bottle, Martin's hand shot out in a backhanded clout that sent the lad reeling.

The ladle shook in Ben's hand, its contents spilling upon the white damask cloth, and blood pounded in his temples. Then a hand, cool and quiet, came to rest over his, easing it down so that the ladle was returned to the punch bowl. "Perhaps I can help you, Mr. Martin." Bryony spoke, her voice glacial, sounding remarkably like Sir Edward Paget's. "I must apologize if the service offered does not meet with your satisfaction."

"Is something amiss?" Sir Edward appeared as if from nowhere. He looked from the lad, still clutching the side of his head, to Bryony, white and stiff, to the crimson, sweating Martin, and then at the motionless figure of Benedict Clare. In the silence, men moved slowly across the grass, drawn by the emanating tension, by the certainty of an impending explosion. It could no more be mistaken than the storm clouds presaging a thunderstorm.

Ben caught Martin by the shoulder in a movement shocking in its abruptness and spun him round to face him. "Brutality may be your creed, Mr. Martin, but it is hardly courteous to practice it upon another man's property!"

Bryony stepped away from Ben, nausea churning in her belly as she felt the shape of an imminent horror. A rustle, maybe of agreement, maybe of disapproval, ran around the gathering circle. Paget opened his mouth to say something in an attempt to end what was about to happen before it began, but the horror could not be forestalled, had passed beyond all possibility of intervention three years since.

"You *dare* lay hands on me!" Roger Martin twisted in outrage, flinging off the hands on his shoulders, his face suffused. There was a moment when the two men were quite alone in a world that excluded the immediate circle of spectators, the plaintive offerings of fiddle and pipe, the excited whispers of servants gathering in an outer circle, the urgent demands for explanation from those in the background wanting to know what had transpired. They were alone in a time and place long past, and Roger Martin gaped as the incredible, unbelievable memory became reality.

"God's blood," he said again. "Nick!"

"What the devil are you talking about, man?" demanded Paget, not troubling to disguise his anger.

Martin extended a shaking finger. Indeed, his entire body seemed to quiver under the force of an ungovernable rage. "A runaway cur!" he hissed. "My bondsman, bought at the dock at Charleston five years ago!"

"Get ahold of yourself, man," Paget insisted, taking his arm. "You babble."

"Indeed I do not." A fleck of saliva clung to Martin's lip as he gazed with sickening triumph at the man he owned. "This piece of scum ran away, owing me twelve years' labor!"

Say something, Ben, Bryony prayed with such intensity that she could not believe he didn't hear. But he just stood there, pale and unmoving.

"What the devil's he on about?" someone demanded petulantly. "Can't say things like that about a gentleman."

"Gentleman!" spat Martin. "He belongs to me, and I demand you put him in irons, Paget. I'll drag him back to Georgia at my stirrup." Suddenly, he grabbed the ruff of Ben's shirt. "D'ye need proof? I'll show you the scars I put on his back. Take your shirt off, cur!"

Benedict stood as if carved in granite, and uncertainty flickered on the faces of those around him. A man would need to be very sure of himself to make such a monstrous accusation, to believe he had in his hand such corroboration.

Bryony never knew exactly what divine hand came to her aid, and she never questioned it. Such gifts one accepted without thought. Her voice rang clear, quiet and utterly assured in the shocked instant of silence — an instant that was about to give way to the baying of the hounds. "I cannot believe, Papa, that you will stand aside whilst a guest in your house is offered such atrocious insult. It is hardly worthy of Paget hospitality."

The cold statement abruptly brought hard-edged reality to the hypnotic trance that seemed to hold them all in its grip. Martin's accusations were those of a madman, and even if, by some aberration, they could be proved otherwise, they were the grossest transgression of all the rules that made life pleasant and possible. Sir Edward, as host, was responsible for restoring order on the instant. If his guest was offered insult under his roof, then it was the equivalent of an affront from himself, and Bryony had reminded him forcibly of his duty.

"You will accept my apologies, Clare." He bowed briefly. "I can only assume that Mr. Martin has a touch of the sun."

"And the brandy," came an added mutter as people began to relax. It was a story that would keep many a dinner table exclaiming for months to come.

"God dammit, man, did you hear what I said? I want this man in irons —"

"Sir Edward." Benedict broke into the enraged bluster, his tone almost neutral. But it was the first time he had spoken, and even Martin fell silent. "I much regret the necessity of causing you further unpleasantness, but I fear that I must insist on satisfaction. Such an affront cannot be borne by a man of honor." No one could guess the deep, warm glow of satisfaction that infused him. His vengeance was there now for the plucking, and quick-thinking Bryony had placed the tool in his hand even as she had saved him.

Martin gobbled like a turkey cock, a corded vein standing out on his temple as he appeared on the verge of apoplexy. Sir Edward, taking advantage of this disablement, said quietly, "The accusation was lunacy, Clare."

"Maybe so, but the terms in which it was couched were not," Ben responded, equally quietly.

"Why, you . . . you . . . you dare to believe I would fight such trash!" Martin seemed to lose the power of speech again, and the gobbling resumed.

Sir Edward did not deign to look in his direction. Instead, with a punctilious bow, he offered, "I would be honored to act for you, Clare."

Benedict returned the bow. "The honor is mine, Sir Edward." He cast a disdainful, dismissive glance at his opponent. "Pistols at twenty-five yards . . . but not until he's sober." Swinging on his heel, he strode down to the beach.

Bryony took a step after him, then recollected herself. Somehow she must contain herself, contain the turmoil and confusion of this revelation that told her so much yet explained so little. He had told her that he was truly Benedict Clare; she had seen the initials on his shirt . . . but a runaway bondsman? There was no sense in it, yet she knew it to be the truth.

Pandemonium boiled around her as explanations were demanded by those who had not been a party to the drama, and Roger Martin continued to rage. But the power of his vilifications and imprecations was somehow weakened by an occasional note of whining bewilderment. Sir Edward cut through the tumult with incisive authority.

"Name your friends, Martin."

The chilling impatience of the demand served to remind everyone of the realities. There was a duel to be fought, and at twenty-five yards — a range that only the most experienced, assured duelist would choose — it would be fought to the death. Clare, as the injured party, had taken with a vengeance his rights to the choice of weapons and to the stipulation of conditions. Some of the choleric flush faded on Martin's cheeks, and he drew himself up. "I'll not fight my bondsman."

A gasp ran around the group. Then, as one body, they turned their backs on one capable of such dishonor, except for Paget, who said with soft insistence, "Do not be a fool, man. You have made such accusations of a gentleman as cannot be tolerated. You must defend them in the only honorable way, as he will defend himself. Name your friends."

There was no help for it, as Martin well knew, even as he raged inwardly at the gross injustice, the quirk of fate that had brought him to this position. To refuse the challenge was to stand dishonored, to be forever spurned by his fellows, an outcast to be regarded with loathing by all honorable men. He wiped his brow with a soiled kerchief and looked around. The group of his peers had turned to face him once more, but no one stepped forward to offer their services, and he was obliged to ask. "Cullum?"

The curt question was directed at Sir Francis, who barely nodded in acknowledgment before saying to Paget, "This is not the place to discuss such matters. I will confer with my principal and meet with you this evening."

The party broke up almost immediately, there being no enthusiasm for further revelry. Subdued, talking in whispers, they all made their way back to the boats, leaving behind on the bank the forlorn remains of the picnic. Of Benedict Clare there was no sign, but an oarsman told them that the gentleman had taken one of the canoes, saying that he would paddle himself back to the great house.

"What do you make of it, Bri?" Francis asked softly, perching beside her on the narrow thwart.

Bryony shrugged. "Martin is crazed — and drunk," she added. "And he's a boorish oaf."

"And Clare will kill him for that?"

She looked up at him, replying casually, "Would you not, Francis, if you had been subjected to such public insult?"

"It is not always easy to put oneself in another man's shoes," he responded soberly. "But there is something devilishly queer about it, say what you will."

Bryony was not about to venture any further opinions. Curiously, she felt no deep repugnance at the idea of Benedict's killing Roger Martin. If, as Martin had admitted, he had put those scars on Ben's back, then he deserved to die. At least he would die in a fair fight. But if he did not die . . . A shudder ran through her. If he did not die, he would have killed Ben, or worse — wounded him so that he could exhibit the marks of the bondsman and drag him back to an existence that she could not bear to contemplate. There was only one possible, bearable conclusion to this. She knew that Ben was a fine shot, and he would hardly have chosen such a range if he had not been sure of himself.

What was to become of *them* now that she knew some of the truth that lay behind those terrifying moods of Ben's, now that she had had some glimpse into the nightmare world that he had inhabited? Surely, it could only bring them closer. Surely, Ben would cease his objections to her plan now that she knew the dreadful secret that he had been keeping with such tenacity. The thoughts tumbled, jumbled, made no orderly pattern. When Ben came to her that night, as he had promised, came to her for the night of loving that was intended to be their last, then she would be able to make sense of this whirling chaos; then, surely, she would learn the whole truth, and Ben would understand that no truth, however dreadful, could make any difference to the way she felt, to her certainty that they were bound to each other by ties that transcended the slings and arrows of fortune.

Throughout an interminable evening, Bryony tried to catch Ben's eye, wanting simply a look, a smile, but he ignored her, although he showed no indication of strain. He smiled, talked, joked, flirted lightly —

in fact, behaved as impeccably as one would expect of a man facing a duel at dawn. Of Roger Martin there was no sign, and Bryony gathered from Francis that he had been persuaded to spend the evening in sober seclusion with his second.

"Such a dreadful thing to have happened. Seldom have I seen your father so upset," bemoaned Eliza. "That abominable man Martin! He'll never be welcome under my roof again."

Bryony regarded her mother with raised eyebrows. "It is to be assumed, Mama, that after tomorrow he will not be in a position to avail himself of an invitation, even should you feel inclined to extend it."

Eliza went white beneath her rouge. "Oh, Bryony! How *can* you be so callous and unwomanly?" She sounded genuinely angry. "I do not know what is to become of you, now that Francis is . . ." Her voice faded and she dabbed at her eyes with a lace-edged handkerchief.

Bryony, filled with remorse, apologized for her sharpness, comforting her mother as best she could. But it was difficult to offer comfort when she needed it herself. Her father had answered her questions curtly, telling her that Clare and Martin would face each other at five o'clock the following morning on the bowling green, with pistols and at the range decreed by the injured party.

The evening ended early and with universal relief. Benedict bade his hostess good night, carefully avoiding the slightest implication that it might also be farewell. The affair would be settled long before the ladies appeared downstairs, and on the surface everyone behaved as if the fair sex knew nothing of this unpleasantness; it was not, after all, a fit subject for delicate sensibilities.

"Good night, Miss Paget." He took her hand, brushed her fingertips with his lips, but still he did not look at her, did not even apply pressure to the hand he held. It was as if she were of no more account than any other young lady in the room.

Bryony curtsied, murmured her own good night, swallowing the sick dread of something that she had not thought possible until this minute. Ben was going to go through this without a word to her. There would be no talking tonight, certainly no loving. It was as if he had lopped her off from his tree trunk, as if she had no part, no right to draw strength from the sap that she had thought they shared. Her soul cried out at the injustice. With her quick thinking inspired by the all-consuming fear for the one she loved, had she not given him the way out? Was there to be no acknowledgment, no understanding, even, of her fear, her need?

It seemed not. The long hours of the night wore on, and she sat at her open window during the slow death of hope. She did not know *why;* but that, after all, was an utterly familiar condition in her dealings with Ben. How many times had she not known why?

The first gray streaks of false dawn touched the eastern sky, and the gilded ormolu clock on the mantel read four-thirty. Bryony dressed again, her eyes dry as sand, her skin strangely tight. She avoided her mirror, wrapping herself in a light cloak, drawing the hood around her face, as much for concealment as for protection against the early-morning dew. Ben's absence in the night had been intended to deliver a proscription on her participation, her understanding of this affair. But Bryony was not prepared to accept that judgment, whether it had been made for some askew reason with her best interests in view, or whether he just wished her out of the way. She was touched as nearly by this as was Benedict Clare. And once those two shots had been fired, she would throw in her lot with the renegade Irishman — with or without his consent.

She fancied that the house held an expectant hush as she slipped from her chamber, pausing on the landing. No sound came from her parents' bedroom, and she surmised that her father was already at the meeting point. The household would not stir for another hour, although the bakehouse and kitchen would be alive and busy in preparation for breakfast. If there was to be an audience to the drama on the bowling green, it would consist only of those men considered necessary to see fair play, and the physician who had been summoned last evening. But Bryony was certain that behind every door in the house lay the wakeful, waiting for the news of the end of one of two lives.

The door to the rear terrace stood open, mute witness to those who had already passed through, and she ran lightly across the grass, the dew dampening her thin slippers. The sound of voices carried on the still, predawn air as she approached the sunken bowling green. A walk bordered by large flowering shrubs surrounded the green, offering both shade and privacy for the players. A gap in the hedge opened directly onto the green, and she stood slightly to one side, partly concealed by the hedge, taking in the scene on the smooth, lush expanse of carefully manicured lawn.

Sir Francis and her father were conferring over a pair of dueling pistols, examining them carefully before loading them, holding them with extreme care at half cock. Lord Dawson and Major Ferguson stood to one side of the green, both immaculately turned out, as if they were paying a morning call. Beside them stood a man in a sober gray coat and neat wig, the black bag he carried as much as his modest dress identifying him as the physician.

Benedict, in shirtsleeves, stood in the center of the green. His hands were thrust into the pockets of his britches, his booted feet set square. The burnished copper hair was drawn into a neat queue at the nape of his neck, well away from his face, and he seemed to have turned in on himself, to be quite unaware of his surroundings. But there was nothing about his stance to indicate tension — quite the opposite — and Bryony felt a quiet confidence fill her, a confidence that she knew was transmitted from Ben. Something for which he had been waiting for a long, hard time was now in his grasp, and he would not drop it. She shivered a little, knowing his ruthlessness, his implacable determination when set upon a goal, and she wondered whether Roger Martin could feel it, also. One could almost imagine that it would be enough to paralyze a man's will.

Martin, unlike his opponent, was not still. He shifted restlessly from foot to foot, a black coat buttoned up to his neck so that not a glimmer of white would give the other man an improved target — a consideration and convention that Benedict Clare was flouting with an insulting confidence.

The two seconds came toward the principals, pistols in their hands. Bryony held her breath, and then suddenly Ben turned toward the gap in the hedge, as if he had known she was there. His dark eyes gave nothing away, but his voice rang clear. "I do not consider this a fit spectacle for your daughter, Paget."

Bryony gasped at this betrayal — no, this rejection. He could not bear to have her near in his moment of trial. Her father stopped, stared, his expression livid. "What the devil are you thinking of, girl? Get back to the house!"

"But, Papa —" she began, taking a step forward.

"If you cannot take charge of your

daughter, Paget, I will," Ben interrupted in glacial accents, moving toward her with a lithe, springing step that declared his purpose. Bryony swung on her heel and left, her heart hammering with mingled fright and fury. That was the second time in twenty-four hours that Ben had banished her from a situation that touched her to her core, and she didn't know whether he had done so because he wished to protect her or because she would be in his way.

Gathering up her skirt, she ran round the path to the far side of the green, where she knew the shrubs had been thinned by old Matt in the hopes that they would grow back stronger and fuller. As she had hoped, it was an easy matter to part the leafy branches, providing her with a bird's-eye view of events on the green below. How could Ben possibly imagine that she would be able to survive the waiting, minding her own business in the house, pretending like the other women that nothing was happening on the bowling green? Pretending — until someone brought them the news of one man's death. He was either insensitive beyond belief or unutterably selfish. Or maybe afraid that her presence might detract from his concentration . . . ? If that was it, then she had been the selfish, insensitive one, but there would be time enough later for apologies and explanations. Dear God, there would be, wouldn't there? Please! Prayers were tumbling from her lips, apposite or not, she did not care. Her hands were clutched together so tightly that they went numb, but Bryony noticed nothing, her eyes riveted on the play being acted out before her on the green stage in the soft cool of early morning.

The two duelists, having saluted each other with impeccable formality, were taking the pistols from the seconds, holding them with muzzles pointed to the ground as they stood back to back. The seconds had retreated to eight paces, and the tableau was for an instant frozen. Then Sir Edward's voice called, "Twenty-five paces, gentlemen." Bryony felt sick with near-unbearable tension as Ben and Martin paced with slow deliberation, each step counted by her father. At twelve and a half, they stopped, still with their backs to each other.

"Turn." Paget held up a white handkerchief, which hung inert in the still air. The two men turned, standing sideways to minimize the target area. "All's ready." So slowly that Bryony thought she would pass out from the agony of suspense, they raised the pistols, taking aim. The white handkerchief fluttered suddenly, and two shots rang out, one a bare fraction of a second after the other.

To Bryony's wild imagining, an eternity passed and nothing happened. Then Roger Martin seemed to crumple, a black shape etched on the grass. Benedict remained on his feet, and Bryony began to shake violently and uncontrollably, her teeth chattering so loudly that she was sure they could hear her. She sank down onto the grass, burying her head in her knees as wave after wave of dizziness washed through her, leaving her too weak to move.

The doctor bent over the fallen man, one finger at the carotid artery in the neck. He straightened slowly, shaking his head. "He does not need my services, Sir Edward." He glanced at Benedict, who still had not moved. Blood dripped from his arm, but he made no attempt to stanch it, just stood, a faraway look in his eyes that brought the doctor over to him in a few quick steps. "You were hit, Mr. Clare?"

Ben shook himself free of his reverie and glanced down at his forearm. "A nick only." He pushed the torn sleeve up to his elbow.

Sir Edward came over, his hand out-stretched. "A fine, clean shot, Clare." It was the quiet acknowledgment that Ben had avoided inflicting the true horror of the dueling ground — the agonizing, fatal wound that would bring a lingering death. They had all seen what happened to gut-shot men.

Hands were shaken, little further was said. The physician bound the flesh wound, and Ben, with a word of excuse, walked away to the guesthouse.

Now that it was over, he was conscious of nothing but a creeping numbness that blotted out all emotion. There was no pleasure, no satisfaction, just the sense of an overdue task accomplished, a debt called in. He had imagined feeling relief, relief from the burden of bitterness once the score had been settled, yet the bitter-ness was still there, no longer directed at the specific individual but at all those who made the inhuman exploitation of their fellow man possible, at those who believed championing the exploited was treason. Every man in this house would have sen-tenced Benedict Clare to a traitor's fate had they been on the bench in Ireland, for all that they had shrunk in horror from the accusations of Roger Martin. They had not been able to believe such a tale. But had the duel gone the other way, had he been disabled, they would have strung him to the nearest tree and lashed him to within an inch of his life without compunction, believing it their duty.

He was packing his belongings as these thoughts tossed in his head. He had not made a conscious decision to leave but knew, as his hands performed the task they had begun without instruction, that he must go at once. He now had his excuse for a breathing space before joining up with Ferguson's Tories. A man who has just killed another in a duel is entitled to some privacy. By the time they wondered why he had not reappeared, he would be well on his way to General Gates. And Bryony . . .

No, he could not think of her. To do so would cloud the real issues. He had a war to fight. She belonged here, in this sheltered, privileged world where bondsmen kept to their assigned places; here, protected by her father's love and all that was safe and familiar to her. She did not belong with an escaped convict, opposed to everything she held dear — prepared to fight to the death for his beliefs.

But he owed her an explanation, a farewell, at least. Ben folded a shirt with extreme care, his movements suddenly slowed. He could not face her. It was as simple as that. She had saved his life with that quicksilver intervention when he had been standing, defenseless, terror-struck, looking into the future that would be his. She knew of his servitude. Could she guess at the humiliations he had accepted, the degradations he had learned to endure without a murmur of protest? She had observed the conditions of servitude, had grown up with it as an intrinsic part of her life. Of course she knew what it would have done to him. And he could not bear the thought that she knew.

The bag was packed. His horse was in the stable. He had only to make his farewells, and those he could make discreetly to Sir Edward, with a word for Ferguson and Dawson. There would be no need to venture near the drawing room, where the women would be congregated, whispering well out of earshot of their menfolk, who would be dealing with the unpleasant business of a dead body and messages that must be taken to the Martin plantation in Georgia. Bryony would be keeping out of the way, presumably. Sir Edward had made no attempt to hide his fury at her shocking and embarrassing presence on the scene, and Ben's angry reaction had been considered perfectly appropriate under the circumstances. It was much better this way. A clean break, a clean death — as clean as he had given Martin.

Picking up his bag, Benedict left the guesthouse and went to the stable to order his horse.

# Chapter 15

"How dared you do such a thing?" Sir Edward spoke to his daughter with a cold ferocity to which neither of them was accustomed. "Such arrant interference! Never have I been so shamed!"

They were in his small study at the front of the house, with no witnesses to the confrontation. Bryony kept her eyes on the floor. The only excuse she had was not one she could use: I love Benedict Clare; we are lovers; there is no life for me without him. All quite valid reasons for needing to witness the moment when that man faced death. Even though the man in question had not himself accepted them.

The angry words broke over her head until, defeated by her lack of response, Sir Edward fell silent.

"I am sorry, Papa. It was thoughtless and I cannot imagine what led me to do such a thing," she said in a wooden voice, still not lifting her eyes.

Paget looked at the bent head in sudden

confusion. This was not the daughter he knew. "What's to be done about young Cullum?" he asked gruffly, as if the previous few minutes had never taken place.

Bryony raised her head, accepting the change of subject without faltering. "He must do what he believes is right. I'll not stand in his way."

"No, of course not." He picked up a letter opener from the tooled leather desktop and tapped it against the palm of his hand. "Every able-bodied young man is needed for this final effort. But it will mean further delay of the wedding." He did not add that the postponement could prove terminal.

"Yes," Bryony agreed quietly.

"Why do you not wish to marry him, child? There is no hostility between you, you cannot pretend that."

Bryony sighed. "I don't love him. I am deeply fond of him, but we do not love each other."

"Love," her father pronounced, "is not a factor in marriage. You have liking already. Attachment will grow from that as you share the joys and sorrows of marriage. Marriage is a duty. If you wish for more, you will only store up unhappiness for yourself." It was said with a degree of sympathy, but Bryony was aware that sympathy was all she would receive. Anyway, the matter was already settled, although her father did not yet know it.

"Major Ferguson will be leaving with his new recruits within the next few days?" she asked reasonably, following the same subject but with a change of tack designed to indicate her acceptance of her father's statement. She also needed to know, since Benedict seemed disinclined to share his plans with her, what he had said to the others.

"He will leave the day after tomorrow," her father informed her casually. "Francis will go with him to join his troop quartered near Gloucester. I understand that Mr. Clare will meet up with them there."

Her heart began that painful hammering again. "Has Mr. Clare left, then?"

"He had business of his own to attend to," Sir Edward said briefly. "It is only to be expected under the circumstances. He left an hour since."

Without a word! He had walked away from her without a word. It defied belief. It certainly defied understanding. However, Bryony found to her amazement that she was relatively unperturbed by the information. Ben was always doing things that she didn't understand, and he always had his own complicated reasons for them — reasons that she didn't necessarily have to accept. It was now quite clear that she was just going to have to take matters into her own hands. There was no possibility of pulling the coals out of this fire in any conventional fashion, as she had hoped. She could hardly seek her father's blessing on the union when the prospective bridegroom was so reluctant that he had absented himself. It was clearly a case of the mountain having to go to Mohammed.

Bryony left the study and went in search of Francis. She didn't know why she should be so certain that Benedict had gone to the cabin in the clearing, but somehow she knew that in the peace of the backwoods, performing the elemental tasks of survival, Ben would heal himself, put the duel into perspective and then behind him, and gather strength for the next move in the game he played. And he was not going to make that next move without her!

She ran Francis to earth in the library perusing the *Virginia Gazette*. He looked up and she gestured with her head toward the open terrace door. He gave a near-imperceptible nod and returned to the paper. Bryony wandered out onto the

410

terrace and strolled in the direction of the thicket.

"Your talent for the clandestine improves hourly," Francis said when he joined her a minute or two later. "Why could you not simply suggest we take a walk in the garden?"

"I don't know," Bryony returned with a smile. "Secrecy becomes a habit. I need your help, my friend."

Francis stroked his beard thoughtfully. "Tell me in what way before I make any rash promises."

Bryony couldn't help chuckling at this caution, which she had to admit was justified. "Benedict has left."

"Without you," Francis agreed. "I had noticed."

"Yes, and I do not know why. Probably because of some absurd scruple about —" She stopped herself just in time. About having been a bondsman, she had been about to say. She was now quite convinced that that had been behind his earlier insistence on the impossibility of their having a shared future — the fact about himself that he had said she could not know. "About the duel," she resumed as smoothly as possible. "So I must go to him."

"I suppose I expected it." Francis sighed.

"You will have it out in the open, then? No excuses, no frills to obscure the hard facts?"

"There seems no other way." She brushed her hair away from her face and looked him in the eye. "I will leave a letter for my father, telling him the truth. You will be relieved of your obligation then. There will be no need to go to war."

Francis smiled a little sardonically. "There is every need. I chose that path, not just because of our situation, Bri. I cannot live a conventional life, I fear, and one day I will be discovered. I do not think I could bear the disgrace, and yet I cannot . . . cannot stop myself."

Bryony reached for his hands and gripped them tightly. "I cannot stop myself, either, Francis, so I am hardly in a position to throw stones. We are what we are."

"Yes," he agreed flatly, releasing her hands after one final squeeze. "So, what do you wish me to do?"

"Can you remember the spot on the Williamsburg road where you found me last summer?"

"I think so." He frowned. "I could probably find it again. This thing between you and Clare goes back to that time?"

She nodded. "I can't give you details, Francis. They are not mine to tell. But if I can find the path I took on that day I will be able to make my way to where I know Ben is at the moment."

"You wish me to take you to where I found you?"

"If you please."

"And then I am to return and face your father, having assisted in the elopement or worse of his daughter?" His eyebrows lifted.

"I think that would be asking too much, even of such an old friend." Bryony chuckled in spite of her own stinging sorrow at the thought of what her defection would do to her parents. But she had to make a choice of loyalties, and in the final analysis the choice seemed not to exist. She went on with her plan, pushing aside the sorrow. "I thought that if you said you were going to join the Tory force at Gloucester tonight, for instance, then I could creep out and ride behind you until we reached the place. You would not be implicated and no one would guess."

Francis accorded the suggestion due consideration, then nodded. "I can see no flaws in it. Besides, the sooner I am away from here, the better. Having settled on this course of action, I'm impatient to implement it. We'll leave after dinner."

"I'll meet you at the end of the drive," Bryony said. "No one will question my decision to retire straight after dinner. It's been an exhausting occasion, after all."

"Quite amazingly so," Francis concurred dryly. "I feel as if I have lived a lifetime in a mere three days."

They went their separate ways, Bryony to lock herself in her chamber and agonize over the composition of the letter she must leave for her father. She could not tell him that she was following Benedict Clare without betraying Ben's Patriot allegiances. If Ferguson knew that a spy had been a participant in their planning discussion, there was nothing to prevent him from changing the plans that Ben was taking to General Gates. Such a betrayal would hardly improve her case with her reluctant bridegroom. Eventually, she settled for a half-true, half-fabricated account of a love affair during her previous disappearance, of the impossibility of now settling for marriage to Francis, of her need to return to the man she loved, whose identity she could not reveal.

Bryony read it through with a grimace. All this talk of love would not appease either of her parents. But what else could she say? It was the truth. She closed the letter with a plea for understanding and forgiveness, although in her heart of hearts she was afraid that both would be denied her. But at least they would not again suffer the hell of not knowing what had happened to her. She could do no more.

Somehow she managed to sit through dinner at the vastly depleted table, where only Lord Dawson, Major Ferguson, and the Cullums remained as guests. Francis's intention to leave for Gloucester that evening met with no opposition, and he and Bryony were rather pointedly left alone in the drawing room once the tea tray had been removed.

"Why don't you run upstairs as if overcome with emotion?" Francis suggested practically. "Then I can make my farewell. I will wait for you on the road."

Bryony nodded. Appearing overcome with emotion was not difficult since tears were very close, anyway. She found her parents on the terrace. They were alone, sitting side by side, Eliza with her embroidery frame, Sir Edward reading to her from a leather-bound book of poetry, and Bryony stood for a second watching this rare moment of complete companionship, glad that if this was to be the last time she saw them, she would have a warm memory. There was no further need to feign sorrow — the tears flowed freely now — and fortunately no need to explain the fervency of her embrace as she bade them good night. Her tears for Francis were considered perfectly understandable and her need for sympathy equally so.

Upstairs, she drew out the doeskin tunic from the back of the armoire, where she had kept it for memory's sake. The moccasins were there, also. She wrapped them and the tunic into a small bundle that she could conceal beneath her cloak, then looked around the room that had always been her sanctuary, where the memorabilia of childhood and girlhood mingled with the appurtenances of womanhood. Was there anything else she should take out of this life? Anything without which she could not live? It was everything or nothing, really, Bryony decided. She would start anew, taking only the few pieces of jewelry that belonged to her. She might have need of money. Ben might have need of money. A small shrug accompanied the addendum. He had not appeared to suffer from shortness of funds these past days, but that didn't necessarily mean anything.

She changed into a plain gown of worked muslin, which could be worn without a hooped petticoat, put on a pair of relatively sturdy leather shoes and the same light cloak that she had worn that morning, laid the letter addressed to her father on her pillow, and slipped out onto the landing. Luck was with her, and she reached the front drive unnoticed. She crossed the lawn into the trees bordering the drive and made her way swiftly down to the road, the screen of trees hiding her from any possible traffic on the driveway.

The road in the gathering dusk appeared empty, and she stood hesitantly. To the right, the road curved, and guessing that Francis was adopting her own obsession with secrecy and was keeping himself out of sight, she ran toward the bend. Francis was standing by the trees, holding his horse, Dirk, and looking anxious.

"There you are. My father and Dawson came down the drive with me to bid me farewell, and I was afraid you might run into them as they were returning to the house."

"No, I saw no one." She went to Dirk, hitching up her skirt as she raised her foot to the stirrup. Dirk stood twenty hands from the ground, but she sprang upward deftly. "Come, Francis. The longer we dally around here, the greater the chance of discovery." She couldn't keep the impatience from her voice, and Francis, with a resigned shake of his head, mounted behind her, reaching around for the reins.

"Dallying, as it happens, was far from my intention. I am as anxious to be done with this business as you."

"I crave pardon," she murmured in subdued tones. "It is just that I am rather scared and I feel like crying. . . ."

"Yes, I know," he said with swift comprehension. "I suppose it would not be helpful to ask what you intend to do if Benedict is not where you expect to find him?"

"He will be," she said with complete confidence.

"And what if he won't take you with him?"

"He won't be able to prevent me," she replied.

Francis snorted a trifle doubtfully. He had formed the impression that Benedict Clare was not particularly malleable, even by one with Bryony's determined talents. However, Bryony had chosen her own course, as he had chosen his, and casting doubts would not be constructive.

They rode in silence for nearly an hour

as dusk became full dark, and Bryony wrestled with something that she had forgotten when she had so blithely made her plans. She would have to make her way through the forest in the dead of night. She shivered in sudden panic and then stiffened her shoulders. She had walked the woods at night with Ben. So long as she didn't lose the path, she would come to no harm. Unless she crossed the path of a bear, of course, or . . .

"It's here, I think." Francis spoke suddenly, drawing Dirk to a halt beside the road. "I remember that configuration of oaks."

Bryony found the beginning of the narrow path with no difficulty. The moon was reassuringly bright, although little light would reach the denser parts of the forest. But she must not think of that.

"I think I should accompany you," Francis said, examining the path in frowning concern. "You can't go into the forest alone in the dark."

"Yes, I can," Bryony assured him quietly, knowing now that she could. "The path is familiar to me." She smiled in an effort to convince him, saying lightly, "It will not help my case with Ben if I trail the entire neighborhood with me."

"What is he doing in the backwoods?" It was a natural enough question, although it was the first time Francis had asked it.

"He goes there when he needs to think," she improvised with a careless shrug.

Francis sighed. "I wish I knew what he was doing thinking in the forest last summer, when he was only supposed to have arrived in the Colonies three months ago."

"Don't press me, Francis. I can't tell you, and yet I know that leaving you in ignorance is fine return for your kindness." Her voice was muffled as the tears again clogged her throat. Francis took her in his arms in a sudden, fierce hug, and she clung to him, letting the tears flow without restraint, wetting his shirtfront.

"It is so hard to bid you farewell," she whispered. "I don't suppose we will ever meet again."

"Don't be so sure of that," Francis replied gently, stroking her hair. "I have a feeling that this is not the last farewell for us, Bri."

A graveyard shiver for some reason prickled her skin, and she stood away from him, smiling with determined bravery. "Will you go first, Francis? I'll watch you out of sight."

"If that is what you wish." He kissed her then, and for a moment, she leaned against him, her body long with his as they shared the same thought: how easy it would once have been to follow the path laid down for them, never to have known the drive of passion, the pain of choice. Then, without words, they separated. Francis remounted as Bryony stood in the dark shadow of the trees, and he rode off down the road to his own resolution, without a backward glance.

Bryony stepped onto the path and allowed the forest to swallow her. She paused long enough to remove her dress and undergarments, and to slip on the tunic, feeling its cool suppleness against her bare skin. Her feet slipped into the moccasins, and suddenly it was last summer again. She stretched, reveling in the freedom of her body, the sense of its belonging in the elemental world of woods and creeks.

Her fear left her with this resurgence of the self who had known these woods. Wrapping her shoes and clothes in the cloak, she set off down the path, looking neither right nor left, not stopping to listen, because the forest noises might alarm her, just continuing doggedly on her way as the night wore on. It took her a little longer this time than it had that sunny summer morning, but she recognized the crossroads where the four paths met, and her heart lifted. It was simple from here — half an hour, perhaps. And yet she was taken by surprise when the trees suddenly gave way to the moon-washed clearing, so achingly familiar, as if no time had passed since last she was here.

She tiptoed across to the firestones. They were still warm, although the ashes were gray, but it told her all she needed to know. Ben was here. The cabin door was closed, and when she pushed tentatively against it, it did not budge. She knew there was a heavy wooden bar that could be dropped across the door, ensuring safety from intruders, but Ben had never used it last summer. Maybe there was more to be afraid of now.

A devastating wave of weariness threatened to engulf her at the knowledge that Ben and the bed were behind a barred door. She could bang on it, call through the window, but if she woke him she would have to talk, and she did not think she could form even the simplest words. She had had no sleep the previous night; had spent the day on a razor's edge of tension;

had been wrung out with the wretchedness of parting from her parents and from Francis; and had triumphed over her fear of the nighttime forest at the expense of her last residue of strength. If she could not creep into bed beside Ben, as she had intended, then she would sleep on the ground beside the firestones.

Her clothes made a pillow, her cloak, drawn tightly around her, sufficed as a blanket. The hard ground was a featherbed — even a bed of nails would have been welcomed so long as she could lie down. Deep, black unconsciousness consumed her, and when the birds burst into their joyous chorus at daybreak, the curled figure, as insensible as if in a coma, stirred not at all.

Ben stood in the cabin doorway, looking down at the sleeping figure before him. Why had he not envisaged this? Had he really thought she would allow him to walk away from her, from the love they had both declared, without a word of farewell? Without a word of explanation? He had been miserably afraid to give her either, and now that piece of cowardice had led to God only knew what complications — complications that he could ill afford. What excuse had she made for her disappearance this time? Or had she simply slipped away in the night? Maybe, so long as she went home within a few hours, no irreparable damage would have been done.

He knelt down beside her, laying a hand on her shoulder, but he realized instantly that it would take more ferocious methods than he was prepared to use to bring her out of this sleep. She was dead to the world, her breathing slow, her body heavy in total relaxation. Ben sighed in resignation and scooped her up off the ground. Not by so much as a flicker of an eyelash did she indicate any consciousness of her changed position. He carried her into the cabin and placed her on the bed, unwrapping the cloak. When he saw the doeskin tunic, he cursed with soft violence as the implications of her chosen dress became clear: Bryony had not come simply to say farewell.

Ben's lips tightened as he anticipated the upcoming confrontation. He tossed the sheet over her and left the cabin, picking up the kettle before going down to the creek. Bryony was so damnably obstinate that he didn't imagine for one minute that she would accept the inevitable with graceful resignation. But he didn't want to part with her in anger; better the clean break he had intended when he had left her father's house — even though cowardice had informed his intention — than acrimony souring the memories. He filled the kettle and returned to the glade, where he lit the fire and began to prepare breakfast. Bryony had a long walk ahead of her back to the Williamsburg road, and he himself had a march of several days through the forest in order to reach Paul Tyler's plantation unobserved. It was much quicker by river, but the water highway was too well used; he could not risk being seen now that he had come out into the open and Benedict Clare was an identifiable figure in the area.

Bryony woke abruptly with a surge of panic. She lay blinking in the dim light of the cabin until consciousness returned fully, bringing recognition of her surroundings and the realization that Ben must have put her to bed.

She swung herself off the bed but found that her body seemed drugged with sleep, her head muzzy. She sat on the bed with a flop and struggled to collect herself. How long had she slept? The smell of wood smoke drifted through the unshuttered window with the unmistakable aroma of bacon. If Benedict was cooking breakfast, then it must still be early. Bryony stood up again, discovered her strength returned, and made for the door.

"Ben, we should leave here soon." She spoke even as she stepped out into the clearing, brushing her tousled hair away from her face. She peered anxiously up at the sky, where the sun was climbing rapidly. Her letter would have been discovered by now.

"Yes, you must retrace your steps," Ben stated with soft decisiveness. "As soon as you have had coffee and breakfast, lass, that is exactly what you are going to do."

Bryony felt the last vestiges of weariness drop from her limbs, the muzziness leave her brain. "No, I am not," she said with a calm firmness to match his. Squatting down beside the hearth, she helped herself to coffee and drank deeply, feeling its revivifying warmth lick her muscles back to life. "I am coming with you. Your cause is my cause, and I will fight for it beside you."

"Don't be absurd." Ben was not, at this point, too alarmed. He had expected as much, and it did not occur to him for one minute that he would fail to prevail in the end. He cut two slabs of wheaten bread, laid several thick rashers of bacon between them, and handed her the substantial sandwich. "Quite apart from the fact that Miss Bryony Paget's destiny does not lie with that of a vagrant with a war to fight and no future beyond that war, a battleground is no place for a woman."

"You are quite mistaken," Bryony informed him, placidly chewing. "It doesn't matter who or what you are now or may become, my destiny is bound inextricably with yours. And women have always followed armies, anyway. I fail to see why this one should be any different."

Benedict began to feel the first hint of apprehension. Bryony's assurance was so absolute. "Finish your breakfast and get on your way. I am leaving as soon as I have closed up the cabin."

"Good," she said. "Shall I put out the fire? The sooner we are away from here, the better, I think." Still munching her sandwich, she stood up and reached for the kettle, tipping its contents onto the glowing embers.

"Bryony, you are *not* coming with me!" He took her by the shoulders, his fingers gripping with painful intent. "We have to say farewell, here and now, and go our separate ways. We have always known that this is the way it would be in the end." His voice softened. "Do not make it more difficult, lass, than it must be."

"It is not going to be at all difficult," Bryony responded. "There will be no farewell. I love you and I cannot envisage my life without you, therefore I am coming with you. You don't quite understand how it must be, but you will soon, I am certain of it — once you have recovered from the events of the last two days and can see matters clearly again. At the moment, you must trust me to know what is best for us both."

Benedict's jaw dropped at this lecture delivered with such utter composure. "I will *not* take you!" was all he could think of to say.

"I am not asking you to *take* me," Bryony pointed out carefully. "I am coming of my own free will, assuming responsibility for myself and my decisions."

"You naive little baby," he said with a scornful crack of laughter. "How can you possibly take responsibility for yourself in such circumstances? Apart from those six weeks you spent with me, you have never done so much as tie your own shoelaces."

Bryony flushed. "That is not entirely true," she said in a low voice. "But even if it is, I will learn. I will not be a burden to you, and I will never interfere with what you see as your duty during this war. When it is over, then we will decide what we must do."

Benedict came to the desperate realization that, short of tying her to a tree in the clearing and leaving her to the wolves, he was helpless to prevent her following him if she insisted. He could, however, ensure that her following was short-lived. Shrugging, he released her shoulders. "Please yourself." He strode into the cabin, leaving Bryony, somewhat surprised at the ease of her victory, to finish her breakfast.

She took the pots and dishes to the creek to wash them, and when she returned, Ben was standing outside the cabin, his sea chest at his feet, cleaning a flintlock pistol. His musket stood ready against the cabin wall, and his clasp knife hung in a sheath at his belt. Bryony noted this overt display of instruments of death. She would have to become accustomed to much more than displays as she embraced her chosen destiny. Maybe Benedict would not survive the war he had to fight; if he did not, Bryony could not begin to imagine what would happen to her. She somehow did not think she would wish to continue living in such a circumstance. She had cast her past aside; abandoned the duties and allegiances she owed those who loved her; and, stripped of all outside supports, dependent only on her own untried strengths, she was embarking on an uncharted future.

Benedict ignored her. He thrust the pistol into his belt, checked the latch on the cabin door, slung the musket over one shoulder, and hoisted the chest onto his other. One last quick glance around the clearing to satisfy himself that there were no identifying traces of his occupancy, and he loped off into the trees at the rear of the cabin, his stride long and easy despite the weight he carried.

Bryony picked up her bundle of clothes with the little velvet pouch of jewelry and followed in his wake.

# Chapter 16

Throughout the day, Benedict strode ahead, whistling to himself occasionally, apparently oblivious of the figure trotting along behind him. At sundown, he shot a pheasant and made camp on the bank of a creek. Bryony watched as he plucked the bird and set it to roast over the fire on a spit he had fashioned from three sticks. She was not invited to draw close to the fire, and it dawned on her that neither was she going to be invited to join him at his supper. To her supreme irritation, this realization brought tears pricking behind her eyelids. She was famished after the long day's march, exhausted, and much in need of a little comforting attention. But none was forthcoming from Benedict Clare, who clearly intended to starve her into submission.

Well, she had told him that she could look after herself, that she would not be dependent upon him in any way, and he had mocked her. Now she was going to have to prove that she could. The determination stiffened her backbone, and she cast a glance about her for something edible. She found sorrel and watercress — the latter a little bitter, but beggars could hardly be choosers.

It was a cheerless supper and did remarkably little to satisfy a hunger that grew intense as the rich aroma of roasting pheasant filled the evening air. When Benedict, with callous indifference to the salivating spectator, pulled the bird apart with his fingers and set to, Bryony discovered that the contemplation of murder produced remarkably few guilt feelings. His meal completed, Ben rinsed his fingers in the creek, tidied his belongings in customary methodical fashion, and lay down by the dying fire, his head pillowed on his cloak. Not so much as a glance had he directed toward his unwanted companion since leaving the cabin that morning, and it was a bereft and forlorn Bryony who finally fell asleep under the stars, on the outskirts of the charmed circle from which she had been so clearly ostracized.

After a restless night, she woke with the first bird call, chilled by the dew, her muscles, accustomed only to feather softness in the last months, stiff and cramped from their unyielding mattress. There was no sign of Ben, and for a second blind terror engulfed her at the thought of finding herself abandoned in the middle of nowhere. Then she saw that his belongings were still neatly stacked and the fire had been rekindled. Was he going to cook something for breakfast? she thought longingly. He'd certainly be making coffee, and at this moment Bryony thought she would sacrifice anything for a cup of that hot, reviving liquid.

When she returned from a necessary trip into the woods, Ben was squatting by the fire, the aroma of coffee almost visible, so tangible was it to her starved senses. Would he give her some if she asked? But even when she approached him across the dew-laden grass, he did not look up or acknowledge her presence by so much as a ripple of a muscle. Pride, Bryony found, was not easily defeated; she could not bring herself to beg. She turned away, going down to the creek, where she splashed her face and drank the cold, cheerless water. She imagined that she was parched in the desert, tormented by thirst and only water could satisfy her — certainly hot, strong coffee would not do so! Another handful of cress served as nourishment while Bryony tried to convince herself that there were many members of the animal kingdom who thrived on a vegetarian diet. The thought that perhaps nature had designed them differently to accommodate such eating habits was not helpful and was summarily dismissed. Variety was clearly the answer. On the march today, she would hunt and gather as Ben had taught her. Yesterday, she had made no provision for her food because it had not occurred to her that Benedict was capable of such heartlessness. Now that she knew the depths of which he was capable, she would be prepared.

Benedict stamped out the fire, stowed away the simple utensils he had used, and cast a final glance around, managing a covert inspection of Bryony, who was standing by the trees, idly examining her fingernails, to all intents and purposes waiting patiently for him to make a move. He was conscious of his admiration for her, despite his anger, which showed no signs of abating. How much longer could she hold out? He had thought when she had approached him and the coffeepot that she was about to throw in the towel. But she was made of sterner stuff than he had anticipated, and Benedict Clare was obliged to admit that he was made of weaker stuff than he had anticipated. He was finding it remarkably difficult to continue with his plan.

The day grew hot and muggy, and the dense forest permitted little movement of air. Sweat stung Bryony's eyes and itched beneath her tunic as she plodded doggedly in Ben's footsteps. Her handkerchief, knotted at four corners, made a makeshift basket for her plunder of nuts and berries collected along the walk. Bryony was not entirely sure how many of them were edible, but Ben's pace was too fast to allow her time to examine before she picked, so she could only hope that when they stopped for the night she would find some in her little store that were at least palatable.

This solitary marching through the backwoods could not continue indefinitely, she told herself whenever her determination showed signs of weakening. At some point, they would come to a place where civilized things happened and where food and drink of an ordinary kind would be readily available to one who would be as prepared to steal as to buy, if that were the only means available. At some point, Benedict was going to have to accept the need to talk. . . . So her thoughts ran on wishfully throughout an interminable, wretchedly uncomfortable day.

The most extraordinary cacophony broke into her miserable trance toward late afternoon, and her head shot up from her intense concentration on her feet's progress along the weed-infested path through the thick undergrowth. Benedict had stopped dead on the path, and she almost ran into him, pulling herself up just in time. Facing him was a phalanx of angrily gobbling wild turkeys, their tails fanned, their wattles shaking. To Bryony's inexperienced eye, they looked most ferocious and certainly sounded it. She stepped back involuntarily. Then Ben, incredibly, put his burdens on the ground and swooped on the foremost bird, tucked it beneath one arm, and wrung its neck.

It was over in an instant, the bird hanging suddenly limp, its neck at an odd angle. Its companions, in sudden panic, scattered, gobbling wildly, and Benedict thrust the dead turkey into his game bag, slung that and his musket over his shoulder, hefted his sea chest, and strode through the bewildered birds, shooing them out of his path. Bryony, still stunned, remained immobile on the path before realizing that the turkeys were re-forming between herself and Ben. With a choked gasp, she plunged into the midst of the crowd, felt them, feathery and warm against her bare legs, felt the sharp peck of a beak, and cursed Benedict Clare with all her might.

Her resentment became overpowering when she realized that Ben was going to cook and eat alone a catch big enough to feed six. He had chosen for his campsite a small glade where a pretty little stream ran limpid and musical over rock and sand. Bryony settled herself some distance from his fire, dabbling her hot, tired feet in the cool, crystal-clear water, and tried not to watch as the bird was prepared. He quartered it and set legs and wings to broil on hot, flat stones over the fire. Presumably, it was quicker that way, she thought glumly, and Benedict must be sharp set after such a long and strenuous day. She, herself, was beginning to feel a little light-headed, but dwelling on the sensation did not help matters in the slightest, so she turned her attention resolutely to the spoils in her handkerchief.

An idea glimmered wickedly as she picked through the assortment of nuts and berries, identifying those she was certain were edible, her nostrils all the while assailed by the luscious aromas of roasting fowl. There was one way to get Ben's attention.

"Is it these berries that look like blueberries that are actually nightshade?" she mused in carrying tones, raising one of the small bright berries to her lips. In no more than the beat of a bird's wing, she was nursing her red, smarting hand, gazing indignantly at her hoard of nuts and berries scattered to the four winds under the force of Benedict's forestalling slap. "That was my dinner!" she reproached, glaring up into his black eyes. "It took me all day to collect those."

"Your father has a great deal to answer for!" Ben pronounced savagely, seizing a thick swatch of hair at the nape of her neck and yanking her to her feet. "Unfortunately, I fear that it is too late to rectify his errors!" Maintaining his grip on her hair, he propelled her across to the fire. "You are the most ill-conditioned, obstinate girl it has ever been my misfortune to meet!" A hard hand on her shoulder pushed her to the ground, and Bryony, well satisfied with this turn of events, sat down.

Ben went over to her original spot and picked through the scattered berries. Gathering some in the palm of his hand, he came back and sat on his haunches on the far side of the fire, glowering at her. "You did not eat any of these?"

"You didn't give me a chance," Bryony said, managing to sound aggrieved. "I am so hungry, I couldn't care whether they are damsons, blueberries, or nightshade."

Benedict sighed, accepting defeat. He tossed the dusky purple berries away. "They are nightshade, as you knew."

Bryony drew her knees up and hugged them, her chin resting atop them as she regarded Benedict quizzically. "You will not be rid of me, Ben. I shall always be beside you, closer than your shadow." She spoke in the same quietly confident tones of yesterday morning, and Ben, reflecting on her performance since then, began to believe it.

"Do you not understand that I do not want you?" he demanded, searching for the most cruelly blunt words of rejection he could find. "I do not want you." He stood up, towering over her as if to reinforce his statement.

"You do not love me?" she asked, seemingly unmoved.

"Love you!" cried Benedict. "What has love to do with it? I am a man who must walk alone, do you understand that?"

"Why?" Her eyes held his unwaveringly. "Because of your past? Because you are ashamed of having been a bondsman? That does not matter to me."

Ben paled beneath his suntan. "It does not matter to *you* — an idealistic, fanciful, privileged girl with her head in the clouds." He laughed, a bitter sound in the quiet forest. "You know nothing of the world, Miss Paget. You have known nothing but indulgence, sheltered by wealth and love from the distasteful realities of the world. You do not know what you are talking about, but I tell you now — it may not matter to you, but do you dare imagine that it does not matter to *me?*"

The angry, bitter words punched her, each one with the power of a body blow, propelled by the depth of an emotion that she had been appallingly guilty of failing first to predict and then to perceive. She didn't know how to apologize for such insensitivity as the full horror became manifest. The Benedict Clare that she knew was a proud man, assured and confident in everything he did. He moved with all the hauteur of one born to an ancient lineage — and he had belonged, in servitude, to a swinish drunkard.

God alone knew what hell he had endured, above and beyond the torture that she knew of, and slowly, on the edges of her soul, she sensed the monster of degradation. Her mind filled with the images of slavery, images that had been an intrinsic part of her life, unquestioned by her or by anyone else that she knew. Benedict had experienced that condition, and the fact that she knew it, could imagine what he had become in that dreadful time, had driven this wedge between them.

She looked up at him with haunted eyes and saw only a twisted mockery in the flat black orbs above, watching as her thoughts played, undisguised, across her countenance.

"Not a pretty picture, is it?" he said in a voice as dry as dust. "Now, perhaps, you understand why I walk alone."

The words of denial rose to her lips, but she swallowed them. Too much pain had been revealed in the last minutes to allow for repetition of her own unmitigated defiance of his determination. Later, after quiet reflection had increased her understanding, she would return to fight the battle on which their love depended. She understood so much more now, but still not everything. Why and how had a Clare become a bondsman in the first place?

441

What heinous crime had he committed for such a sentence to be passed on an aristocrat? And even a bondsman's past did not truly explain that puzzling, unfocused hatred that she had felt so often and that he had said had nothing specifically to do with her. He loathed everything her father stood for, but she would swear that Sir Edward was not simply tarred with Roger Martin's brush. There was something else.

After a minute, when it became clear that Bryony was not going to respond, Ben turned his attention to the rapidly crisping turkey. "You will find dock leaves by that patch of nettles," he said matter-of-factly. "Bring me some that we may use to hold the meat. It's too hot for bare hands."

It was an instruction of a kind that she had received often enough in the past, delivered in much the same tones. To that extent, it offered reassurance, but reassurance that Bryony suspected was false. She brought the leaves and obeyed the curt order to fill the kettle at the stream so that water for coffee could heat while they ate.

"Eat slowly," Ben adjured, passing her a leaf-wrapped drumstick. "I don't wish you to be sick. The meat is rich, and you have not eaten properly since yesterday morning."

As if she was unaware of that fact, thought Bryony with a flash of ordinary irritation. Her mouth filled with saliva as she looked at the succulent leg, steam rising from the charred, crisp skin. Her tongue ran over her lips and she cast Ben a quick glance. He was smiling unconsciously and her heart flipped. But his expression became stern and forbidding the minute he caught her eye, and Bryony, pretending that she had not noticed that momentary softening, took a large bite of turkey.

A full belly was a miraculous possession, she thought, half an hour later, wiping turkey grease from her chin with the dock leaf. She never would have realized how miraculous if she had not experienced the opposite condition quite so thoroughly. There was something to be said for the appreciation — it certainly enhanced one's pleasure. The coffee that followed was the elixir of the gods but did nothing to alleviate the overpowering drowsiness that struck without warning. Her eyelids, weighted with lead, dropped, but she forced them open, staggering to her feet, hoping that action would provide sufficient stimulus to avert the threatening unconsciousness. Somehow, she managed to wash the beakers, but all the cold-water splashing in the world could not infuse her drugged limbs with life.

"What on earth are you doing?" Benedict pulled her up as she knelt by the stream, quite unable to force her limbs to perform the motions necessary to get her to her feet. Water dripped from her face and hands, dampening her tunic. "You're dead on your feet. Go and sleep by the fire."

Bryony shook her head. "I am afeard to sleep."

"Why should you be so, lass?" It was suddenly the old Ben speaking. "I am here. Nothing is going to harm you."

Bryony gnawed her lip and spoke with some difficulty. "I am so tired that I am afraid I will not be able to waken when you leave in the morning."

There was a moment's silence, then Ben said roughly, "I will not leave you here, and I do not deserve that you should believe such a thing of me. Now, go to sleep!" He gave her a shove in the direction of the fire, and Bryony stumbled over, too exhausted for further argument. It seemed an eternity since she had last enjoyed a full night's sleep. Her cheek pillowed on her hand, her body curled toward the comforting glow of the embers, she passed into dreamless slumber.

Benedict lay down beside her, arms flung above his head as he gazed up at the wedge of night sky revealed in the opening of the trees. By noon tomorrow, they would reach Tyler's plantation, and he would ask Paul's help in returning Bryony to Sir Edward. It was not going to be an easy request. And it would not be an easy parting, either. Bryony, beside him, suddenly moaned softly and rolled over into the hollow of his shoulder. Quite insensible, she had traveled in her sleep like a bee returning to its hive; feeling the familiar warmth and shape and automatically cuddling in the remembered fashion. With a little self-mocking smile, Ben moved his arm to enfold her, adjusting her warm, malleable limbs against him. Her hair brushed his chin, and the scent of her filled his nostrils — a scent composed of earth and sweat and the eternal richness of her skin. He smiled again, but it was a pleasanter smile, as he thought of the different vision this Bryony presented from the elegant young lady, exuding rose-water fragrance, rustling in satin and lace. And he didn't think he would be able to state a preference if such a choice were ever demanded of him.

Benedict fell asleep eventually, as determined as ever to pursue the course he had laid down for them both. They would part painfully, it was true, but as friends, and Bryony now understood much that had been hidden from her. That understanding would surely ease the parting and resign her to accept the inevitable.

Bryony woke to the smell of coffee and the most wonderful sense of bodily ease. Even though Ben was no longer beside her, the shape and feel of him remained imprinted on her body, and she knew that he had held her throughout the night. She stretched and yawned luxuriously, before hitching herself onto one elbow and regarding him sleepily. "I give you good day, sir."

"Good morrow, lass." Ben smiled at her over the lip of his beaker. "I was beginning to think you would sleep forever. If you wish to have time for breakfast, you had better see to your ablutions with all speed."

Bryony got to her feet and stretched again, feeling her muscles expand as she breathed deeply of the fresh morning air, which was as clear and heady as champagne. "Am I not to receive a good-morning kiss, Mr. Clare?" she teased, going over to him and dropping onto her haunches beside him.

Benedict kissed the tip of her nose lightly. "Hurry up, now."

"That was not a kiss," she protested, putting her arms around his neck. "*This* is a kiss." It promised to be a remarkably thorough demonstration until Ben broke her hold abruptly and took her face between his hands.

"It will only make matters worse, lass," he told her gravely. "In a few hours we must part, and I cannot bear to be reminded so powerfully of what is now finished."

Bryony's mouth set, then she shrugged and stood up. "I will go and wash." She took her time over her preparations, her mind trying to separate and order the ideas jostling for precedence. It did not seem sensible to confront Ben prematurely, here in the forest. She didn't know the destination that was to bring the parting of the ways, and she didn't know how Ben intended to leave her. Presumably, he intended making some provision for her return home, but Bryony couldn't begin to imagine how a self-styled vagrant, moving undercover to join the American forces, could possibly do such a thing. When she understood his plan, then she would be better able to counteract it.

They walked in silence, but it was not a hostile silence today; rather, it was one indicative of their absorption with private thoughts. When the forest quite suddenly gave way to a stretch of meadowland, Benedict halted, waiting for her to come up beside him. "We walk for about two miles in the open now," he informed her. "We will reach the house from the back."

"Whose house?" Bryony peered into the distance, but the sun was too bright for her to see very far ahead.

"A friend of mine," Ben told her without expansion.

"A Patriot?"

At that he chuckled. "What do you think, Miss Paget?"

"A Patriot," she stated. "Will he assist you in joining up with General Gates?"

"I trust so." Ben set off across the meadow. "I need a horse, that is all." And a little help in restoring Miss Bryony Paget to her own, he added silently.

"Does he have a name, this Patriot?" Bryony pressed, half running to keep up with him. It seemed most unjust that, loaded down though he was, he could move so much faster than she, who carried nothing but her cloak bundle.

Ben looked at her. "If he wishes you to

know it, he will tell you himself."

She shook her head at this implication that she was an unsafe confidant, but she swallowed her irritation, prepared to harbor her resources for the greater battle.

A solid two-storied brick house roofed with red pantiles came into view, set amid green lawns. There was no elaborate landscaping, though, Bryony remarked, unlike her own home, and the lawns gave way naturally to paddocks and meadowland. It seemed an affluent establishment, although not lavish — more that of a wealthy farmer than a planter.

"We will use the side door," Ben said, swinging to the right in the direction of the paved yard beside the house. Obviously, he was utterly at home in this establishment, Bryony reflected as she followed him, a prickle of unease undermining her earlier assurance. Benedict was presumably expecting some potent reinforcements to lie within doors, and one woman, even with all the determination in the world, could not hope to prevail against superior numbers.

"Ben, my friend! I have been expecting you since the news of Charleston reached us!" a deep voice boomed from the doorway, and a tall, sunburned man with a shock of white hair and powerful shoulders came into the yard with a seven-league stride.

"Paul." Ben dropped his burdens and the two embraced with a warmth that bespoke a friendship of more than ordinary depth. Bryony stood to one side, feeling slightly awkward, like an unwitting intruder, until they stepped apart and Paul Tyler noticed Ben's companion for the first time.

"And who is this?" Bushy eyebrows rose, but the question was asked in a kindly fashion, and the man's bright, intelligent eyes smiled a greeting.

"I will explain when we are alone," Ben said swiftly. "For the moment, do you have a bedchamber where she may rest? We have had a long walk."

"I am not in the least fatigued," Bryony said stoutly. "And I am not going to be shut up whilst you plan how you may manage to be rid of me, for I have told you, I do not know how many times, that I am coming with you."

"You are *not!*" exploded Ben, seeing the end of his patience looming.

"I *am!*" she reiterated just as forcefully, folding her arms and glaring at him.

"Perhaps we should repair within doors,"

Paul suggested tactfully. Intrigued though he was by this amazing scene, he was also conscious that others might find it equally fascinating, and an audience of laborers and servants was to be avoided. "Miss . . . uh . . . ?" He gestured politely to the side door.

"Paget," Bryony informed him with a firm little nod. "I am Bryony Paget." Tossing the raven-black cascade of hair over her shoulders, she marched ahead of them into the cool dimness of the house.

Ben swore under his breath. "I am going to need your help, Paul."

"Yes, I can quite see that you might," the other mused, a ripple of laughter in his voice. "As determined as her father, it would seem. That is the connection, is it not?"

"Aye," Ben agreed dourly, following Sir Edward's daughter into the house.

"Let us go into the parlor." Paul opened a door onto a sunny, front-facing room with a canvas floor covering of black and white squares. Pretty checkered curtains hung at the windows, and the couch and cushions were covered in the same material. The furniture was for the most part solid and workmanlike, with none of the elaborate carvings and inlays that characterized the European styles with which Bryony was most familiar. "Ye'll take some ale, Ben. Miss Paget, you would perhaps prefer lemonade."

"Thank you," she replied politely, taking a seat on a straight-backed chair against the wall and clasping her hands in her lap. Paul Tyler's lips twitched at this picture of patience and resolution. Ben, however, looked like a volcano on the point of eruption.

The door closed on their host, and Ben strode over to the empty hearth, staring down at the brass andirons as he brought his temper under control. Slowly, he turned back to the still figure by the wall and spoke as reasonably as he could manage. "If you are going to persist in this foolishness, Bryony, we are both going to be left with a memory that we shall always regret. Let us draw what has been between us to a graceful close."

"I am coming with you," Bryony declared simply.

As she said this, the door opened on Paul Tyler bearing a laden tray. "Ah," he said, setting the tray on an oblong cedar table. "We are back where we began, I gather."

"Since Benedict has neglected to introduce us, sir, perhaps you would be so good as to tell me whose hospitality I am accepting." Bryony took the pewter mug of lemonade with a smile of thanks.

"Paul Tyler, ma'am." Her host bowed formally. "And you are most welcome under my roof." He handed Ben a foaming tankard of ale and perched himself on the corner of the table, a smile lurking in eyes and voice. "You had better tell me the tale, children."

Bryony hid her smile at this sobriquet applied so casually to Benedict. Mr. Tyler, for all his lean strength, did look old enough to be his father, certainly. Seeing Ben for once somewhat taken aback, she decided to put her oar in first. "Benedict is going to join General Gates, taking him information about Major Ferguson's plans," she said. "I have left my home and my family to throw in my lot with Ben's. Only he is being a little difficult about it."

"And you are about to find out just how difficult I can be," Ben said dangerously. "I warned you that if you persisted in this, we would both regret it." He crossed the room, seized Bryony under the arms, and hauled her to her feet. "Paul, I would be grateful if you would direct me to a room with a key that I may turn upon this importunate woman. She will stay there until I am well on my way; then, perhaps I may count upon you to arrange for her return home."

"If you lock me up, Benedict Clare, I will jump out of the window," Bryony said fiercely. "It will not matter to me if I break my neck, since I no longer have a life apart from yours. I have severed all —"

"One minute," Paul broke in hastily, suspecting that Ben was about to resort to lamentably primitive methods to achieve his point. "Benedict, my friend, there are many around the house who would be glad to see you again. Why don't you go and greet them and leave me to talk with Miss Paget?" Although couched as a suggestion, it was an unmistakable instruction, and Bryony, who had never before heard anyone give Benedict orders, waited breathlessly in the sudden silence to see how he would take it.

His expression did not lighten but his shoulders relaxed somewhat. "Be warned, Paul, she can talk you around her little finger. But since nothing will be achieved if I lose my temper, I'll leave you to persuade her back to her senses." The door clicked shut on his departing figure, and Paul, who had not moved from his perch on the table, turned to Bryony.

"I think you began your explanation in the middle of the story, my dear. Benedict cannot have spent more than a few days in your father's house. It seems a remarkably short time for one to throw one's hat over the windmill as thoroughly as you appear to have done."

Bryony frowned. "Indeed, you are right. I will begin at the beginning. . . ."

At story's end, she said, "So, you see, Ben has always maintained that there was something about him that I could not know, and that this something made it impossible for us to have a shared future. When Roger Martin made his accusation, I finally understood the secret, but now I think it is the fact that I know what he has been through that is causing all this muddle. He is very proud." She gave him a tentative little smile. "I decided I would have to make the decision for both of us, since Ben doesn't seem to be able to see things clearly at present. It is most unmaidenly of me, is it not, sir?"

"There is little about your tale, my child, that could qualify as maidenly," Tyler said bluntly, frowning at her. "Do you know why Benedict was sent here as a bondsman?"

Bryony shook her head. "I have not

asked because I am sure he won't tell me — not yet, at least. But *I* do not care what he has done. I know what he is, and that is all that matters."

This simple statement drew a short nod from her audience. "I will not tell his secrets for him. But that is not one that should lie between you. It could create much unhappiness for you both." There was another silence while he contemplated the fact of Roger Martin's death, its manner, and the part this girl had played. It all seemed quite fitting. He said slowly, "Forgive me, but are you convinced that Ben's love for you runs as deep as yours for him?"

"But of course," she replied with calm assurance. "If I were not, I wouldn't be pursuing him in this fashion. I have given up everything, Mr. Tyler. Wounded my father so grievously that I am certain he will be unable to forgive me. That is a great loss, but I had a choice to make between losses. I made the only one possible."

Miss Paget had a head upon her shoulders older than her years, reflected Paul, pulling at his chin. He loved Benedict Clare as the son he'd never had, and in any other circumstances would have rejoiced that his son should have won the love of such a girl as this. But, unlike Bryony, he understood all the ramifications. However, if they parted at this point, they would never find each other again. If they went on together, the future was uncertain, could easily hold death for either or both of them, could hold the loss or death of their love, but it also contained the possibility of eventual happiness. The other way promised only loss. He nodded slowly, his mind made up.

"Campaigning is a dangerous activity for a woman, Bryony."

"As it is for a man." She shrugged. "I am prepared for the danger and discomforts."

That almost made him smile. He very much doubted that one as gently bred as Miss Paget could begin to imagine the discomforts of marching with an army fighting for survival.

"Will you help me?" she asked directly.

"I will not hinder you," he replied carefully, "and I will not help Ben with his plans for you. But I cannot make up his mind for him."

"Indeed you cannot." Ben spoke vigorously from the doorway. They had not heard him come in, and Bryony started, but Tyler merely nodded at him.

"Good, you are well come, Ben. Bryony

has told me her tale in some detail, and she is determined, it seems, to become a campaigner in Gates's army."

"God dammit! No!" But in spite of the force of the negative, a look of uncertainty had crept into his eyes. He had not, for one minute, imagined that his dearest friend would fail to take his part in this. "It is quite impossible."

"Why is it impossible?" asked Bryony. "I will not be in your way. And I can keep up with you. Women have followed armies since men first went to war."

"Camp followers, maybe," Ben growled. "That is not a role you will play."

"No, I think it would be best if you regularized your arrangement before you left here," Paul agreed calmly. "Pastor Williams will be glad to perform the ceremony."

Benedict paled and spoke with soft intensity. "You know why I could never be wedded with a Paget, Paul."

Before the other man could reply, Bryony spoke up. "I do not know why you cannot, but it doesn't matter. I am no longer a Paget. I have severed those ties and bear the name in name only. Your cause is mine, love. Whatever future is in wait for you, I will share. I have no other."

Benedict looked helplessly at Paul. "What am I to do?"

"If you love her, Ben, the answer seems simple enough."

Ben studied Bryony as she sat in her tunic, her hair tumbled about her shoulders, her face set, the pansy-blue eyes meeting his gaze with fearless clarity. What she wanted was insane. She could not wed a traitor, a vagrant, a soldier of fortune with a legacy of hatred for those like her father who were destroying his homeland — a legacy that she could not begin to understand, never having acknowledged that part of her heritage. But, dear God, he did love her; would count himself thrice blessed if he could spend some part of his life with her, could postpone the parting. For love of him, she had cut herself off from every support, had yielded herself totally to whatever passions drove him, prepared to embrace them as her own. A feeling of awe at the monumental decision, at the enormity of the sacrifice that she had made for love of him, filled him with a slow sweetness. He had no right to reject the offering, and no desire to do it, at all.

Into the silence, Paul spoke, as if accurately reading the other man's thoughts. "You cannot take her unwed, Benedict."

It was true, Ben knew. If he accepted what she was so freely offering, he must do so honorably, must offer her the legal and moral supports she had relinquished when she had followed him. He would tie her to a traitor, as he would tie himself to a family who abused the land and people for whom he had forsaken his freedom, and for whom his friends had given their lives. It was a bitter thought, a secret bitterness that he must hold tight within him, for its revelation could only hurt Bryony more deeply than he had yet wounded her.

"Come then," he said, holding out his hand. "If you will throw in your lot with a vagrant who has neither family nor fortune to protect you, then so be it. You come in freedom, and if ever you choose to leave, it will be in the same way. I will not hinder you, should you ever remember that passion makes a poorer master than reason."

"I have not forgotten it," she said softly. "Nevertheless, I will go where passion drives." She placed her hand in his.

"And I, also," he replied, his fingers closing over hers. "We will take that road together."

# Chapter 17

"Vainglorious fool!" pronounced Benedict Clare, several weeks later, fastening the strap of his saddlebags with a vicious tug.

"What has he done this time?" Bryony was in no doubt as to who had earned Ben's derision. General Horatio Gates, since winning the Battle of Saratoga three years previously, seemed to believe that he was invincible, much to the dismay of the officers and troops under his command.

"He intends taking a shortcut to meet Cornwallis at Camden," Ben spat. "And the road lies through a —"

"Anyone home?" a cheery voice hailed as a chubby, rosy-cheeked young man pushed through the tent flap. "The smells coming from this region tell me it's dinnertime." He beamed at Bryony. "What has the hunter caught for us today?"

"You are a scavenger, Charlie Carter," Bryony accused with a chuckle. "You have your own mess tent."

"But it never produces victuals like

yours," Charlie replied with truth. "The commissary is all to pieces, and no one has Ben's skill with the knife and the musket."

"They could always take the trouble to learn," Ben said shortly, bent double in the confined space as he stacked the saddlebags against the tent wall. Charlie's eyebrows shot up at the curt tone, and he looked to Bryony for enlightenment.

She smiled slightly. "Ben is in a temper because General Gates wants to take a shortcut to Camden. And I imagine he would not listen to Ben's impeccable advice, delivered, I would suppose, in his customary uncompromising language."

"It is no laughing matter!" Ben exclaimed. "And I'll thank you to be a little more respectful to your commanding officer, madam."

Bryony, who was already kneeling on the tent floor, bowed her head in elaborate obeisance. "I crave pardon, your high and mightiness, for forgetting my place. One must not make mock of a newly appointed colonel." Her voice quivered with mischievous laughter, and Ben, his eyes dancing, seized the heavy black braid hanging down her back and yanked her head up.

"Disrespectful hoyden," he scolded. "It is fortunate that my sense of consequence is sufficiently great to withstand your raillery."

Bryony, laughing helplessly, flung her arms around his neck and kissed him, blithely paying no heed to their audience. Charlie, however, was well accustomed to these unconventional displays, as, indeed, were all the officers in the First Virginia Brigade. The unorthodox couple had caused a few raised eyebrows in the early days, but Benedict Clare had rapidly won the respect and admiration of his fellows, to whom it seemed there was nothing he could not do better than anyone else. A natural modesty and an easy manner had completed the charm. As for his lady, and she was undoubtedly a lady, for all the oddity of her present lifestyle, it had taken little more than that warm smile, the ready laughter, the friendly willingness to listen to woes and fancies, to win her an undisputed place in the brigade. She also had one skill that was much appreciated by men and officers alike. When Benedict Clare, who did not suffer fools gladly or otherwise, was put out, life could be most unpleasant, but his wife could generally be relied upon to tease him back to good humor — a skill she had just demonstrated to perfection.

"Ben, have you heard what that infernal

idiot intends to do?" The exasperated question heralded the arrival of a lanky redhead who crawled into the crowded tent without waiting for invitation. "Oh, hello, Charlie, might have guessed you'd be here. It's suppertime, isn't it?"

"Go and stir the stew, lass," Ben said. "We have guests, it would seem."

"Well, someone else will have to provide the ale," Bryony declared. "We have but a half barrel left after the last party."

"I can supply cider," John Davidson, the new arrival, offered. "Managed to buy it off a farmer."

"*Buy* it?" Bryony scoffed. "When did you ever pay for anything, John?"

They all chuckled. The young cavalry officer was well-known for his foraging abilities, which more often than not crossed the fine line of legality. "This I paid for," he lamented. "Miserly old codger couldn't be persuaded to donate the butt in the interests of the health and spirits of the American army, and he didn't take his eyes off me until we rode out of there, so there was no hope of slipping it out."

Ben sniffed the air suddenly. "Bryony! If that stew burns, I shall hold you responsible!"

She rushed out of the tent to where an

iron pot hung over the fire, aromatic steam curling in the gathering dusk. It was summer and game was plentiful, although keeping an army of three thousand adequately provisioned in the Carolina back country was no easy task. She prodded the contents of the pot with a metal spoon, glad that the long hours of slow cooking had reduced the brace of squirrel, and the other unidentifiable furry creature that Ben had tossed in, to innocuous chunks of good-smelling meat.

It was a warm, midgy night, the air filled with the scents of crushed grass and wood smoke from other campfires. The force was camped on a hillside, and almost as far as she could see were tents and bivouacs, voices raised in altercation or laughter carrying through the gloom. It was a strange life, campaigning, but Bryony had long ceased to question or examine the circumstances of her daily life. For, as long as she had Ben, the old laughing, loving Benedict, she wanted for nothing — except, occasionally, news of those she had left behind. When the ache rose, and her mind was filled with thoughts of her parents, of Francis, of how they were faring, she forced them away, reminding herself that she had made her choice and had accepted the consequences with open eyes.

A violent oath from the tent behind her shook her out of her reverie. "I do not believe it, John!" Ben catapulted through the tent opening, his two comrades following. "This time he has got to listen to me. It's suicide!"

"Ben, what on earth's the matter? Where are you going?" Bryony reached up and grabbed the tail of his coat. "The stew is ready."

"Save some for me," he said brusquely.

Bryony hung on to his coat. "Tell me what is the matter. It can't be so imperative that you can't eat your supper first."

Ben looked down at her where she was kneeling, still clutching his coat. "I think I am the best judge of that, lass."

Bryony bit her bottom lip and let him go. Ben accepted her teasing, asked for her advice frequently, always listened when she offered an opinion, but he would not tolerate unwarranted interference, and when he had made up his mind about something, there was nothing she could say to alter it. He walked off and she turned her attention back to the stew.

"I'll go and fetch the cider," John said. "Ben'll be in need of it when he comes back."

"It's Gates again," Charlie informed Bryony, squatting beside the fire. "He's going to take this shortcut to Camden through a damn swamp infested with Tories, and John says he intends doing it at night!"

Bryony absorbed this news in silence. She needed no expansion to understand Ben's fury. A forced night march through enemy-held territory would weaken the inexperienced force dreadfully and would hardly equip them to face Cornwallis's disciplined, fresh troops. But Gates would not take into consideration the fact that his soldiers were green troops for the most part, unused to fire, not yet broken in to army discipline. He saw only that he had vastly superior numbers to Cornwallis, and, after all, he had won a magnificent victory against the British three years before, so his own prowess as commander was proven beyond question.

She ladled the stew into bowls, and the three of them sat around the fire making desultory conversation while they ate, all of them imagining the scene in the general's tent. Ben was not one to mince his words, and it was only the fact that Gates relied upon him absolutely that had saved him from charges of insubordination on countless occasions. He came back after half an hour, his eyes blazing.

"Damned murdering lunatic!" He took the flagon of cider and drank deeply before passing it back to John. "Told me that if I did not wish to risk myself in such a venture, he would excuse me from participating!" He took the bowl Bryony handed him without acknowledgment, but she was not about to insist upon the courtesies.

"When is this march to take place?"

Ben sighed wearily and let the unconstructive anger run away from him. "Tomorrow night. And I don't know what in God's name I am to do with you."

Bryony stared. "Whatever do you mean?"

"I mean, lass, that I do not want you on that march, but I do not see how I can leave you behind since Gates is intending to take the entire force. You will have to travel in the rear with the baggage and supplies."

"The *hell* I will!" exclaimed Sir Edward Paget's daughter with all a trooper's vigor. "I'll not travel with the pack mules."

A stunned silence fell over the little group, and Bryony — with a shudder — heard her voice repeating the oath in her head. The words had just popped out of her mouth. She heard them all the time — that word and many worse. It was hardly surprising that she should slip up once in a while.

"Well, I think it's time to turn in," Charlie said with unconvincing carelessness. "That was an excellent supper."

"Aye, indeed it was," concurred John heartily, following Charlie's example and getting to his feet.

"Stay and finish the cider," Bryony said hastily, shaking the flagon. "It is silly to leave this small drop." The pretext fooled no one. Although Benedict had said not a word, they were all well aware that he was simply biding his time until their guests had left. Bryony watched them go, wondering whether to allow the storm to break or to attempt to avert it. The choice, however, was not given her.

"How dare you say such a thing!" Ben demanded almost before the others were out of earshot. "Don't you ever let me hear such language on your tongue again!"

"Oh, pah!" Bryony found herself returning the fire before she had time to consider whether a meek apology would have been a sounder tactic. "Don't be such a self-righteous hypocrite. We are not in my mother's drawing room."

"It's at times like this when I bitterly regret having removed you from that place,"

Ben snapped. "You seem to have forgotten every vestige of decent conduct."

"May I remind you, Mr. Clare, that *you* were not responsible for my leaving my mother's drawing room," she said icily. "In fact, if you'd had your way, I would still be there, and I do not grant you the right to be arbiter of my behavior or my language, even if you are my husband."

Ben's eyes narrowed on a sudden wicked gleam. "My old nurse used to wash our mouths out with soap when we came into the house with stable talk," he mused thoughtfully. "It was remarkably effective, as I recall, and the old remedies are frequently the best." He rose to his feet in a deceptively leisured manner that did not fool Bryony for one instant.

"Ben! Don't you dare!" She gathered up her calico skirts and fled, skipping over guy ropes with desperate agility, hearing him pound after her, and knowing that she could not evade capture for long. The chase drew laughing comment from those around, as well as a few ribald remarks. Bryony veered into a small copse on the outskirts of the camp, where whatever should ensue when she was caught would at least take place in privacy. She tripped over a tree root and fell, sobbing for breath, onto the mossy ground.

"It was not so very bad," she protested in laughing defense, as Ben walked slowly toward her. "I could have said much worse. And it is a little absurd of you to object like some high stickler for decorum, under the circumstances. I am marching with an army."

"John and Charlie were deeply shocked, nevertheless," he said, although his eyes sparkled merrily. "Have you hurt yourself with that tumble?"

"Yes," Bryony said wickedly. "I think I have broken my ankle, and it's all your fault."

He dropped to the ground beside her. "Let me see."

"That is not my ankle," Bryony protested faintly as his hand slipped up the inside of her leg, pushing up her skirt.

"Is it not?" inquired Ben in wide-eyed innocence, flattening his palm against the inside of one thigh, parting her legs. "For thirty years I have thought it was!"

A soft moan escaped her, and she fell back on the grass as his fingers whispered over the cambric of her drawers, teasing the exquisite sensitivity with a warm, knowing friction through the thin material.

"Take them off," he demanded, drawing

back for a minute, lifting his hand from her with almost demonic knowingness the instant before she was about to slide over the edge of bliss, so that she lay, taut with arousal, suspended in joy, needing completion, yet lost in expectant glory. His eyes were hooded, an expression of determined intensity on his face as he looked down at her body, her skirt rucked up around her waist, legs sprawled in wanton abandonment. "Take them off," he repeated, unfastening his britches. "I want you *now*."

Her tongue ran over her lips, her muscles tensed under the powerful wave of passion swamping her at the rough statement, at the revelation of the hard shaft springing from the base of his flat belly in vigorous readiness. She fumbled with the string at her waist, then raised her hips from the grass as she pushed off the offending garment. Ben did not take his eyes from her — neither did he help her, just knelt over her supine figure, waiting with every sign of impatience. It happened like this sometimes, when his desire became invincible almost without warning. Play would cease, to be replaced with a hard, urgent ardor that demanded instant satisfaction. It was as if, sure now that they both trod the same path, Ben felt able to yield to his desire in whatever form it took. And when he needed her in this way, Bryony felt a curious self-defining power fill her, becoming inextricably, fervently entangled with her own arousal.

He came down to her, taking her mouth with a sweet savagery as in the same breath he thrust deep within her body. Bryony quivered and was instantly lost; her body, kept in suspenseful thrall, finally climaxed in shuddering release, and she cried out against his mouth. She looked up into the ebony eyes, sliding her hands around to grip his buttocks, her fingers biting into the hard muscles driving him within her, as she concentrated with every stretched nerve on Ben's progress along his own road to joy. At the right moment, she lifted her hips slightly and tightened her inner muscles around him. His face dissolved in ecstasy and he spoke her name in lingering syllables.

They lay for long minutes in the darkness on the hard, unyielding ground before Ben murmured, "I hope your ankle is cured now."

Bryony chuckled weakly. "Was that what that was, then? A novel cure for hurt ankles?"

"Well, it wasn't what I had intended when I followed you in here," Ben said, getting to his knees with a reluctant groan. "Making love was far from my mind."

"It is never far from your mind," Bryony retorted, reaching for her discarded undergarment. "Except perhaps when you are battling with General Gates."

"Did you have to remind me?" Ben tugged on his britches, a frown creasing his brow again. "You will ride at the rear tomorrow night, lass, and I don't want to hear any more nonsense."

Bryony stood up and tossed her disheveled braid over one shoulder. "If you think I am going to ride through a Tory-infested swamp in the pitch dark with only mules and sutlers for protection and company, think again. I will be a great deal safer at your side, surrounded by Charlie and John and the others. Unless it is not my safety that concerns you, and you simply wish to be rid of me." A glare accompanied the accusation.

Ben scratched his ear thoughtfully. Bryony had a point and it was one that had not occurred to him earlier. The rear of the army might be less vulnerable to attack, but it was not immune, and in such an event she would be lamentably short of protection. He shrugged and in customary fashion yielded gracefully. "I think you have the right of it. However, I must have your promise that you will do as I bid you, instantly and without question, throughout the march and the engagement. I cannot afford to be distracted with argument or unnecessary worry."

"I am yours to command, Colonel Clare," she said, grinning in the dark. "You will find me perfectly obedient."

"I wish I could be as lighthearted, lass," Ben said somberly. "I have a fearful premonition about this ill-conceived business."

Bryony shuddered, all desire to laugh leaving her instantly. "What do you think will happen?"

"Defeat at best, a rout at worst," he replied succinctly. "Cornwallis has a highly trained, disciplined band of regulars with him. And there's no knowing how our men will react under fire, particularly if they are weakened by fatigue and panicked by skirmishes during a night march."

Bryony swallowed. Knowing that she must not add to his burdens with her own weakness, she controlled the urge to cling to him, to beg him not to take part in this exercise in which he had no faith, to ask him what would happen to her if he should be killed.

If Ben sensed her fear and uncertainty, he gave no indication of it. But when they reached their tent and the straw palliasse that Bryony now considered to be as comfortable as any featherbed, he wrapped her in his arms, surrounding her with the warm reassurance of his body so that she fell asleep, convinced for the moment of the safety and continuity of their little corner of a world riven by turmoil and conflict.

The following day, chaos became manifest as an army, three thousand strong, broke camp and prepared to meet the enemy. Small groups of men were being drilled about the hillside while others milled around, taking down tents, loading up the wagons and pack mules. General Gates had set up his headquarters under a spreading beech tree, pandemonium reigning supreme around him. With him, poring over the giant map spread out on a trestle table, were Ben and three other high-ranking officers. Bryony, needing to ask Ben a question regarding their luggage, approached the group cautiously. Gates had never treated her with anything less than courtesy, but in general she endeavored to avoid bringing herself to his notice.

"The First Maryland should be in the front line," Ben was stating crisply.

"No," Horatio Gates interrupted. "They will hold the rear behind the North Carolina militia."

"And you will have untried, raw recruits in the front line?" Ben brought his fist down on the table in disgust. "If they break, they'll take the center with them."

"Sometimes, Colonel, I think you forget who is commanding this army," the general said coldly.

"General Gist? Baron de Kalb? What is your opinion?" Benedict appealed to the two veteran commanders, who were frowning over the map.

Mordecai Gist shook his head. "It's a matter of tactics. A strong rear guard or a strong front line? There are points to be made on both sides."

Bryony, deciding that now was perhaps not an opportune moment to bother Benedict with a domestic question, turned to slip away, but he caught sight of her and called her back.

"Is there something you want, lass?"

"It's not important," she said hastily. "I didn't mean to interrupt you." She smiled in hesitant apology.

"You're not interrupting anything, Mrs. Clare," boomed Gates heartily. "The matter is already decided. Perhaps you can persuade this obstinate young man that he would do well to listen to his elders."

Benedict flushed a deep crimson. "Excuse me, sir." Taking Bryony by the arm, he drew her away. "I do not know how long I am going to be able to keep my hands off him," he hissed. "What do you want?" The question was snapped, but Bryony did not take it personally.

"Why do you not just give up?" she asked. "He is determined not to heed you, so you only create aggravation for yourself."

Ben sighed, rubbing his temples wearily in a manner that tugged at Bryony's heartstrings. "I daresay you're right, but I cannot stand aside and say nothing when so many lives are at stake. Now, what is it that you wanted?"

"Only whether the portmanteaux are to go to the rear, or whether we should take them up with us." It seemed a dreadfully trivial issue in the light of Ben's wrestling with life-and-death matters. "It affects what I put in them, you see," she explained lamely. "If they are to go to the rear, I will keep some necessities out. . . . Oh, I beg

478

your pardon. I should not be bothering you with such petty problems."

Some of the tension had left Ben's face, and the corners of his mouth quirked slightly. "Let me ask you a question, lass. This is an army, marching into battle. The horses on which we shall be riding are also going to be facing the guns and bayonets. Does it strike you as reasonable that they should also be weighted down with cooking pots and clean clothes and sheets and —"

"Oh, do stop!" Bryony begged, flushing to the roots of her hair at this absurd image. "I didn't think of that."

He tipped her chin with a long forefinger, saying seriously, although with a smile, "Next time you have a question of such a nature, think around it a little. I am sure you will come up with the answer yourself."

"Yes," Bryony mumbled, feeling more stupid than she could ever remember. "I am sorry to have interrupted you."

"Oh, that doesn't matter in the slightest," Ben said. "You may interrupt me in such a circumstance as often as you please. It might serve to keep my sanity, or, at least, to ensure that I am not court-martialed for assaulting a superior officer!"

"Well, I am sorry for being so stupid, then."

"You won't be, another time," he replied, a lot more cheerfully. "Now, you had better go about your business and leave me to mine." He pinched her cheek in careless affection and returned to the men under the beech tree.

Bryony returned to her task of rolling their clothes into tight sausage shapes so that they would fit into the rounded, oblong leather portmanteaux supplied by Paul Tyler. He had also procured her expanded wardrobe, he and Ben having pronounced the doeskin tunic to be quite unsuitable for a wife living among soldiers. Bryony now had several serviceable gowns and a riding habit of the kind worn by respectable bourgeois women. Eliza would be shattered at the thought of her daughter in calico and kersey, with pinchbeck buckles on her shoes. . . .

Bryony stuffed a cotton stocking into a spare corner and dashed a recalcitrant teardrop from her cheek. The effect of her present wardrobe on her mother was hardly important when compared with the basic facts of her present existence. She sat back on her heels and surveyed her handiwork. She was still lamentably unhandy at these tasks, and it had taken much pushing and scrunching to put back in the bags what had originally come out of them. Everything would be horribly creased when they were unpacked. *If* they were ever unpacked. The thought rose unbidden. Who was to know whether they would both be alive on the morrow? Certainly, a few creases in their clothes would not be regarded. Why did she keep having these silly, trivial thoughts when the world was teetering around her? Probably just because it *was* teetering, she thought gloomily. The mind responded in the strangest ways to fear.

The fear did not abate as the day wore on. Indeed, once she had completed the packing and could find nothing else useful to do, it threatened to fill her mind, lurking in dark corners like some dream monster waiting to spring out and swallow her. She wandered aimlessly around the now dismantled camp, but everyone she knew was enviably occupied, harassed frowns on their brows, voices slightly sharpened. There were other women with the army — many wives, and some not dignified with that status — although none that Ben considered fit companions for his own wife. But today she felt a great need for the companionship of those who must be feeling much as she did. Her position was the same as theirs — the woman of a man who was going to face death on the battlefield. Like her, they would bear no part in the business of war, but hung on the periphery, performing the little domestic tasks that needed no engagement of the mind and merely served to emphasize the ephemeral quality of life.

A knot of women, surrounded by a wall of kit bags, sat in the shade of a willow tree, and Bryony's steps, without conscious prompting, went in that direction. As she approached, they looked up curiously but without hostility, and when she smiled, nodded at her in friendly fashion.

"May I sit with you?" she asked. "I find myself somewhat . . ." She sought for words to explain her present distress but saw instantly that they were not necessary.

"Sit ye down," an angular woman with a sharp nose invited promptly. "There's nuthin' to be done but wait, and waitin's better in company."

"Yes," Bryony agreed gratefully, and sat on the grass within the circle of kit bags. She had little to contribute to the conversation, concerned as it was with people and events that were unfamiliar to her. She knew nothing of life in the ranks, as they knew nothing of an officer's life, but she was content to listen and to admire the stoic resolution of the women who marched with the army's backbone. They had left behind farms and cottages; children, in some cases; parents and siblings. And they were all frightened, and all resigned to living with that fear.

Bryony found herself drawing strength from her honorary membership in this strange sisterhood and allowed her mind to drift as the long hours of the afternoon wore on. Whatever happened would happen. Then suddenly the elusive peace was shattered. Charlie Carter, out of breath, his young eyes anxious, appeared suddenly on the outskirts of the circle.

"Bryony, in the name of the good God! We are about to start out! Ben has been looking for you for this last hour."

"But he did not say . . . tell me to be . . ." she stammered, apologizing profusely as she tripped over legs and feet on her impetuous way to join Charlie. "What time is it?"

"Near six," he told her. "You have not eaten and there is all hell to pay. Gates is already mounted, and the first column is set to move out. He has already told Ben that he will not wait any longer and —"

"Oh, don't say any more." Bryony groaned, needing no expansion to imagine the scene that would be laid before her in a very few minutes.

"Ben, I cannot tell you how sorry I am," she said swiftly, going to where he stood white with anger and mortification, holding the bridles of Bryony's mare and the magnificent plantation horse, both given to them by Paul Tyler. "I did not realize the time and did not see any signs of —"

"Well, now that you *are* here, ma'am, perhaps Colonel Clare would be so good as to fall in, so we may get this army on the march," General Gates declared with biting sarcasm.

Ben went, if anything, even paler and his black eyes blazed. "Get up," he snapped, holding his cupped palm to receive her foot as she took the reins. He tossed her onto the mare's back and mounted his own horse without further word. From somewhere behind them, a drum began to beat, slowly at first, then with rousing fervency, and General Gates spurred his horse.

"Ben, please," she whispered, her mare nudging the gelding's flanks. "I would not have had that happen for the world."

He looked sideways at her. The expressive blue eyes were liquescent, radiating distress and penitence. The soft mouth quivered anxiously, and he could not hold on to his anger. "Where were you?"

"With some of the women. I was a little afeard." She shrugged in self-deprecation. "I found their company comforting, and the time just disappeared."

"I do not need to be glaringly in the wrong with Gates," he said ruefully. "It's bad enough when he picks fault without justification, but when he has just cause . . ."

"Yes, I know. Am I pardoned?"

A reluctant smile tugged at the corners of his mouth. "Aye, lass, you are pardoned. I know it was not done on purpose, and I was not there for you, although I wish that I could have been. You have cause to be afeard — we all are."

# Chapter 18

Night fell all too soon as the unwieldy army found itself squelching across squishy ground, their boots settling in at each step, requiring a heave to bring them free with a reluctant gurgle. It was slow, painful going, as hard for the cavalry horses as for the infantry, and conditions were not improved by the constant whining torment of mosquitoes, rising in clouds from the unhealthy swamp-ground to feast with a glutton's delight on the sweat-slick skins of three thousand burdened men.

Bryony drew the hood of her cloak around her face, preferring the misery of near suffocation to that of exposure to the vicious darts that left great itching lumps — more virulent than those she remembered from home. All around her, men swore and slapped, and horses tossed their manes and flicked their tails. To add to the entire wretched discomfort of it all, her belly began to make vociferous complaint at its missed supper. The Lord only knew when the next meal would appear, or where from; food seemed a thoroughly incongruous reality in this stinking, squelching, midnight oven.

"I daresay you now wish you had joined the ranks of the wise virgins and supped when you had the chance?" Ben spoke with mock solemnity at her side as her stomach growled.

"Do not gloat; it's most disagreeable," Bryony told him. "It was not as if, with foolish improvidence, I passed up the opportunity when it was offered. It was not offered."

"You were not around when it was," her husband corrected with remorseless truth. "However . . ." He leaned sideways to unfasten a saddlebag. "Being a caring and considerate commander, I thought of your welfare." He handed her a small package. "This will serve to keep the wolf at bay."

"My thanks." Bryony smiled gratefully and unwrapped the offering with eager fingers. Cheese, a hunk of manchet bread, and an apple did much to restore her spirits, and she was beginning to feel that maybe they would get through this dreaded march without mishap, when an explosion to the right, accompanied by a sheet of flame, brought a bellow of fear and anger from somewhere behind her.

"What is it?" Even as she asked, the crack and whine of musket balls rent the air, and all hell broke loose.

"God dammit! We are under attack!" Benedict swore, wheeling his horse. "Get down low over the saddle. Whatever you do, stay mounted and keep up with the front line. I will be back as soon as I can." He galloped off to the rear, intent on rallying the dismayed troops. Bryony crouched in the saddle, bereft and terrified. General Gates and his headquarters staff, as one body, spurred their horses onward, hoping to outdistance the fighting.

Instinctively, she drew back on the reins as the fear of separating herself from Ben took precedence over her fear of the firing. Charlie Carter appeared at her side. "You're to keep up with the general's party," he panted. "Ben says he'll have your hide if you lose them."

"But I don't want to lose Ben," she protested, then pulled herself together smartly and urged the mare forward again. "I crave pardon, Charlie." Brilliant flashes of light stabbed the dark night and the explosions of grenades mingled with the incessant snap and crack of muskets as they were primed and fired. Commands were shouted on all sides, and Bryony could not begin to imagine that there was any order in the seething bubble of confusion that had filled the night.

"Ben will be all right," Charlie comforted. "But he's needed where he is. If the men lack leadership, they'll cut and run in panic."

"Then, had you better not go where you are also needed?" She smiled, her face pale, but her eyes shining resolutely in the reddish glow that had replaced the darkness.

Charlie looked doubtful. "Ben said to stay with you if you wanted me."

"I do not require a nursemaid," she responded firmly. "I will stay with the general's party, and Benedict will find me when he is free."

"If you are sure?" It was clear that Charlie could not wait to be off to the action himself, and Bryony reiterated that she was quite certain and sent him on his way.

The rest of the night passed in a nightmare of shouts and shots, interspersed with the shrill screams of horses and the cries of wounded men as the attackers hounded the army, cutting down stragglers and keeping up an incessant barrage of fire into the columns of marching men who could not see the enemy in order to defend themselves with returning fire. Benedict and his fellow officers could do little but keep the columns moving, shouting encouragement where it would help, and curses and threats where they seemed more appropriate. Men fell on all sides, but Ben, his face blackened with gunsmoke, deeply etched with lines of fatigue and fury at this senseless carnage that could so easily have been avoided, rode in the midst of the slaughter as if protected by some talisman. On one occasion, a musket ball almost clipped his ear, but he simply brushed the air as if a mosquito had attacked him, and then hurtled down, sword raised, at a group of the enemy who had fallen upon a pair of wounded troopers. Miraculously, they fell back, making no attempt to cut down his horse, and vanished into the swampy darkness. A ragged cheer rose from the column at the sight, and Ben forced a grin on his face as he galloped past them, waving his sword in victory and encouragement.

Dawn did eventually come, even to those doubters who had become resigned to an eternal night of sudden death. With the first gray streaks in the sky, the attack ceased, the enemy fading into the landscape. Benedict rode the length of the column, taking note of the damage. The walking wounded struggled on with the aid of their fellows, but those who were down stayed down, littering the path on both sides, together with the bodies of horses and mules. On the faces of all but the veterans, sullen anger, resentment, and fear showed. What had happened in the night was not war as they had believed it to be; it was murder and they had been offered up like pigs to the slaughter.

"Do you think they'll ever fight again?" John Davidson, his face as black and weary as Benedict's, appeared out of the dawn gloom.

"Not with much heart," Ben replied grimly. "Can you blame them?"

John shook his head. "Where is our illustrious general?"

Ben's lips tightened; his eyes became ebony pinpricks of contempt. "Safe and sound, it is to be assumed, well ahead of all this mess. I only hope my wife is with him." He turned his horse toward the head of the columns. "I think, if you will excuse me, John, I'll go and find out."

Bryony, however, once the firing had ceased and it became clear would not be restarted, couldn't contain her anxiety and dropped behind the front line, where she had ridden throughout the long dark hours, crouched low in the saddle, her hood drawn tight around her as if she could block out the sounds of fear and death, trying to master her own terror — a terror that was for Ben rather than for herself.

"Mrs. Clare?" an adjutant, seeing her fall back, called imperatively. "Is anything the matter?"

"No, nothing," she replied. "I had thought to go in search of my husband."

"He'll be along soon enough with his report," General Gates said briskly. "You'd do much better to keep your place with us. No sense getting lost. Clare will not be best pleased if he cannot find you."

There was certainly sense in this, Bryony reflected, but she knew she could no longer ride in ignorance with this group who showed no imperative need to discover the worst. True, throughout the night, riders had brought reports of events behind them, but Bryony couldn't understand why, now that they could draw breath, the general did not halt the army and take stock. "I will not go far, sir," she said, and turned the mare. She was halfway down the column when she recognized Ben's horse first, the blackened rider second.

Her heart leaped with relief, and joy seeped into her toes. "Ben!" She set the mare to gallop, pounding up to him, waving with frantic abandon.

"Dear God! What are you doing here?" demanded Ben, the need for discipline taking precedence over his own joyful relief and the overpowering urge to sink into her softness, drawing from it the strength he knew would be forthcoming. "I told you to stay with the van."

"Oh, never mind that!" Bryony held up her arms imperatively. "You look like a sweep, but if you don't kiss me immediately, I shall not be able to believe you're alive."

"I do mind it," Ben groaned, yielding to what was both demand and invitation, leaning down to catch her face as she clasped her arms around his neck, her lips opening on a soft exhalation of pleasure as dread and terror finally were vanquished. "If I cannot trust you to obey orders, I will be prey to anxiety, and I cannot afford to add to my worries."

"I left the general's side but ten minutes ago," Bryony declared in stout defense.

"There seemed to be no further danger, and I couldn't stand to wait in idleness and dread another minute. You cannot have just cause for complaint."

"No, I suppose I cannot," Ben agreed. "But, oh, lass, it was a damnable night's work." Weariness stood out in every line of his body, for all that he held himself as straight in the saddle as if he had just mounted after a long night's sleep. She touched his gloved hand in silent empathy. "Come, I have to make my report." His voice became strong again, and he urged his tired mount forward. "As soon as we are free of this damn swamp, we must halt and rest."

It took much persuasion, however, before General Gates could be brought to see the necessity for a brief respite. Benedict was amply supported by others who had seen the devastation and dismay among the ranks, and at mid-morning a halt was called on the banks of the Wateree River. The pause allowed the surgeons to do what they could for the wounded, and allowed the hale to eat what they could scavenge and to rest bodies that had been pushed unmercifully for sixteen hours.

Ben's saddlebags yielded a slab of bacon; John appeared with six duck eggs, laughingly refusing to account for such a possession. But no one was prepared to question the arrival of such bounty. Charlie, bewailing the fact that he had nothing to contribute but his labor, collected sticks and lit a fire, then begged the use of a skillet from a group of troopers who had contrived to tickle two good-sized trout from the river and were willing to share their skillet in exchange for use of the fire.

"I think that perhaps I should cook," Bryony offered tentatively. "Since everyone except me has produced something. But Ben is a great deal better at it than I am."

"Your presence is sufficient gift." John bowed formally, offering the heavy pleasantry with a wicked gleam, and Bryony laughed as she curtsied.

"My thanks, sir. But I must protest, you do me too much honor."

"Far too much," agreed Ben. "We have no platters. See what you can contrive."

"Dock leaves?"

"Or some such." He cracked the eggs into the bacon fat sizzling in the skillet, and Bryony went off to hunt for broad, firm leaves that could serve as platters.

Eggs and bacon maneuvered off a leaf with the blunt edge of Ben's clasp knife tasted better than anything Bryony had ever eaten before. That morning, with the hot sun on her neck and the cheerful raillery of her companions, deliberately creating an atmosphere of ease and relaxation to combat the hell of the previous night and the anticipation of the hell awaiting them in the battle to come, would remain forever in her memory. She fell asleep on the grass, as suddenly and as easily as a kitten, exhausted with play, will collapse where it stands.

"We should try to do the same," Charlie said soberly. "There's no telling when we'll have the chance again." The earlier lightness dissipated as it must. It had been chimera only, a moment to be snatched from a fearful uncertainty; a moment that would stiffen the backbone again.

Ben lay on the bank, closing his eyes, feeling the sun's heat against the lids, creating a red glow that filled his internal vision. He put a hand out to touch the curled figure beside him. His palm flattened against her hip, and just the feel of her was sufficient to remind him to count his blessings. But how long would it — could it — last . . . ?

"Colonel, General Gates wishes to see you immediately." The adjutant had spoken only the first word of his sentence and Benedict was instantly awake. He glanced at the sun and judged that he had perhaps been asleep for thirty minutes — not much to recompense for a sleepless night, but better than nothing.

"Very well, Adjutant. I am on my way," he replied quietly, anxious not to disturb Bryony, although she looked as if it would take an earthquake to return her to the land of the living. He went over to the river and splashed his face with cold water before reporting to the general for orders that he already knew he would not want to follow.

Half an hour later, a bugle sounded its imperative note, and Ben shook Bryony awake, ruthlessly ignoring her protests, her pleas for five more minutes as she curled tighter on her side. "I will be quite awake then," she begged, her words slurred with sleep.

"No!" Ben yanked her over onto her back. "You have to be on your horse in three minutes!"

Bryony's eyes shot open, and she blinked into the set face above her. Something had made Ben exceedingly angry. With a hasty apology, she scrambled to her feet and stood swaying in the sunshine as her blood rearranged itself in her body. The bugle sounded again, and all around her men were running to fall into the columns already re-forming. "I feel dreadful," she groaned, stumbling over to her mare.

"No more so than anyone else," Ben snapped, catching her around the waist and swinging her into the saddle.

"I was not asking for sympathy," she retorted, gathering up the reins and swallowing her yawn. "Why are you so angry now?"

"I don't have time to explain. You will ride in the van again, and this time you will stay there — is it understood?"

"Where will you be?" Bryony found that she was waking up rapidly; indignation was a powerful spur.

"Wherever I am needed," he replied curtly. "Is it understood?"

Bryony nodded. "I suppose so. Quite frankly, when you are in this mood, I cannot imagine wishing to go in search of you. I am just as tired and irritable as you, as it happens, but I do not take it out on *you*."

She looked so rumpled and pink in her indignation that Benedict could not help a sudden chuckle. "It is most unjust of me, lass, I agree, but I have no time for either apologies or explanations at the moment."

He swung onto his own horse and cantered off without further expansion.

"He makes me so cross!" Bryony declared to John Davidson, who had been audience to the spat. "I have done nothing to my knowledge to annoy him. It is always the same when something has angered him. I always have to play whipping boy!" She glared into the middle distance, then recollected that it was perhaps not decorous to discuss one's husband in such fashion. A sideways glance at her companion, however, was reassuring. He did not appear in the least embarrassed by her confidence.

"He's greatly concerned for your safety," John said after a minute. "Gates is insisting on meeting Cornwallis head-on as soon as we come up with him. His battle plan, Ben is convinced, will be a disaster, and the men will have been granted no respite to recover from the march. Ben wishes to find a safe place for you, well away from the battlefield, but he cannot do that if he doesn't have the time to reconnoiter."

"Oh." Bryony absorbed this information, then said carefully, "I think it would be best if you forgot what I just said, John. If you please."

John grinned at her. "He does have a regular pepper pot of a temper, doesn't he?

But he is under a great deal of strain at present."

"Well, I wish he would not worry about me," Bryony declared. "I have told him all along that I will have a care for myself. He has his duty to do, and I will not interfere."

It was mid-afternoon when they approached the small town of Camden and the British army encamped in a field outside. Bryony sat on her horse and observed the enemy with a mixture of awe and anguish — the clustered tents beneath the fluttering flags; the red-coated figures, tiny in the distance, going about their business, presumably as much a prey to fear and uncertainty as those who stood around her, gazing in their turn, for the moment silent. It was the first time that she had beheld the British as enemy, and if it had not been for Benedict Clare, she would be looking in the opposite direction, seeing enemy in those with whom she now marched. In a few short hours, these two forces would join battle, and she wondered whether there were any familiar faces to be found under the British flag. Her father, perhaps? But he would not have left her mother, surely? Not so soon after her daughter's defection.

"Yes, it is a somber spectacle." Ben came

up suddenly on her right. "Cornwallis has only highly disciplined regulars with him, each one with years of battlefield experience." He sighed bleakly. "They will make mincemeat of our men if they get the chance."

"I was wondering if there was anyone I knew over there," Bryony said, still following her own train of thought.

Benedict shrugged and gave a short laugh. "That is the reason for the tragic mien, then?"

"I cannot somehow see the comic aspects of the situation," she retorted, nettled at the sardonic tone.

Ben, plagued by anxiety for her safety, racking his brain for a solution that Gates seemed determined to deny him, said sharply, "If you are regretting your choice, it is a little late, I fear."

Bryony flushed with anger. "I did not say that. But I do regret the necessity for having to make it," she returned sharply. "I do not myself give a tinker's damn whether King George rules the Colonies or not, and I wish I understood why it is a matter of such desperate importance to you. It is not your country. Why must you fight someone else's battles?"

It was the first time that she had expressed these sentiments, and her tone was far from conciliatory. Fatigue, sorrow, uncertainty, fear for those she loved on both sides, and indignation that Ben could not understand how she might feel torn, even though she would never go back on the decision she had made, lent an unfortunately truculent note to her voice.

Benedict's eyes flattened in that dreaded fashion as the old bitterness welled, and he forgot his resolution to keep her safe from its bite. "Because I can no longer fight the battles in my own country," he pronounced coldly. "But why should a Paget question the foundations of her wealthy, privileged world? Of course you do not give a tinker's damn for injustices visited upon others, only insofar as it disturbs your own peace."

He swung his mount and rode off, leaving Bryony sickened at the suddenness and viciousness of the attack. He hadn't spoken to her in that manner since the afternoon in Paul Tyler's house when they had pledged themselves to tread the same path. And she still did not understand why her admittedly snappish question should have produced such a savage reaction. Unless it had something to do with what had earned him the sentence of bondage. Paul Tyler had said that it was a secret that should not lie between them — that it would bring them unhappiness. But how could she force the confidence?

Tears pricked behind her eyes — a familiar sensation that she now always associated with Benedict's seemingly unprovoked attacks. She dashed the tears away with the back of her hand and sniffed vigorously. "Charlie!" She hailed the young man who had dismounted and was talking with a group of officers. He came over immediately, smiling although his eyes were grave. "Charlie, I am going into the town," Bryony said briskly. "Will you tell Benedict that he may find me there when he is finished with this . . . this killing? I will be quite safe, and he need not concern himself in the least."

"You cannot just go," Charlie said, aghast. "Ben will have made plans for you."

"I have made my own," she said, wheeling the mare. "I do not wish to be a burden to him." Before Charlie could say or do anything further, she went off at a gallop down the dusty road. She had no idea what she would find in the town of Camden, but Bryony did not think she could bear another such encounter with

Benedict with the battle so close; the possibility of the end to love and the end to all that was familiar was now so tangible as to seem almost inevitable. The hurt went too deep — that he should turn upon her when she was already vulnerable, prey to confused sorrows and the sharp edge of panic.

So lost was she in this slough of despond that the pounding hooves behind were almost upon her before she noticed. Benedict seized the mare's bridle and hauled her to a stop. His eyes blazed in a whitened face. "How *dare* you do such a thing!" he rasped. "To leave such a message!"

"I merely said that I would take a care for myself and you were not to concern yourself," Bryony protested, as white as he. "You have weighty matters on your mind; I wished simply to lighten your burden."

"Don't you play such a game with me!" he raged. "How could I possibly not know where you were and be unconcerned? As bad as it is, at least when I put you somewhere, I'll know where to find you afterward."

"If there is to be an afterward," she said, the fight suddenly leaving her. It had been absurd to ride off like that and expect him to put her out of his mind while he concentrated on the business of war. But that had not really been the motive, anyway. Anger and hurt tended to muddle clarity.

"There will be!" he said with fierce intensity. "Sweet Jesus, Bryony, I cannot explain what happens to me sometimes. I am afraid for you, for me, for every man on that damn field, and I can do nothing about it."

"You could explain what happens to you if you would tell me why you sometimes hate me. I understand that it comes out when you are worried or distressed in some way, but I don't understand anything else, and I don't think I can go on living with you if you will not tell me." She was horrified by the words of ultimatum even as she recognized them to be the truth.

Ben swore, a short barnyard oath. "You have a fine instinct for picking your time, don't you, lass?"

"I am sorry," she said in a wooden voice. "I realize this is not a convenient time or place, but I just thought I would mention it."

"Well, now that you have mentioned it and I have duly taken note, the matter must rest. We are going back to the column, and if you break rank again without my permission, I daresay that I shall discover I cannot live with *you*." Still holding the mare's bridle above the bit, he turned both horses on the narrow road.

"I am quite capable of guiding my own mount," Bryony declared frigidly.

"Just so long as you guide her in the right direction!" He released the bridle, however, and they rode back to the army in grim silence. Benedict hustled Bryony to the rear, where a makeshift camp had been made and women and a few children milled around among the supplies and pack mules.

"You will be as safe here as anywhere," he said. "And at least I'll know how to find you."

Bryony looked at him, desolation etched on every feature. "I do not wish it to be like this, Ben."

He gripped her hands in a painful squeeze. "Sweeting, forgive me once more. I cannot do what I must unshriven."

She swallowed the lump in her throat. "Forgive me, too. I should not have laid such a burden upon you at this time."

"I will not let such a thing happen again," he promised softly. "There is nothing to tell you, and you must not think of it further." Then he kissed her in hard affirmation and rode off without a backward glance, because he dared not take one.

Bryony watched until the bright copper head was swallowed in the press. *Why* would he not tell her? She knew so much already, what could there possibly be that he did not consider fit for her ears?

Throughout that night, three thousand men took up battle positions, facing an army half their size. It was no wonder that General Gates, in the gray light of dawn, should have surveyed his massed troops with a complacent eye as line upon line stretched before him. Two thousand men of the North Carolina militia formed a solid center. Maryland and Delaware veterans under General Gist and Baron de Kalb brought up the rear. But Benedict Clare could feel no justification for complacency as he rode the front lines, sensing the uncertainty, the anxious shufflings, the whisperings, and the movements within the lines — all manifestations of fearful and untried men facing fire for the first time.

The redcoats, ranged in orderly lines, stood with apparent relaxation despite their numerical disadvantage. For several minutes, time ceased and this corner of the world hung suspended in absolute silence.

Bryony heard the silence as if it were a fanfare, the ominous presager of battle.

She had spent the night soothing a fractious baby whose mother was burning with fever and unable to nurse the child. It was a task that gave Bryony some purpose, a much needed sense of usefulness, and she found, although she had had little experience of babies or small children, that she was quite successful. Now she stood in the dawn, the sleeping baby in her arms, waiting for the silence to break. Then a bugle called, a drum began to beat, and the first cannon bellowed.

Brushing her hair away from her face with her free hand, she walked wearily over to a fallen tree stump and sat down to wait, as women had done since the dawn of civilization while their men dealt and received death in the name of religious conviction or territorial aggrandizement — rarely in the name of anything worthwhile, she reflected, absently allowing the babe to suck on her little finger. In a minute, the milkless finger would cease to satisfy and she would have to resort to the rag soaked in goat's milk to answer the most basic need of this pathetic scrap of humanity. Perhaps, if one was forced to pay more attention to the basic needs of survival, one would be less willing to sacrifice survival for concepts, Bryony thought, knowing that by these abstractions she was somehow distancing herself from what was happening a mile or so away. Contemplation of the reality was not possible if she wished to retain her sanity.

Suddenly, she could no longer ignore the events around her. Men were running through the camp, running and yelling, throwing away their muskets as they hurtled in blind panic, trampling upon those who were in their path. It was only a few to start with, but as she stood, hand to mouth, eyes wide with incomprehension, the few became a torrent of wild-eyed humanity, shouting incoherently while the sounds of battle continued behind them. Bryony did not think she could ever have imagined such a sight, as she ran instinctively with the baby onto a hillock out of the path of the floodtide. Three thousand men marching in column or camped in a field was one thing, but three thousand men on the run was a heart-stopping, petrifying sight. Surely it was not the whole three thousand? But she recognized the insignia of the North Carolina militia and knew that Ben's worst fears had been realized. The center was broken.

As she watched, a sight that filled her with a dull fury burst upon her incredulous vision: General Gates, astride a lean, powerful racehorse well-known for its speed, tore across the camp, a few members of headquarters' staff, not so well mounted, trailing him. They vanished in a cloud of dust up the road to the north as his routed army poured forth in his wake. Dear God, where was Ben? He would not flee, she knew it, even as she cursed him for the stiff-necked pride that would keep him knocking at death's door in the face of impossible odds. . . .

Benedict had not seen Gates leave the field; he had seen only the breaking of the front line when the green troops had thrown down their muskets and fled in panic at the first major salvo from the British ranks. He had seen the center disintegrate and the First Maryland veterans in the rear thrown into confusion as their ranks were burst asunder by the fleeing multitude. He spurred his horse with desperate resolve, rallying the veterans, finding himself alongside Baron de Kalb as they charged forward onto the field, a small band of soldiers with them. Across the field, he saw Mordecai Gist with his own band, also fighting hand to hand as one bayonet charge succeeded another. None of them realized until later that they were fighting the entire British army in a battle already lost, their commander in flight miles to the rear.

All around him was carnage as men fell before the enemy bayonets. Benedict saw de Kalb go down under a cavalry charge that at last broke the American ranks. A groan of despairing fury escaped Benedict's lips as he finally accepted the overwhelming odds. "An organized retreat is all that is left to us," he said to Charlie, who had been at his side throughout. "Although God knows how many of us are left to retreat." He looked grimly around at the decimation. There could not be more than sixty men of Gates's army left standing on the field.

But those sixty would leave in good order. The bugler sounded the retreat, and the Americans fell back, still fighting, but were not pursued beyond the field. All around them was a scene of devastation and confusion, bodies and weapons marking the path of the rout. Benedict, numbed by the sights he had already witnessed, thought only of Bryony now. She would have been much safer in Camden than in the path of the fleeing troops who might have swept her along to God knows where, if she had not been trampled underfoot.

He reached the camp and looked around in despair. A few women remained, their faces blank with shock, eyes stunned. Wagons were overturned, their contents spilled higgledy-piggledy; sacks of flour were split, pouring over sides of meat in a pathetic heap; mules were tugging at their tethers in search of uncropped ground.

Bryony came slowly down from her hillock, the baby in the crook of her arm, brushing hair away from her face in that characteristic gesture that twisted his heart. She looked ten years older, eyes haggard and deeply shadowed, shoulders sagging as she surveyed the wreckage. Then she saw him standing beside his horse and came running, tripping heedlessly over guy ropes and debris, yet maintaining her hold on the babe even as she threw herself into his arms.

As her cheek touched his, she felt the wetness of his tears and drew back slightly, looking into the haunted face. "Such carnage, sweeting," he said softly as she stroked the tears from his cheeks with a caressing fingertip. "A slaughterhouse. We did not know we fought alone."

"Even had you known, you still would have fought," she said gently, running her salt-tipped finger over his lips.

512

"Gates left hours ago on his racehorse."

His face darkened and the tear-brightness of his eyes dried. "He has surrendered South Carolina to Cornwallis. There will be no organized resistance, so the fight must go underground again."

"You will not follow the army?"

"What army?" he said with a sharp crack of disdainful laughter, looking around. "No, it is time to return to the backwoods." He looked over her shoulder, saying with difficulty the words he knew he must say. "Will you go under flag of truce to Cornwallis? You will be safe, and he will restore you to your father."

Bryony managed to produce a watery smile. "You said you would be rid of me if I broke rank again without permission. But I am still here, am I not? Your wife, when all is said and done."

"My life." He cupped her face with his battle-grimed, callused hands and she turned her lips into his palm.

A thin wail came from the burden in her arms and Benedict looked down. "Whose is this?"

Bryony shook her head in a gesture of defeat. "Her mother died of the fever a while ago. Her father could be anywhere — dead on the field, or in flight. I do not

513

know what to do with her, except to take her with us."

"An unweaned babe-in-arms! Lass, have some sense," Benedict exclaimed, shaken out of bleak despondency by such an impossible suggestion. "We must hide by day and move by night. Wage war by stealth. It is no business for a woman, let alone for a child."

"But what are we to do with her, then?" Bryony looked at him helplessly.

"Give her to me." Charlie Carter stepped forward, and they both realized that he had been standing to one side, patiently waiting for the intensity of their reunion to abate. "I have a little money, and one of the women will be glad to take the child, I am certain, in exchange for coin."

Bryony looked doubtful. "Are you certain that one can buy fair treatment for her, Charlie? It is a life's burden you lay upon someone."

"They would take her without pay," Charlie replied quietly. "They take care of their own. But it would ease matters for many if there was payment for her keep."

"I have some jewelry," Bryony said swiftly.

"Keep your jewelry." Ben stilled her hand, which had begun to grope beneath her petticoats. "Here, Charlie." He handed him two gold sovereigns. "That should be enough."

"Aye." Charlie nodded and took the coins and then the baby. "You will wait for me?"

"Do you take this fight into the underbelly, then?" Ben asked, his eyes serious, holding the younger man's gaze. "It is not clean fighting, Charlie. No heroics, no glory."

"After what I have seen today!" Charlie spat on the ground. "I have no truck with heroics or glory. I will fight as it is necessary."

"Very well, then. We will gather together supplies."

"Where is John?" asked Bryony, reminded with a powerful stab of the laughing, redheaded forager.

"Cut down with de Kalb," Ben said, the curt tone masking his grief. "He cannot have suffered. He was dead when I reached him."

"Yes," Bryony said. There was nothing else to say. Those who were left would continue the battle in whatever way was open to them, and they would fight, informed with the spirits of those who had died, so that their friends would not have died in vain.

# Chapter 19

"Murdering bastards!" Benedict Clare surveyed the smoking ruins of the tiny hamlet in sick disgust. Picking up a large stone, he hurled it at a rooting hog, and Bryony turned her head away, retching. The hog had been feasting on human flesh. Unburied bodies lay in the gardens, along the cart track running through the center of the hamlet, stretched across doorways where they had fallen, blood blackened, the limbs twisted in rigid death, and flies rose in clouds in the warm September air.

"Ferguson's lot again!" A bearded rifleman in leather jerkin and baggy britches spat disgustedly. "They've left nothing that could be carried away."

Bryony wondered if her breakfast of goat's milk and blackberries was going to remain in her belly. Somehow, she could not become inured to these sights, although she had seen plenty similar in the weeks since their band of frontiersmen, hunters, and riflemen had tracked the course of Major Patrick Ferguson's Tories and Loyalist militia in his plundering sweep across western South Carolina.

Ben looked around, then said with resolution, "Well, let's stick one or two pigs. There's worse dinners than fresh pork."

"You cannot!" Bryony stared in horror, her hand over her mouth. "They have been feeding on human flesh. We can't eat them."

Benedict spoke with his customary realism. "Lass, when one is hungry, one cannot afford to be too nice in one's notions. If you choose not to eat it, no one will force you." He took his knife from his belt, running his finger over the blade to test its keenness. "I used to chase pigs across the fields when I was a lad. It's to be hoped I haven't lost the skill. They're the very devil to catch."

An enormous bear of a man, his skin tanned to a deep mahogany, tough as leather after a lifetime in the Carolina hills, chuckled richly. "Let's be at 'em, then!" The two men crept stealthily into the garden where the pig still snuffled and grunted. Bryony shuddered and turned away.

"Poor girl," Charlie said with soft sympathy. "I don't think he means to be unkind."

"No, of course he doesn't," Bryony said swiftly. "And you have to admit, if it were up to me, we would all starve." A reluctant smile glimmered in her eyes.

Charlie laughed. "Ben is so damnably competent," he said. "How does he know how to stick pigs?"

Bryony shrugged. "I do not know, Charlie. For an Irish aristocrat, he possesses the oddest assortment of skills." But then, Irish aristocrats were not usually sentenced to bondage, and they did not, in general, bear the marks of the whip upon their backs. The thought came and went as it often did. A shrill, piercing squeal came from the garden, and Bryony paled beneath the sun's bronzing. "That's the pig! They are hurting it."

"Well, I don't imagine it's possible to avoid doing so," Charlie said thoughtfully.

"Oh, I am being a fool! We are surrounded by dead people and I am concerning myself with a pig!" Angry tears clogged her voice and threatened to spill from her eyes. Bryony turned away abruptly. "I am going for a walk."

The stench of corruption hung heavy over the hamlet, and soon the air was rent with more squeals as other members of the band followed Ben's example and set about a slaughter that would provide much needed replenishment of their peripatetic larders. There had been many times in the last weeks when she had ached for home, for the time long gone when she had not known these horrors existed, had not believed what man was capable of doing to his fellows. But now she had seen gibbets by the paths, entire villages put to the torch, men and women staring sightless into the unfeeling blue sky. She had wept with exhaustion even as she put one foot in front of the other, wept with anger, wept with misery. More than once, she had turned on Benedict in her rage and wretchedness, blaming him for the horrors because he was a part of this dirty fight that seemed without honor on either side. Not once had he retaliated but had reacted with limitless patience, holding her until the storm had expended itself and she was cleansed and renewed.

Because he had borne her anger and her accusations with love and tenderness, had looked at her only with the eyes of love, and had touched her only with the touch of passion, she had put away from her those moments when the hatred that he bore someone . . . something . . . became focused on her. The business of living from minute to minute was raw enough without resurrecting old sores.

She walked down the mud-ridged cart track, keeping her eyes on the verge, where, incongruous in the midst of this charnel house, wildflowers massed in a profusion of blues and pinks, yellows and whites. A sudden movement behind a clump of bushes flickered across her vision. What could possibly be left alive among this carrion? Then she heard the sound. It was a human sound, part sob, part cry. Bryony pushed through the bushes and then stopped, staring.

A child — a ragged, tattered scrap of human flotsam — cowered in the grass. Brown eyes, huge in a pinched, dirty face, gazed at her in terror. His scrawny body and sticklike limbs poking through the torn shirt and britches were evidence of deprivation, as were the open sores and scabs where flies clustered. Bryony had been campaigning long enough to know what happened when flies found open wounds — the child would be crawling with maggots.

She dropped to the grass beside him. "Don't be afraid. I am not going to hurt you." There was no response. The terror-struck gaze remained unmoving. "Where do you live?" she asked gently. Again no response. "In the village?" she guessed, gesturing over the hedge. This time there was a barely perceptible nod. No one was alive in the village. The child must either have been left behind when his family fled, or somehow he escaped the slaughter. "What is your name?" She risked reaching out a hand to touch his arm, but the tiny figure recoiled as if he had been burned. What had he seen? she thought with a shudder of revulsion; it required little imagination to guess.

Nonplussed, she sat beside him, then almost instinctively picked a handful of daisies, piling them in her lap before beginning to thread them into a chain, not watching the child, who at least made no attempt to run from her. Perhaps he could not. "Are you hurt?" she asked in a casual tone, still not looking directly at him, although her eyes slid sideways. His head shook a negative. "Hungry?" Again her tone was casual, as if the question were of no real importance. There was an affirmative nod.

Bryony held up her daisy chain. "This is pretty, is it not?" She turned to smile at him. "But then, little boys don't make daisy chains, do they?" There was no response, but she could sense the slight re-laxation, a flicker of life in his eyes. "My name is Bryony." She strung the chain around her neck. "It's the name of a wild-flower. Will you tell me your name?"

It was barely a whisper. "Ned."

"Well, Ned, I think we had better find you something to eat." Bryony stood up and reached down for the child's hand. He shrank away, but this time she took the clawlike hand in a firm grasp. "You would like some bread and milk, would you not?" Their scrawny goat could be induced to produce another cupful, she thought. And there was half a loaf of barley bread that they had been saving for their supper.

The child came up as she pulled on his hand, but he hung back when she pushed through the bushes and took a step toward the village. "It's all right," she reassured. "No one will hurt you now."

Benedict, wiping his bloody hands on the grass, looked along the cart track and saw a sight that made his heart sink. Bryony, some disreputable creature in tow, was striding along with the determined vigor that always spelled trouble. The baby at Camden had been the beginning. Ever since, she had been constantly collecting the living debris of this war. There had been starveling kittens and three-legged dogs, pregnant women who must be given food and coin, wandering children who must be found homes, which also required the outlay of coin. Ben's financial resources were much depleted as a result of this philanthropy, but he could not find it in his heart to refuse her when her distress at what she saw and experienced was so vital a force.

"His name is Ned," Bryony declared without preamble as she reached Ben. "He is half-starved and utterly petrified. I think he must have been in the village when this —" she gestured around her, searching for words, but none adequate came to mind "— when this happened. Can you imagine the effect on such a baby? He does not seem able to speak."

Ben scratched his head, surveying the pathetic mite. "He needs cleaning up. Those sores will be infested."

"I know. But I thought I would feed him first. It might help to ease his fear."

"What are you going to give him?" He could not help a slight smile, even in the face of this further war-torn misery. Bryony was so very intense.

"The goat will yield a little more milk today, and we can spare the barley bread," she said with determination.

"Then *you* will have to eat pork or go hungry, lass," Ben pointed out with a quizzical lift of an eyebrow.

She shrugged. "I daresay I shall not regard it when the time comes. There are worse things."

"Undoubtedly," he agreed solemnly. "Well, see to your protégé. The pig has to be butchered, and we must bury these bodies before we go."

It was two hours later before the band was ready to move on, their booty packed in haversacks, the dead buried in a deep communal pit that would deter the scavengers for a while. Ned still had not spoken a word, but he had consumed the bread and milk with a single-minded concentration, and had endured Bryony's ministrations as she stripped off his rags and cleansed the worst of the dirt from him with water drawn from the village well. She had used a paste of wormwood on the open sores, which would kill the maggots and keep away further flies, then regarded her handiwork, frowning.

"Stay here, Ned. I will be but a minute." Leaving the child by the well, she had gone in search of Ben, who was busy with the grisly business of burying the dead. "I don't know what to put on him, Ben. His clothes are torn beyond repair."

Ben had sighed. "Since we won't be taking him farther than the next hamlet, Bryony, surely they will do?"

"If the next hamlet looks like this one, we'll be taking him a lot farther."

So little Ned, wrapped in a shirt of Ben's, as if in swaddling clothes, was clutched tightly in Bryony's arms when they left the hamlet and continued on their way in pursuit of Major Patrick Ferguson.

"You had better let me have him," Ben said, after they had been walking for an hour and Bryony's step was beginning to flag. He made to take the child, but Ned wailed in sudden terror and clung to Bryony, burying his face in her neck.

"It's all right. I can manage." Bryony smoothed the dirty thatch of hair in soothing fashion.

"I beg to differ," Benedict said dryly. "Come along, Ned. Either you let me carry you, or you walk." He pried the scrawny arms from Bryony's neck and hitched the trembling boy onto his hip. "The sooner we find a home for this stray, the better."

"We have seen nothing but wasteland," Bryony said. "I do not understand it, Ben.

Francis is with Ferguson. He would not be a party to such inhumane savagery. You know he would not. I broke bread with the major. My father called him friend. I cannot make my mind go around it. . . ." She sighed. "I don't know how to explain."

"I understand," he said, brushing a speck of dirt from her nose. "But in war, people behave in inconceivable ways."

"Francis would not have been a party to this," she repeated sturdily. "What are you doing to my nose?"

"I thought it was dirt." He chuckled, attempting to deflect her train of thought. "But it's only a freckle, it seems. You are so thoroughly bespeckled that there is barely a free centimeter."

But Bryony was not to be deflected. "I suppose he may be dead."

"Yes, he may well be." Ben was never one to ease matters with prevarication.

Bryony said nothing further, just tramped at his side until the falling of dusk signaled the moment to make camp. These backwoodsmen and frontiersmen were expert at creating a degree of comfort out of the most unyielding surroundings. Fires sprang to life in a circle that allowed for privacy even as it offered companionship. Groups had formed long ago, and foraging, hunting, and cooking took place within them. But no one team would refuse to share with another less fortunate.

The minuscule addition to the Clares' cluster of themselves, Charlie, and two burly, monosyllabic Carolinians remained mute, although his mouth opened to roast pig before he tumbled, still swaddled in the voluminous shirt, onto a pile of leaves and instantly fell asleep.

"Poor little bugger," one of the Carolinians muttered. "What d'ye intend doing with him, Ben?"

"The same as the others," Ben said. "There'll be someone in the next village who'll take him in."

"How old do you think he is?" Bryony yawned deeply. "He seems such a baby, but that's probably because he will not speak."

"Four or five," hazarded Charlie. "Young enough to forget, it's to be hoped."

"In which case, he is more fortunate than I." Bryony wiped their knives clean on the grass, concentrating on the chore with a little frown.

Ben threw more sticks on the fire. He knew that frown from experience, and it had nothing to do with the task at hand. "Bedtime, I think."

The others rose instantly, bidding them good night and seeking their own beds at a discreet distance. Bryony sat looking into the fire, her expression bleak.

"Sleep on it, lass," Ben advised quietly. "Things always look less grim in the morning."

"I do not believe that Francis is dead," she said, poking at the fire with a twig. "That night, when he left me on the path to the clearing, he said it was not our last farewell. And something tells me that it was not."

Ben sighed. "Basing hopes on feelings and premonitions, sweeting, is not sound practice. You merely set yourself up for more grief."

"That is easy for you to say. You have not left behind all those whom you love, who informed your childhood and your growing —" She stopped, shivering at the look on his face.

"Have I not?" he asked, a mocking note in his voice. "You know more about me than I do myself, it would seem. Or are you simply assuming that I sprang without family assistance into the world?"

"If I were to assume such a thing, it would hardly be surprising," Bryony said, meeting the challenge head-on. "I dare not ask questions. As far as I am concerned, I am married to a man who has no family and no history. I have said that I am content to have it so, if that is what you wish. I do not know whether you are a murderer or a thief, or whether you were wrongly accused and sentenced. I know that Roger Martin put those scars on your back, and that you are a runaway bondsman. Which means that you are an outlaw, but I do not suppose that will matter once this war is over. I don't suppose anything will matter anymore." They were brave words, but the tremor in her voice could not be hidden.

"You are not content to have it so," Ben heard himself say. "And I fear that I was not wrongfully accused and unjustly sentenced. I have committed both murder and theft in the name of justice — but they call it treason." Why he started on this road after all his resolutions, he would never know, but his feet were firmly on the path now, and he did not think they would stop until the tale was told. Perhaps it was better. She had given up so much for him that maybe he no longer had the right to withhold what he knew she needed so desperately. And there would be a relief for him in the telling.

"You are talking in riddles." The firelight

caught the bright spark in her eyes as she leaned closer to him. All around them was the silence of sleeping men, broken only by the crackle of a fire, the occasional, desolate hoot of an owl, the rustle of the night breeze in the trees.

Benedict looked into the fire and saw tumble-down hovels and starving children; women, aged beyond their years by incessant childbearing; men, bowed and broken by the struggle to wrest a livelihood from land that was loaned on sufferance and taken away at whim. He saw families standing by the wayside, their pots and pans and the few sticks of furniture around them, evicted from their homes because their landlord, who had probably never set foot on his land, had another use for it, condemning them to the slow death of starvation.

"What do you know of Ireland?" he asked quietly.

Bryony frowned. "Very little. We have considerable land there, I believe. Papa says the people are lazy and ignorant, drunk most of the time —"

"And on what does Papa base this judgment?" Ben interrupted harshly. "When did he last visit his land and his tenants?"

Bryony touched her lips with her tongue,

feeling the edge of the precipice with a dreadful fascination, wondering if she dared step closer, knowing now that this was what it was all about. This was the stain with which she was tainted. But it was too late to draw back even if she wished. "I don't think he has ever been there," she said hesitantly. "He has a steward who sends him monies and reports."

"And where do you think that money comes from?" he demanded. "Perhaps it grows in the fields, in the hedgerows, there for the picking?"

"I think you had better tell me where it comes from," Bryony said, keeping her voice steady with effort as the fearful foreboding cast its slimy tendrils around her. "I appear to be very ignorant."

"It comes from the labor of those lazy, ignorant drunkards," he said with low-voiced bitterness. "They pay your father rack rent for a plot of land too small to feed their families. They work your father's land for no wage to help pay their rents. And if they fail . . ." He shrugged with seeming nonchalance, and the tendrils took hold of her, became tentacles of dread. "Or should your father's steward decide that he needs their little plot of land, then he will tell them to leave. If they protest, the roof will be burned over their heads, the crops they have planted will be destroyed."

"Please . . ." Bryony broke in, her eyes clouded with distress as she looked into the picture being painted for her. "You cannot be telling the truth. My father would not knowingly permit such things."

"Of course he permits them! How else is he to get his rents? Rents that have kept *you* in silk and satin; your belly filled with delicacies; a blood horse to ride." Benedict laughed derisively. "And your father will defend to the death his right to do as he pleases with his land and with his tenants, who have no legal redress and mostly cannot read or write because Catholics are denied the right to education."

"But what of *your* family?" she demanded, unable to contemplate the image of her father created by Benedict's descriptions without making some attempt to defend or to explain — at least to lay his sins at the door of a community rather than an individual. "Are they any better?"

His face was in shadow, and she could not make out his expression as he said, "I have no family."

"They are dead?"

"I am dead to them." And then he told her, sparing neither of them a single nuance of detail.

"So, you are wedded to a traitor who should have paid the traitor's penalty," he finished with a bitter laugh. "Hanged, drawn, and quartered . . . because I questioned the right of men like your father to starve families to death — a right that your father would consider inalienable and the traitor's penalty well visited on those who would deny him."

"It could have been my father who sentenced you. That is what you are saying, is it not?" The puzzle was now in place, and Bryony felt as if she were sitting on some cold, gray beach, contemplating the wreckage of a ship of illusions.

"Do you deny it?"

"No, I cannot. And I am guilty by extension. As you said, I have enjoyed the fruits of those labors. No wonder you didn't wish to marry me." She shook her head and the black hair swirled, hiding her face from him. "Why did you?"

"I am not married to your father," he said quietly. "And I love you."

"Not always. Sometimes you hate me. But at least now I understand why." She looked up and offered him a travesty of a smile, which held so much weariness and hurt that he wanted to weep.

"I should not have told you." He reached for her, pulling her into his arms. "I never intended that you should know. I do not really blame you. It is only when the bitterness rises as it does."

"Yes, yes, I understand that now," she said, almost impatiently. "Your friends have died a dreadful death, you lived in slavery . . . endured such degradation that I cannot bear to think of it. . . ." A tremor ran through her. "And still it continues. How can you help but be bitter? How can you help but find loathsome those who perpetrate by omission or commission —"

"Enough!" he said fiercely, crushing her to him, alarmed by her extreme pallor, the haunted distress in her eyes, the sudden fragility of the body he held, as if all the stuffing had gone from her. "You are to say nothing more, do you hear me? It will never be mentioned between us again." His hand stroked her hair away from her brow, but she began to shake, her teeth chattering as if she were in the grip of an ague, and he cursed himself for the self-indulgent insensitivity that had led him to tell her what he had known all along would cut her to the quick.

"It may never be mentioned, but it can never go away," she said with low intensity, resisting the comfort of his hold, turning her jaw against the fingers that would bring her face to his. He could feel the retreat of her self, a shrinking deep down into the core that he could only reach when her body and spirit met and matched his on the ephemeral plane of pure sensation.

With grim deliberation, he forced her to meet his eyes, his fingers bruising against her jaw as he refused to yield to her mute wish to crawl into her own place, to lick alone the wounds that she should not have to bear. The words of denial were on her lips as he brought his mouth to hers, stifling the negation. Even then she held her mouth closed against him, as if to permit him entrance would expose her to yet more pain. But he explored the tender curves with the tip of his tongue, tasting the sweetness of her lips, the fingers on her jaw holding her immobile. His other hand was behind her, unfastening the hooks of her gown. The soft September night air, tipped with mountain freshness, brushed her bare back, and she struggled against him, in confusion and distress, knowing that he offered sweet annihilation and the loss of hurt, yet resisting the gift in strange, irrational anger.

The gentle exploration of her mouth changed, became a searing, thorough invasion that forced her lips apart. Her breasts were flattened against his chest as he held her against him as if his heart would beat for them both. His free hand roamed down her bared back, reaching farther to caress her buttocks, lifting her so that she lay sideways across his lap and could feel the hard maleness of him pulsing against her hip. She tried to push against his chest, but the hand on her buttocks gripped tight, clamping her to him as his tongue continued to ravish and plunder her mouth. And within this captivity, this forcing of her self, lay the peace of final surrender, the healing that he would compel her to receive.

When he felt the fight go out of her, Ben released his hold on her jaw, although his mouth still held hers and his other hand remained firm and warm on her bottom. He pushed the loosened gown from her shoulders, baring the proud mounds of her breasts, moving his mouth to the hollow of her throat, then burning a teasing, tantalizing path to her bosom. The straight black eyelashes swept upward, and Bryony gazed into his face, where the fire's glow created planes of light and hollows of shadow. He let her fall backward on his lap so that she lay, still now, in offering.

"I love you," he whispered. "You must never forget that. It is all that matters, do you understand?" He drew the wadded material of her gown from under her so that she lay naked, the tender symmetry of her body, the pearl softness of her skin brushed by the night air, opalescent in the fire's glow. "Do you understand?" he repeated with gentle insistence, spanning the slender indentation of her waist with the callused hands of the woodsman fighter.

Bryony nodded, reaching a hand to touch his face, laying her fingers lightly across his cheek, tracing the strong angle of his jaw, down to his neck, where the tendons stood out, in taut evidence of his urgency and the muscular restraint of that urgency. "I love you."

A tiny sigh escaped him, and he began to move over her body with sweeping caresses, his words, expressing his sensuous delight in the glories that he found, filling her with liquid enchantment. He drew from her the murmured responses that he required, obliging her to reveal for him the sites and touches that gave her greatest pleasure. And she was no longer isolated, alone with the pain of a self-imposed responsibility and its guilt. She was fired with the brand of his love, that was taking her, ever ascending, to the moment of obliteration.

She was still lost when he laid her upon the grass, his black eyes charcoal embers as they devoured her where she lay, awash in languor. He stripped off his clothes, then knelt between her widespread thighs, his body a bronzed and powerful shadow in the deeper shadows of the night. He drew her legs onto his shoulders, slipping his hands beneath her buttocks to lift her to meet the slow thrust of his entry, which seemed to penetrate her core, to fill her with a sweet anguish that she could barely contain, yet could not bear to relinquish. The fire had burned low and the woodland sounds had yielded to the silence of profound night before they came back to themselves, the sweat cooling on their entwined bodies. Bryony cuddled closer into Ben's embrace, and he reached for her cloak, wrapping her soundly before rebuilding the fire, so that they lay in a circle of warmth and light within the deep dark of the wood. Their companions' fires had died long since and, before sleep finally claimed them, the lovers could believe that they still existed on their own plane in their own universe, where words were not necessary; their eyes locked in love and the touch of their skins expressed all that ever needed to be said.

# Chapter 20

"It's to be hoped we'll find a likely family here." Benedict hitched Ned higher on his back, where he was riding piggyback, and frowned at the farmhouse and the cluster of outbuildings that appeared beside the bridle path.

"Ye take one step on my land and ye'll be feeding the vultures!" The threat bellowed from the top of the barn and a shot punched into the trunk of a tree behind them. Ben had dropped Ned to the ground and swept Bryony behind him almost before the echo had died.

"We come in peace," he called, raising his hands, showing them weaponless.

Bryony stepped forward. "We would ask for your help for a child —"

Another shot whined overhead, and Benedict, a violent expletive rending the air, grabbed her roughly, shoving her behind him again. "Stay where you are put!"

"But I only thought that if they could see Ned and me, then they wouldn't be

540

afeard," she explained reasonably. "If Ferguson's men have come this way, then it is hardly surprising that they don't welcome strangers."

"When folks are scared, they are inclined to shoot first and ask questions later," Ben pointed out.

"Then they are as likely to shoot you as me."

Ben's laugh quivered in his voice. "You are a damnably argumentative lass." He looked around again, then shook his head. "I think we are on a fool's errand here. We had best rejoin the others."

They had broken away from the group earlier that morning, since the pursuit of Ferguson's band was now taking them off the beaten track, away from the possibility of hamlets or even the lone farmhouse, like this one. Ben was anxious to be rid of the boy, who still had not said a word, although he came trustingly enough into Ben's arms when his little legs grew weary. But campaigning of any kind was no activity for a child, and this stealthy creeping up on the plundering Tories was fraught with more than ordinary dangers and privations. Bryony seemed to thrive on this hand-to-mouth existence, her body grown lean and taut where it had been slender and fragile, her skin bronzed and freckled instead of cream and rose. Her hair was always tangled and frequently dirty, but Benedict did not think he had ever known her more beautiful — or more achingly desirable.

"Wait!" Bryony said suddenly as Ben turned to go back the way they had come. "Someone is coming." A woman, a rifle beneath her arm, appeared in the doorway of the house. Bryony, dodging Ben's grasping hand and ignoring his imperative shout to come back, ran over to the house. Ben swore again, waiting with jarring heart for another shot from the watcher in the barn. None was forthcoming, however, and Bryony reached the house unmolested. Hoisting the child into his arms, Ben followed her.

Bryony was deep in explanation when he reached the house. Her audience was a gaunt woman with sharp eyes and gnarled hands, iron-gray hair scraped back from an angular countenance. She held the rifle with the ease of one well versed in its use, and she stood, legs apart, with all the stolidity of one who had broken the sod of the frontier and knew its hardness and intractability. She listened to Bryony and eyed Ned, who gazed with his habitual, wide-eyed mistrust from the shelter of Ben's arms.

"Scrawny!" the woman pronounced when Bryony had fallen silent. "But he'll learn to work soon enough."

"But he is only a baby," Bryony said, shocked into protest. "He can't work."

The woman snorted. "There's no food for idle hands! He'll chop wood and fetch water, clean out the stables and do most anything for a bed in the barn and his keep."

Bryony turned to Benedict, who said quietly, "It is the life he would have had, lass, if he had not lost his family."

"But he would have had it with people who loved him," she said in a low voice, looking around the bleak property, then into the expressionless eyes of the woman. There was no love here. Maybe no cruelty, either, but such a little mite, already battered by the world's ferocity, would shrivel in this thin, ungiving soil where there was no nurturing warmth.

Ben set the child on his feet and said, "I will pay for his keep, ma'am, until he is older and stronger . . . and for a bed in the house." Drawing one of his few remaining sovereigns from his pocket, he held it out to the woman and said to Bryony, "It has to be, lass." Taking her arm, he turned her back to the path. She went without protest, knowing that he had done what he could, but she had not taken three steps when a sobbing wail came from behind. Spinning on her heel, she saw the child hurtling toward her.

"Bryny . . . stay with me!" Ned flung himself at her knees, clinging and sobbing. It was the first time he had spoken since she had found him.

"Sweet Jesus!" muttered Benedict, in no doubt as to what was going to happen now. "Bryony, I cannot be saddled with a child."

"You will not be. I will," she said firmly.

Benedict sighed. "Listen, lass. It is hard enough for me to do what I must when I have a woman in tow."

"I am not in tow!" Indignation sparked in her eyes.

"You are," he stated, "and I would not have it any other way. But *not* a child!"

"Then I shall stay with him, and you may come back for us both when you have done what you must and what you cannot do with women and children in tow." She faced him on the narrow path with all the resolution that he knew so well, but a resolution now hardened with the wisdom and experience of maturity.

Benedict looked down at the child, who still clung to her skirts, peeping up at him with an anxious yet unusually trusting stare. He accepted defeat. "Then retrieve my sovereign. We don't have so many that I can scatter them at random around the countryside, for all that you seem to think I can."

"Mayhap, she will have some clothes that would do for him," Bryony said thoughtfully. "For a small payment —"

"There will be no more payments," Ben interrupted, "for anything that is not essential. You will have to turn seamstress, I fear. You were taught to sew, were you not?"

"Well, yes," Bryony said doubtfully. "But I'll lay odds I am not as good as you are."

"As it happens, I am not at all handy with a needle," he stated, dashing her hopes.

"Oh." Bryony shrugged. "Then, I daresay I will manage." She ran back to the house, where the woman still stood, as if carved in granite. "I must thank you, ma'am, but the child, it seems, wishes to come with us." She smiled, hopefully placating. "If I could have the sovereign."

"Givin' in to children never did any good," the woman said, but she handed over the gold coin with a tiny shrug, then turned back into the house without a word of farewell, the door banging shut with a desolate finality.

Bryony left the bleak, unfriendly spot with a sigh of relief, and the three of them set off down the path, Ned, his articulate moment apparently just that, trotting silently between them. Bryony looked up at Benedict. "We could not have left him there."

"We could have," Ben replied. "*You* would not. Warfare and children make ill companions. And warriors who have to concern themselves with the day-to-day conditions of women and children make less than single-minded soldiers."

"You would be rid of me, then?"

Ben glanced down at the brown, set face and shook his head ruefully. "Only when there is danger and I worry about your safety. But I could do without the child, I'll admit."

"I will care for him," she declared with determination. "I am quite capable." A mischievous chuckle suddenly escaped her. "After all, in any other circumstance, I would have had half a dozen of my own by now."

Benedict, for some reason, did not seem

to find the idea as amusing as she did. Indeed, the thought of fathering a child filled him with trepidation, and he could not imagine a time when it would not. He was hardly in a position to found his dynasty, and it seemed highly unlikely that that position would change, even if he survived the war. He had no land, no fortune, no family to fall back on — nothing to give a wife, let alone children. But such contemplation produced gloom, and time was too precious these days to waste in despondent reflection upon a future that might never materialize.

"It is to be hoped you don't regret your charge," he declared with an assumption of briskness. "For he is most certainly your charge. I shall hold you responsible for any mischief he may get himself into and for ensuring that he does not trouble anyone else. Is it agreed?"

Bryony peered down at the trailing mite. "He doesn't look as if he could possibly get into mischief."

"It is the nature of the beast called child," Ben told her. "Once he has recovered himself somewhat, you will have your hands full, I guarantee it."

Charlie greeted their return with raised eyebrows. "Still got him, then?"

"He didn't want to be left," Bryony explained. "He actually said so."

Charlie whistled in surprise. "So, what are you going to do with him now?"

"First I must find him some clothes." Bryony tapped her teeth with an impatient fingernail as she pondered the problem. "I can cut down Ben's shirts easily enough, but what are we to do about britches?"

"I don't recall giving you permission to make free with my shirts," Ben stated.

"Well, you would not allow me to buy him clothes, so what else are we to do?" She caught the raised eyebrow. "What else am *I* to do?" she amended.

"That's better. You may have one of my shirts in addition to the one he is already wearing, but that is as far as I am prepared to countenance the depletion of my already scant wardrobe." Shouldering his musket, Ben veered off into the woods in search of game for their supper.

A week later, they crossed the border into North Carolina and knew they were close now to their prey. The houses were still smoldering, the bodies barely cold, and those they spoke with told bitter tales of systematic looting and murder. The band of backwoodsmen and frontier riflemen was almost nine hundred strong, each and every one filled with a savage fury, vengeance their only goal. Bryony felt the grim purpose rise to exclude all else as the men grew silent, the lines of their faces set as they turned inward, drawing from their own wells for strength and courage.

"We have him, Ben." It was said with satisfaction, just after they made camp early one evening, and Benedict looked up from the rifle he was cleaning.

"The scouts have found him?"

"Aye. Atop a hill at Kings Mountain. About a thousand of 'em." The young rifleman squatted down by the fire. "They'll have the advantage, being atop of us."

Bryony's fingers became suddenly clumsy, and the needle she was using slipped, pricking her thumb and leaving a bright spot of blood on the shirt she was hemming. She swore a backwoods oath that did not even draw a glance from her companions, and sucked the injured thumb.

"There are more ways than one of skinning a cat," Ben mused. Bryony abandoned her needlework. Her fingers were trembling too much. She clasped her hands firmly in her lap and waited for Benedict to share his thoughts.

"Ben! Ben! Look what I got!" The excited shriek came first, the small body catapulting through the bushes in its wake. Ned, tripping over the bottom of the shirt that Bryony had managed to cut but had not yet got around to hemming, rushed over to them, his hands clasped to his scrawny chest.

Putting thoughts of battle strategy behind him in the face of this clearly more urgent matter, Benedict said, "What have you got there?"

"Look!" The child extended his cupped hands, a delighted beam on the dirty little face.

"Oh, it's a lizard." Ben gave the captive due consideration. "What do you intend doing with it?"

"Eat it," the child replied matter-of-factly. In his recent experience, the acquisition of animals meant supper.

Bryony choked, her eyes meeting Ben's amused glance over the boy's head. "I don't think it has enough meat on it, Ned," Ben said seriously. "Lizards are a bit bony."

"Oh." Ned's face fell. "Could put it in the pot."

"Well . . ."

"No!" Bryony cried when it looked as if Ben was about to agree to the suggestion, presumably on the grounds that so many things went into the pot, what difference would a little lizard make? "I refuse to eat reptiles."

"You ate snake the other day," Charlie pointed out.

"I did not!" She glared with growing suspicion around the circle of laughing faces.

"I'm afraid you did," Ben said. "And pronounced it very tasty."

"Sometimes, Benedict Clare, I dislike you intensely." Bryony stood up, smoothing down her faded dimity print skirt. "Don't you dare put that lizard in the pot." She stalked off, hearing their laughter behind her. Her annoyance died fairly rapidly as she strolled around the camp. What did it matter if they made fun of her once in a while? She didn't really mind and knew that sometimes, like just now, the teasing provided an outlet when tensions or excitement were running high. It was probably the last laugh any of them would have until the grisly business that had brought them so many miles was completed. If any of them were left alive to laugh.

She tried to shake off the thought. They were all sworn to see Ferguson and his men dead or prisoners. There would be little quarter offered those who fell into the hands of these enraged Carolinians. But Ferguson's army was well trained and had never been accused of lacking in bravery, and they held the superior position, even if they were trapped in it.

"Bryny . . . Bryny . . ." Ned's shrill accents interrupted the unpleasant reverie. Since the boy had found his voice again, his incessant chatter continued every waking minute. He did not really seem to mind if there was no audience beyond birds and flies, and his imperative shrieks for either Ben or Bryony were constantly heard.

She waited for him to reach her, then asked, smiling, "What did you do with the lizard?"

The little face screwed up with intense concentration. "Ben says we're not goin' to eat it, so you can come back. Charlie says he didn't mean to tease you."

"What a splendid messenger you are," Bryony said, taking his hand, and they walked back to their campfire.

"Still cross?" Ben stood up as she reached him, tilting her chin to plant a kiss on her freckled nose.

"You are quite horrid sometimes," she declared, trying to maintain her severity. "Did I really eat snake?"

"Do you really want to know?" He laughed.

"Probably not." Bryony sighed. "There is much that I do not think I wish to know, but that I must."

"For instance?" The laughter had left the black eyes, his gravity matching hers.

"How you intend skinning this particular cat — and when — and what Ned and I are to do while you go about it."

"You and Ned, sweeting, will stay in the village," he said. "The people have no love for Ferguson and his bandits, and you will be quite safe."

"When?"

"We leave before dawn and attack at first light." As usual, Ben answered her questions with no wasted words and, as usual, he would offer her no false comfort, no promises that he could not be certain of keeping.

It was still dark when the band of nine hundred stamped out their fires, shouldered their rifles, and slipped through the trees to the base of the mountain that formed a natural fortress for the enemy. The gray October dawn saw them swarming up the mountainside, taking their lessons from Indian strategies that they had learned painfully over the years.

Expert marksmen to a man, they hid behind trees, firing with deadly accuracy into the Tory/Loyalist lines as they charged, bayonets poised. The backwoodsmen fell back beneath the charges, only to re-form and press ever closer to the camp, forcing Ferguson's lines backward, his men dropping like flies beneath the sniping fire.

"By God! We have them on the run," Charlie exclaimed, dashing the sweat from his eyes as he joined the wave of men breaking from cover to surge across the field, firing as they raced forward, overrunning the Tory lines. For a minute there was chaos as the two forces mingled, trampling over the dead and wounded, trying to sort themselves out; voices yelled orders, screamed pleas, roared in savage fury as bayonets slashed and rifles cracked.

"A surrender flag," Benedict gasped as two white flags appeared out of the tumult, waving forlornly above the bloody field. "By God, he's surrendering."

Then the flags vanished as Patrick Ferguson cut them down with his sword. Bellowing defiance, he charged down the field, riding directly at the American forces standing massed in his way. Fifty men raised fifty rifles, leveling them at the figure. A volley exploded and the major fell from his horse, quite literally shot to pieces.

Benedict Clare thought for a fleeting instant of the time when he had sat at table with the major, had shared a toast. Then a great roar went up as white flags again appeared, this time to remain fluttering in the cold, early-morning mountain air. The battle had taken one hour, and the field was littered with bodies bearing Tory uniforms and Loyalist insignia.

Francis Cullum drifted in and out of pain. When it came, it was too intense to be endured, and he would sink into oblivion, returning to his senses but to a confused awareness of the hard ground beneath him, the misty blue of the sky above, the sounds that could have come from hell's inferno — men pleading for water, for surcease; men cursing in broken voices; men weeping. There was a great heaviness on his chest, as if someone had rolled a boulder onto him, and when he breathed, a funny bubbling sound came forth and he did not seem able to draw sufficient air to satisfy his body's craving. Clearly, he was going to die, he thought with calm detachment. He had been seeking death in this war, after all. But somehow he had not envisaged this reality. Did it have to be in this manner? So slowly and so lonely. Then he heard a voice — a voice from the past, piercing the fog that was coming to claim him again. He opened his mouth and thought he said the name. "Clare." But then the fog came and he did not know whether he had spoken or not.

Benedict heard his name, or something approximating it. It had come forth as a weak croak from somewhere below him. He looked down. The band he had marched with and fought with showed no interest in the wounded. They would leave them on the field to die or to be cared for by any who chose to come among them. The living were their main concern. Seven hundred of them were to be herded and marched off in captivity, back into the mountains. When he saw Francis Cullum, his first thought was that he was dead, that he had to be dead with such a wound in his chest. Then he saw the eyelids flicker.

He dropped to his knees beside him, feeling for a pulse. It was there, but fast and feeble. "Charlie?" He beckoned to the younger man, who was standing, surveying the devastation, the look on his face so clearly expressing grim satisfaction — they were revenged for Camden and for all those left dead in Ferguson's wake. "I want to get this man down the mountain," Ben said. "I do not know if he will survive being moved, but he will not survive here."

"Why bother?" Charlie knelt beside him. "Throw him in the pit with the others."

"You do not combat gratuitous savagery with its like." It was a cold rebuke from a man who knew its truth, and Charlie felt the blood rush hot to his cheeks.

"Clare?" Francis spoke with sudden clarity, startling them both. "Thought I heard your voice." His eyes closed again. "How is Bri?"

"Well," Ben said. "Do not talk. I am going to take you to her."

"You . . . you . . . know him?" Charlie stuttered.

Ben tore off his shirt and began to roll it into a flat oblong. "He is a childhood friend of Bryony's. Now help me lift him so that I may bind his chest with this. It may serve to keep the wound closed." Charlie obeyed the rapid instructions without further demur. They fashioned a rough stretcher from material they found within the Tory camp and together bore the now unconscious Francis down the mountain.

Bryony had left the village the minute the firing had started and taken up a position at the base of Kings Mountain. She had left Ned behind with a motherly soul who had enticed him with the promise of gingerbread. It was impossible to tell what had happened until news of the resounding defeat was brought down the mountain by local lads who had followed the frontier force. Bryony, without further reflection, set off up the slope at a run. There were casualties on the American side, she knew, although her jubilant informant had said nary a one compared with the slaughter of the butcher's men.

It was a chilly autumnal morning, and the sun had not the power to warm the mountain air, but the sweat was trickling down her rib cage and plastering her hair to her brow when Benedict saw her clambering at great speed up the mountainside toward him, hampered by her skirts and her ill-shod feet. He wondered whether remonstrance would be a worthwhile exercise and decided that it would not. The minute his back was turned, she went where she chose, as she had done since the night she had followed him to the armory and warned them of the redcoats.

"You are safe!" Breathlessly, she came up to them, smiling mistily. "I could not wait below . . . not when I heard that the battle was won."

"So I see," was all he allowed himself to say. He did not allow himself to touch her, either, and saw that she also held back, as if just the moment of reunion was precious enough and sufficient unto itself, after the agonizing uncertainty when the image of his death was as real as the memory of his presence.

Then she dragged her eyes from his, smiled at Charlie, including him in her joy, before their burden intruded on her consciousness. The color left her face. "Francis?"

"He is sore wounded," Ben said swiftly. "We must take him to the village."

"Yes. I'll go ahead and make preparations." She turned immediately, then stopped with her back to him. "Will he live, Ben?"

"I do not think so," he said quietly; there were things he would not tell her, but he would never lie to her. Her back was still and straight, her head slightly bowed so that her neck curved, open and vulnerable, and he ached to hold her through the grief. But then she raised her head, tossed her hair over her shoulder, and went ahead of them, running down the mountainside.

The woman in the cottage where Bryony had left Ned raised her eyebrows at the request that she receive under her roof a wounded Tory, but the pain that stood out in the younger woman's eyes could not be denied, and she gestured to the bedstead that stood against the kitchen wall. "Ye can lay him there."

Ned crept into the inglenook when Ben and Charlie appeared in the doorway, the stretcher between them. There was fear and dread in the kitchen where before there had been the hot fragrance of gingerbread; rich, embracing laughter when he had said or done something that seemed to amuse; hands that stroked or patted carelessly. Now it was like it had been when the soldiers had come and his mother's eyes had opened wide in terror and his father had cried out. As he had done then, he hid in the far corner of the fireplace, so close to the fire that it scorched his cheek, and he closed his mouth tight, lest a betraying sound should come forth.

Francis was laid as gently as possible on the bedstead, but all the care in the world could not prevent the groan of anguish as he returned to consciousness. Bryony knelt beside him, her eyes filled with pain at her own helplessness. One look at the wound had told her that Ben had been correct. There was nothing they could do but attempt to ease his death and make it a little less lonely.

"Bri?" A tiny smile cracked his lips. "Said we'd have another farewell."

"Yes, you did. I have remembered it all this time," she replied, laying a damp cloth on his brow, taking his hand, trying not to squeeze too tightly. "But I was sure you could not be with Ferguson's force."

Pain scudded across his face. "Such savagery, Bri." He coughed, and she wiped the bubble of blood from his lips, watching despairingly as the bright fountain welled from his chest to soak the makeshift bandage.

"Do not talk, Francis."

"I must while I can. If it hastens death, then I am not sorry." He sounded stronger, as if marshaling those resources that remained hidden until the ultimate need. "I tried to stop it, Bri . . . but . . ."

"How could one in a thousand stop it?" she said soothingly. "I have always known you could not have been a part of it."

His lips twisted in a grimace of disgust. "I was a part of it because I was there."

"In war, things happen that one cannot prevent or even mitigate." It was Ben who spoke in quiet compassion for the dilemma he understood so well. It was a dilemma that had nothing to do with the causes and principles for which one fought — it had to do with the simple facts of warfare.

"My thanks for those kind words." Francis coughed again, and the self-directed cynicism in the green eyes was vanquished by suffering. His eyes closed and there was silence in the small, hot room. Bryony blinked back her tears. They would not help Francis, and she would not indulge in weeping while he was still here to see and be sorry for it.

"Happy, Bri?" His eyes opened again, searching her face as she bent over him to catch his words.

She nodded. "As much as it is possible to be at such a time." She wiped the trickle of blood from his mouth again and smiled effortfully. She wanted to ask him about her parents, about how they had reacted to her disappearance, whether he knew if they were well, but she could not frame the questions.

But Francis read her thoughts, as he had often been able to do. "Your father is with Cornwallis," he said, then stopped as he struggled to draw air into his shattered lungs. "On their way to Charlotte to rout

out the rebels there. Then to Virginia . . . knock the South out of the war . . ." Another pause before he said in barely a whisper, "Things different now — after today." Blood filled his mouth, and he had barely the strength to spit into the bowl Bryony held.

"Do not talk anymore, I beg you," she pleaded in unutterable distress, wiping his mouth.

But Francis gathered strength again. "Your mother . . . heartbroken, Bri, but she knew."

"Knew what?" She leaned over him, so startled by this revelation that she forgot the horror for a minute.

Francis almost managed a smile. "Knew that something had happened that summer — that you would go back, in the end."

"Yes," Bryony whispered. "I think I always realized that she knew." Her fingers gripped his. "But my father?"

"Went to join Cornwallis . . ." He coughed again. "Couldn't stay still . . . Your mother said it was better that way. . . ." His voice faded and died as the last reserve of strength was exhausted.

Bryony sat beside him for the two hours that it took before life finally left him. He did not regain consciousness, but the

563

broken body perversely struggled on, trying to do what it was supposed to. Benedict stayed with her, in the far corner of the room, knowing that she was oblivious of him, that he had nothing to offer her as she mourned, yet unable to leave her to suffer alone. When she finally placed the hand that she held onto the bed and stood up, he went to take her in his arms, but she pushed away from him and went outside into the village street. She returned in about ten minutes and spoke in a strange, wooden voice that carried no expression.

"There is a weeping willow by the stream. I would like to bury him there, please."

Ben nodded, and he and Charlie followed her to the spot, where they dug the grave in silence. Francis Cullum was laid beside the murmuring stream under the soft shade of the graceful tree.

Bryony sat near the fresh mound of earth and did not seem to hear Benedict when he gently said they must prepare to leave. Ben, for once at a loss, turned and went back to the house in the village. A short delay would not make much difference. He had already decided that they would not continue with the Carolinians who were heading back into the mountains with their prisoners. He had two choices: to make his way to Charlotte to join the remnants of Gates's army where they waited in the hope of reinforcements from the North; or he could join up with another of the bands who slipped through the backcountry, harassing Cornwallis's army in the undercover war that was proving more successful than pitched battle.

It was only when he reached the cottage that he remembered Ned. There was no sign of the boy, and the woman said that she had not seen him since they had brought the wounded man inside. Benedict and Charlie hunted high and low. No one in the village had seen a small, ragged child who did not belong there, although there were plenty who did belong.

"He must be somewhere!" Ben flung himself onto a stool in the cottage kitchen and looked in exasperation at Charlie. "Bryony is in a bad enough state as it is, without this."

The woman went to stir the contents of a pot hanging from a hook suspended from the lug pole over the fire. "Well, I'll be! He's in 'ere . . . been 'ere all along, I'll be bound." She grabbed the child's arm and hauled him out into the kitchen. "Young varmint! Turned the place upside down, we 'ave, lookin' for ye."

"You knew I was looking for you, Ned," Ben said, drawing the child toward him. "Why were you hiding?" There was no response, and Benedict sighed as he recognized the child they had first found — a mute, petrified scrap of humanity. "Charlie, keep an eye on him, will you? I have to fetch Bryony. It's time to put this place behind us."

He walked down to the stream, where he found Bryony, still unmoving beside the grave. "Lass, we must leave now." Bending, he took her arm and raised her to her feet.

"I want to go home," she said in that same wooden voice that sounded as if a spring had broken.

He felt the sorrow seep into his pores. She had had enough of the choice she had made; he could hardly blame her. "I had thought you were home with me, but I said that I would not hold you if you changed your mind. As soon as it is possible, I will arrange for you to return to your mother."

She looked up at him, shock and incredulity chasing away the paralysis of grief. The black lashes were sticky with tears, but the eyes were now clear. "Of course I am home with you. How could you think I would change my mind? I meant only that I wish it were possible to go back to a time when none of this . . . oh . . ." She smiled, a faint little smile, but it was an attempt. "I would not change loving you, Ben. But I wished, just for a minute, that I could be a child again, with the future ahead, waiting to be made — back to a time when one believed that one *could* make the future, that it would not make itself and tumble you along with it." Her shoulders lifted in a tiny shrug. "Such childishness, I know, but I do not think I could bear to be scolded for it at the moment."

He caught her chin, lifting her face to his scrutiny. "You deserve to be scolded for thinking that I would, sweeting. There is nothing childish about wishing things undone. The foolishness lies in behaving as if they can be." He kissed her, sensing — with a flood of relief — that she was at peace. There was no passion in her response, but he had not been trying to elicit that reaction, merely to provide the comfort and reassurance of his loving presence. It was a comfort and reassurance that she did not reject.

"Come." He put his arm around her shoulders, turning her back to the village. "Something about today has badly upset Ned. He was cowering in the inglenook, while Charlie and I turned the village upside down looking for him. And he has lost his tongue again."

"I expect it was the proximity of death," she said, as if it were the most obvious thing imaginable. "Go on. I will join you in a minute. I would bid a last farewell to Francis."

He studied her carefully, reluctant to leave her to renew her mourning, but her eyes were calm, her features composed, and he nodded his agreement. "Do not be long. The living have need of you."

# Chapter 21

"Well, that is a piece of news worth having." Thomas Sumter regarded with scant interest the unconscious figure of the redcoat who had been induced to part with the useful information.

Benedict Clare shivered in the December night, shrugging deeper into his greatcoat, grateful for a garment that few of Sumter's band of guerrillas possessed. "What do you want to do with him?" He gestured to the straggler they had cut out from a party of Cornwallis's troops who had strayed too far from the army's winter quarters at Winnsboro, South Carolina.

"Leave him here, the wolves'll have him. . . . Take him with us, we'll have to feed him." Sumter shrugged as he laid out the alternatives. "We've enough mouths to feed."

It was true enough, Ben knew. Game was scarce in the dreary winter months, and stockpiling supplies was impossible, as Thomas Sumter's band was perpetually on the move, attacking British outposts, snatching stragglers like the man before them, stinging Cornwallis in hit-and-run raids that required his constant attention and the constant deployment of troops all over the province. Ostensibly, the British earl was in control of South Carolina, but it was an uneasy possession, one that threatened to slip from his grasp if he dropped his guard for a minute.

One of the band solved the problem without further analysis. A shot rang through the dank wood, and the group left, sliding between the trees, as soundless and as deadly as any mountain lion.

Bryony gloomily surveyed the sole of her once sturdy leather shoe. The hole was enormous and this time past even Ben's ingenuity, she reckoned. But it was too damn cold to go barefoot! The turf fire in the hearth spluttered, sending evil-smelling smoke curling up to the clapboard roof of the mountain cabin that had been home for the last three days. The turf fire was Ben's innovation — it was the fuel of the Irish peasant, he had told her, and she supposed she should be grateful. After two weeks of incessant rain, there wasn't a dry piece of timber on the mountain, and during this time she, Charlie, Ned, and Ben would huddle around the smoking hearth, taking what comfort they could from the flameless smolder that threw out little heat, although a pan of water would warm eventually.

The door banged open and a sheet of rain blew in, ice-tipped. Ben had slammed the door behind him before the yell of protest left her lips. "It couldn't be helped," he said. "It's blowing a gale!" He bent to warm his hands at the thankless hearth. Bryony held out her shoe, wordlessly inviting his examination. Ben sighed. "Maybe I can patch it again. But take heart, lass. This time next week, you shall find your bed in a town."

"What! You mean we may leave this god-forsaken mountain?" Bryony bounced to her feet, holey shoes and smoking fires for the moment forgotten. "Oh, I love you, Benedict Clare." Seizing his arms, she danced across the earthen floor with him.

"What brought this on?" Charlie stepped into the hut, letting in another icy blast. "Have we killed a goose for Christmas?"

"No, but we are going to spend Christmas in town," Bryony declared. "Where houses have shutters and doors that fit, and one can buy things . . ." She dropped to the floor again, in front of the fire.

"What with?" Ben asked, loath to dampen her excitement but not willing to deny reality. "Anyway, even if we had the wherewithal, lass, I doubt very much that there will be anything to buy in Charlotte. Gates's army has been quartered there since their defeat at Camden. The country-side will have been picked clean."

"I am all in favor of a change of dwelling, Ben, but why this dramatic shift?" asked Charlie, surveying the con-tents of a cooking pot with singular lack of expectation. "What is this, Bryony?"

"Maize," she said. "It's all we have. I nearly sent Ned out in search of lizards." It was a gallant attempt to make light of things, and Ben bent to stroke her hair. She reached up and caught his wrist, squeezing strongly. "So, answer Charlie's question."

"We picked up a straggler this after-noon." He sat down beside her and ladled the thick, tepid maize porridge onto a wooden trencher. "He was persuaded to tell us that General Washington has sent Nathanael Greene to take command in the South. The Quaker is the ablest of Wash-ington's men." He smiled through a mouthful. "Children, I think we are back in the fight."

"When were you ever out of it?" Bryony demanded, taking a spoonful of maize from the pot and swallowing with effort.

"An organized fight between equal opposing sides," Ben explained, although she did not really need the explanation. "If Greene can pull Gates's army together, then we stand a chance against Cornwallis on the open field."

"And we are going to join the army, I suppose?" Bryony sighed heavily, and Ben cuffed her playfully. She fell forward onto his lap, chuckling. "You will have to carry me. I cannot walk all the way into North Carolina without shoes."

"I will carry both you and Ned, if necessary," he said, stroking her back, and she heard the underlying seriousness behind the light tone that matched her own. They both glanced toward the little mound on the far side of the fire. Ned was like any other small animal. He fell asleep wherever he happened to be, and stayed asleep through any degree of turmoil for as long as he needed to.

The three adults talked until late into the night, making the plans that would take them into the next phase of the grim game they played. Later, when they lay curled around the fire, and the even breathing of their companions told them that they were alone, Ben turned her onto her side, facing away from him beneath the concealing blanket. As he joined them in a soft, sweet slide of delight, Bryony pressed backward, molding herself to the curve that contained her, surrendering her self with her body to the deep well of pleasure that never ran dry however often they drew from it.

Ned woke them, as he always did, at first light, doing his usual dance expressive of the urgency of his need as he demanded that they open the door and let him out. "For all the world as if he's a puppy," Ben said, grinning as the child scampered out into the rain, disappearing into the bushes behind the cabin.

Bryony rose and went to peer out of the door. "Will it ever stop raining? The thought of walking to Charlotte in this does not fill me with enthusiasm."

"The sky's lightening up a little," Charlie ventured. "It's a good sign. Do we have any breakfast?"

"Maize porridge," she told him. "If there's any left over from last night."

"Unless you'd prefer fish," Ben remarked

casually, and both the others spun round, eyes eager, mouths watering. He was examining a hook on the end of an improvised fishing rod. "There's a stream up yonder. It may yield something."

"I'm hungry," announced a childish treble, as a very moist but visibly relieved Ned appeared in the doorway, fumbling with the fastening of his britches, " 'n' I don't want porridge."

"A sentiment with which I heartily agree," said Charlie, bending to help him do up his buttons. "But Ben has promised us fish."

"No promises," Ben protested. "I cannot catch them if they're not biting. Do you want to come with me, Ned?"

"He'll get dreadfully wet," Bryony pointed out, but more as a matter of form than as serious objection.

"Not exactly an unusual condition." Ben chuckled, and went out into the gloomy morning, followed by a prancing tot.

The fishing expedition having proved successful, it was a well-fed group who left the cabin several hours later, their few possessions bundled into the two portmanteaux, battered now but still sturdy. Bryony's shoe was patched with a lumpy piece of leather that Ben had begged from a member of the band they were leaving behind. It kept out the water but rapidly rubbed a sore place on the sole of her foot. However, she had learned to endure discomfort with some stoicism in the last months and plodded on, hiding her limp as best she could from Ben's sharp eyes.

It was a forty-mile hike through rough country, since they had no desire to run into one of the groups of redcoats who patrolled the main thoroughfares of the province. Once into North Carolina, however, they could relax their guard somewhat. After the defeat at Kings Mountain, Cornwallis had reacted with caution and had withdrawn his plan to roll up the South in one bold sweep, retiring instead to winter quarters at Winnsboro to wait out the bad months. This left North Carolina for the moment free of British invasion. But what they found in Charlotte, when, footsore and exhausted, the four stumbled into the American-held town, was not a situation to inspire confidence.

Bryony forgot the pain in her foot for the moment as she stared in dismay at the ragged, half-starved scarecrows thronging the streets. "This is the army?"

"It would appear so," Ben said grimly. He walked over to a small group and addressed a man leaning on a crutch. "Where can I find General Greene?"

The man gestured with his thumb down the road. "Big house on the corner is headquarters. Ye'll find 'em all there."

"My thanks." Ben came back to his own party. "All? I wonder who 'all' are?"

"The sooner we find out, the better," Charlie said practically. "Maybe there'll be rations, now that we're back with the regular army."

"Ever hopeful!" Bryony leaned against a wall and lifted her foot, examining the sole of her shoe. Blood stained the leather, and the thought of what she would find beneath made her feel a little sick.

"Stay here with Ned," Ben instructed briskly. "Charlie and I will seek out Greene."

"Why can't we come, too?" Bryony looked doubtfully down the dirt road, where groups of men wandered aimlessly.

"Because, sweeting, I do not wish to present myself to my new commanding officer surrounded by a gaggle of women and children," he said bluntly.

Bryony glanced around, eyebrows raised. "Gaggle?" she inquired. "I see no gaggle. Just us."

Charlie chuckled but said, "Ben has the

right of it, Bryony. It doesn't look very soldierly for a colonel to report for duty with a child on his hip."

"Well, how are you going to manage to keep us hidden?"

Ben spoke more sharply than he intended. "I have no intention of keeping you hidden, but until I find out what the position is here, I do not intend to parade you in front of the army's high command." With that, he turned on his heel and strode down the road.

Charlie handed Ned to Bryony, offering her a hesitantly sympathetic smile, which she returned with an obvious struggle. "It's only because he is worried about you," Charlie said. "He has been dreadfully concerned about your foot, and now he must find lodgings and food —"

"Yes, I know," Bryony broke in swiftly. "It's always the way when he is harassed."

"Yes," agreed Charlie with a slight shrug. "I had best not be dilatory in presenting myself to Greene." He went off at a trot in the wake of the rapidly disappearing Benedict, and Bryony, finding a relatively dry spot, sat down by the side of the road, holding Ned on her lap, both of them huddling into her cloak for warmth.

★ ★ ★

"There's but three days' rations, General, and the country is almost laid waste. The inhabitants plunder one another with little less than savagery." The staff officer finished his gloomy report to Nathanael Greene as Benedict Clare and Charlie Carter were shown into a square parlor that served as staff room.

General Greene turned from his contemplation of the small fire in the hearth and looked at the new arrivals. "Who have we here?"

Benedict spoke for them both, and the handsome, florid veteran listened attentively. "You were at Kings Mountain, you say? Then you'll do best to join Daniel Morgan's men. He's gathering together groups of local militia, men who've been fighting as you have been. He's in dire need of regular officers who understand the frontiersmen and their style of battle." Greene turned to his staff officer. "Ask the brigadier general to join us, will you, Lieutenant Bates?"

The staff officer left, and Greene frowned thoughtfully. "We're in a mess, Clare, as I expect you've gathered. A few ragged, half-starving troops in the wilderness, destitute of everything. We live from hand to mouth. There's no morale, the armory is all but bare, and we face an army three times our strength. We will make but a poor fight, I fear. It is difficult to give spirit to troops that have nothing to animate them."

"Do not underestimate the backcountry folk, sir," Benedict said. "They are bold and daring above the ordinary. With leadership and a purpose, they will fight for you."

"Well said, sir!" Booming agreement came from the door, and Brigadier General Daniel Morgan strode in. The old Indian fighter, who had commanded riflemen in the Northern campaigns until sent with Greene to rebuild the Southern forces, regarded the tall, lean Irishman with approval. "Bates tells me you've both been with Sumter's raiders."

"Aye, General, but when we heard news of your arrival in Charlotte, it seemed time to return to the open again."

"You are well come, indeed." Morgan clapped them both on the shoulders. "We'll be spending some time organizing ourselves before we'll be fit to fight. The officers' billet is not the lap of luxury, but you're welcome enough."

Charlie coughed and looked at Benedict,

who said carefully, "We'll need to find a billet of our own, General. I do not travel alone."

"Oh?" Nathanael Greene's bushy brows shot up, and all eyes were on Ben, who found himself unaccountably embarrassed.

"My wife is with me, sir." He settled for the plain, unvarnished truth. "Also a small child whom we found in one of the villages that Ferguson had passed through — the only survivor and a remarkably tenacious lad." A slight smile touched his lips. "He does not choose to be left."

"They've been with you all winter?" Morgan seemed incredulous. He had little difficulty imagining the kind of living they would have had with the guerrillas in the mountains.

"My wife has been with me since I joined General Gates before Camden. She is quite a campaigner."

"She must be," muttered Greene. "Well, you know your own business best, I daresay. We do not have sufficient rations for families, I should warn you. We may be able to feed the two of you —"

"That will be my concern, General," Benedict interrupted, a little stiffly. "I will look to my own."

"Yes, well . . . uh, good, good. That is all

settled, then." General Greene, restored to his customary cheerfulness, rubbed his hands together over the fire. "I am sure you will be able to find lodgings in the village or nearby, for a small outlay."

"It will have to be very small," murmured Charlie, only too aware of their scant resources.

"There's a cottage near the church," Lieutenant Bates said suddenly. "A bit tumbledown, and deserted because the men are afeard of ghosts from the cemetery. It's said they walk during the full moon." He shrugged. "I'd not care for it myself, but it could be made habitable with ingenuity."

Ben smiled. "That is a commodity we *do* possess, for all that our pockets are thin. And I'm sure we'll find only friendly specters. My thanks, gentlemen." He saluted, beaming now that his major problem was a fair way to being solved. Charlie saluted in turn and followed Benedict from the house. "Now," Ben said, "let us first look at this cottage, then we can surprise Bryony with a home."

"I think you should fetch her first," stated Charlie. "She is sitting at the road, in all this wind. I am sure she would prefer to be doing something."

"I don't want her walking unnecessarily on that foot." Ben frowned. "But I daresay you're right. She will be mad as fire if I leave her alone any longer than I need to. Fetch her and bring her to the church. It's down that lane." He gestured to where a small spire rose above the stone roofs. "I'll reconnoiter."

Charlie loped off up the street to where a very impatient and disinclined to be placated Bryony remained, huddled against the wind. "We think we have found us a house," he said, helping her up, wincing in sympathy as she flinched when her foot touched ground. "Shall I carry you?"

"Oh, don't be absurd!" Bryony bit back both a low moan and the tears of pain and weariness, choosing acerbity as an effective mask. "I should warn you that if Benedict is inclined to be snappish, then we shall have an uncomfortable time of it, because I am not at all in a good temper."

"No, I can see that." Charlie swung Ned onto his shoulders. "But if the house will do, then Ben will be as happy as a sandboy, and you will not be able to provoke him, however hard you try." That drew a chuckle from her as she hobbled at his side, accepting the support of his arm.

The cottage by the church was most definitely tumbledown, the roof sagging, the windows glassless, weeds choking the tiny garden. But there was a well and, to Bryony's unbridled joy, a necessary house at the end of the garden. Sanitary arrangements when one moved with a marauding band tended to be limited, and she was heartily sick of bushes and ditches and trees.

"I think we are in luck." Ben appeared in the cottage doorway, smiling happily. "I shall have a fire going in no time, and there are a few sticks of furniture that can be pressed into service. The roof needs some patching, but it's no great matter."

Bryony stepped through the door into the small, dark, one-room interior and burst out laughing. "Only you, Benedict Clare, could say that *this* is luck. Cattle are housed with more decency."

Ben's face fell. "I will do what I can, lass, to make it habitable."

"Oh, you silly!" She flung her arms around him, hugging him fiercely. "I was only funning. I didn't mean to hurt your feelings. It's a veritable palace after what we have been used to. And there is a privy! Just imagine that."

"I don't think you are going to want to use it until we have rid it of the spiders and other crawlers." He laughed, his spirits restored. "But before I do anything else, I am going to look to your foot."

"I don't think that that will be very easy," Bryony said doubtfully, sitting on a rickety three-legged stool. "The shoe seems to have become stuck with blood to my sole."

Ben looked a little grim. "Ned, go outside and collect sticks for the fire. Little ones for the kindling. Can you do that?" The child nodded importantly and disappeared at a run. "Charlie, we are going to need water. There is a bucket by the well. It's to be hoped it doesn't have a hole in it."

Charlie followed the instruction as cheerfully as Ned had done. One did not object to receiving orders from Benedict Clare. He knew too well what he was doing, and without his skills, they would none of them have survived the past few months.

"Now, let me see." Ben knelt down and lifted Bryony's foot, subjecting the mess to a frowning examination. "I am going to have to cut the shoe off, lass, and then try to soak off the patch. But I'll need hot water."

"I got some sticks." Ned, with a gap-toothed grin of satisfaction, stood in the doorway, his arms full of twigs.

"Good lad." Ben took them from him. "We'll get the fire going first." He knelt before the chimney and peered up it. "Of course, if there's a bird's nest up there, or some such, we'll be smoked out. Ned, see if you can find a long stick that I can poke up the chimney."

Bryony smiled to herself, feeling the relaxation seep into her despite her raw, bloody foot. Benedict Clare, with a job to do, was a joy to watch, and it did not occur to her for one minute that he would fail to turn this abandoned hovel into a haven of warmth and comfort. Such doubts did not occur to Ned or to Charlie, either, and their trust was not misplaced. The chimney was poked and pronounced free of obstruction, kindling laid, flint struck, and fire created. The lug pole over the fire was intact, and a kettle of water was hung over the blaze. A straw broom made an appearance in a gloomy corner, and Charlie was set to sweeping while Ben, at Bryony's insistence, went to render the privy usable.

"I am going to the officers' billet to scrounge a lamp," Charlie announced, replacing the broom in its corner. "I am certain they will be able to spare one. Shall I ask for anything else, Ben?"

"How about a couple of chickens, some milk, and some coffee?" Bryony suggested, only half joking.

"Bring what rations they will allow us, Charlie," Ben said quietly. "They will at least form a base, and we'll see what we can buy to augment them."

Bryony examined her fingernails with a concentration that their cracked and dirty condition did not encourage. Ben could be remarkably sensitive sometimes, when his ability to provide was hampered by conditions outside his control; at such times, she and Charlie needed to be especially careful with their teasing complaints. She exchanged a rueful look with Charlie as Benedict turned away to test the temperature of the water heating in the kettle.

"I come, too, Charlie." Ned jumped to his feet, holding out his hand imperatively.

"No," Ben stated in the soft voice they all knew. "We'll not play on sympathy."

"What's that?" demanded the child, although he resumed his seat at Bryony's feet without argument.

"What Ben means is that after one look at your big brown eyes, Ned love, the soldiers will give us all the milk and food we need," Bryony said, stroking his hair.

"They don't have sufficient for their own needs." Ben hoisted the kettle off the fire. "This is ready now."

"I'll be about my business, then." Charlie disappeared, and Bryony gritted her teeth, facing the upcoming ordeal.

The silence in the room was disturbed only by the sound of water being wrung from the cloth that Ben was using to soak the leather glued to the wound, and the occasional shuffle of his knees on the earthen floor as he shifted position. Ned sat watching, the tip of his thumb between his teeth. Bryony's eyes were closed. It seemed easier that way to separate herself from the excruciating pain as Ben tried to ease away the leather that was embedded in her flesh. She spoke only once, in a tiny voice. "I do not think I want you to do this anymore, Ben."

"I must, sweeting," was the only reply, uttered in a quiet, matter-of-fact tone that did more to bolster her courage than all the sympathy in the world. The task was done at last, and the torn, soggy mess of her foot could be washed and bound. Ben wiped her tears with his grubby handkerchief and kissed her. "You are a grand campaigner, my sweet, but you'll not walk on that foot for a few days. We must fashion you a crutch."

For the next three days, Bryony hobbled around the cottage doing what she could to make it more comfortable. They now had straw palliasses, which were a great improvement over the bare earth. Ben and Charlie patched the roof and tightened the shutters, so they were warm, at last. There was no shortage of firewood, but there was a shortage of food. That problem, and trying to induce Ned to use the necessary house rather than a bush as he was accustomed, became Bryony's main concerns during the long hours that Benedict and Charlie were about the business of pulling together this weak and disparate force.

The store rations allowed two soldiers were scant and could not begin to feed four, even when one of them was a mere five-year-old. Ben and Charlie had pooled their resources, and Bryony, once her foot healed, went out on daily foraging expeditions armed with a few pennies, to see what could be bought. She discovered soon enough that those who had were not prepared to share, except for an extortionate sum. There were chickens, cows, and goats in the hamlets outside the town, producing eggs, milk, butter, and cheese. There were smokehouses, where bacon and hams hung. But the possessors of these riches wanted more than Bryony's pennies. She was by no means the only one in search of scarce provisions, and the atmosphere in the countryside was sullen, fear and mistrust on every face.

The first time she stole, she found herself flooded with an amazing conflict of emotions — primarily, incredulity at how easy it had been, followed by a strange excitement, then sheer joyous satisfaction at the thought of the four eggs at the bottom of her basket. Guilt, when it came, was not powerful, and Bryony decided that hunger and privation were excellent tutors when it came to replacing the moral values of a lifetime.

She glanced down at Ned, who was trotting along beside her. He had seen her take the eggs from the bowl on the shelf in the dairy when the farmer's wife had grudgingly gone off to fetch a cup of milk for Bryony's proffered penny. He had said nothing, however, and she was unsure whether she should mention it. She did not want him blurting her new profession to Benedict, but neither did she want to involve such a child in a conspiracy of silence. In the end, Bryony decided to leave well enough alone. If it came out, then so be it.

As it happened, either Ned had not found anything strange in Bryony's behavior, or he forgot what he had seen. There were delighted exclamations when Bryony placed a dish of scrambled eggs upon the table that evening, and her airy explanation that a kind farmer's wife had found Ned irresistible went unchallenged. After that, Bryony turned thief with careful deliberation. She took only enough for the four of them and only from places where her coin met grudging acceptance and bought little. Bacon and cheese began to make regular appearances on the table in the little cottage, ham bones enriched pots of broth. Only on one occasion did she overreach herself.

A cold chicken stood on a kitchen table, inviting possession. An old woman, grumbling about beggars who could not provide for themselves or their children, took six pennies in exchange for a cup of flour and a jug of milk. She had tottered off to fill the jug when Bryony whipped the chicken into her basket, grabbed Ned's hand, and flew out of the kitchen and across the yard. A loud yell came from behind, and she looked over her shoulder to see the woman making remarkable speed in pursuit. Ned's little legs were going like pistons, but he

591

could not keep up with Bryony, who was obliged to swing him up onto her hip. Sobbing for breath, she rounded a corner in the lane and dived behind a bramble bush, burying them both and their ill-gotten gains in a muddy ditch. The woman came round the corner, swearing vigorously, but the lane was empty and she was clearly at the end of her strength. After what seemed an eternity to the cowering fugitives, she turned and went muttering back home.

Bryony began to laugh as relief not unmixed with satisfaction at her audacious coup swept over her. Ned started to dance, singing gleefully, and they made their way back to Charlotte, laughing and singing, the prospect of cold chicken for supper adding piquancy to the excitement of the aftermath.

"Where the devil did this come from?" Ben walked into the cottage at dusk, Charlie on his heels, and stared at the bird sitting proudly on the table.

"Sit down," Bryony instructed. "I am going to demonstrate my carving skills. I spent many hours with the carving master in my other life and am determined to show how well spent they were."

"*Where* did it come from?" Benedict repeated. "Chickens cost a great deal more than six pennies."

"I worked very hard for it," said Bryony. "Do not question gift horses, Benedict. Sit down, or you will not have any."

"Well, I don't care where it came from," Charlie stated fervently. "I think this is an occasion to broach the ale." He filled three beakers from the keg that formed part of their rations and sat down, rubbing his hands together in hungry anticipation.

"Lass, where did it come from?" Ben sat down and laid his hand over hers, which was poised to begin cutting up the prize. "What do you mean, you worked very hard for it?" His voice was softly insistent, and she could feel the flush creeping up the back of her neck.

"Well, I did not sell myself, if that is what you're afraid of." She tried to laugh airily, but neither the laugh nor her casual shrug could make up for the fact that she would not meet his eye. "Ned and I coaxed and cajoled and pled starvation. But you do not want to hear about that."

Benedict sighed. He didn't want to picture the scene where his wife and the child who was also his responsibility had to go begging. The idea that Sir Edward Paget's daughter was roaming the countryside like a mendicant, cadging and cozening to put food on a Clare's table, filled him with a dull anger, but he knew he could not reasonably forbid it; there seemed no other way to ensure an adequate food supply.

Bryony read his thoughts with little difficulty. "Please, Ben," she said softly. "Enjoy it. Ned and I were so happy, and now you are spoiling it."

"I am sorry." He took a mouthful, but it tasted like ashes on his tongue. He chewed and swallowed and tried to smile, but the attempt fooled no one. Neither Bryony nor Charlie made any attempt to stop him when, the meal over, he pushed back his chair and went out into the night.

"That damned, stiff-necked Clare pride!" Bryony exclaimed in frustration. "It is hardly his fault that we have so little money. If it's anyone's, it's mine. I made him spend so much on the march."

"I don't think he begrudged it, Bryony." Charlie stacked the wooden platters. "There's another meal on that carcass, I reckon."

"Yes," she said, as if the subject was of little interest. "I can boil it for soup."

"Why don't you go and find him." Charlie gave her braid a friendly tug. "I'll clean up in here."

"You will have to take Ned to the privy before he goes to bed. He is afeard to go on his own in the dark."

"But he is using it in the daytime now?" Charlie glanced at Ned, who, sublimely indifferent to the goings-on around him, was sitting on the floor by the hearth, playing with a set of pegs and a board that Ben had made for him.

"Not unless I'm watching him." She chuckled, forgetting her sorrows for a minute. "He doesn't seem to see the point . . . not when there are all those bushes." Still smiling, she went out to the deserted lane.

"What has amused you?"

"Oh!" She jumped. "You scared me, Ben. How could you tell I was smiling? You couldn't see my face."

"I don't need to," he said, putting his arm around her shoulders. "You smile with your whole body when you're amused."

"Oh, Charlie and I were just laughing about Ned and his antipathy for the privy." She leaned into the cradling arm. "We have to try to civilize him, or I don't know how we shall manage when things become normal again."

"What is normal?" Ben asked into the darkness above her head.

"Well, houses and proper privies and baths . . . things like that."

"And sufficient food upon the table."

Bryony chose not to respond, and there was a short silence as they stood in the lane in the January cold, the sky clear and bright — the same sky that also watched over another world, an ordinary world; the same sky that had watched over them both in the other world; the same sky that would watch over the future world, wherever and however it was fashioned.

"Enough said." Benedict turned her into his embrace, holding the fragile line of her jaw between finger and thumb. "There is only one thing I wish for at this moment. Do you know what it is?"

Bryony nodded, her eyes gleaming mischievously in the starlight. "The cottage to ourselves. It is so frustrating not being able to make any noise." She looked around speculatively. "Do you think we will get the rheumatics if we stay out here?"

"We will on the grass." The black eyes were dancing responsively now. "It's icy cold and very damp. However . . ." He took her hand and marched with her into the churchyard. "There is a good broad oak tree over here."

"We cannot make love in a tree," Bryony

protested, although her feet tripped along beside him.

"Not in it," he said with another wicked gleam. "Against it."

"Like a whore on the waterfront!" Bryony could not hide the ripple of excitement in her voice, even as she exclaimed in feigned shock at such an outrageous suggestion.

"I won't ask what you know of whores and waterfronts," Ben said, standing her firmly against the broad trunk of the tree. "But you have the right idea." He pulled her skirt up and her drawers down in one movement, and Bryony felt herself begin to tremble as the deep recesses of her body moistened. She pressed herself against him with low murmurs of urgency, wanting him with a sudden, wild outpouring of lust, impatient as he freed himself from his clothes. She took him in one hand, stroking, squeezing, expressing her need, before guiding the erect, throbbing shaft within her hungry body, receiving him with a soft cry of pleasure.

"Sweet heaven!" Ben murmured. "To be inside you, my love, is to be buried in sweetness." His hands were on her shoulders, holding her skirts up against them as he pressed deep within her, their eyes locked in wonder in the dim starlight.

"Nothing matters when we have this, does it?" Bryony whispered. "Nothing could ever matter, could it?" Her eyes sought affirmation in his — affirmation that the trivialities of pride were as nothing compared with this magical combination of love and lust with which they were blessed.

"Nothing," he said. His lips took hers, and she felt the rough bark of the tree rasp against her scalp under the possessive pressure of his mouth. Then the maelstrom took them and she shuddered against him, spent but fulfilled.

# Chapter 22

It was two days after their miraculous joining in the churchyard that peace was shattered, and all the affirmations in the world were rendered powerless against the force of an explosion that tore apart the fragile edifice of love, exposing the skeleton in all its grinning inevitability.

Benedict was standing outside headquarters, deep in conversation with Harry Lee, whose legion of Virginian cavalry held undisputed position as the army's crack band of raiders and scouts. The two men had much in common when it came to skills and styles of warfare, and Harry was a frequent visitor to the cottage by the churchyard. It was a sunny morning, freakishly warm, and Benedict was feeling remarkably at peace . . . until the sounds of commotion broke upon them.

Ben instantly identified Ned's high-pitched shriek. He swung round to look down the street. The child was running as if all the devils in hell were after him, yelling at the top of his voice, and, indeed, pounding after him was a burly trooper whose virulent curses and scarlet face were ample evidence of Ned's need to flee.

"What in Hades . . . ?" Ben ran forward and collared the screaming Ned, whose legs continued to race even while he was held fast.

"Light-fingered little varmint!" The trooper, breathing heavily, came to a stop beside them. "That's my cheese, 'e's got! Whipped it outta my pack, quick as a flash, 'e did. Born to thievin', 'e is."

"It's for Bryny!" Ned shrieked, still kicking. "It's for Bryny!"

The elusive pieces slowly drifted and fell into place, forming the complete, horrible picture. "Give it back, Ned," Ben commanded quietly. "And say you are sorry for taking it."

With obvious reluctance, the child handed over the piece of cloth-wrapped cheese, since the hand on his collar was making a very definite statement. He mumbled words that could have been taken as apology, and Ben offered his own as simply as he could in the face of his hideous embarrassment. Everyone in Charlotte knew that Colonel Clare had two dependents, his wife and a stray child. It would not take many minutes for the story to be around the town. He could only hope and pray that the incident would be put down to an understandable aberration of childhood and the blame not laid where it was due — at least, not by anyone but himself.

"He needs a good wallopin', if you ask me," the soldier said, recovering his property.

Not *he,* Ben thought with savage emphasis. How could she have been so blind to every personal consideration? To his position? To the child's outlook? Still holding Ned by the collar, he stalked off in the direction of the cottage.

Bryony was darning a much-darned stocking of Ben's when the cottage door crashed open. Ned began speaking, the words tumbling from his lips. "I got some cheese, Bryny, but Ben made me give it back."

"And if you ever again take anything that does not belong to you, my friend, I'll skin you alive!" Ben said with a quiet ferocity that could not be ignored. "Go outside, but you are not to leave the garden." He sent the boy through the door with a smart tap on his rear and shut the door, turning slowly, placing his back against it, to look at Bryony.

She was rather pale but laid down the stocking, saying, "He was only trying to help. It is not his fault."

"I am well aware at whose door to lay this!" His black eyes were pinpricks of fury. "Do you know the punishment for thievery and looting in this army?"

She did. "Thirty lashes. But I am not in the army."

"But *I* am!" he rasped.

"Ben, listen to me." She spoke quickly now, sensing that they were teetering on the brink of an abyss of some unknown depth. "I have done nothing that is not routinely practiced."

"Why do you think Greene is imposing such harsh penalties?" demanded Benedict. "Because it has become an epidemic."

"And with good reason." She continued to find her words easily, to speak calmly, explaining the position as she saw it — unpleasant, certainly, but unarguable. "Some people have food, Benedict, and they will not share it. I cannot pay what they ask for even one egg, after I have bought milk. It is robbery of another kind. I have merely evened the score."

"You have wantonly deceived me!" The voice did not sound like Ben's. She had seen his anger in various manifestations

602

but never this naked blade that she knew with a sick conviction would strike at the jugular. "You have forced my connivance in a crime."

"It is not a crime in the ordinary sense," she cried, losing her calm. "We were hungry."

"God dammit, my wife does not steal to put food on *my* table!" He seized her upper arms, forcing her to her feet, and Bryony felt the quickening of real fear.

"It is *our* table," she said.

Outside, Charlie Carter stood for a minute, a bleak look on his face as the raised voices carried. Ned's hand slipped into his, cold and small. Charlie looked down at the child and saw fear of the unknown standing out in his eyes. "Come on, Ned, let us go for a walk."

"It is *my* table." Ben's fingers bruised her arms, bringing tears to her eyes. "I have said that I look to my own. And I will do so."

Something snapped. Whether it was the anger and fear brought on by the fact that he was hurting her, whether it was the injustice of it all, the blind refusal to acknowledge reality, she didn't know. But she hit back. "You do not have the wherewithal to look to your own." She regretted the words the instant they were spoken.

"You think I am not conscious of that?" His voice grated, and he shook her with each word, almost as if he were not aware of her as living flesh. "You would throw such a failure in my face! Well, let me tell you that while you remain as my wife, you will have to manage on what I *can* provide! It may not suit a Paget, but I fear that this Paget will have to learn her place as the wife of an indigent soldier! Do you understand me?" He let her go with an abrupt push that sent her reeling against the table. She stood looking at him, arms crossed over her breasts as she rubbed her bruised flesh, her eyes wide with shock.

Grim-faced and breathing heavily, Ben fought to bring himself under control, and the silence stretched between them, throbbing with the raw emotion of the last few dreadful minutes. "I beg your pardon, I did not mean to hurt you," he said in a deadened tone. "When Cornwallis comes within marching distance, I will send you over to your father. Until then, you must make do with what is available."

Every word was a stab to the heart. "I do not wish to leave you," she managed to say at long last, through a throat dry as if clogged with sand. "I wished only to play my part. It does not seem reasonable that you should carry the full burden alone."

"You are my wife," he said, as if that was answer enough. "If you find that you do not care for what that means in its entirety, then you must leave."

"And may a wife not attempt to share her husband's burdens?" she asked quietly. "The role of parasite sits uneasy in my craw."

"Your misguided actions have simply added to my burdens," he told her with cold, flat finality. "In future, I would be grateful if you would confine your aid to those areas in which I request it. And you will account to my satisfaction for every-thing that comes into this house."

"And what of later? When this damnable war is over and we must make a life to-gether? What then, Benedict? Must I sit in a corner and twiddle my thumbs because your damned pride will not allow you to accept aid from those in a position to give it?" She heard her voice as if from a great distance. She did not wish to be following this path, not now, when Ben was this cold, angry stranger. But they had somehow found themselves upon it, and it had to be faced at some point. There was so much anger and hurt between them already that maybe it could not be worsened by this related issue.

"And whose aid do you have in mind?" he asked, his eyes opaque, his body very still. "I was under the impression that you had thrown in your lot willingly with a vagrant who has neither family nor fortune to protect you. Did you perhaps not fully understand what that would entail?" Mockery laced his voice. "I have no plans for when this war is over — if I am still here to make plans. But I do not foresee a life of ease, in the great house on a large plantation, for myself or for my wife."

"I do not ask for it." She swallowed, trying to find the right words. "I pledged myself to embrace your life and your cause, Benedict. But that does not have to mean that I can bring nothing of my own, does it?" A spurt of flame from the fire lit the dim room for a minute, and Ben looked at her, seeing the worried eyes, the taut leanness of her body, the rough skin of her hands, the broken nails, the ragged gown. She did not even have a decent pair of shoes!

"And what have you to bring?" he demanded, his voice harsh. She was not to know that the harshness was directed at himself for having reduced her to this pauper's state.

"I am an heiress —" She stopped as all trace of color left his face and he looked as if felled by a body blow. Summoning every vestige of courage, she continued. "When this war is over, I can make peace with my father."

"You think for one minute that I would accept Paget blood money?" His voice shook and he took a step toward her. Bryony shrank back against the table. "Money that is wrested from the pores of those wretches . . ."

"I am sorry," Bryony whispered, feeling the hard edge of the table pressing into her thighs as she bent backward, desperately trying to put some distance between herself and this livid stranger. "Please, Ben, let us not mention it again. I only thought that perhaps when it was all over you would feel differently."

He gripped her jaw, and his eyes, no longer opaque, were sword points of contempt. "I do not understand how you could have thought such a thing, after everything that I have told you. You are no different from the rest of your breed, Bryony Paget. You imagine such things as I have told you can be banished at will in the interests of expediency?" He flung her face from him with an expression of disgust and left the cottage, the door slamming in his wake.

Bryony turned and crouched over the table as sobs wracked her, welling, it seemed, from the depths of her stomach, filling her whole body to overflowing. One day he would have to lose the hatred or be forever corroded by bitterness. She had thought, oh, so foolishly, that this war would exorcise the demon — had almost done so. But never before had he looked at her like that. Even when she had got in the way of his hatred, she had known that it was not really her he was seeing with such bitter distaste. Today, it *had* been her.

"Whatever is it?" Charlie, his voice resonant with distress, stepped into the cottage. He came over to her, stroking her back as she huddled bent over the table. "Bryony, what is it? Do not cry like that. You will do yourself some harm." Helplessly, he continued to pat her back, but the weeping would not stop, shuddering the slender frame. Ned began to wail in fright at this collapse of one of the props of his existence, and Charlie swore, violently but uselessly. Ben had caused this, whatever it was, and Ben was going to have to put it right.

Charlie stormed out of the cottage, for once furious with the man whom he loved and admired as if he were an adored elder brother. Bryony's stealing at this juncture in the reestablishment of regular army discipline had been enough to make anyone annoyed; Charlie was more than willing to concede that, but Ben must have done something dreadful to cause such piteous distress.

Benedict was in the churchyard, and there was nothing about his countenance to encourage confidence, but Charlie was not deterred. "What did you do to Bryony?" he demanded without preamble.

Ben frowned as if the younger man were an impertinent subordinate. "I fail to see what business it is of yours."

Charlie flushed angrily. "She is weeping as if her heart is broken, and now Ned has started. You must have done something."

Ben sighed with weary irritation. "What are you accusing me of, Charlie — beating her?"

"Of course not." Charlie shuffled his feet restlessly on the grass. "It's none of my business, and she should never have done it, I know. But I am sure she just did not think —"

"Charlie, that is not really the issue. While I appreciate your concern for Bryony, I must repeat, I do not welcome interference in my affairs."

Charlie, thoroughly discomfited, could only mutter an apology and walk away with as much dignity as he could muster. When he returned to the cottage much later, it was to find Bryony white-faced and red-eyed but perfectly composed. Ned was subdued but showed no other ill effects of the morning. Benedict greeted them all in neutral tones when he came in, his face showing neither anger nor pleasure.

Supper was a meager, cheerless meal of watery broth and a heel of rye bread that Bryony had toasted over the fire. She toyed with her soup and gave her share of the toast to Ned, whose appetite was unimpaired by the day's events. Ben's lips tightened as he saw her slip the bread onto the child's platter, but he said nothing. They lay that night, side by side as always, beneath the same blanket. But the distance between them was like a frozen tundra — icy and infinite.

The following morning, Nathanael Greene revealed the plan for his first move against the British. It was breathtaking in its audacity, and most certainly guaranteed to take Cornwallis by surprise.

"We go west and you go east," announced Daniel Morgan with a rich chuckle at the end of the exposition. "You reckon the earl will divide his own forces, Nathanael?"

"What would you do?" Greene's eyes gleamed. "Unless I very much mistake the matter, he will send Banastre Tarleton after you — a small force, for why would he need an army against such a puny strength? If you can deprive him of his light corps, then our sinews will be much braced."

"To horse, gentlemen." Morgan stood up, a hard, sturdy rock, radiating energy. "We'll crack a whip over Colonel Ban, I swear it."

Only Benedict Clare showed no responsive enthusiasm, and Charlie knew well the reason. What was to be done about Bryony and Ned? Horses would be found for Ben and Charlie, but the army could not be expected to mount a man's family.

In the evening, they went back to the cottage in silence. The march westward into South Carolina would begin at dawn. Greene would take the rest of the army along the heights of the Pee Dee River, some one hundred forty miles to the east. There would be no place for an unmounted woman and child with that force, either.

"If only Cornwallis were closer." Ben spoke his thoughts, startling in the heavy silence. "Her father is with him."

"Is that what she would wish?" Charlie ventured hesitantly.

"Wishes have little relevance at the moment." There was no sharpness in the comment, and Charlie realized that it was not meant as rebuke. "If I leave them here, at least they have a roof over their heads. We can perhaps scrounge some provisions from the stores, and, after all —" he gave a short laugh that did not convey humor "— my wife is not unable to care for herself."

Bryony listened in silence as Benedict told her of the situation. He spoke to her as if he were briefing a troop of soldiers, calm, matter-of-fact, explanatory. It was not the way a man would propose a separation of untold hardship to his wife. When he had stopped talking, waiting for a response, his face without expression, she got up and went over to a portmanteau in the corner. She drew from it the little velvet pouch that she had taken from her bedroom in another life.

"These belong to me. They did belong to my mother — baptismal gifts — so do not bear the Paget taint." She laid on the table the chased silver filigree fillet that had confined her hair on the evening that Benedict Clare had walked into her father's house. Beside it, she placed the matching silver pendant. "I imagine one may purchase a horse with such coin. Ned will ride with me."

Charlie did not quite understand what she had said, understood only that she referred to whatever abyss lay between her and her husband. Benedict looked at the silver, winking in the gloom, a shocking brilliance, an excess of riches in this hovel. Ned clambered onto a stool, reaching eagerly for the pretty toys, demanding to know what they were and if he could play with them.

Ben moved them out of the child's grasp, then looked at Bryony. "One of these will be sufficient. Which do you choose to keep?"

She shrugged, still refusing to meet his eye. "It matters not a whit. I have no use for either of them and cannot imagine a time when I will. I brought them with me simply to serve as currency should the need arise. It appears to have done so."

Ben put the pendant in his pocket and left the cottage without another word. Bryony replaced the fillet in the pouch, and looked around the room. "Do we take everything with us, Charlie?"

"I think so." He tried to make his voice as calmly matter-of-fact as hers, but the atmosphere remained charged with currents that he could not identify. "We are on the move again, and I suspect that this time we will not stop until this is over, one way or the other."

"Then it's fortunate we do not have much to take. There is little to be gained by being overburdened." She moved around the room, gathering up their few possessions, examining clothes to see if they required any last-minute mending. All the while, she was quiet and contained, enclosed in a world that Charlie could not penetrate, so he occupied himself with Ned, preparing the child for bed.

It was late when Benedict returned. He looked tired and drawn as he placed a bundle on the table. "Try these." He held out a pair of riding boots to Bryony. She took them in the same manner, as if they were being proffered by an acquaintance. He watched her put them on, a frown buckling his brow. "Do they fit?"

"They are a little big." She took several tentative steps. "But it is better that than too small. I will wear two pairs of stockings." The boots were serviceable, the leather good quality, but they had clearly spent some time on someone else's feet — a fact that Bryony did not regard in the least. "Did you find me a horse?"

"Yes, an ugly brute but with stamina. He has an uneasy gait, but you will become accustomed. He will carry you without flagging, and that was my main concern." It was almost as if he expected her to object and was forestalling her, Bryony thought distantly, examining the rest of the bundle on the table. In addition to the boots, Ben had procured for her a heavy hooded cloak and gloves. And somewhere he had found a pair of sturdy woolen britches and a jacket that would drown Ned, but would at least keep him warmer and dryer than anything in his present makeshift wardrobe.

"You didn't purchase anything for yourself?" Ben was also in dire need of stockings and boots.

"I have no need of anything," he replied shortly, laying a small heap of coins on the table. "That is yours, what's left over."

She bit her lip. "It is ours, Benedict. Why would you not buy yourself some stockings, at least?"

He turned on her, his voice low but intense. "Have you learned nothing?"

Bryony walked out of the cottage, unable

to bear the proximity of such animosity any longer. It was cold, but she hardly noticed as she walked aimlessly along the lane. What sort of a life could they possibly have together in this wasteland that had sprung up between them? Maybe it would pass; but if it did, there were no guarantees that it would not arise again. Just by being who she was, she could provoke it, for as long as Benedict clung to his bitter, vengeful hatred.

"Bryony!" His voice rang out behind her, sharply imperative, but she ignored it, maintaining her pace. "Bryony, wait! You will catch your death of cold." He broke into a run, coming up with her. "Did you hear what I said?" The heavy cloak went around her shoulders, and he turned her, pulling up the hood and fastening the clasp at the collar. "Why will you not do as you're told?"

Something extraordinary had happened. His voice was lightly teasing again, his eyes were inhabited by himself again, instead of that neutral, expressionless stranger. She shook her head in bewilderment, confusion filling her eyes.

"If you fall ill, you will not be able to keep up on the march," he scolded in the same tone. "I cannot be distracted by worrying over you."

"You will not have to be," she managed to say, wondering if she would ever understand anything again. Part of her melted with relief at this incredible volte-face, yet a deep-seated wariness remained, showed on her face.

"I will if you are insubordinate and careless." He touched her mouth gently with his little finger. "Let us put it behind us, lass. It happened, but it is over."

Until the next time, she thought wearily. "I do not seem able to forget as quickly as you, Ben."

"It is not forgotten," he said quietly. "But it is over. We cannot live under that shadow. I beg forgiveness for my part, Bryony."

He was waiting, quite clearly, for her own apology, but she did not know how to apologize for being herself, for having sprung from tainted seed. She could only promise to try to refashion herself upon the anvil of love, to drive out of her all symbols and reminders of her antecedents, to submerge herself in Clare.

The next morning, Morgan's body of frontiersmen, a thousand strong, marched westward, back into South Carolina. The presence of a colonel's wife and a child, both on the back of a raking gelding, drew from the brigadier general only the comment that their mount's rolling gait was like to render them both seasick. Bryony simply laughed and said that she had always been a good sailor. It was a response that clearly pleased the old Indian fighter, who nodded with approval and told her to stay at his side when her husband had business elsewhere in the column.

The second evening brought the return of the scouts, with the news that Colonel Tarleton, with a force not much larger than their own, and two small cannons, was riding to meet them. Bryony, wrapped in her cloak, sitting beside a brazier, heard the rapid discussions and felt the familiar tightening in her gut as she contemplated the upcoming battle. Strangely, she had found the raids and the skirmishes when they fought undercover less fearful than the pitched battles. She seemed to feel that Ben was in his element in the former, but that on the battlefield he had no more advantage than anyone else.

"Lie down and try to sleep, lass." Ben came over to her, his face grave. "We march at first light in search of good ground."

"Ground for battle?"

"Aye. We will wait then for Tarleton to reach us."

Bryony shivered — thinking, like lambs for the slaughter. But she kept her own counsel. Benedict did not need to be burdened with her anxieties; he had enough of his own. The ground at Cowpens that Daniel Morgan chose for the confrontation did nothing to improve her spirits.

"Why here?" she asked Charlie, looking aghast at the open hillside, exposed in front and on the flanks, without undergrowth, even, to provide concealment. "It is so unprotected."

Charlie nodded. "It was suggested to Morgan that he move elsewhere, but he says the men must have no opportunity for retreat. When they are forced to fight, they sell their lives dearly."

"Harsh judgment, but correct nevertheless." Benedict appeared beside them. "Bryony, you and Ned must wait behind the rear lines. There will be no rout this time." It was said with grim satisfaction. "Morgan has ordered riflemen posted in the rear to kill deserters."

"Where will you be?"

"Where I am told to be, lass." He would not tell her in which line he was to fight, in case stories of the battle positions filtered through to the rear and might alarm her unnecessarily. "As *you* will be, it is understood? This time there's to be no moving the minute my back is turned." The black eyes bored into her until finally she submitted with a little shrug.

She did not see Benedict that night. Having escorted them to the rear, he had left her with Ned and gone to join Morgan and the other officers, who were making the rounds of the men, bolstering their courage, joking with them, raising their spirits as they prepared them to meet the fast-approaching enemy in the morning. Bryony found space for Ned in a covered wagon, and rolled him in his blanket, then she left him sleeping, knowing that he would not stir until sunup. She skirted the lines of soldiers, looking for a place from which she would be able to watch the battle. It didn't matter that her plan was in direct contravention of Ben's orders. She could not stay in the rear, hearing the cries and the firing, not knowing which way the tide turned.

Thus it was that when Colonel Tarleton arrived on the field in a cold, clear January dawn, Bryony was crouched, chilled and stiff, but with a bird's-eye view, in the crotch of an oak tree at the top of the hill.

After the first charge by the British cavalry, she lost her fear completely, becoming utterly absorbed in the awesome beauty of a scene that seemed to have broken away from reality. The sun rose, shedding a weak, wintery benediction on the field as the British line of dragoons advanced at a trot toward the massed American ranks. Bryony could make out General Morgan galloping along the files, flourishing his sword. Then a loud, challenging cheer went up from the advancing dragoons. Bryony felt the hairs on her scalp lift. There were shouts coming from the American lines, and she could see officers pounding down the rows, gesticulating. They were telling the riflemen to hold their fire and for a breathless instant, as the British line advanced inexorably, they did. Then the air was rent with a sheet of flame as the regulars fired simultaneously in one devastating volley. It was a sight of the most magnificent destruction. Still, for Bryony, it was unreal, as if she were looking into a painting.

Then the clear strokes became blurred as if someone had smudged the picture. A troop of American cavalry plunged in among the dragoons and all was confusion, impossible to sort out for the watcher in the tree. The American infantry seemed to be falling back, up the hill. The redcoats broke ranks and charged after them. As one body, the Americans turned and another volley cut their pursuers to ribbons before they charged after them, down the hill, scattering them to the four winds. It was over in a few minutes — the complete destruction of Tarleton's army. To Bryony's eyes, the field was littered with redcoat bodies, and she could see no others. There would be some, though, she knew, and as the dreamlike wonder dissipated, cold reality took its place.

She climbed stiffly down from her tree, stretching her cramped muscles, wondering at how she had been able to watch that violent destruction of men by men and find it beautiful. But she had and it had been. The cries of the wounded reached her as she skirted the field, making her way back to the wagons at the rear, worried now about Ned. If he had woken and found her gone, he would be scared. Catching up her skirt, she began to run through the cold.

"Well, where the devil is she, Clare?" Morgan was demanding as Bryony came into view. "We don't have time to scour the countryside for her."

"I am here." Bryony arrived, panting, cheeks pink with exertion and cold air. "I hope I have not delayed you, sir."

"*Where the hell have you been?*" demanded Ben. He was bleeding from a long scratch on his cheek, and his jacket was ripped, but apart from that he looked whole, Bryony thought, taking rapid, automatic inventory.

"Up a tree." She beamed at him, unable to contain her joyous relief. Ned was plucking insistently at her skirt, and she bent to pick him up. "Are we to move out now? I am quite ready."

"How very fortunate for the rest of us," Ben said sardonically. "I was once advised to put a leash on you. It was advice I should have heeded."

"Oh, don't be stuffy, Benedict! I was not in any danger, and I cannot have kept you waiting. You have all only just left the field yourselves."

Morgan chortled. "Quite right, my dear. But now we are on the run, so unless you wish to fall into Cornwallis's hands, since he'll be on our tail in no time, you had best keep up with us." He swung onto his horse and rode off.

"You are a constant embarrassment," Ben declared, taking Ned out of her arms and setting him on his feet. "Would you get on that horse, please."

"Are we really in retreat?" She scrambled onto the gelding's broad back, assisted by a flat hand on her bottom, shoving her upward.

"Nothing else for it." Ben handed Ned up to her. "We're not strong enough to fight the entire British army, and they'll be after us once Tarleton gets back to Cornwallis with news of this day." He turned to mount his own horse and did not see the sudden stricken expression on her face as the mischievous amusement borne of relief died abruptly and the little cold spot in her soul that she usually managed to ignore began to ache.

With Cornwallis rode Sir Edward Paget. As she fled with the Americans before the British pursuit, she fled her father. And she knew, despite the love and loyalty she owed and felt for her husband, that she did not wish to run from her father . . . that there had to be some way of reconciling the two parts of her.

But throughout the remainder of that bitter winter, she did run. Greene joined Morgan, and the American army raced from river to river, Cornwallis on their heels, sometimes so close that they had barely snatched their last wagon from the flood-swollen torrents before the first redcoat line appeared. Bryony came to understand the true meaning of fatigue. Her horse fulfilled all Ben's expectations and carried her without flagging through the freezing rivers, Ned clinging to her if Ben was not there to take him up himself. But there were days when Bryony did not know if she was asleep or awake. Her knees gripped the saddle, the reins were imprinted upon her hands, her eyes saw nothing but the crude road ahead. Occasionally, Ben or Charlie would take Ned and lead her horse so she could doze uneasily in the saddle. But mostly, she had to manage for herself. Ben was too busy with the men who tramped the frozen ground, barely clad, their feet leaving bloody prints as shoes wore down and the cloth that they used to wrap their feet shredded.

They crossed the Dan River into Virginia at the beginning of March, and there, for the first time, paused. They were not followed. Ben wrapped Bryony in her cloak as if she were a baby and put her to bed in one of the wagons. She took his hand, her eyelids fluttering as she struggled to stay awake for one more minute. "I miss you, Ben."

He smiled and squeezed her hand before tucking it under the cloak. "I miss you, too, lass." She fell asleep as he kissed her, and he sat on his haunches for a minute, looking at her. He missed her to a point beyond pain, sometimes. The splendor by the tree in the churchyard seemed to have happened to two other people in another lifetime. He had not even seen her naked since then. And he longed for her body, would sometimes feel her movements against him, hear the little whimpers and cries of pleasure. But they were waking dreams that brought him to an erect and throbbing arousal despite exhaustion, and had to be banished with stern resolution.

When Nathanael Greene took his rested and reinforced army back into North Carolina to await battle at Guilford Courthouse, Bryony was left in Virginia. Nothing she could do or say would persuade Benedict to take her.

"I will come back for you, sweeting," he promised, holding her as she wept angry tears.

"You may not be alive to do so!" she reminded him, pulling out of his embrace.

"Then you will be better off here." He took her shoulders, looking into her eyes awash with grief and foreboding. "If I do not return, you may make your way to the British army or go on to your home. Either option will be possible for you. The horse will carry you, and you still have the silver fillet. It will buy you what you need."

"I need *you*," she said with fierce passion, rising on tiptoe to take his mouth with hers.

"And I need you." He groaned, tasting her sweetness, feeling her body, taut and demanding, against him. As one body, they moved backward into the wagon, heedless of who should see and guess their intention. They came together with the desperate hunger of the long deprived, pushing garments out of the way, mouths locked as their bodies twisted to fit into each other with the wonder of a long-lost but ageless familiarity. And when the summit was reached, it held the sharp piquancy of a climb that perhaps would never again be made by these two together.

Ned beside her, she watched the army out of sight. It took a long time for over four thousand men to disappear, but they went eventually, and the woman and child were left with the wounded and the unfit. For a week, they waited, news reaching them sporadically, the accounts inconsistent, so that it became impossible to judge the truth. There had been a big battle. The British had won — no, the Americans had won. . . . Cornwallis had camped on the battlefield and issued a victory proclamation, calling on "all royal subjects to stand forth and take an active part in restoring good order and government." But there had been no response. British casualties had been heavy — no, they had been devastating; the army was destroyed . . . but still the earl claimed victory. . . . American casualties were negligible . . . but the Virginia militia had run from the field in disorder. . . .

Bryony eventually ceased running when each new messenger arrived; battered by conflicting reports, she let the tales wash over her. Whichever side could really claim victory, the possibility of loss was as great for her. Her husband and her father would have met on that battlefield, and through the long days of waiting, she had come to see clearly that one could not submerge a fundamental part of one's self because another part demanded it. She was still Bryony Paget even while she was Bryony Clare, and her father's death in battle would strike as deep into her core as that of her husband.

Benedict Clare came back, unscathed and bearing the truth. Technically, it had been a British victory, but another such

Pyrrhic victory would ruin the British army. Cornwallis had lost a quarter of his force, whereas General Greene had counted only 78 dead and 183 wounded.

Bryony searched Ben's face and knew that he did not have the answer to her question. If he had news of her father, he would not have been able to hide it from her — good or bad. "So, where do we run to now?" she asked, looking around the disorderly camp that had become home. "Ned has settled well here." She laughed. "He has become a great favorite with the men who were left. I rarely see him from sunup to sundown."

"Are you wearied of running, lass?" One eyebrow lifted quizzically, but the deep seriousness of the question could not be hidden.

"Not I," she said firmly, meeting his gaze. "For as long as you run, Benedict Clare, I run with you. Have I not always said so?"

"Always," he said, drawing her into his arms.

"Ben! Ben! I can ride a mule, Ben!" Ned raced over to them, plunging between them, wrapping his arms around Ben's knees, bouncing on his toes, eyes shining. "Come and see!"

"I think you'll have to settle for me, Ned." Charlie, with an amused chuckle, yanked the bouncing child out from under. "Ben will come later. Won't you, Ben?" Laughter and conspiratorial understanding glimmered in his eyes, and they laughed back at him.

"Word of honor," Ben said, tickling the child beneath his dirty chin. "And if you really can ride, then you shall do so, all the way."

"All the way where?" Bryony returned to the original question as she returned to his embrace.

"To Tidewater, Virginia," he said against her ear. "The endgame will be played there."

# Chapter 23

"For pity's sake, Ned, stop whining!" Bryony snapped in exasperation as the child's insistent voice finally penetrated her preoccupation.

"He wasn't," Ben said without looking up from the pistol he was cleaning on the plank table.

"Wasn't what?" Frowning, she turned to observe him, noticing absently how the bent copper head caught a finger of evening sun coming through the small window.

Ben sighed and put down the pistol. "He was not whining, Bryony. He has been asking you the same question for the last five minutes, but you have taken not a blind bit of notice." His eyes probed her face, and she felt her cheeks warm under the scrutiny that, while it was far from unfriendly, was uncomfortably minute.

She resumed her scouring of a skillet, asking casually, "What is it you want, Ned?"

"My ball," the boy said. "It's after supper."

Bryony's expression was blank, and Charlie reminded her, "You took it away from him because he was throwing it through the window."

"And you said I could have it back after supper," Ned put in, an unusually aggrieved note entering his voice.

"Oh, I forgot. I am sorry." Bryony dried her hands and reached up to the top of the dresser. "Here." She handed the prize to Ned, who ran out into the August evening with it. "Could you not have given it back to him?" Bryony asked Ben, trying not to sound irritable.

"You took it away from him, lass, not I," Ben replied, reasonably enough.

"And I suppose I should not have done so?" This time she could not prevent the irritation.

Benedict rubbed his chin thoughtfully. "On the contrary. Indeed, if it had been I, he would have lost it a great deal sooner and for much longer."

Bryony chewed her lip. "I didn't mean to snap. I beg your pardon."

"What is troubling you, sweeting?" Ben stood up, coming over to put his hands on her shoulders.

"I think I'll go and play ball with Ned." Charlie, with his customary delicacy, left the little waterside cottage on the outskirts of Williamsburg.

"What is it?" Ben tipped her chin, peering into her eyes, which slipped away from his inspection.

"It's nothing." She fixed her gaze on a crack in the clapboard wall of the cottage. "Just the heat. It is damnable, is it not?"

"Yes," he agreed quietly. "But it has been so for the last three months, when we have trailed across Virginia under the broiling sun, and you have not once complained — even on a twenty-four-hour forced march."

"I expect it's just an excitation of the nerves." She attempted a smile, a little shrug. "The time of the month."

"No, not that," he contradicted. "I know your cycle as well as you do yourself, lass."

"Better, it would seem," she muttered, moving to twist away from him. Ben's grip on her shoulders tightened.

"I wish to know what's troubling you, Bryony."

"Do you not have to post pickets at the line?"

Ben sucked in his breath sharply and ignored the question. "Ever since we have been quartered here, you have been like a bear with a sore head. Now, what is it?"

"I have told you, there is nothing the matter. But if you keep worrying at me like this, there soon will be!" She pulled back, and this time he let her go with a gesture of exasperated frustration.

"You are as stubborn as a mule! But I am warning you that if you do not snap out of this mood before I return in the morning, you will tell me what is the matter if I have to wring it out of you." With that, he picked up his pistol and banged out of the cottage on his way to post pickets for night duty at the line of men that stretched across the peninsula just outside Williamsburg, where the bulk of the Marquis de Lafayette's Continental Army was quartered.

Bryony sat down at the table, dropping her head wearily into her hands. How could she tell him what had happened to her almost the moment they had reached this part of the world that was so achingly, hauntingly familiar? They had marched down the Williamsburg road, right past the entrance to her father's house, but Ben had not been beside her. He had ridden ahead with the marquis, and she doubted whether he had even made the connection, so involved was he with matters of warfare.

She could understand his engrossment. For the last five months they had dodged around Virginia, meeting up with the Frenchman and his force at Richmond at the end of April, and from then on they had skirmished, sometimes fleeing the British, sometimes pursuing them. They had fought last-ditch battles and marched day and night, but now Cornwallis had taken up defensive positions at Yorktown and across the river at Gloucester. From Williamsburg, Lafayette was trying to hold him fast in the trap until General Washington arrived with reinforcements from the north.

It was an exciting time for this army that had gone through so much hardship and had battled near insuperable odds. Lafayette was full of youthful enthusiasm, bubbling with energy, and his spirit infected all those who worked with him. The French fleet was approaching the Chesapeake Bay, and so long as Lafayette could hold Cornwallis in Yorktown, the allied concentration would bring victory.

But for Bryony, it was a wrenching time. Her father was seven miles away, facing the humiliation of defeat, and she was joined with those who would defeat him. She could express none of this turmoil to Ben, who saw the matter with such clarity, with no emotional tangles, no division of loyalties, none of this exquisite anguish. She had pledged herself to his cause, had renounced the other loyalties, or so she had believed. It was something he believed, at least, and bitter experience had taught her that if they were to live in peace together, he must continue to believe that she had disavowed the tainted blood of the Pagets.

So, she could not tell him what she had done this morning, could not tell him how she had agonized over the decision but in the end was unable to keep herself from making the six-mile walk to her childhood home. She had found it closed up, only old Mary in residence as caretaker. Mary, weeping tears of joy and sorrow, had told her that her father had sent a message, instructing Eliza to go to friends in the North once the raiding had begun in Tidewater, Virginia. She had exclaimed in horror at Bryony's thinness, her sunbrowned complexion, her threadbare attire. She had wept bitterly over the heartbreak that Bryony's disappearance had caused in the household. And, as Francis had done, she had demanded to know whether the girl was happy.

Bryony had been hard-pressed for a

truthful answer because she no longer knew whether she was or not. To be with Benedict was happiness, but to be torn in this way was misery. She had tried to write to her mother, but it had been impossible to say what was in her heart, and anything less would add insult to the injury she had already done her parents. So, she had simply asked Mary to say, when the next messenger came, that she was well and that she loved her.

Then she had walked the six miles back to this little cottage, which Benedict had found for them with such smug satisfaction. Its owners had fled during the raiding and burning of the Tidewater country by the traitorous Benedict Arnold and his men, and Ben, riding in the van into the town, had staked his claim to this snug little dwelling. There was no shortage of food, either, these summer days. Now that they were settled, Ben was able to hunt and fish when not on duty, and the game augmented their army rations, which were more generous here than in Charlotte. After the privations, the fears, the endless journeying, Bryony thought that she should find her present circumstances idyllic. Benedict was still in danger, but it was not as acute as it had been so often in the past, and the one-room cottage had a loft where they were assured of some privacy. It was the presence of these luxuries that made her miserable preoccupation and snappish impatience inexplicable to Ben — and to Charlie and Ned, although they were less importunate in demanding to know the reason.

It was time to pull herself together. All this weary glumping was achieving nothing! And if she could not rid herself of the depression, then Benedict would become very difficult. He was not in the habit of making idle threats. Bryony stood up, straightened her shoulders in a gesture of resolution, and went outside. It was dusk and Ned's squeals of laughter, interspersed with Charlie's more moderate tones, rang in the late-summer air. The ball came flying toward her and she leaped, catching it deftly.

"Bravo!" Charlie applauded and she laughed, tossing the ball to Ned, who missed it and went scampering along the riverbank in pursuit, shrieking gleefully.

"Do you think he ought to be in bed?" Bryony asked Charlie, curling her bare toes into the grass, feeling it dry and scratchy, still warm after the day's sun.

"He'll go when he's tired." Charlie

wiped his brow with his handkerchief. "He always does."

"Yes," Bryony agreed. "Campaigning doesn't exactly lend itself to a nursery routine, does it?" She walked to the edge of the little stream. "I cannot imagine what is to become of him when all this is over."

"He'll stay with you and Ben, will he not?" Frowning, Charlie joined her on the bank, where she sat, idly dabbling her toes in the cool water.

"But where will we be, Charlie? Doing what?"

"Is that what has been troubling you these last days?"

She sighed. "A little, but don't tell Ben. He has enough to concern him."

"I think he would be less concerned if he understood." Charlie stood up. "Baron von Steuben has demanded my presence at a drill to be conducted at nightfall. I do not quite understand the significance of such an exercise, but one does not argue with the inspector general."

"No, indeed not." Bryony laughed, getting to her feet. "The Prussian has proved himself too good a soldier for his tactics to be questioned."

"He's an irascible bastard, though," Charlie stated with absolute truth. "Therefore, I do not care to be late." Calling good-bye to Ned, he strolled off into the town.

Bryony was asleep in their loft bedchamber when Ben came back in the early hours of the morning. The raven's hair lay tumbled across the pillow, one bare arm curled above her head. Her face, even in repose, showed the determination and the humor that had carried her through the hardships of the last sixteen months. He had once said that her father had a lot to answer for, Ben remembered with a tiny smile as he shrugged out of his shirt. Sir Edward Paget had certainly fashioned a most extraordinary daughter — undeniably unique. He came down onto the bedstead beside her, and she rolled instantly into his arms in her warm soft nakedness. He was content to lie in the moonlit loft, holding her, feeling the suppleness of her frame, her breath rustling across his chest, her hair tickling his chin. Ben smiled to himself, inhaling the fresh, clean fragrance of her skin and hair. Cleanliness was a luxury they had gone without for the better part of the last sixteen months. . . .

He woke slowly, wonderfully, to the awareness of his body coming alive beneath whispering caresses. He heard her soft murmur of satisfaction as he rose beneath her ministering hands, and he reached down dreamily to stroke her head, resting on his belly as she concentrated on her task. She made love to him with languid pleasure, taking the time to taste every inch of him, to revisit the planes and hollows of his body before moving above him, drawing him within her, moving at her own pace as he yielded to her orchestration, allowing her to play upon them both in the soft, lyrical morning. Afterward, they lay, still unspeaking, savoring this moment when they were alone in their own universe, until the peace was abruptly shattered.

Running feet sounded on the lane outside and then there was a hammering on the door. Ben was on his feet, pulling on his britches almost before the echo had died. They heard Charlie's voice, struggling with sleep, and then Ben, barefoot, had plunged down the stairs, which were really no more than a ladder. Bryony, too anxious to take the time to get dressed, bundled herself into her cloak, it being the nearest to a wrapper that she possessed, and followed.

"What has happened?" She pushed her hair out of her eyes and blinked at the young trooper standing in the doorway. The sound of drums and the shrill call of the bugle came from the town.

"A big fleet has been sighted in the Chesapeake," the messenger told them. "The marquis has issued a general alert."

"French or English ships?" Benedict snapped, turning back to the ladder.

"We don't know yet, sir. They are too far away."

Bryony went over to the hearth, filling the kettle with water from the stone jar that stood beside it. She set the kettle over the fire and poked at the embers, performing the domestic actions automatically as she absorbed the implications of the news. If it was a British fleet, then Cornwallis was out of the trap. If it was the French, then he was cut off by sea and entrapped on land. She did not know which she hoped for. "Do you wish for coffee before you go?"

"No time, lass." Ben, now dressed and booted, clattered back down the ladder. "God knows when I'll be back." He lifted her hair and kissed the nape of her neck. "If it's the French, sweeting, this business will be over in no time." He did not wait for a response and left with Charlie, hastening toward headquarters, where they would receive their orders.

It was an anxious day as they waited to discover the identity of the fleet. Late that night Benedict returned to the cottage, weary but triumphant. The French Admiral de Grasse was in the bay with twenty-eight line-of-battle ships, several frigates, and three regiments of French soldiers.

Within weeks, General Washington and his army had arrived in Williamsburg.

As September continued in days of blazing heat and suddenly chilly nights, the embattled Cornwallis worked incessantly on fortifying his position, clearly prepared to defend himself to the last extremity, and General Washington planned that last extremity with great care. Williamsburg filled with troops as the Americans gathered from across the country for the last campaign of the war, and Bryony Clare retreated within herself.

To all outward appearances, she was calm, cheerful, uncomplaining at Benedict's constant absences on patrols. When he returned, exhausted, hungry, dirty, but always exuberant, she listened to the descriptions of the skirmishes, the stories of spies, the attacks on the small British fleet on the beaches of Yorktown. And her heart grew cold as she pictured her father, cornered, preparing himself for the humiliating surrender that he must know was inevitable — if he was still alive.

There was smallpox in Yorktown, Ben told her, supplies were down to a minimum. Starving horses had been driven out to die on the beaches because they could no longer be fed. Women camp followers and their children had been sent away to fend for themselves. The damn arrogant British would swallow their pride this time! It was said with that fierce intensity, with the disfiguring smile that she had seen so often before; the first time was when he had contemplated the capture of the group of redcoats on the lane by the armory, and she had wondered then what demons possessed a man of such tenderness and humor, who had so much love to give and who gave it so freely. She knew the demons now, and she knew her own. And she knew how they must be exorcized.

On the evening of September 27, Benedict and Charlie, the gravity of their expressions belied by the excitement in their eyes, came back to the cottage with the news that Washington had drawn up his order of battle. They were to march at dawn to strike the final blow that would win America.

"There will be a garrison of two hundred remaining here with the sick, the wounded, and the stores," Ben said, drinking deeply of his tankard of ale. "You and Ned will be quite safe until we return."

"Yes, I am sure we shall," Bryony said calmly, without the flicker of an eyelid. "Do you have time for supper, or must you go back to headquarters?"

Benedict glanced at her. There was something amiss, something not quite right about her voice, her manner. But it was probably the prospect of the upcoming battle, he told himself. He crooked a finger at her, and she came over to him, unsmiling, though her body as he held her was quite relaxed. "It will be the last time, sweeting," he promised gently, touching her lips with his finger. "I know it is hard for you to bear, but you have borne so much, you can manage this last."

"Have I said that I cannot?" There was a tinge of indignation in her voice that quite reassured him.

At five o'clock the following morning, the troops moved out of Williamsburg and took the sandy woodland roads to Yorktown, seven miles away. It was already warm and, as the morning wore on, the heat grew intense and clouds of gray powdery dust filled the air under the steady tramping of twenty-six thousand men, clogging noses and throats and obscuring the countryside on either side of the narrow road.

Bryony left Ned with Claude Blanchard at the hospital in Williamsburg. The Frenchman accepted the charge with an easy shrug. He had three hundred men to care for with only one helper; a small boy would make little difference. Bryony rode out of Williamsburg on her raking gelding, adapting with the ease of familiarity to his awkward gait. She kept well to the rear of the marching column, holding a handkerchief over her mouth to prevent choking on the dust. At noon a halt was called, and she sat under a giant cypress, waiting patiently as cooking fires sprang up along the roadside despite the heat. Ben, she presumed, would be with his mountainmen, tramping stolidly in their baggy britches and bare feet. They were marching ahead of the French column in whose rear she had found herself, so she was quite safe from detection at this point.

A chill message came down the line from General Washington as the men sat eating and laughing in the broiling heat. It was a message to remind them forcibly that this respite was but brief. If the British came out to meet them, they were to fight hand to hand, using the bayonet.

Bryony ate her bread and cheese, drank a little water from a trickle of a stream, and turned her attention to the tricky matter of how and when she should disclose her presence to Benedict. There was nothing he could do about it once she was in the siege lines, but if his anger was very great, it would make it even more difficult to persuade him of her need — a need that she had little reason to believe he would understand, anyway. But if she left him to do what she must without his understanding, without his agreement, then only the bleakest of futures lay ahead for them — if, indeed, they would have a future.

Once the march was resumed, the column divided, the French moving off to the left, the Americans to the right. Bryony also went to the right. It was late afternoon when the American column was halted at a swamp where the bridges had been burned. A troop of green-coated horsemen rode out of Yorktown but were turned back by a few rounds of grapeshot, and the army settled down to make open camp while the bridges were rebuilt across the swamp.

Benedict was with Washington and his staff officers, meeting under a mulberry tree that served to take the place of a headquarters tent, when Bryony rode up. "Good evening, gentlemen." She swung off her horse. Her face was pale and set as she walked over to them, leading her mount. "I beg your pardon for interrupting, General Washington, but may I talk with Colonel Clare?"

Benedict's first thought was that something dreadful had occurred. With a low exclamation, he strode over to her, not waiting for a response from the general. "What has happened, Bryony? Whatever could have brought you here?"

She looked uncertainly at the group under the tree. They were all regarding her with a mixture of curiosity and annoyance. She had little difficulty understanding both reactions to the presence of a woman at this moment and in this place. "Please, I must talk with you," she said in a low voice that throbbed suddenly with intensity. Her gaze locked with his, urgent with appeal and with something indefinable that filled him with a deep foreboding.

He turned back to the general, offering a word of excuse, then took the gelding's reins and walked toward the concealment of a small wood. "I am having difficulty believing that you could do this," he said. "I cannot imagine what could have happened to have brought you here." There was sharpness in the words, but his tone was puzzled rather than angry, and the eyes probing her face for answer were quiet and warm.

"Nothing has happened," she said slowly, feeling for the words that she had rehearsed over and over, but that now had deserted her. "There is something that I must do."

Ben felt a little chill run up his spine as his foreboding expanded, emptying his mind of all else. He said nothing, just waited.

"I must go into Yorktown." There, she had said it. With none of the softening explanations or pleas for understanding, she had said it.

The gelding lowered his head to crop the grass at his feet, and the rein tugged in Ben's hand. He let it slip through his fingers while his mind tried to encompass what she had said. "Why?" The word hung in the hot, muggy air.

"My father is there." She reached a hand to pull at the horse's rough mane as if the little gesture could restore normality between them.

"Go on," Ben said, coldly now.

"I am a Paget, Benedict. I have tried to deny it, to submerge myself in Clare so that I will not remind you of what you hate, but I cannot do it." She looked at him, seeing the cold rejection in his face and accepting it, sorrowfully but with the knowledge of its inevitability. "I must reconcile the two parts of me. I love my father and cannot deny him, not even for you, who I love more than life itself."

She searched his face for a response to this declaration, but his eyes had flattened and there was no emotion to be read. She swallowed and continued. "I must make peace with my father before I can live in peace with you. I do not ask that you do so, also. I would not expect that. But I wish you to understand my need. Afterward, I will return to you, to go again where passion drives . . . if you will have me." She looked over his shoulder and into the rapidly darkening wood, where the whine of swamp mosquitoes rose to promise misery.

"You cannot go into the town," Ben said flatly, concentrating on the one issue of which he was certain. What she had said, he could not grapple with at the moment. "Washington intends blasting them into submission. He has ordered the heavy guns

650

brought up, the battering cannons and mortars. There will be nothing left of the town if Cornwallis does not surrender."

"Then that is all the more reason why I must go. If my father is killed and I have not made peace, I will not be able to live in harmony with you, or with myself."

"I cannot let you go!" It was a cry of anguish. "Into such danger, Bryony. I will not risk losing you for such a whim. Afterward, you will find him. . . ."

"He may not be there," she said with quiet stubbornness, burying deep the hurt that he should judge as whim an imperative of such magnitude. "You once said, when this began between us, that you would not hold me." This time there was defiance and challenge in her voice. If he would deny her his understanding and acceptance of this need, then she must fall back on his promise, which he was bound to honor. It was a bleak substitute for a lover's compassion, but all that was left to her. And she would not dwell upon the paucity of a spirit that embraced only bitterness.

Had he ever expected her to invoke that promise, made at a time when he did not know her as he now did? He had loved her then, certainly, but she had not yet entered his soul, become one with him. Now she would sever the bond of love, cut herself out of him, leave him mutilated by loss. And she would do this because she was ultimately a Paget, and those ties had proved more binding than any with which he had tried to hold her.

Disillusion chilled him. Despair stood stark in his eyes. Dull anger infused his voice as he bowed to compulsion. "In the morning, when we have crossed the swamp, I will send you under flag of truce."

And so it was that a small figure, accompanied by two soldiers, crossed the barren, sandy plain between the opposing armies, to be received within the enemy fortifications. Benedict Clare, filled with an aching sense of loss, betrayal leaden on his soul, watched her go, back to her own people.

# Chapter 24

Sir Edward Paget stood in the dining room of Thomas Nelson's handsome Yorktown house, listening to the wrangling. "If we cross the river by night, we can destroy the allied boats on the north shore, drive back Choisy's force, capture their horses, and be one hundred miles inland before Washington realizes." The plan was described in impassioned accents by a bewigged staff officer.

"Indeed, then we can join Clinton in New York," another stated with a sage nod.

"Or go south and regain the Carolinas."

The plans of desperate men flew around the room like locusts, and Sir Edward wandered to the window, looking out over the York River, where the French fleet threatened and their own few remaining ships bobbed at anchor in the harbor. He was tired, sick to death of this campaign. Sick of the fight, of the cause, of the rhetoric. There was no savor to life. But then, there hadn't been for longer than he could bear to remember.

The door opened and the contentious buzz in the room paused. "There's a woman, my lord." The lieutenant addressed the earl, in such haste that he was in danger of forgetting the courtesies. "Came under flag of truce from the enemy lines. Wishes to speak with Sir Edward."

Paget swung round as the buzz broke out with renewed vigor at this extraordinary piece of news. Deserters on both sides were a plague to which they were all accustomed, but women, bearing the white flag? . . . "Who is she, Lieutenant?"

"Won't give her name, sir. Says she must speak with you alone."

"Well, go to her, man," Cornwallis said testily. "She may have valuable information." Sir Edward hid the sardonic gleam in his eye with a punctilious bow and a formally uttered excuse.

Bryony stood in the hall, between two troopers, and as her father appeared she drew herself up and looked steadily at him.

For a long moment, he returned the look, searching her face for clues. He saw a slender woman in a threadbare riding habit — a woman from whom all the frills and the fancies had been pared, revealing the essence that shone clear and candid from adult eyes. Then the weariness dropped from him as if by magic. This *was* a kind of magic — this miraculous apparition; his daughter, for all that she bore the marks of one who had gone through the fires and emerged, honed, tempered, strong enough to take what was allotted her. He held out his arms and she ran into them with a little sob of pain and joy.

A coughing and shuffling of feet brought Paget back to a sense of reality. "That will be all," he said crisply to the soldiers. "Come into the parlor, child. Whilst I am overjoyed to see you, I could wish you had chosen a more orthodox method of reappearance."

Bryony began to laugh weakly. "Oh, Papa, you are not in the least changed."

Her father paused on the threshold of the parlor, regarding her with a quiet gravity. "We are all changed, Bryony. In many cases, out of all recognition." She bowed her head in silent acknowledgment and preceded him into the graciously furnished room, whose handsome appointments seemed somehow incongruous in this besieged town.

"Tell me," her father invited. "You are not here because you have run away from anything."

She smiled slightly. "How can you know that?"

"Just by looking at you. You have found what most of us seek and few discover." He took her hand where the thin gold band encircled her ring finger. "Is it Benedict Clare?"

"How did you know?"

"Your mother knew immediately." He shrugged. "When I thought about it, of course, it seemed obvious — odd moments that I recalled as puzzling . . . your outrageous appearance at the duel. But I am not blessed with a mother's intuition." He released her hand. "He is with Washington?"

Bryony nodded. "There are things I cannot tell you, but he has no love for the British."

"Then why are you here?" There was a sudden sternness to the question that took her aback. "He is your husband. You made your choice and you cannot renege."

"I wished to see you." Bryony opted for the simple truth. "If only to say farewell."

"And he permitted this? Permitted you to enter a doomed town?" Sir Edward's eyebrows lifted. "I do not know what kind of a rogue your husband may be, daughter, but I suspect that he is not the kind to see his wife go into danger without remonstrance."

"He is the kind of rogue, Papa, who will

not stand in the way of a personal imperative." It was a bare statement that her father sensed left much unsaid, but he would not probe. Bryony spoke again, her voice low. "Do you feel that I have betrayed you?" It was the question she had come here to ask. He had received her as his daughter, but that did not necessarily mean that he was untouched by her defection.

Sir Edward seemed to take a long time considering his answer. Then he shook his head. "After what I have seen these last months, differences in principles and beliefs seem singularly unimportant beside the ties of family and love. That is your belief, also, is it not?"

Slowly she nodded. "But not my husband's."

So, that was it. Sir Edward nodded. "Mayhap, he will learn it."

How long could it go on? Ben could almost feel the earth shudder as the barrage continued to tear apart the village. From where he stood, on the browning grass, amid bear-paw cactus and sere sedge, he could see the tall houses of Yorktown shuddering as the cannonballs plunged through roofs and shattered walls. Where was she in that kitchen of hell? On the riverfront below Yorktown, a torrent of fire raged, enwrapping the British ships as the French lobbed red-hot shot in among the crowded vessels, and cannon and mortar bludgeoned the town from behind. Now and again, a shell would sail over the town to plunge into the river, exploding in a foaming jet that shot into the sky, cascading down, tinged with the flame-brightness of the night. How could anyone still be alive in there? he thought with stabbing desolation. Close to four thousand shot had fallen upon the town and harbor in the last twenty-four hours, and the slaughter within must be horrendous.

Hour by hour, American and French troops dug the trenches that would bring them close enough to the town to force the British surrender. Only two British redoubts, far in front of the defense line, stood in the way of allied advancement, and they were to be taken that night in a concerted attack. Benedict was to join Lafayette's men, storming the Rock Redoubt, and he was under no illusions about the danger of the mission. It would be a desperate battle with cold steel in hand, no quarter possible in the confined space. They had been told to empty their muskets, relying only on the bayonet to achieve their goal. But he would play his part with grim determination, knowing that success would bring this damnable business to an end all the sooner, and if Bryony was still alive, then her chances of staying so until he could reclaim her would be greatly increased.

During the days since her departure, he had made endless bargains with fate, with God, and with the devil. If she was alive and well, he would care for nothing else. And he knew now that nothing else mattered beside her love. He had said and done things that should have destroyed that love, but it had remained as shield and buckler for both of them. She had struggled to steer a path between abiding loyalties while maintaining her personal integrity, and he had made it as difficult for her as he could. She was who she was — his wife, his lover, his friend and companion. And she was also the daughter of Sir Edward Paget — just that and nothing more. At last he could see her clearly, separate from the entanglements with which he had insisted she be bound.

Benedict was filled with a deep peace even through his terror that he would be denied the chance to share the peace with her, to tell her that he had laid down the burden of hatred because she had shown him its insignificance beside the gift of love.

Bryony had seen carnage in these last months, but nothing as dreadful as this. The village was a ghastly landscape; bodies littered the main street; bits of bodies lay scattered — heads, arms, legs. It was impossible to take more than a few steps without running into huge shell craters and half-covered trenches. The houses were devastated, riddled with shot, windows smashed, roofs caved in. And still the cannonade went on. It was like living in the midst of a never-ending earthquake, her ears bruised by the constant, deafening battering, her body almost fragmented by the violent shaking.

Thomas Nelson's house had been so severely battered that Cornwallis had been obliged to move his headquarters. They now cowered in a shallow cave below the marl cliff, looking out over the river, where two blazing ships drifted across the black water to the far shore.

Bryony sat huddled at the back of the damp grotto. She had not wanted to come down, feeling her position anomalous in this tense and desperate group. But her father had assumed his mantle of parental authority. She had endangered herself sufficiently, he had stated, and she owed it to her husband to protect herself as she could. There had been little to be gained in argument, so now she sat and listened to the debate, the comings and goings of grim-faced men bearing the incessant reports of the slaughter at the fortifications, and she wondered where Benedict was; if he still lived; what he was thinking. He had not bidden her farewell, had not given, by touch or look, any hope of a softening. As far as he was concerned, she had simply regretted her choice of loyalties and wished to embrace the old ones. She had tried to explain that it was not that, but his face and heart had been closed to her — as they always would be closed to a Paget.

She blinked back the tears and wished she could sleep. That state had been denied her so long that to attain it seemed like an impossible dream.

"If you lose your gun, don't fall back — take the gun of the first man killed." The whispered instruction went around the assault force, halted a quarter mile from the redoubt. Benedict took Charlie Carter's hand for a minute in silent farewell — the acknowledgment that in less than a quarter of a mile, their days on earth could come to an end.

Charlie was to take part in the "forlorn hope" that would launch the first attack, climbing directly over the wall. Ben watched him creep off into the fog and wished that Bryony had been given the chance to bid their longtime friend and companion farewell. She would have wished for it, he knew.

Then there was no time to think of anything. A flaming volley burst from the British lines. Obviously they had been alerted by something, and the American force now stood exposed upon the field. With a bellowed command, he led his own company at a run to the trench below the parapet of the redoubt where the first assault was already in progress. Men fell all around him, and he thought for a minute that the British volleys were wiping out the force. But in the yellow light of the powder flashes that illuminated the scene, he realized that the men were falling into shell holes, scrambling out to rush forward again, and again falling. He led the way through the palisade and saw Charlie in the eerie light, half a dozen bayonets lunging down at him from above. Ben rushed to his aid, and the two beat off the attack with their own bayonets. Hand grenades fell into the trench, lobbed by the British from the wall above.

"Up!" Ben yelled. "Let me use your shoulders, man." The soldier bent, and Ben leaped from his shoulders, over the wall and into the redoubt, the rest following his example. And then it was impossible to think of anything but the need to slash and not be slashed in a few moments of violent, hand-to-hand fighting that eventually cleared the redoubt.

Ben found Charlie bleeding copiously from a bayonet thrust to his thigh, but he was conscious and capable of a feeble grin, so he left him to await the surgeon, who was already being led through the darkness to attend to the wounded of both sides.

The second redoubt fell to the French in much the same manner, and in the gray light of the following dawn, a stunned Cornwallis stood on the parapet at Yorktown and stared at the new enemy siege line, a stone's throw from the town. The bombardment increased in violence, and Bryony, in a weird trance that was neither sleeping nor waking, listened in the cave throughout the day as finally it was agreed that matters had become unendurable.

Sir Edward, his face bleak, eyes sunken with grief, came over to her. "There is no hope left here. Cornwallis is going to attempt a retreat across the river to Gloucester. It seems the only way to avoid the mortification of surrender. I am bound to go with him in the second wave, but you stay here and await your husband."

"I doubt he will welcome me," she said wearily. "But I will not run from him."

The first wave of men went across the river just before midnight, but they were the only ones to achieve the south shore. A freak storm blew down the river, whipping the water into a turbulent boil that made further sailing impossible. At sunrise, the bombardment began again, a hundred cannons ripping through the fortifications, forcing the embrasures closed, so that no offensive response was possible.

Cornwallis, in the headquarters cave beneath the cliff, faced the prospect of sacrificing the few soldiers left unwounded or not sick of the fever, and he bowed his head in submission. Bryony felt and shared the aching grief in those desperate moments of acceptance. It showed on every haggard, disillusioned face. Six years they had fought to be brought to this moment.

It occurred to Bryony, through the mists of her own exhaustion, that if Benedict Clare could have witnessed this scene, he would have found his revenge sweet. Was the appetite for vengeance insatiable? Would this satisfy him, leave him purged?

Benedict Clare was in the front line when the drummer boy clambered upon a British parapet and began the steady drumroll. The sound could not be heard above the firing, and Benedict sent the word to silence the guns. Into the abruptly shattering quiet of a cold early morning in October, the call for parley sounded, the most beautiful sound that Benedict thought he had ever heard.

It was the next morning, however, before he was free to enter Yorktown. His eyes took in death and destruction on all sides as he looked fearfully in the craters, among the bodies for the shape that was imprinted upon his own. It seemed impossible to believe that anyone could be alive in this charnel house.

He saw her at the end of the street and knew that she had seen him, was waiting for him. His soul expanded to receive the rush of joy, of love, of unutterable relief as he walked steadily toward her. She brushed her hair away from her face in that gesture of uncertainty that wrung his heart.

A man appeared at her side. A man who stood tall in the face of defeat, the white hair shining in the cool autumn sunlight, the blue eyes as direct and fearless as his daughter's. Paget laid a hand on her shoulder. A hand of reassurance or affirmation? Benedict wondered as he approached them. What would she say to him?

But when he reached them, he saw in her eyes that it was up to him to speak first. She had already spoken when she had told him of her need to make herself whole again. He had offered her nothing then. Now he held out his hand to her father, knowing that it was the only statement he could make.

"Sir Edward."

"Clare." The hand that gripped his was warm, dry, and firm — not the hand of a beaten man. And not the hand of an ungenerous man. "It seems that I must give my daughter away in rather unusual circumstances." An eyebrow quirked. He took Bryony's hand and laid it in Benedict's. "Go with your husband, daughter. It was the choice you made freely, and you must now return to his side. When there are no longer divisions, then we will come together again."

"Come," Ben said softly to her. "If you will." She lifted her face in answer, to receive her husband's kiss.

That night, as she lay in his arms in a tiny tent beneath a clear, star-decorated sky, in the amazing stillness that followed the battering of the last days, she said softly yet firmly, "I cannot go to watch the surrender, Benedict. I will return to Williamsburg and retrieve Ned. You can join me there when the formalities are done."

He stroked her hair in the darkness, thinking of the scene that would be played out on the surrender field: the columns of British and German soldiers, marching to the drum that would beat the dirge of vanquishment, marching between the conquering lines of American and French to lay down their arms, regiment by regiment, following the inexorable rule of defeat; to return empty-handed between the same victorious lines, back to Yorktown to await disposition as prisoners. It was not a spectacle that he would witness with any satisfaction, he realized.

Tranquillity settled upon him, bright and gauzy as a blanket of butterfly wings. "I have neither need nor desire to be there, either, sweeting. We will return to Williamsburg together."

# Epilogue

"Bryony really should not be running around in this heat. And she does not even have a hat on." Eliza Paget fanned herself vigorously. The May afternoon was hot, and the waters of the James River shimmered below the overlooking garden. "Cannot you do something about it, Benedict?"

Ben looked up from the chessboard. His opponent offered him a small, conspiratorial smile, which he returned before staring across the garden to where Bryony was instructing Ned in the intricacies of the croquet lawn. "I could try, ma'am," he said. Sir Edward Paget chuckled, and then moved his bishop, uniting his rooks in preparation for a concerted attack on the queen's file.

"Lass?" Ben called, his voice carrying easily. Bryony knocked her ball through the hoop and straightened up, swinging her mallet as she squinted against the sun.

"Do you want me?"

"Aye." He crooked a finger and she

crossed the grass, smiling, Ned at her heels, remarkably unwaiflike in his nankeen britches and pristine linen.

Ben could feel his mouth curving with pleasure, his eyes filling with his joy as he watched her approach. He had loved her as a bruised and battered stray with no identity; as the beautiful, cultivated daughter of the privileged; as the lean and hungry campaigner, dirty and tattered, yet always unbowed; and now, as the bearer of life, her skin translucent with an inner radiance, the inhabited eyes glowing, the unmistakable swell of her belly thrusting against the muslin of her gown, her breasts pressing, full and rich, against her bodice. He would never be able to decide which facet of his wife he loved the most.

"Your mama wishes you to sit in the shade and rest," he told her with the utmost gravity. "It is a very hot afternoon."

"Oh, pshaw! I have endured much worse than this, Mama!" Bryony expostulated.

"Yes, that may be so, but you were not then in a . . ."

"Delicate condition." Bryony rescued her mother, who still could not manage to refer to intimate matters, even in this male company. "I am perfectly well and not in the least need of coddling."

Benedict surveyed his options on the board and shook his head. "I cannot seem to avert a mate in two, sir." He toppled over his black king with a flick of his finger, and held out his hand to his father-in-law. Then he turned back to his wife, a wicked gleam in the hawk's eyes. "If you will not sit in the shade, sweeting, then I fear you must rest upon your bed during the heat of the afternoon."

Her mouth formed a mischievous pout. "But I am not in the least fatigued."

"Nevertheless, I must insist." He rose from his chair.

"Yes, you are quite right to do so," Eliza said with a nod of satisfaction, quite missing the laughter in her husband's eyes, occupied as he was with the chessboard while he replaced the pieces.

"Ned, is it not time you returned to Mr. Blake?" Ben glanced down at the boy, who had clambered onto his vacated seat at the chessboard and was assisting Sir Edward in setting up the board, a frown of concentration on the small face as his fingers moved unerringly.

"I do not like Mr. Blake," Ned announced in tones that could not be gainsaid. "He hurt my hand." A small palm was up-turned, revealing the blister of a ferrule.

"Oh, I will not permit that!" exclaimed Bryony, outraged. "Why did he punish you, Ned?"

The child's frown deepened as he thought. Then he shrugged as if the matter were of no further interest. "Can't remember."

Ben chuckled. "Clearly it did not make a lasting impression. But I will speak to Blake later."

"He will learn more by playing chess with me this afternoon than he will in the schoolroom," said Sir Edward.

Since no one was inclined to argue with Sir Edward's views on education, they left a contented Ned and an equally contented patriarch, and made their way to the guesthouse, where they had been in residence for the last few months, Benedict, for the moment, content to have it so. Bryony needed to reestablish much with her parents, and if she wished to give birth in her family's home, the new, unburdened Benedict would not stand in her way.

"I have tried to explain to Mr. Blake that Ned is not an ordinary child," Bryony said, her forehead puckered, as they went into the cool, dim hallway. "He is not yet accustomed to the usual rules. But Blake cannot understand."

"Then, we will find a tutor who can." Ben flicked his fingertips against her bottom, encouraging her into the bedchamber. "Ned's affairs are not uppermost in my mind at present."

"Oh?" Her eyebrows lifted. "And what could be more important, pray?"

Benedict did not answer the question, which was purely rhetorical, anyway. He unbuttoned her gown, sliding it off her shoulders before brushing away the thin straps of her underdress, baring her to the waist. His palms, gentle in their awareness of the tenderness of pregnancy, globed the full swell of her breasts. His lips pressed into the hollow of her throat as he pushed her clothes to the floor, a rich, lace-edged puddle around her ankles.

"Ben, there is something I have been meaning to ask you since this morning." Bryony caught his chin and pulled his head up firmly. "I cannot concentrate until you tell me. My father wanted to talk about marriage settlements, and I did not know how to answer him. Did he mention it to you?"

"Lie down," he instructed softly, stroking the round hardness of her belly.

"But did he?" Bryony insisted, her hand instinctively covering his as they both made contact with the life within. "I told him that he must talk to you alone, because it was something that lay between you and him. . . ."

"Lie down!" An imperative crackle entered his voice, and he pushed her backward onto the soft featherbed. The sweeping strokes continued over her belly, and his tongue dipped into her navel.

"Tell me!" She struggled to resist the creeping melt that would erode all clarity. Her fingers curled in the burnished hair, shining dark against the white of her abdomen.

Ben raised his head but cupped his hand over the moistening apex of her thighs. "I told your father that he should make whatever settlements he chose upon you, including the estate upriver. I would not, through selfish pride, oblige you to live as the wife of a pauper. I will manage the estate, but I will have nothing in my name."

Bryony lay very still. It was only what she had expected, after all. But she had hoped for a yielding.

Benedict smiled and a finger probed with soft insistence. Her body stirred in response. "Your father said that he did not feel it appropriate for a man to be his wife's pensioner. Particularly when the wife in question was as strong-willed as mine. A sad fact, for which your father confessed that he bore considerable responsibility." A teasing note was in his voice, his eyes holding hers as the questing finger continued its work and he could feel the tension leave her. "He wished the man who will father Paget grandchildren to stake a claim on some part of his estate."

"And . . . ?" Breathlessly, she searched his face, saw only serenity, touched with amusement.

"And, lass, I said that if it would satisfy him, then I would lay claim to the Paget land in Ireland." He bent his head to nuzzle the rosy crest of one breast, but Bryony pushed him from her, struggling upright.

"Do not play games with me, Benedict Clare. Not about such matters!" Her eyes sparked fire, and he laughed softly.

"I am not playing games, sweeting. It struck me — belatedly, I will confess — that if I cannot cure the ills of a nation, I can, at least, ease the lot of some."

Bryony examined it and found it good. "So, you will use the revenues to improve the lives of the tenants?"

"There is much that can be done, if the land is farmed right and the goodness not wrung from it."

She touched his face. "You will remain a poor man."

"But I will have a wealthy wife, will I not?"

It was said with such mischievous satisfaction, such complete tranquillity that Bryony knew without the shadow of a doubt that the chains he carried had finally been laid down. Her arms went around his neck, drawing him to her. "For all time. Whenever and wherever passion drives, my love. As it has always been between us."

He smiled, his lips brushing over hers, moving to trace the outlines of her face as he whispered:

*"Misled by Fancy's meteor-ray,*
*By passion driven;*
*But yet the light that led astray*
*Was light from Heaven."*

# Author's Note

The story of Bryony and Benedict takes place against the background of the War of Independence and particularly the southern campaign of 1780/81. The events depicted are historically accurate to the extent that I have been able to make them so. In the interests of the fictional narrative I have, however, taken two liberties with historical chronology. Charleston fell at the beginning of May, 1780, and General Gates was appointed to his command in June of that year. These events, thus, could not have been known at the end of April during the house party described in chapters 10–13.

The lines that close the story are from "The Vision," Duan II, by Robert Burns (1759–1796).

# About the Author

*Jane Feather* was born in Cairo, Egypt, and grew up in the New Forest, in the south of England. She was trained as a social worker and — after moving with her husband and three children to New Jersey in 1978 — pursued her career in psychiatric social work. She started writing after she moved with her family to Washington, D.C., in 1981. Five contemporary romances wre followed by two Regencies and historical romances, of which *Chase the Dawn* is the third.